The Gathering of the Clans

The Storm-Bringer Saga: - Book Two

By Nav Logan

*****

Published by Nav Logan

*****

Original Copyright August 2013 Nav Logan

Reformatted and re-edited March 2014

*****

ISBN eBook Version: 978-0-9928521-2-2

ISBN Paperback Version: 978-0-9928521-3-9

Other books by Nav Logan:

The Storm-Bringer Saga: -Book One

The Storm-Bringer Saga: -Book Two

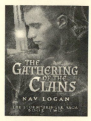

The Storm-Bringer Saga: - Book Three

(Due for release in the summer of 2014)

Learn more on: -

https://www.facebook.com/

And on my website: www.navlogan.com

*****

Cover Artwork by Clarissa Yeo

Book Cover Art: http://yocladesigns.com/

*****

Editing and proofreading by: Storywork Editing Services

www.storywork.co.uk.

*****

Map Illustrations by: Nav Logan

*****

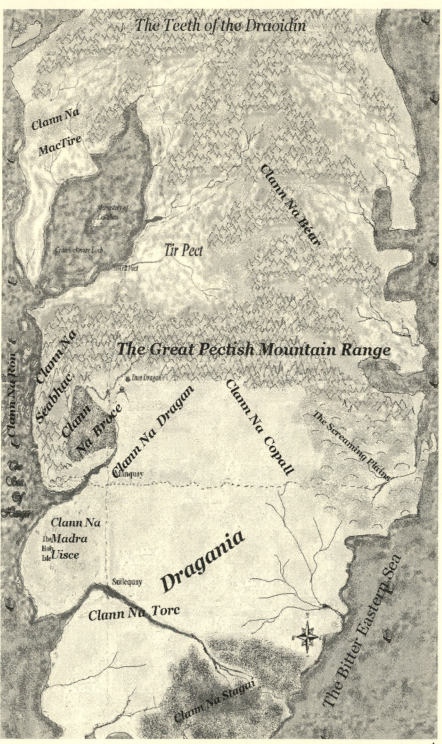

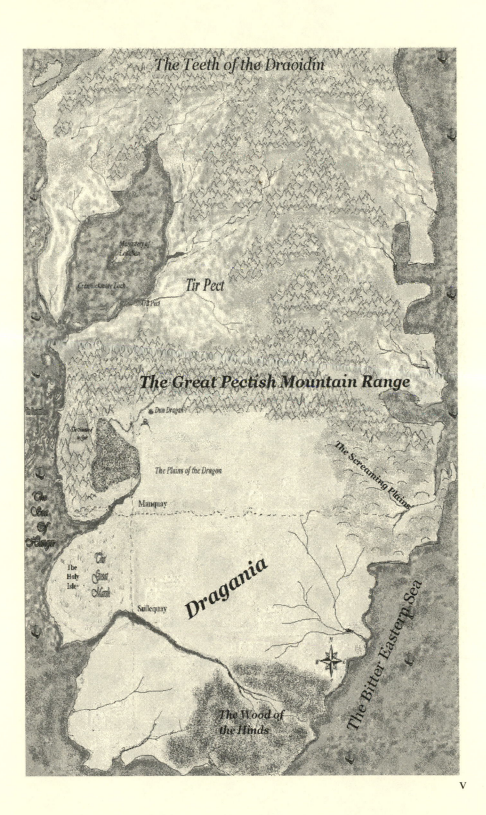

The Teeth of the Draoidin

Monastery of
Luichan

Crannockinate Loch

Ard Pect

Tir Pect

The Great Pectish Mountain Range

Dun Dragan

Cronasay Isle

The Plains of the Dragon

The Screaming Plains

Manquay

The Sea of Hunger

The Holy Isle

The Great Mark

Dragania

Suilequay

The Wood of
the Hinds

The Bitter Eastern Sea

Author's Note

This book is dedicated to the many people who gave support, feedback, and reviews for Book One of this series. Without your kind words of encouragement, this book would never have seen the light of day. Thank you all so very much.

It is also for the free spirits, the dreamers, the black sheep, and the misfits. Let your freak flags fly. You have always been an inspiration to my wandering soul, and therefore, this is for you. It is for the wooden cabin within our heads, where we can find our own Walden.

Hopefully, everyone else worthy of credit will fit into the above, so there is no reason to mention them as individuals. They already are.

*****

...And also...

The people and places mentioned in this book are purely a work of fiction, but some influence may be accredited to historical events, folklore, and the legends on which I grew up. These images of the past have always inspired me. The power struggle and social upheaval caused by the invaders in this story could easily have been the Romans in Celtic Britain, or the Danes of Brian Boru's Ireland.

I have used some Gaelic words, such as *'Fear Ban'* and *'An Fiacail Dragan'* to help distinguish the use of the 'Old Tongue,' of the Pectish Clans, who once reigned over Dragania. I hope that this adds to the texture of the story. I have also used italics to differentiate the use of the 'Old Tongue', as well as for telepathy and 'Dream-catching'.

Prologue

I pause at the top of the hill to catch my breath and to look around at the mystical vista before me. The sun has not yet broken through the low lying fog, giving the landscape a haunting effect, as the low hills of the drumlin countryside peak up out of a sea of mist. On mornings such as these, you can easily imagine the Great Marsh as it had once been. That was, of course, before the cataclysmic events that drained the water from this once great marshland.

Behind me are the ruins of the Temple of Deanna, my life's work. Within its library vault there are still so many secrets yet to be discovered. Even after all these years spent studying within its haunted walls, I still have so much to learn. The sheer quantity of knowledge, carefully stored to survive the years of neglect, is mind boggling.

I am only one man, and my eyes feel worn out from decades of reading. The locals call me the Mad Professor, due to my obsession for the hidden secrets of the Temple. I cannot ... will not, walk away and abandon the knowledge I have found.

The locals were right about the ghosts. They haunt the ruins, and their curses protect the once majestic structure, but for some strange reason they have not harmed me, far from it in fact. Do they want me to find the truth? Were they waiting for a lunatic like me to wander in on that stormy night when I stumbled through the illusory wall that had protected the Temple's vault for so long? The wealth that I found here has kept me going, gold and jewels aplenty for a man with my simple lifestyle. It has provided me with the food and equipment that I need while I complete my studies, but for an avid historian like me, the mass of ancient parchment I found there were the real treasures. Was this the reason that I have been allowed to survive when so many other treasure-hunters had fallen to the curses? Could the ghosts have seen the truth within my heart? Had they sensed a kindred spirit, and not an interloper, to their sacred domain? Instead of madness and death, the ghosts, or perhaps the goddess herself has given me a blessing of longevity. Despite having spent over three decades living and working within the vault, I am still blessed with a relatively youthful appearance and vigour. It seems that the powerful life magic of the Holy Isle still lingers, despite the neglect to the Temple over the centuries.

Stretching my back until it cracks, I turn away from the morning mist, and I head into my dilapidated home, ready for another day of researching. Hopefully, before I die on this isolated hilltop, I will know the truth, the whole truth about the Storm-Bringer who saved the world.

Some of the locals believe that the story should start with the dawn of time, with the coming of the Seven Greater Gods, but perhaps it started long before that in the darkness that existed before.

Others are convinced that the story only began with the Great Invasion, when the once-great nation of *Tir Pect* was torn asunder by the land-hungry Reavers. They stole the lower half of the country and settled on the lush farmland they found there. This was the time of the *Fear Ban*.

Both of these arguments are valid, but it was only later, much later, when we heard about the Storm-Bringer. In fact, after years of studying in this dusty ruin, some of the truth has become clearer to me. There was not one Storm-Bringer as we have been taught. There were, in fact, two. I now firmly believe that it was not the legendary Uiscallan who saved the world from disaster, as the history books would have us believe, it was another Storm-Bringer, a later one. It was a small girl called Maerlin Smith, from the remote mountain region of High Peaks.

When I first read this amongst the confusion of scrolls, I was astonished. I couldn't believe what I was reading, but the weight of knowledge attests to its truth. The facts cannot be denied. This young girl, hardly into her womanhood and raised far away from the political mire of Dragania, was the one who changed Dragania forever. With little or no formal training in the arts of magic, she turned the world upon its head. Was it her very ignorance of the ways of the world that allowed her to do what countless others could not? They would have accepted defeat as inevitable and passed quietly into obscurity but not her. She had the spirit of a lioness ... or maybe even a dragoness.

Single-handedly, she defeated the greatest sorcerer to ever walk the lands: Dubhgall the Black. The hidden scrolls attest to this quite clearly. They tell of how she rose up from the Maiden Stone and called upon the heavens to release their vengeance unto the Dark Mage for the evil he had perpetrated. With a power that shook the world and made the very gods awaken from their slumber, she blasted him into oblivion. With her indomitable spirit and fearsome magic, she saved the young Dragon prince and her other companions from their doom ... but the tale does not end there; far from it in fact. I have found more, much more, hidden within the vaults. I have found scrolls that tell of the time after the defeat of the Dark Mage. If only I can find some order amidst the chaos of parchments, I might be able to decipher the full truth and finally know...

This is my mission and it haunts me, much more than the ghosts ever could.

Chapter One: The Dark Visitation

Long ago, deep in the land of Tir Pect...

The Monks of Leithban were an isolated community, living on a small island within Crannockmore Lough. They rarely received visitors to their wild haven, and they tended to like it that way. It gave them more time to study the gifts of nature and the stars, gifts given to the world by the Seven Greater Gods. They spent their days in quiet contemplation while doing the menial tasks of everyday life and adhering to the rituals of the various deities. Occasionally, a visitor would come to the island. Most came to buy their renowned Leithban mead, but occasionally one would come seeking a life of quiet isolation. The monks would greet them warmly and make available what simple comforts they had to offer. Some of these visitors later became monks themselves, thus perpetuating the Order and bringing new lifeblood into the small community.

It was, however, with some surprise that the Order came across its most recent arrival.

It happened early one winter's morning. It was the sort of morning where foggy mists crept into every nook and cranny, and it brought aches to broken bones. Abbot Gearoid opened the huge oaken gates of the monastery to let out his herd of goats. Every morning, he would walk them up the hill, where they could graze on the rocky ground of the island until it came time for evening milking. He would walk as much for the joy of it as anything else. Wolves and bears were not a threat on the island. It had become a habit for the portly monk to hike up the hill with his charges, carrying any newborn kids that were not fleet enough to keep up with the wily old puck goat and his herd of nimble nannies. In truth, most of the kids were quite able for the hike, but some were amenable to being carried.

Abbot Gearoid was startled to find a woman at the entrance. She had not rung the large bell as visitors normally would. She simply stood there, waiting.

He recovered quickly. "Can I help you, Milady?"

"My apologies, Druid. Did I frighten thee?" The woman stepped close, too close for decorum. She stopped when she was almost touching the monk, but her body leaned even closer, forcing Abbot Gearoid to take a step backward.

He cleared his throat and shook off his discomfort. "Nay, Milady ... surprised perhaps."

She was tall and rake-thin, angular, and yet strikingly beautiful. Her hair was as dark as a raven's wing, and her skin was as pale as alabaster. Looking into her eyes, he could detect no colour, merely obsidian pools that bored deeply into his soul. He shivered involuntarily. Her voice had a rich timbre, and his eyes were drawn to her thin, blood-red lips.

"Forgive me if I startled thee. Thou look like thou hast seen a ghost," she teased. A smirk floated fleetingly across her pallid features.

"No," Gearoid assured. "It's just ... it's rare that we have visitors and even rarer for them to be ladies of regal birth." He inadvertently referred to the black, satin cloak that she wore. No commoner could afford such a garment.

The lady watched him silently through her haunting ebony orbs. Her silence was making him nervous.

"My apologies," he stammered. "We didn't hear your boat arriving. Are you alone?"

"I came with my ... father ... I need to speak with thy Head Druid," she replied after another long painful silence.

He could not place her accent. She spoke fluent Pectish, but in a strange archaic form. Looking closer, her features were unlike any of the local Clans from around the Lough. Whoever this strange lady was, she must have travelled far to reach the monastery. Gearoid cleared his throat, wondering why her presence upset him so. He must have been living for too long in the isolated community. It had been some time since he had the uncomfortable fumbling of his youth when dealing with women.

"That would be me, I guess. That is to say, I'm the leader here now. Our revered Abbot Guerin passed on to the Otherworld only last week. It was a gift perhaps after his long illness. Blessed be Macha," he added, making a warding gesture with his fingers.

"Then it is to thee that I wish to speak, Gearoid." Her eyes bored into him, invading his aura with her presence. Placing a hand on his broad chest, she purred "Perhaps thou canst be of some use to me."

Gearoid tried to recall when he had introduced himself, but the more he thought about it, the murkier his memory became. Eventually, he lost his chain of thoughts altogether.

Another long silence ensued.

"Forgive me. I'm lost in a daydream this morning. I fear I didn't sleep well last night. The Samhaine spirits must have troubled me."

Silence fell, and he wondered why the topic of death kept intruding on their conversation.

"I need the assistance of thy Order, Druid."

Confused, Gearoid shook his head. "I'm sorry Milady, but there must be some mistake. We're a strictly male order. We strive to keep temptations from cluttering the younger monks' minds, if you'll excuse my frankness." He felt blood flush into his cheeks, and she seemed amused by his discomfort.

She smiled a strange lurid smile and then broke into haunting laughter. "Thou dost misunderstand me, Gearoid. I don't wish sanctuary for myself. I wish for thee to aid my ... father. He has recently fallen upon misfortune, and he needs a place to heal."

The monastery rarely accepted the sick within its walls, though not from any lack of charity. "We are not equipped with gifted healers, Milady. You might do better to take him to the Temple of Deanna, at *Ard Pect*. It's only a few leagues farther down the Lough. The priestesses there are adept in the healing arts."

A shadow crossed the woman's face. "Dost thou deny him sanctuary?"

No religious order could afford to annoy the nobility, and Abbot Gearoid, although new to the job, was wise enough to realise the implied threat. "Nay Milady, that's not what I meant at all. We'd be honoured to look after your father. I was merely concerned that he should receive the best possible care. As I said, we are not gifted in the healing arts. We mainly devote our time to meditation, study, and prayer."

This seemed to placate the woman. "The hustle and bustle of *Ard Pect* would ill suit his condition, I fear. He needs solitude more than he needs soothing balms. Though the accident has caused him some physical ailments, his mind needeth healing more. The intrigue of *Ard Pect* would be detrimental to his constitution."

"Very well, then. We'll gladly care for him, if that is the case. He'll have plenty of time to recuperate here. Did you plan on him being here permanently?" Gearoid asked as diplomatically as possible. This would not be the first time an ageing relative had been put aside, so that a young heir could inherit his title.

This seemed to amuse the woman, and she grinned wickedly at him. "That's for him to decide ... not me. If he recovers and wishes to leave, then so be it. If he chooses to stay and ferment within thy leaky walls, then he's of no further use to me. He can rot here until eternity for all I care."

Gearoid blinked in surprise at her harsh words.

"Here. These wilts recompense thee for his time here." She offered Gearoid a doeskin purse, heavy with coin.

"That won't be necessary, Milady." Gearoid declined for the sake of politeness, though he was well aware of the list of items that were needed from the mainland. Although the monks survived on the fruits of their own labour, and they even made a small profit from their mead produced, some things needed money to purchase; the beams and slate for the roof of the chapel, for example. It was well overdue for repair. These materials would need to be purchased from *Ard Pect*.

"Give it to the poor if that is thy wish, or have thy roof repaired. I care not." She dropped the bag of coins in the dirt at his sandaled feet.

Another haunting silence ensued. Finally, Gearoid conceded and gathered up the offered alms. "The gods bless you for your charity, Milady. Your father ... where is he?"

"Thou wilt find him lying in the Lough ..." Her pale hand pointed through the mist toward the jetty "... In a boat, that is."

"By the Seven! He could catch pleurisy lying out there at this time of the year! I'd better go and fetch him immediately." Abbot Gearoid hurried down to the shoreline. He could feel her presence behind him as he scampered down the slippery stone steps to the jetty. There, he found a small fishing boat, one of the traditional *currach* used by the local fishermen. In it, he found a man, or at least what was left of one. He was in a sorry state.

"What on earth happened to him?" Gearoid asked, gazing with horror at the man's wounds. Silence answered him. He was sure that he had felt her presence behind him, but there was no trace of the lady in the fog.

"Hello! Where are you?"

His voice rebounded off the Lough, coming back at him through the cold fog. That, and the lapping of the waves, was his only reply. Shaking his head, he pulled off his cloak and covered the sick man before hurrying back to the monastery, hoping to find the mysterious woman. She was nowhere to be found. Confused, he reached up and yanked on the bell chord, summoning help.

It didn't take long for the other monks to come running.

"What's the matter, Abbot Gearoid?" a younger monk asked.

"Have any of you seen a lady around here? She was here a moment ago," Gearoid asked, but no one had seen the arrival and departure of their visitor. Shrugging off his confusion, he pulled himself together. "Brother Niall, fetch a stretcher and take Brother Fionn with you, down to the pier. There's a man down there who needs our assistance. Bring him to the infirmary at once."

"Aren't you going to send him to *Ard Pect*?" Brother Seamus asked.

Gearoid stuffed his hands into his robe. His fingers brushed against the coins resting there, reminding him of his earlier conversation. He tried to recall more of it, but for some odd reason it eluded his grasp. Desperate to make sense of the situation, he tried to recall the features of the noblewoman, but again, the details eluded him. He could only remember the vaguest description of the woman, and the more he strained, the more his thoughts slipped away. One thing came back strongly though and that was her insistence that the man to be kept here, rather than at *Ard Pect*.

"...Gearoid?"

9

Sighing, Gearoid shook his head. "No, Seamy, I'm placing him in your care. You've always had a gift for healing, so his life is in your hands. We'll pray that he can recover but some of those wounds would challenge even Deanna's priestesses. He may yet feast in Macha's Hall by day's end."

Chapter Two: The Coming of Winter

They huddled in their clothing against the evening chill, wary of lighting a fire on the open plain. They were not sure if they were still being hunted, but a fire was sure to attract unwanted attention, so they suffered the cold and tried to sleep.

They were all weary after the previous fortnight of walking; only pausing for long enough to catch a little sleep during the ever-shortening days of early winter. Vort had advised them against travelling during the day. It would be better to hide in the long grass and trust to Vort's night vision to guide them through the darkness. Vort's Clan, the Brocians, had long since lived a nocturnal existence like their Clan's totem-beast, the badger. Because of this, they could see much better in the dark than the other Clans of Dragania.

Winter was rushing toward them. It came earlier and harsher this far north where the cold winds slipped down off the Pectish Mountains and wandered unhindered across the Plains of the Dragon.

Chewing on some horse jerky, Cull sat, looking out at the last rays of the sunset on the prairie. He was pondering their next move. "How far is it to this Sett, Vort?"

"It's another night's walk ... maybe two. It's at the very edge of the mountains."

Cull grimaced, not liking the situation but seeing no viable alternative. "Is it always this damned cold up here?"

"The winter's only just starting, Cull," Taliesin said. "I grew up a little to the east of here, on the Pectish border. Soon, the snow will come down from the mountain and then you'll know just how cold it can get. You can hear the trees cracking as the sap freezes, and occasionally, you'll find animals frozen solid by a sudden blizzard, unable to find shelter in time."

They looked up at the snow-capped mountains on the northern horizon, slowly growing as they slogged nearer, day by day.

"We'd better get going," Cull grunted. "The sooner we get there, the happier I'll be. I don't like how Maerlin is looking. I've never seen someone look so pale."

"Maybe we should wait a while longer, Cull. Cora is nearly spent. A few more moments isn't going to make much difference, one way or another," Taliesin suggested.

Cull looked over to where the others huddled around their makeshift stretcher, and he knew that the bard was right.

*****

"Here, Cora," Conal urged, offering her his ration of horse jerky. "Eat this."

Cora smiled wearily at the Prince. "You should eat it yourself, Conal."

"I'm fine. I've never had much taste for horse meat anyway. Eat it, Cora ... please."

She looked over at him, seeing the worry in his blue eyes. She couldn't resist his penetrating orbs for long. "I'll tell you what ... I'll share it with you." She broke the jerky in half. Placing her share in her mouth, she held the other piece out to Conal. Opening his mouth, he allowed her to feed him the morsel, and they chewed in companionable silence.

Cora studied him as she ate. Already his blonde locks were showing close to his scalp, beneath the dye. "I think we need to wash that dye out. It's marring your good looks." She watched Conal flush. Leaning forward, she kissed his reddened cheek, making him flush even more.

"What was that for?"

"It was just to say thank you."

Conal looked away, trying to hide his burning cheeks. He was not used to girls being nice to him, let alone kissing him. He looked over at the sleeping form on the stretcher. Maerlin lay wrapped in blankets, with the magpie still cradled in her arms. She was sleeping restlessly, occasionally moaning or crying out. She had been like this since the battle on the burial mound, never waking from her catatonic state and never releasing the bird from her grasp. Maerlin had never kissed him or flirted with him.

Most of the time they seemed to be arguing or sitting together in sullen silence, but Conal missed her nonetheless. He longed for her to wake up so that they could find a quiet place, away from the others, and just sit together. He even looked forward to their next row. Conal smiled, remembering the way her eyes flashed and sparkled when her temper flared.

"I miss her too," Cora said, reading his mind.

"Do you ..." Conal stopped, afraid to speak out loud what they'd all been thinking. Taking a breath, he tried again "Do you think she'll be alright?"

Cora followed his gaze. "I hope so. I discussed it with the High Priestess yesterday, during my dreams. She said that it was probably just exhaustion, but even she wasn't sure. Using Wild-magic can be dangerous, especially for the untrained. Maerlin has had some training, but what she did back there was truly awesome! None of the priestesses could have done that! It would have taken the concerted efforts of a number of well-trained priestesses to even attempt what Maerlin achieved. Ceila had always said that Maerlin was exceptional, but I wouldn't have believed it if I hadn't seen it for myself. Even my Water Elementals rushed to do her bidding! Until recently, I didn't understand the difference between an Air-sister and a Storm-Bringer, but seeing Maerlin working her Wild-magic has given me a new perspective on the legends about Storm-Bringers."

She could see that Conal still didn't understand the enormity of the magic wielded by Maerlin, during her battle with Dubhgall the Black. "Let me explain, Conal. If you lift a boulder that's too heavy for you, your body will ache afterwards, and if you strain too much, you may do some permanent damage. Sometimes, the ache will go away, but other times it'll persist or it'll need treatment to cure it. Wild-magic is like that. It's like a muscle in your brain, or your spirit. You need to exercise it and build your strength up to stop you overexerting yourself. People have gone into comas or become gibbering idiots from overreaching their magical abilities."

Conal turned to Cora, his eyes wide with concern. "You mean to say that Maerlin could..."

"...I don't know, Conal. No one will know until Maerlin wakes up," Cora replied with exasperation.

Conal silently pondered Cora's words. "What about the bird? Where did it come from, and what does it mean?"

"I don't know that either, Conal," Cora replied. "I haven't a clue, but there's something strange about that magpie."

Conal looked questioningly at her.

"Every living thing has an aura, Conal. You, me, Maerlin, even trees and grass. If it lives, it has an aura. Magic has an aura too, so I guess you could say that magic lives. That sword you carry, for example, has an aura."

Conal looked at the legendary sword, *An Fiacail Dragan*. Its silver, dragon-shaped hilt shimmered in the half-light.

"Your sword has a golden glow to it, which means that it's steeped in Wild-magic. That magpie also glows, but not the way a magpie should. Its aura is different. It has an almost human aura with the myriad of colours in it that you'd see in a person, but there's something else, a depth that I've never seen before. Perhaps Ceila could tell me more. I'll ask her about it the next time we speak."

"That's something else that I don't understand," Conal said. "How do you speak to Ceila in your dreams?"

"I can't contact her as I'm not a Dream-catcher, but she can contact me while I'm sleeping. It's like going into a room in my dreams, and she's sitting there. It's like I've been transported to the Holy Isle. Once she's contacted me, we can talk for a while."

"But you said that she talked to you during the battle. Were you asleep then?"

"No." Cora thought for a moment. "Maybe it was the root that Orla gave me, or maybe it was because the Dream-catchers were working together. I don't know."

They didn't get a chance to consider it further; however, as Cull interrupted them "It's time to go. Are you up to another hike, Cora?"

Cora nodded. "I'm fine. I ache all over, and my feet are blistered, but that's all. Let's get this over with so that we can find some shelter. I need a hot bath and some clean clothes. Other than that, I'll live."

Cull knew that she was putting on a brave face, but he said nothing. He headed over to the stretcher were Vort was waiting. Together they lifted it up and set off into the darkness...

*****

Just before dawn, the plain gave way to rolling hills, and they sank wearily to the ground.

"We'll be safe to light a fire today," said Vort, "a small one. I'll go hunting while you set up camp."

Cull dug out a patch of ground for a fire pit while the others gathered what little firewood was available in the vicinity. The hillside contained some small shrubs and the occasional scrawny willow tree. It would provide enough fuel to cook with, if not enough to warm them.

A short while later, Vort returned with a brace of rabbits. The group ate them hungrily before settling down to sleep. Cull volunteered for the first watch, knowing that the others were all exhausted. As they slept, he watched the sky redden in the east as the sun rose.

Sitting quietly with only the whispering wind for company, he assessed their options. Soon, winter would set in, and they would be trapped until spring. Vort had assured him that he had relatives living on the edge of the mountains, who would offer them shelter. If he were confident of their support, then Cull trusted his judgement. After all, Vort had effectively become an exile from his own people since the incident of his shape-changing.

This had happened during a Blood-truth, which was a challenge to his title as War-leader of his Clan. Vort had won the fight, but they were not sure how the High Council had viewed his victory. Shape-changing, or Form-melding as the Brocians called it, was traditionally a shamanistic ritual, and Vort had no wish to become a shaman under Dorcha: the High-shaman.

As things transpired, Dorcha had turned out to be Dubhgall the Black in disguise. The ramifications of this could only be guessed at, but with

Dubhgall's demise during his battle with Maerlin, the Brocians would now be seeking a new High-shaman. Vort, he was sure, would not be applying for the job, even though his ability to Form-meld would make him a likely candidate. Vort had instead opted to leave his Clan, in order to help Conal obtain the Dragontooth sword: *An Fiacail Dragan*. Vort believed that by assisting Conal to his throne and denying Lord Boare's claim to the High Kingship, he would help to bring peace to the kingdom of Dragania.

This was also why the priestesses of Deanna had assisted Conal, with help from Nessa MacTire and the two novices: Cora and Maerlin. This was also why Cull's own liege: the Beggar-lord had assisted. He only hoped that the young prince would be given enough time to rally his forces before the fateful day when Conal would meet Lord Boare in battle.

By heading into Pectish territory, Cull hoped to delay that meeting, at least until next spring. Then, they would gather together an army of the different factions who opposed Lord Boare's claim to the High Kingship. Still, uniting these factions would be no simple matter, even for the son of the Dragon-lord, and even with the legendary *Fiacail Dragan*.

The High Priestess, Ceila, had told Cull that Maerlin was the key to the success of their mission, and that her fate and Conal's were entwined. Cull looked over at Maerlin, lying pale and withdrawn. If Maerlin was to play any further part, she would first need time to recover from the mental and physical ordeal that she had suffered during the battle on the burial mound.

Though not a religious man, Cull offered a silent prayer to Deanna for Maerlin's recovery.

Gritty-eyed, Cull stayed awake for as long as possible before getting to his feet. Stretching to ease his aching limbs, Cull wandered over to where Taliesin slept, curled up with his harp nestled protectively against his chest. Nudging the gangly bard's feet, Cull murmured "Hey Tal, wake up. It's time for your watch."

Taliesin groaned, opened his eyes a sliver and waved a hand at Cull in acknowledgement. Cull waited, knowing that the bard was not easily stirred from slumber. Only when Taliesin had roused himself enough to sit up and stretch did Cull finally relax.

"Brrr! I swear it's getting colder by the day."

"Are you awake now?" Cull asked, even though Taliesin's eyes were open.

"Yeah, yeah, I'm fine."

Cull nodded and headed for his bed-roll, "G'night then, Tal."

"Sleep well, Cull."

Moments later, Cull was snoring lightly.

Taliesin sat shivering, struggling toward wakefulness. A cold breeze was coming down from the mountain, so he pulled his blanket tighter around his lean frame. He blinked a few times against the daylight and decided he was awake enough to risk closing his eyes, if only for a moment. The light was hurting his eyes. He opened them again, and the world was still the same: cold, bleak, and boring. As if weighed down, his eyelids closed again.

When he opened them, the world had suddenly gone white. He blinked, thinking that he had slipped into a dream, but the snow stayed, enveloping the landscape and smothering the bodies of his companions.

"Wake up!" he yelled, realising that he must have fallen back to sleep. He tried to gauge the time of day while he shook snow off his blankets, but the sun had disappeared beneath the heavy flurries. "Wake up, it's snowing!" he cried. He knew the peril of snow this far north.

*****

"How's our patient?" Gearoid asked.

Brother Seamus looked up from the manuscript he had been studying. "I think he'll live, but other than that it's hard to say."

The patient lay motionless on a cot. He was sleeping under a light blanket with a fire burning nearby to warm the austere room. His upper body lay uncovered, and he was heavily bandaged. He reeked of burned flesh and medicinal ointments.

"Have you any idea how he got into this state, Seamy?" asked Gearoid.

Brother Seamus shrugged. "The lacerations around his face suggest a possible attack by some creature perhaps. As for the burns, they are a mystery. His back is completely unblemished, but his chest is covered in scorched flesh. The swelling hasn't even gone down yet. Only then, will the true pattern of the burn reveal itself. Unless our patient comes to and tells us how he got into such a state, it will always be a mystery."

"I see," Abbot Gearoid replied. "Is there any sign of consciousness?"

Brother Seamus chewed on his lower lip. "I'm sure you've heard him screaming, Gearoid. I think they must have heard him in *Ard Pect*. It gives me nightmares just listening to him, but the strange thing is, even though he sits up yelling his head off, he isn't aware of me or Brother Fionn's presence. It's like he's in a different world, haunted by some inner demons."

"Perhaps he's haunted by his own memories. Whatever caused those injuries would be enough to give any man bad dreams."

Chapter Three: The Snowstorm

Maerlin tossed and turned on the stretcher as her companions carried her through the snow. Occasionally she would cry out or mumble gibberish. Other than that, her body showed little sign of the struggle that went on inside her head.

Again, she found herself on Dragon's Ridge, witnessing the battle between the forces of *Clann Na Dragan* and Lord Boare's army. This time, however, there were subtle differences in the scene.

The wind blew strongly from the west, bringing the scent of blood and terror to her nostrils as she stood beside the White Sorceress on the ridge. Below her, the White Knight was charging forward, his sword held high as he charged toward the Boarite leader.

The Dark Mage stood on the Burial Mound chanting a spell, but somehow, Dubhgall the Black looked less confident, less arrogant.

When the Sorceress looked toward Maerlin this time, Maerlin noticed a change there, too. Maerlin struggled to compare this dream to the previous dream. She tried to spot the differences between the two dreams, but was unable to do so. The battle drew her attention away. Looking at the Maiden, Maerlin felt some empathy there, but not the connection that she had previously felt and when the Maiden turned to look her way, their eyes did not meet. Instead, the Maiden looked through her, as if Maerlin was not there. Maerlin felt like an outsider; somehow disconnected from the scene.

Her spirit was drawn downwards to the battle, and she flew over the heads of screaming horses and cursing men as she glided to the mound were Dubhgall the Black stood. Suddenly, before she was fully aware of what was happening, she was pulled into Dubhgall's body and looked out at the battle through his eyes. Thunder rumbled across the sky as the White Maiden worked her Wild-magic, and lightning danced around the Dark Mage.

The image blurred, and she could see herself standing naked on the Maiden Stone at the centre of the burial mound, summoning lightning down from the tempestuous skies. She watched, through the Dark Mage's eyes, as he deflected the first few bolts, but they continued to come, faster and more powerfully, as the Elementals obeyed her wishes. Finally, the first bolt of white-hot heat seared into Dubhgall's chest, and Maerlin screamed as pain shot into her mind. Each bolt that hit the Dark Mage caused Maerlin to scream and shudder. Maerlin struggled to free her Dream-spirit from his body as she relived her attack on the Mage, but it was to no avail. She could not break free, and was forced to endure each agonising blow, until eventually, the killing blow came and Maerlin's spirit was knocked free.

*****

The crone had been sitting in her cottage, looking out of her window at the growing storm, ignoring the silent rebuke of her companion. She could feel the cold wind and the icy snow in her arthritic bones, and she watched as her well-tended rose garden shrivelled away and vanished under the snow. Still, she did nothing.

She heard a rustling behind her, but she refused to acknowledge his silent stare. Even when he moved closer, and she could feel him beside her, she would not meet his eyes.

Finally she could stand it no longer. "Perhaps they'll find shelter somewhere else, Fintan."

Fintan did not reply. His silence was filled with disapproval.

"Damn thee, Fintan! Why dost thou get me into these things?" she grumbled when the first crash of thunder sounded overhead. It was quickly followed by a flash of lightning. Now she knew that her senses were not deceiving her. This was no ordinary storm. Snowfall should appear like a light out-breath, whereas this snow was a tension-filled gasp.

Fintan remained silent; knowing that words would not change the old woman's long-held aversion toward visitors. Only his silent disapproval could move her to shame.

"Damn thee, and damn thy meddling, Fintan!" she cursed, retrieving her stout staff. Pulling her shawl tighter around her head so that only a vertical sliver of her ancient face showed, she yanked the door open and headed out into the storm.

*****

They had been running all day, racing toward the shelter of the mountains while the snow storm worsened. Cull was the first to notice Maerlin's troubled expression, but soon it became apparent to them all. Maerlin was having another nightmare. She shuddered violently as she screamed out and wept in her sleep. Try though they might, they could not rouse her, and Cull suspected that Maerlin's dreams were the cause of the ever-worsening weather. When thunder rumbled overhead and lightning clashed through the blinding snow, they all looked at the pained expression on Maerlin's face and prayed for help.

"How far is it, Vort?" Cull asked, panting from the exertion.

"We're still a half a day away. We need to find shelter soon or we'll be lost. This storm might blow over, and we'll be able to continue when it's gone."

Cull looked around, but all he could see was white flurries of snow on a bare landscape. He considered splitting the party up to look for shelter, only to dismiss the idea. In this storm, it would be easy to lose someone. They would be better off sticking together.

Again thunder crashed overhead, as if in response to Maerlin's screams, and lightning followed an instant later.

*****

The crone marched angrily across her beloved garden and up the nearby hill. Listening to the wind and watching the lightning flashes, she focused her attention on the storm and looked for the strangers that Fintan had warned her were coming. She could see no one in the storm, and she cursed her companion. For years, they had lived in happy isolation, but now, she would be forced to step back into the mad world of mankind and face the haunting shadows of her own past.

Using her special abilities, she focused on the storm, feeling it lurking just behind her consciousness. It crept up her spine and tingled into her brain. Finally she knew enough. Taking a deep breath, she raised her arms wide and yelled at the top of her lungs "STOP THIS!"

The storm bucked like a startled colt before rumbling on as if nothing had happened. Glaring at the sky, she tried again. This time she did not try to out-shout the storm, merely *out-will* it. Focusing sharply on the storm's epicentre, she let her command out in a short bark.

"Stop it!" Her tone was that of a schoolmistress who had found a child scrawling on his desk, and the storm flinched back in surprise.

The winds stumbled to a halt, leaving the snow to fall gently to the ground like feathers from a burst pillowcase.

Looking around, she still could not see the visitors, but she sensed that they were close by. They would surely see her once the snow had settled. Lifting her staff, she muttered a simple spell, and the gnarled tip glowed brightly.

"Over here," she croaked, still secretly hoping against hope to go unheard. If they passed her by, her conscience would be clear, and Fintan would stop glaring at her with that all-knowing look that he had perfected over the years.

"Hello?" the surprised response came from out of the settling blizzard.

Her shoulders slumped, and she reluctantly accepted the will of the goddess. "I pray this is worth it, Deanna," she mumbled as she stood waiting for the strangers to come toward her. They were a pathetic group of wretches, huddled against the bitter cold. Although the crone preferred her solitary existence, she was not an evil woman, and pity soon filled her.

"Who is foolish enough to have thee out in this weather?" she demanded.

"The gods be with you," the man who carried the forepart of the stretcher responded "Are we glad to see you!"

"Well, I can't say that the feeling's mutual," she replied with a touch of bitterness. "What, by the Nine Hells, art thou doing out here at this time of year? Didst thy mother drop thee on thy head when thou wast a nipper?"

The man had expected a warmer welcome, and her question left him dumbstruck. The other stretcher-bearer finally answered "We were heading for the Sett of *Clann Na Broce Snochta*, when the storm caught us out in the open. It's still a little early for such a blizzard."

Her attention shifted to the second man. "Thou keep strange company for a Pect, Brocian."

The Brocian shrugged. "We're seeking shelter from the blizzard, Ma'am. The wee lassie's not well." His head indicated Maerlin, lying on the stretcher.

"Which of thee is the fool who summoned that storm?"

"Erm ... that'd be Maerlin, Ma'am," the first man answered, also indicating the girl in the stretcher.

The crone looked at each of them in turn and finally down at Maerlin. With a sigh she turned away. "Come along then, if thou must." She led the way back to her cottage and indicated the cot beside the fire. "Put the wee *cailín* down there. I'll go and fetch my medicines."

Fintan looked silently down from the rafters, ruffling his feathers against the sudden cold draught.

*****

"What's all that shouting?" Abbot Gearoid asked, marching into the infirmary.

Seamy and Fionn were tending to their patient. They both looked wearily up at Gearoid, clearly unhappy.

"It's Balor, Gearoid. He's had another one of his nightmares ... the worst one yet," Brother Seamus explained.

Gearoid did a mental jig to keep up. "Balor?"

"Well ... we had to call him something. We couldn't just keep referring to him as the stranger or the 'mystery man, could we? It's ... it's just not right!"

"Ah, I see. I guess it'll have to do for now, until he comes around ..." said Gearoid.

"...If he ever comes around," Brother Fionn added.

Abbot Gearoid looked at the freckle-faced youth and smiled. "There speaks the optimism of youth, eh, Seamy!"

Brother Seamus grinned and Fionn flushed.

"We'd all better pray for his recovery, Fionn."

The young monk nodded apologetically. "Yes, Abbott, I'm sorry."

"It'd certainly make your task easier, what with the feeding and the bedpans, Fionn," Seamy joked. "I'm sure that it'll get tedious after the first couple of hundred."

They smiled in agreement before Gearoid brought them back to the reason for his visit.

"These nightmares, Seamy, is there something you can give him for them? Some of the monks use this wing for study, and it certainly doesn't help their contemplation."

Seamy considered his options for a moment. "It's not that easy, Gearoid. The mind is a delicate thing. I'm not sure if these nightmares are helping the healing process, or hindering it. It's very hard to say. The priestesses of Deanna have skilled magicians that can slip into a person's dreams and interpret them ..."

Gearoid could see where this was leading and frowned at his friend. "We're not sending him to the priestesses, Seamy. I've told you that!"

"But why not ...?"

Abbot Gearoid couldn't give him an answer. It was a question that he'd pondered on a number of occasions. "Just leave it, Seamy ..." he begged "... please?"

Seamy chewed his lip, dissatisfaction written all over his face, before he sighed and rubbed the frown away. "Very well, then. It was just an idea."

"What about moving him to more isolated quarters?" Gearoid asked in order to change the subject.

"I'd prefer not to move him unless it's absolutely necessary. I'll try a mild sleeping potion on him and see if that helps."

Gearoid smiled at his friend. "Seamy, you need some rest yourself. I'm sure Fionn will be able to manage the bedpans and feeding for a short while. You've hardly left the man's side since he arrived."

"I'll be fine."

"No, Seamy, you won't!" Gearoid argued. "That's an order from [ ]
superior. Go and get some rest. I don't want you keeling over [ ]
exhaustion. You're too valuable to us all."

Seeing the Abbot's determined face, Seamy nodded and left the bedsid[ ]
It was rare for Gearoid to even mention his new status as leader of th[ ]
community. When he did, the other monks were usually so surprised tha[ ]
they immediately gave up any resistance.

"Thank you, my friend. I'll have Fionn wake you for supper."

Seamy gave Gearoid a sidelong glance, but offered no further resistance
as he headed to his cot.

When he lay down and pulled the covers up over his head to block out the
light, weariness overtook hold, and he slipped into troubled sleep.

"I'll be fine."

"No, Seamy, you won't!" Gearoid argued. "That's an order from your superior. Go and get some rest. I don't want you keeling over with exhaustion. You're too valuable to us all."

Seeing the Abbot's determined face, Seamy nodded and left the bedside. It was rare for Gearoid to even mention his new status as leader of the community. When he did, the other monks were usually so surprised that they immediately gave up any resistance.

"Thank you, my friend. I'll have Fionn wake you for supper."

Seamy gave Gearoid a sidelong glance, but offered no further resistance as he headed to his cot.

When he lay down and pulled the covers up over his head to block out the light, weariness overtook hold, and he slipped into troubled sleep.

Chapter Four: Seabhac and the Hawk

The crone shuffled outside and filled a kettle with fresh snow, rather than wade through the drifts to her well. When she returned, her visitors were still standing, dripping water onto her battered rug.

"Don't just stand there getting my house wet. I've enough to deal with with one patient, without the rest of thee coming down with something. Take those cloaks off and hang them on the porch to drip. When they've stopped dripping, thou canst bring them in and let them dry by the hearth."

As they shuffled out to obey, the crone put the kettle over the fire, and added wood to the embers. "Best fetch some more wood in while thou art out there. Thou wilt find some in the lean-to at the side of the cottage," she ordered. If she had to have guests, the least they could do was help out.

Pulling off her damp shawl, she hung it on a hook beside the fire to dry and turned to inspect her patient. As she pulled the damp locks away from Maerlin's face, her heart did a back-flip. "Sweet Deanna!"

Looking up into the rafters at her companion, she glared balefully at the old harrier. "Didst thou know about this, Fintan?"

Her companion remained silent. Standing with his claws embedded in the rafters, the ancient hawk ignored her accusing glare. His plumage had long ago lost its sheen, for the bird was ancient in hawk years. His strong connection to the crone helped the harrier to communicate with her through a melding of minds. She had taught him far more than she would ever reveal to another living soul. After all their years together, there were few secrets between them, but somehow the harrier had kept this news from his companion.

Muttering curses under her breath, she turned back to his patient and studied Maerlin's face more closely. It was a face that she had seen in her mind, long before Maerlin was born. To see it now, lying so pale and sickly, struck a chord in the old woman's heart. Laying her hand on Maerlin's forehead, she felt the heat there.

The other girl appeared in the doorway. "How is she?" she asked timidly.

The crone had not heard the door open and hurriedly wiped the moisture from her eyes. Her first words were a little choked, and she had to clear her throat before trying again "She has a slight temperature," she replied. She could see the genuine concern on the girl's face.

"Have you any feverfew?" the girl asked. "We've lost all our own herbs, and I haven't had the time to gather more."

The crone looked at her in surprise. "Thou hast been taught the healing arts?"

"...A little. I'm a novice of Deanna. I learned a few things while I was on the Holy Isle."

The crone raised an eyebrow. "Thou art a long way from home, girl," she said, noticing the seashell necklace. "What do they call thee?"

"Cora, Ma'am, Cora *Ni Rón*. I'm a Water-sister of the Western Isles."

"Come then, Cora. Thou canst help me undress thy friend. We'll need to get those wet clothes off her before she gets consumption."

"Yes, Ma'am."

"I'm a bit long in the tooth to be called, Ma'am," she replied. "You can call me ..." The crone hesitated. It had been a long time since she had used her name "... You can call me Seabhac, and that smelly old bird in the rafters is Fintan." She gave the hen harrier a baleful glance, which he studiously ignored.

"Ma'am?" Cora asked. "I mean ... Seabhac?"

"What is it?"

"It was you who stopped the storm, wasn't it?"

Seabhac looked sharply at Cora, and then, around the room to make sure that they were alone. "Cora," she said, her voice becoming very serious. "I want thee to promise me that thou wilt keep that to thyself. Dost thou hear?"

"Yes Ma'am, of course, but why?"

Seabhac looked off into the distance for a moment before answering "I have my reasons, believe me. I want thee to promise me that thou wilt not tell a living soul about this. Wilt thou grant me this small boon?"

Cora looked confused, but reluctantly nodded her head. "I promise."

A small smile spread across Seabhac's face for the first time that day, and she patted Cora's hand. "Thank thee, Cora. This must be our little secret. Now, we'd best get to work."

Carefully, Seabhac prised the magpie from Maerlin's grasp and laid it near the fire. Together, they undressed Maerlin, pulling the wet clothes from her body and throwing them on the floor. Seabhac tutted with disapproval as she discovered the various bumps and bruises that were revealed on Maerlin's body. Suddenly her face went pale, and she let out a gasp of shock.

"What's the matter?"

Seabhac's fingers brushed the silver medallion that nestled between Maerlin's breasts. "Dost thou know how thy companion came by this?"

"No. Maerlin has always had it, at least, as far as I know. Why?"

"Maerlin ... is that definitely the child's name?"

"Yes. She's called Maerlin Smith of High Peaks."

"That's a powerful name for such a small girl. Has she also been blessed by the goddess?"

"Yes, she's a Dream-catcher and an Air-sister. She hasn't had much training, but she's very gifted. They say that she could be the next Uiscallan."

Seabhac looked sharply at her. "Uiscallan was nothing more than a foolish legend, child. Such stories tend to get exaggerated over time."

They heard the door open, and their conversation ended. Quickly, they covered Maerlin with a blanket. Lifting the unconscious magpie from the fireplace, Seabhac placed it carefully back into Maerlin's hands, before turning to the door.

The older man entered first, still wearing his broad-brimmed hat. His arms were laden with firewood. The others followed, carrying their packs and more firewood. Seabhac watched them enter and pointed toward a stack of dry timber near the fire. One by one, she took in each of their faces, noting their clothing and mannerisms. Once they had all settled, she spoke. "From the look of all of thee, there's a tale to be told here, and a bard to tell it. What brings thee this far north, so close to winter?"

Cull spoke quickly before the bard-Taliesin-could blurt anything out. "There's trouble brewing down by the ridge, so we came north to avoid it. We've banded together for safety against bandits. My name is Cull, and this is Conal ... my nephew. The harper is called Taliesin, and the Brocian is Vort. The girls are Cora and Maerlin."

Seabhac's tawny eyes met Cull's hazel ones and bored sharply into his. She was not fooled, and they both knew it. "Thou wilt find few bandits this far north, especially at this time of the year. There are lean pickings around here, even for the wolves. Apart from the Snow Badgers, there's no one else around here."

"Snow Badgers?" Cull asked.

"Clann Na Snochta Broce ..." the Brocian, Vort, explained. "My Clan brothers. Like the badgers that dwell around here, my cousins are albino. We believe that it's a blessing from Cernunnos, so they are known as Clann Na Snochta Broce to the Pects, or the Snow Badgers to the Fear Ban."

Seabhac was looking closely at the boy named Conal. Muttering a whispered curse, she commanded "Come closer, boy. My eyes are not what they used to be."

Conal looked up at the crone, and then toward Cull, his eyes questioning. Cull nodded, and Conal stepped forward. Seabhac looked long into his piercing blue eyes, and the room fell into silence, save for the crackling of the fire. Lifting her gnarled hand, she stroked his hair, and her eyes drifted to the silver dragon-hilted sword, hanging from a baldric on his shoulder.

"So, they still treat that old thing like a sword, eh?" she muttered. Her gaze bore deep into his soul. "Why hast a Dragan chosen to darken his golden locks, pray tell?"

Conal gasped in surprise, and Cull cursed as Seabhac held the Prince's gaze.

"Thou canst try and hide thy hair, but thy eyes blaze like the sun, and don't bother telling me a whole heap of lies either. Thou can save thy breath," she said, her hand rising to stem off Cull's protestations. "Thy secrets are safe with me, *Dragan*. Who would I tell anyway? Fintan is my only company, and I don't intend to go marching off anywhere. I'll tell thee this though. Much though the boy may wish to keep that pathetic excuse for a sword near to hand, it'd be wiser for thee all if it were hidden, especially if thou art going to spin feeble yarns to strangers. I may be an old hag, but I'm far from senile. I can smell horse dung when it's wafted under my nose."

Cull cleared his throat, clearly deciding to offer at least some of the truth. "The boy's in danger, Ma'am. We're heading north to find a safe place to hide out for the winter."

"How old art thou, boy?" Seabhac asked, ignoring Cull.

"I'm due to claim my manhood at the spring gathering, Ma'am."

"Ah! So thou still must face thy Rites of Manhood before thou canst claim thy crown. Is that it?"

Conal nodded, pale-faced at the perceptiveness of the crone.

"Well, don't worry, my bonny prince. Thou hast nothing to fear from this old hawk. Thou can consider me a loyal servant of *Clann Na Dragan* ... just don't expect me to be there for thy coronation. I'm happy enough right here. If thou needeth any service from me, then thou will just have to come up here and get it thyself."

Conal smiled hesitantly. "Thank you, Ma'am."

"Deanna! What's with all this Ma'am business? Please, call me Seabhac."

Seabhac looked again at Conal, her mind drifting back in time. "If thou wilt take the advice of a mad old hag, Conal, let me give thee some."

"Yes?"

"Wash that dye out of thy hair and grow back thy golden locks in all their glory. Thou wilt need to look like a *Dragan* come springtime, when thou comes down from the mountains. Thy people wilt not follow a nervous-looking boy, no matter what sword he wields. They wilt want to see their King: *Ri Na Dragan*."

"But he'll stand out like a sore thumb if he does that. He won't be safe anywhere near *Tir Pect*..." Cull protested.

Seabhac rolled her eyes at Cull. "Thou hast nothing to fear on that front. Thou art a long ways from *Ard Pect*. King Conchubhar, and that wily Queen of his, may have eagle eyes and long ears, but they don't hear all that well in these parts of Dragania. It's true, Conchubhar has aspirations to reclaim all of the previous Pectish lands, but I doubt he's ready to invade the *Fear Ban*. His mind is sharper than a razor, even if his wife's madder than a jack-in-the-box. He knows that his Pects will never defeat Lord Boare while he has his pet wizard at hand."

Seabhac sensed the sudden unease in the room, but she knew not the cause. She had a lot on her mind and needed some time alone to consider all that was happening. Firstly though, she needed to tend to Maerlin's wounds. Turning to Cora, she changed the subject "Canst thou cook, lass?"

Cora nodded.

"Well, thou all hast the look of winter-wolves about thee. Canst thou rustle up a hearty stew? Thou wilt find vegetables in the outhouse and a fresh hare hanging in the rafters. Fintan brought it back yesterday, along with the news of thy coming."

Cora prepared their first good meal in days, while Seabhac dressed Maerlin's broken fingers.

"It's been a long time since I've heard a bard's tale," Seabhac said over her shoulder. "We don't get many visitors in these parts. Could thou play us all a little something, bard? There isn't a whole lot else to do around here with all that snow out there."

"It would be an honour, Ma'am," Taliesin agreed, pulling his harp from its protective case. As Seabhac bound Maerlin's fingers to a straight stick, the singer tuned his harp.

"What would you like to hear?"

Seabhac shrugged her shoulders in a non-committal fashion. "I don't care. Whatever comes to mind."

"Do you know any legends about my sword, Tal?" Conal asked.

Taliesin frowned. "I'm sorry, Conal, but I don't really know all that much. The origins of the sword are shrouded in mystery. Only two people knew the full tale and neither of them ever revealed their secrets."

"Who were they?"

Taliesin stroked his harp strings, and the room hushed in expectation. "I'll tell you what I know, although it isn't much..."

"It was a long, long time ago, in the darkest part of the history of Dragania. It was a time of poverty and deprivation, a time of pestilence and famine. The common folk hid within their hovels and prayed to the Seven for salvation. They claimed that the High King had gone mad, and the kingdom was falling into darkness.

It all started when a young sorcerer arrived in the mighty city of Suilequay. No one knew from whence he came, but his arrival heralded the coming of the Dark Age, and the decline of the once-prosperous kingdom of Dragania.

It was whispered that the sorcerer dabbled in forbidden arts, dark and ancient practises long since forbidden by the guild of Magi. There finally came a day when the guild formally accused the sorcerer of Necromancy: a crime that was punishable by death. The young man did not deny his crimes, far from it in fact. He laughed in the faces of the leaders of the Magi Guild, and challenged them to a duel.

A terrible battle ensued, a magical battle that had never been witnessed before or since, and one that left the once-magnificent city of Suilequay as a smoking ruin. Many of the citizenry of the city died in the days of fighting, and not just the mages. Hundreds of innocent bystanders were engulfed in the inferno that swept across the city. The High King barely escaped with his life, and it is said that this was the cause of his later madness.

Fire wept from the heavens, and lightning bolts destroyed whole streets as the battle continued unabated. Finally, from out of the smoking ruins a victor emerged. It was the young sorcerer, and he strode forth to take up the seat of the High Mage.

An immense unkindness of ravens descended on the smoking ruins of the city, and they feasted on the poor unfortunates who had not escaped. The people named the sorcerer: Dubhgall the Black, due to the ravens that followed in his wake. Since then, he has become the most feared sorcerer in the land.

As the Mage's powers grew, so too did his influence over the High King, and the Boare fell further into bouts of madness. Taxes rose to levels that no man could pay. Crime became rampant in the cities, and poverty was seen everywhere. It didn't take long before plague spread through the land, decimating the population. The Clans became fractious and petty wars broke out due to the lack of any strong leadership from the High King.

One of the Clan leaders was a young northern prince called Luigheagh. His Clan was a small insignificant one from the wild northern plains. His ancestors had been bequeathed the land for some service to a previous High King. They had also been given the arduous task of defending the realm against the marauding Pects, who regularly swept down from their mountains.

It was a harsh land that the Prince had grown up in as the Pects constantly harried his boundaries, and with King Boare's mind steeped in madness, reinforcements failed to arrive from the south.

Nevertheless, Luigheagh was a brave man, and although young, he was powerfully charismatic. His clansmen fought fiercely at his side to keep the Pects at bay. It wasn't long before the Pectish High King retreated and for the first time in recorded history, the northern border settled into a wary peace.

The rest of the Kingdom, however, was falling further and further into chaos.

Eventually, the High Priestess of Deanna was reluctantly forced to intervene. Seeing the darkness spreading throughout the land, she summoned her Dream-catchers together to search out for possible solutions.

34

The following spring, a young priestess arrived at Luigheagh's stronghold with a message from the High Priestess. She told him that a new High King was needed, and that he had been selected from all the available candidates.

Naturally, Luigheagh was a little surprised at the news. What she was proposing was nothing less than an act of high treason. He also had reservations about challenging the High King's mage. Even in the far north, they had heard of the prowess of Dubhgall the Black.

The priestess: Uiscallan led Luigheagh outside onto the plain and showed him her own magical abilities. She explained that the High Priestess had decided to intervene, and if necessary use the full might of the Order of Deanna to help defeat the Boare and his mage.

Luigheagh was impressed by her magical ability, as it far surpassed the skills of his own hedge-wizards. Although he was still reluctant, he agreed to consider her proposal. He asked her to be his guest at his Dun while he sent out scouts to the four corners of the Kingdom to assess the situation further.

Reluctantly she agreed, and the summer passed them by while she waited for his decision. When the scouts returned, they brought with them dire stories of war, pestilence, and famine.

Finally, she was summoned to his private chambers...

*****

Maerlin drifted through the fog of her dream and found herself in Prince Luigheagh's private chamber.

The handsome prince was lounging in a chair, drinking mead from a horn and scratching one of his wolfhounds' ears. Before him stood Uiscallan. Maerlin recognised her immediately from her other dream; the one from the Battle of the High Kings. The priestess looked younger, but there was no mistaking her, or for that matter, the young knight with his piercing blue eyes.

"I've been thinking about your proposal," he said, coming quickly to the point.

"It wasn't my proposal, Luigheagh. I told thou before, it came from the High Priestess," Uiscallan pointed out.

"Whatever," he dismissed. "Anyway, my scouts have returned. Their news is grim. Dragania is falling apart, and my spies in Ard Pect report that the Pects are growing restless. They sense the weakness in the High King. Only the threat of Dubhgall the Black's magic is keeping them at bay, that and my own vigilance. The peace with the Pects is looking shaky, and therefore, I've decided to agree to your request. I will raise an army and challenge Lord Boare for the High Kingship."

Uiscallan cleared her throat, looking decidedly uncomfortable

"Is something the matter?"

"Prince Luigheagh, as I explained to thee previously, the Dream-catchers of the Order of Deanna have foretold thee as the next ruler of Dragania. They have had visions of thy defeat over Lord Boare and his Dark Mage. However, there is something that thou must do, before the time is right for thy challenge."

Luigheagh waited for further enlightenment.

Uiscallan played with one of her long dark braids. It signalled her nervousness. Taking a deep breath, she looked boldly at Luigheagh and ploughed on "They have foretold that thou must journey on a quest for some mystical item. When thou hast gained possession of it, the path to the throne of the High King will be open to thee."

"Quest ... I can't go on a quest. Who would guard the northern passes while I was away? Who would be the guardian of my Clan?"

"Prince Luigheagh. Unless thou complete this quest, thy challenge for the High Kingship wilt be doomed to fail ... and with thee, the whole Kingdom."

Luigheagh frowned. "What is this item?"

"Alas, that I do not know, I am not a Dream-catcher."

"I see," Luigheagh said, though clearly he did not "And where will I find this item?"

Uiscallan twisted her braid again and would not meet the young prince's eyes. "That too is hidden from me."

"Why did the High Priestess choose you to come here, if you don't know these things?"

"Because a Dream-catcher cannot help thee like I can."

"So what can you offer me?"

"I can help thee to gain the High Kingship, but the quest will not be easy. All I know for certain is that we must venture far to the east, across the Bitter Eastern Sea, in order to fulfil thy destiny. Our journey will be fraught with perils, but I will protect thee during thy quest, and I will know when thou hast found that which thou must seek. We must leave soon, however, before it is too late for Dragania."

"You want me to go now? But the summer is nearly over. Soon, the snows will be upon us. When are we expected to return?"

Uiscallan sighed. "This journey could take us many moons, Sire."

"Moons!"

"Years, perhaps."

"But it's only a two week ride to the coast!"

"I know this."

"You aren't suggesting sailing across the Bitter Eastern Sea in the middle of winter, are you?"

"Hast thou heard of a place called the Ice Plains?" Uiscallan asked.

"Yes, of course I have. My mother told me tales of it when I was younger. It was one of many such scary stories she told to frighten the children with, but surely such a place does not exist."

"Art thou sure?"

"Of course, I'm sure."

"Prince Luigheagh. The Ice Plains do indeed exist, and we must travel through them to reach our destination. We must seek out the legendary Palace of the Frost Dragons," Uiscallan declared.

"Are you mad? Ice Plains ... Dragons! Those are all just fairy tales."

"Hast thou never wondered about the origins of such legends? Can they all be figments of the imagination?"

"Clearly the High Priestess and her Dream-catchers have very fruitful imaginations. I believe none of it. Go back to your Holy Isle, and tell them to find another fool for this errand. You're all mad ... "

The mists swirled and the scene vanished, only to be replaced by another.

Maerlin saw the priestess, stony-faced, riding away from the small fort. In the distance, she saw a rider galloping out of the gates and racing after the priestess. It wasn't long before the Luigheagh pulled up alongside the priestess.

"Good morning, Luigheagh," she greeted, though there was little warmth in her tone. "What brings thee out, so early in the day? Didst thou wet thy bed after too much ale?"

Luigheagh slowed his mount and they rode on in sullen silence for a few moments. Finally he spoke "I had a very strange dream last night."

Uiscallan rode on in silence.

"I saw things that shook me to the core, things I wouldn't wish on my greatest enemies."

"I can recommend a good tonic for thee to prevent such dreams," she offered, "... though it is said to leave one a little dim-witted on the morrow." Uiscallan glared at the Prince before adding "I'm sure that you'd hardly notice the difference."

Luigheagh bit back an angry retort and gripped his reins tighter to control his temper. "Surely, you can understand my apprehension."

Uiscallan again said nothing.

"Look, perhaps I was a little rude yesterday," he offered as an apology. "Please, come back to the fort and we'll discuss your proposal further."

"I've already told thee, Luigheagh, this was not my proposal." Uiscallan pulled up her horse and looked pointedly at the Prince. "Let's get one thing straight, shall we. I'm not exactly enamoured with the idea either."

The Prince looked confused.

"I'd be much happier sitting in the great library studying ancient tomes, rather than riding halfway across Dragania to meet some loud-mouthed, unwashed Hinterlander. That's to say nothing of thy squalid fortress and thy warriors' barbaric concepts of personal hygiene. I mean, is it really necessary to have thy pigs and thy dogs living in thy throne room? Hast thou not noticed the smell coming out of that place?"

"But ..." Luigheagh began.

"...And while we're on the subject, I've seen the way that thy men leer suggestively at thee, every time I walk past. I have no intention of sleeping with thee, nor with any of thy men for that matter. I'd rather sleep with that blind old boar thou keep as a family pet. At least he doesn't snore and fart while he sleeps ... well ... not as much anyway."

"But ..." Luigheagh began again, but Uiscallan was already riding back toward the fort.

"...Thou hast one week to get thy affairs in order, and then I shall leave, with or without thee," she ordered over her shoulder.

"How many men should I bring?"

"Men! What dost thou want thy men for?"

"The plains to the east can be dangerous," Luigheagh explained. "We'll need an honour guard of twenty warriors at the very least. Perhaps fifty would be better, to discourage bandits."

"Thou hast no need for thy men, Luigheagh. I wilt protect thee from any bandits foolish enough to waylay us."

"But ..."

Uiscallan pulled up and turned to look back at the Prince. "It appears that thy herbalist has already proscribed that sleeping draught we spoke about earlier, but I fear her measurements were incorrect. Thou seemeth extremely dull-witted this morning."

The mists swirled and obscured Maerlin's vision, dragging her back to her body...

*****

"What happened next?" Conal demanded. He was eager to learn more about his ancestors.

"Well, that's another tale," Taliesin replied. "I'll tell you about their return tomorrow, Conal. Alas, no one knows the full story of their actual quest. King Luigheagh and Priestess Uiscallan never revealed the details of their expedition. They took the secret to their graves."

Seabhac groaned as she got to her feet. "That was a powerful tale, bard. It was almost as if I was there."

Taliesin smiled at the complement.

"I think thou hast earned some mead to wet thy throat," Seabhac declared. "How's that stew coming along, Cora?"

Chapter Five: Dreams, Nightmares, and Reincarnation

"Abbot Gearoid! Abbot Gearoid!"

Gearoid, who had been catching a few moments of peaceful meditation after a busy day, turned to look at the young monk. "What's the matter Fionn?"

"Abbot Gearoid!" Fionn gasped. "It's Balor. He was dreaming again!"

Gearoid rolled his eyes skyward. "...And?"

"Abbot, I ..."

"Come, Brother Fionn, sit yourself down and catch your breath," Gearoid suggested, patting the wooden pew beside him.

Fionn opened his mouth to speak again, panic in his eyes, but he was forestalled by Gearoid's restraining hand. "Sit with me and pray for a few moments, Brother, and then you can tell me all about it."

Fionn nodded and tried to still his beating heart.

Abbot Gearoid closed his eyes, as if to will calmness into the youth beside him. After a few moments, he could sense Fionn's continued agitation and opened them again. "Alright, Fionn, let's start at the beginning."

The young monk nodded, still eager to get to the brunt of the problem. "Brother Seamus had gone to his cell to catch up on some sleep, and I was sitting by the fire in the sickroom keeping an eye on our patient. Anyway, I looked over at Balor as he was groaning in his sleep again."

"Did you give him some more sleeping draught?"

"No, Abbot. I thought it better to wait for Brother Seamus to come back as I'm not sure of the dosage."

"I see," Gearoid replied. "So, the patient was getting restless. Was it another nightmare?"

"I don't know. He was tossing about on his cot and moaning. He didn't start screaming though, like he's done before."

"Then, what's the matter?"

"Well, I thought it best to go and wake Brother Seamus, just to be on the safe side. He might want to give him a sedative before things took a turn for the worse." Fionn looked over at Abbot Gearoid anxiously.

"What happened, Fionn?"

"I was ... I was only gone for a few moments. I ran down to Brother Seamus's cell, as quick as I could, Abbot, honest, I did."

"I'm sure you did," Gearoid assured. "So what happened?"

"Well, Brother Seamus and I hurried back to the sickroom, but when we got there, Balor was gone."

"Gone?"

"Yes, Abbot, gone, disappeared!"

"How can a blind, old man just get up and go, Fionn?" Gearoid asked. "Where's Seamy?"

"He's in the infirmary, Abbot. He's got some of the other monks out looking for him. He told me to come and fetch you."

"By the Seven!" Gearoid exclaimed, getting to his feet.

The Abbot hurried along the corridors and opened the door to the infirmary, Brother Fionn tagging along behind like a lost puppy.

"Ah, Gearoid!" Seamy greeted, concern written all over his face.

Gearoid looked at the sickbed, now empty and dishevelled. Clearly, the patient was not there. Gearoid crouched down to look underneath the cot.

"I've tried that," Seamy explained, "... and in the cupboard too."

Gearoid frowned and walked to the window. "Was this already open?"

"Yes, Abbot. I opened it a short while ago," Fionn explained. "Brother Seamy told me to let fresh air in regularly, so I open it for a while every morning and again just before dusk. It releases the foul poisons that can eke out of the sick."

Gearoid nodded his understanding. He had always found a strange smell lurking around sickrooms. He leaned on the windowsill and looked out across the small island. The room was on the third floor, and the patient could not have climbed down the smooth walls. Looking off into the distance across the lough and to the south, he noted heavy clouds covering the mountains. "There's some snow already on the mountains," he informed the others absently. "We could be in for a long winter."

The door opened, and another monk stepped in. The monk was about to speak to Brother Seamus when he noticed Gearoid, standing by the window. "Ah, Abbot Gearoid. We've searched the building, and he's nowhere to be found."

"Are you sure?"

The monk nodded firmly.

"Have them searched again," ordered Gearoid, "and send some of the men out to search the island. It's nearly dark. I don't want to find him frozen to death in the morning. Fionn, go with him and organise a complete search of the island. Seamy, you organise a systematic search the monastery. Leave nothing unturned."

They hurried out, leaving their spiritual leader alone in the sickroom. Gearoid walked over to the bed and looked down at the messed up blankets, lost in thought. It was only then that he noticed something sticking out of the top of the bedding. Frowning, Gearoid pulled back the covers and inspected the strange object.

"How did that get in there?" he asked, examining the black rectrix feather closely.

*****

Maerlin slipped back into the dream mists, which swirled and revealed a fortified ridge upon a sea of flowing grass.

Dragon's Ridge was lit up with many torches along its crest and around its outer perimeter. Soldiers hurried to and fro with final preparations. Men sweated digging fortifications before the coming battle, needing to have them completed before the onrushing dawn. Below on the plain waited the enemy, the myriad campfires signalling their presence. Here, the two armies of Dragania would decide its destiny.

Farther back within the defensive rings on the hilltop stood two marquees. Outside of one, flew a majestic war banner depicting a Frost Dragon. The other tent held no banner, and yet, it was just as spacious and luxurious as its counterpart. Maerlin was drawn toward this tent. Within it she found the young priestess, resting on a canopied bed while she read from a scroll.

Uiscallan pulled a stray black lock away from her face, absently tucking the errant hair behind her ear. She appeared distracted and eventually she threw the parchment aside in frustration.

Maerlin watched the scene unfold...

*****

Standing, Uiscallan pulled down the figure-hugging gown of white silk and moving toward the entrance. Peering out for a moment, she frowned, frustration marring her exotic good looks. She paced back and forth on the rich rugs beneath her feet.

"Damn him!" she cursed. "Why does he toy with my emotions?"

Moving to the dresser, she studied herself, doubt in her eyes. Lifting a brush, she brushed her hair, although it looked as if she had already done so innumerable times that evening.

"Thou art a fool, Uiscallan, to think that he holds thee in his affection," she berated herself. "Thou art just his pet magician. He hast no more care for thee than he does for his stallion, probably less. Why would he choose thee, when he has all those Fear Ban maidens whimpering for his affections?"

Frustrated, Uiscallan hurled the brush aside and turned away. Throwing herself onto the bed, she pulled one of the long cushions towards her and hugged it. "Damn him!"

Uiscallan lay there, tossing and turning, her mind replayed recent events. Since returning, the young prince had been distracted and often moody. One moment he was warm and attentive, and the next he shunned her company. He left her feeling foolish and confused. Could he have forgotten all that they had been through together? After all that she had given him, surely he was not intending to choose another for his bride? Had the smoky-eyed look he gave her earlier that evening been imagined? She was sure that he had hinted of slipping into her chambers after dark, or perhaps she had misheard him. Doubt filled her. It was only a few bells until dawn, and she had been waiting all night. The perfumes, with which she had adorned her body after bathing had long since lost their allure and her make-up had worn away from her constant fidgeting.

She heard a scratching sounded on the canvas, and a hushed voice spoke softly "Uiscallan, dim the lights lest we be seen."

Uiscallan gasped. Quickly, she shuttered down the oil lamp beside her, surprised at the strange request.

"My Lord!" she greeted, straightening her gown.

He slipped in, and even in the dim light she could see his roguish smile. "Am I disturbing you, Uiscallan?"

"No, please come in Sire." She climbed off the bed and moved forward to greet him. She was thankful now for the dimness of the light as she could feel her skin blushing.

"Do you always have to be so formal, Uiscallan, even when we're alone?"

The night suddenly felt warm as the priestess swallowed and moistened her lips. "No Sire, I mean ... Luigheagh."

Speaking his name sent a shiver down Uiscallan's back, and his smile gave her a glow inside.

He stepped closer until his vivid blue eyes dominated Uiscallan's vision. She felt herself slipping into those orbs when he reached for her. Breathing became difficult for the priestess. Shaking herself, she struggled to regain control of her emotions.

"Thou art not disturbing me, Luigheagh. I couldn't sleep."

"Neither could I," he confessed. "But it wasn't the coming battle that has kept me turning in my sleep. It was you, Uiscallan. I can't concentrate for thoughts of you."

Uiscallan flushed, lost for words. Never had the Prince spoken so openly of his affections for her.

"Forgive me for being so blunt, but my heart aches for you, Uiscallan. I want you for my wife. Tomorrow, if all goes well, I will announce it to the court and all will know you as my future Queen."

Uiscallan stepped back in shock, her eyes welling up. Only in her deepest dreams had she envisioned him saying those words to her. They were her greatest secret, and she had never believed that this day would come. From the first time she set eyes on the Prince, she had thought of this. She dreamed of being swept up in his arms. She longed for him to kiss her passionately until she was breathless with desire. She wanted desperately to look up at him and see the same deep love in his eyes that she felt in her own heart. She found her dreams coming true when he pulled her toward him, his hands strongly confident as he dragged her into his embrace and kissed her fervently. The surprise made her hold back, but only for a moment, before fully committing herself to her desires.

He lifted her as if she weighed no more than a bird and carried her over to the bed. Clinging to his neck, they kissed as she sank into the soft lambskin cover. His mouth probed hers while his hands roamed over her bodice, and her emotions soared when his weight pressed her down into the mattress. She shuddered as he undressed her, his rough manner surprising her. As her passions overtook her fears, she tugged at his clothing until they both lay naked, wrapped in each other's arms and locked in a passionate kiss...

... Later, she drifted into sleep, exhausted but content.

He rose quietly and dressed, and then being careful not to wake her, he laid a pendant on the pillow beside her and turned away. Quickly, he slipped into the night where the shadows hid his movements. There, his form blurred.

It was nearly dawn, and the first rays of the sun were lighting up the sky when a raven rose into the sky. It circled and climbed for a moment, looking down at the tents below, before arching away toward the enemy camp.

Maerlin dreamed on, wondering about the strangeness of her vision. Slipping back into Uiscallan's tent, she moved closer to the bed. She studied the priestess's contented face, and then she noticed something else. Coming closer still, she saw the necklace that lay beside the priestess. It was a silver hawk, a merlin.

Maerlin shuddered at the sight of her silver pendant.

"It cannot be!" she muttered, "Oh, sweet Deanna!"

"*Ah!*" a voice said. It was a voice then Maerlin knew well. "*Finally you stir.*"

Suddenly the dream vanished, and Maerlin found herself in a white room. Sitting there, calmly smoking her pipe was Nessa *MacTire*.

"*Ness!*" Maerlin exclaimed, rushing forward.

Nessa embraced her warmly.

"*Where are we?*"

"*We're in your head, dear,*" Nessa replied in her usual matter-of-fact manner.

"*So you survived?*"

"*Sit down, Maerlin. We need to talk.*"

Maerlin frowned and looked about. Suddenly, an additional chair appeared in the room.

"*Why are we here?*"

"*It's easier for me to talk to you here,*" Nessa explained.

"*It's a bit dreary,*" Maerlin commented.

"*It's your head, dear. You can decorate it any way you like. I just needed something to start with, and I've always had a fondness for white.*"

Maerlin looked around the white room, noticing its lack of doors, windows, and anything that made a room feel homely. *"You mean I can change it?"*

Nessa sighed. *"Yes dear, but can you pay attention? You can fiddle about later."*

Maerlin had been thinking about a window, a nice big one with flowery curtains around it. She had never owned her own home before and was already considering a cosy fireplace to sit beside.

"Maerlin!"

"Oh yes, sorry Ness." Maerlin apologised, and the fireplace disappeared as quickly as it had appeared. *"I was just..."*

"Yes dear, I know, but I need you to listen to me for a moment."

"Okay."

"Can you remember the last time you saw me?" Nessa asked.

Maerlin thought for a moment. *"Yes. We were in this room. You showed me how to summon the storm that defeated Dubhgall."*

Relief washed over Nessa's face. *"That's good. I was worried that there might have been some damage."*

"Damage?"

"You used an awful lot of 'Wild-magic', summoning that storm, Maerlin, and you know how dangerous that can be. You've been sleeping ever since."

Maerlin frowned. Images of her battle with the Dark Mage came back to her. Suddenly she gasped. *"Nessa, you nearly died!"*

Nessa pursed her lips. *"Yes, well, that's one of the things we need to talk about."*

Memories flooded into Maerlin's mind. *"I found you. You were dying. I put some life force into you to keep you alive. It worked, didn't' it?"*

Nessa took a deep breath. *"I'm afraid that it's not that simple."*

"But you were living. I saw your aura," Maerlin protested. She relived her last moments of consciousness, over and over again, feeling her magic soaking into Nessa's burned crow form. *"The aura was faint, but it was still there."*

"It isn't that simple, Maerlin. Few things are, especially death."

"Are you a ghost then?" Maerlin asked.

"No, Maerlin, not exactly."

"I don't understand."

"How can I put this? I'm afraid that I did die that day, but all's not lost."

"What do you mean?"

"As I'm sure I've told you before, death claims us all in the end. That's an unbreakable law. Some of us live a little longer than others, but we all have to embrace the goddess of death at some point."

Maerlin nodded, unable to speak.

"I was a servant of Deanna. That means I was blessed with a longer lifespan than most, but even a servant of Deanna can't overstep the Laws of Death. To make matters worse, I did a foolish thing. I took the form of one of Macha's angels."

"You changed form into a crow? What's wrong with that? Dubhgall did it all of the time."

"Dubhgall the Black was a servant of Macha, as I was a servant of Deanna. It wasn't just any crow's form that I took. It was that of the raven, a Death Angel. Macha demanded retribution for that."

"So you died?" Maerlin blurted, still confused. *"I still don't understand what you're telling me. What exactly happened?"*

"I've been reincarnated."

"What?"

"Reincarnated, you know, reborn."

"Does that mean that you're just a baby, and that you need to grow up?"

"No, Maerlin. Deanna and Macha made a pact, and I was given a second chance at life, but there's a problem. Now, I must serve two mistresses."

"Does that mean you're stuck as a raven? Is that it?"

"Sort of ... you'll see when you wake up."

"Am I still dreaming?"

"In a way ..."

"Will we be able to talk again, when I wake?"

"I'll be here in your head, though over time my form will change as your memories fade."

"Fade? They won't fade. How could I forget you?"

Nessa smiled. *"You're like a daughter to me, Maerlin, but believe me, over time your image of me will change."*

Maerlin frowned.

"Anyway, it's time for you to wake up, Maerlin. You need to gather your strength. Deanna needs you, and so do your friends."

"Hang on, Nessa. There's still so much I want to ask you!"

Nessa's image faded.

"Nessa, wait!"

Maerlin sat up, and the blanket fell away, letting the night air chill her. Looking around, she probed the darkness. The embers of a small fire glowed nearby, and she could hear the sounds of people breathing. Maerlin tried to remember where she was, but no memory came to her. She could smell food, wood smoke, dried herbs, and human sweat. As her eyes adjusted to the darkness, she could make out dark clumps on the ground around her. People were sleeping there. She felt a rustling beside her, and a quiver of fright ran up her body.

"Hello Maerlin," croaked the voice in her head.

"Ness?"

The bird made a noise that sounded faintly like mocking laughter. Nessa was laughing in her head.

"Ness?"

"Yes, it's me, Maerlin," Nessa's croaky voice replied in her head.

"A magpie?"

Again the bird cackled, and again, Maerlin heard the eerie echo of the laughter in her mind.

"This was the image chosen by Macha. This is the body I must wear for this incarnation."

"Maerlin?" a sleepy murmur came from the darkness "...Maerlin, is that you?"

"Cora!"

Maerlin threw back the blanket and rushed toward the sound of Cora's voice. Her body was not ready for such a rash action, however, and refused to coordinate itself property. Maerlin crashed to the floor after two steps, landing heavily on Cull.

Cull woke up cursing, and soon everyone was helping Maerlin back to bed and asking her questions she could not answer. She clung fiercely to Cora, not wanting to let go.

A candle was lit and light flooded the room. "Stand back and let the poor lassie breathe. Shoo! Break it up. Let me have some room to examine her," a new voice demanded.

Maerlin looked up at the old woman who had pushed her companions aside. She looked ancient; her skin dark and wrinkled like a walnut, and her long hair flowed like snow down her weather-worn face. Nevertheless, her eyes were still sharp. Something about the woman struck a chord of familiarity, although she knew that they'd never met. Perhaps it was the confident manner, so reminiscent of Nessa and the other powerful women on the Holy Isle. Maerlin realised that this old woman, dressed in a simple nightgown and woollen shawl, emanated power. People naturally bowed to her commands ... but could it be something more?

"Cora, why don't thou heat up some of that broth for Maerlin? I'm sure that she'll be hungry after her long sleep."

"Yes, Seabhac," Cora replied, and with a squeeze of Maerlin's hand, she scurried over to feed sticks to the embers.

Seabhac lifted Maerlin's head and inspected her in the candlelight. "Lie back and rest. We'll get thee some food and then thou can talk to thy friends briefly, but don't go overdoing it. Thou need to get thy strength back first."

The mention of food made Maerlin stomach rumble, and the smell of heating broth made her ravenous. However, Seabhac would only allow her a small bowl of watery rabbit stew.

"It'll make thee sick if thy eats too much, too soon, Maerlin," Seabhac explained. "Thou can have some more in a while, after thou hast rested."

"But I'm fine! I don't need to sleep," Maerlin protested.

A few moments later, as she sat back watching the others, her eyes became heavier and heavier, and she slipped into unconsciousness.

Seabhac carefully wrapped her up in the blanket. "Sleep well, lass. Thou wilt need all that thy can get."

Chapter Six: Departures

"We've found him!" Brother Fionn reported breathlessly.

"Where was he?" Abbot Gearoid asked.

"We found him on the top of the hill, Gearoid. He was lying there, fast asleep. He'll be lucky if he doesn't catch pneumonia."

"How, in the Nine Hells, did he get all the way up there?"

Fionn shrugged. "I haven't the foggiest, but they're bringing him down now."

Gearoid tapped the black feather against his lips in thought. "I want him watched at all times. Seamy, I want him dosed with a good, strong sedative and tied to his bed with restraints, if necessary."

Brother Seamus nodded and started mixing an elixir.

"Did he wake up when you found him?" Gearoid asked.

"No," replied Fionn. "He was lying there like a dead lamb."

"But he still lives?"

"...For now!" Fionn replied, clearly doubting the patient's ability to survive the ordeal.

A short while later they could hear the sound of approaching feet, and Balor was carried into the room. He was shivering in his sleep and looked deathly pale, but his breathing was steady. Seamy went to work at once.

*****

"How soon will she be ready to travel?" Cull asked.

"It's too soon to say. It'll be a turn of the moon or maybe two, if thou art lucky," Seabhac replied.

"But she seemed fine! Surely a day or two would be enough?"

Seabhac turned on Cull, anger flaring in her piercing eyes. "And what dost thou know about such matters? Hast thou any idea of the amount of Wild-magic she tapped into, or what that can do to someone? She's lucky to be coherent at all, but believe me when I tell thee, this girl will get worse before she gets better. Soon, the headaches will come; headaches that'll make her feel that her brain is ready to explode. Even candlelight will hurt her eyes, and she'll be so weak that she'll have to be spoon-fed. It'll be at least a moon before she can make her way outside to the privy unaided, and the winter could pass her by in the blink of an eye."

Cull turned to Cora. "Is this true?"

Cora was reluctant to agree, but she remembered her time in the pool. She had used only a relatively small amount of 'Wild-magic' when she hid herself in the water, but still, far more than she was used to. It left her exhausted, and she still suffered headaches from it. On the battlefield at Dragon's Reach, she had felt Maerlin's magic from over a mile away, so great was the power being summoned. Maerlin had even stolen Cora's Water Elementals away. They had abandoned her to follow Maerlin's summoning. Cora wondered at the power used to draw Elementals from so far away, and they had not just been Water Elementals, either. There had been Air, Fire, and probably Earth Elementals too. She was only just beginning to understand the amount of power wielded by a Storm-Bringer and why they were so rare. "I'm sorry Cull, but I think Seabhac's right."

Cull had not until recently considered the possibilities of an invasion from the Pects. Now, he realised that they were stuck between two opposing forces. It wouldn't take Queen Medb's spies long to learn of the demise of Dubhgall the Black. The avaricious rulers of *Tir Pect* may decide that the time was right to drive the *Fear Ban* back into the Bitter Eastern Sea and reclaim the rich fertile lands that belonged to their ancestors.

This revelation had brought changes to their plans. Cull knew that he would need to travel to *Ard Pect* and gather whatever intelligence he could from the Beggar-lord's spy network. Vort and Taliesin had come to the same conclusion and worry marked their faces. It would be a tough journey, now that the snows had started to fall.

"By Cliodhna's curvaceous bosom!" Cull cursed "We can't wait that long! We need to get to *Ard Pect* before the snow blocks the pass."

"...If they haven't already," Taliesin added.

"The passes will still be open," Seabhac assured them. "This blizzard was localised."

"How do you know that?" Cull demanded.

Seabhac looked at him for a moment and explained "Maerlin was the cause of the blizzard. She was its epicentre. The farther away thou art from her, the less snow thy wilt find. I can ask Fintan to check for thee if thou want, once it's light."

They all looked at the old harrier, sleeping in the rafters. "Can he do that?"

"It wouldn't be a problem," Seabhac assured "It's about time he did something useful around here, rather than sticking his nose into other people's business."

"We can't leave Maerlin behind," Cora protested. "Don't you remember what Ceila told us? She is the key to the success of this quest."

"Cora," Cull replied "We already have the sword, so the quest is over. Now, I need to get to *Ard Pect* and find out what's going on there, or Conal might not have a Kingdom left to rule come springtime. Queen Medb will have Conchubhar's army marching south at the first thaw if something isn't done to distract them. My job is to see Conal safely to his throne, and I can handle that. I don't need Maerlin's help for that."

"I'm not leaving her behind," Cora protested "She'll need someone here when she wakes."

"That's fine. You can stay with her, Cora. I'm sure she'll be happy to see you when she wakes," Cull agreed, his mind already working on the journey ahead. "We'll come back this way as soon as the snow thaws from the mountain pass. We can pick you both up then and escort you back to the Holy Isle."

"Is that okay, Seabhac?" Cora asked "Can I stay until Maerlin gets better?"

Seabhac sighed and nodded. "Very well, I guess so."

Cull turned to Taliesin and Vort. "Well ...?"

"I'll guide you to the Sett of *Clann Na Broce Snochta*. We'll be able to find a guide through the pass from there," Vort replied. "I've chosen this path, and I won't turn away from it now. I'll aid the young *Dragan* to his throne in any way that I can."

Cull nodded, glad to have the Brocian at his side. Over the last moon or so, a bond had grown between the two men, as it had with all the companions. "What about you, Tal?"

"Do you think I'd leave and let this story go untold ... or even worse, be told by someone else? Anyway, I know *Ard Pect*, and I could be useful to you there."

Cull grinned and turned to Conal. "Well boy, it looks like I'll have to teach you some new tricks."

"What tricks?" Conal asked.

"You'll become my beggar apprentice for the winter. I hope you can do better at that than you did at thievery."

Conal's face fell. He had considered himself a good thief, but Cull was a master-thief, as well as a spy, a beggar, and much more besides. Conal had some reservations from his previous experiences as a student. Cull had proven to be a tough mentor and demanded only the best.

"We'd better get some rest. It's a while yet before dawn, and we've a busy few days ahead of us. We'd better make good use of a dry bed while we can," Cull instructed.

They settled back down to sleep and Seabhac's candle was extinguished. Few of the companions managed to sleep, however, as their minds were on the day ahead. When dawn finally arrived, they crawled sleepily from their beds and ate a quiet breakfast. As they ate, their eyes drifted regularly over to Maerlin, but she slept on, pale-faced and unmoving. Only the magpie on Maerlin's chest returned their silent gazes.

"Will she wake up soon?" Cull asked Seabhac, his voice hushed.

"It's hard to say."

They waited for a while longer, hoping that Maerlin would stir, but the morning dragged painfully by with no sign of movement. Finally, Cull rose and signalled to the others. "We'd better be leaving, if we're going to make it to the Sett before nightfall."

"Aye," Vort agreed.

Cora bit her lip and looked at the men through watery eyes.

"We'll come back this way, Cora, as soon as the snow thaws."

Cora nodded. "I'll tell her."

Chapter Seven: The First Steps to Recovery

They watched in amazement as the man climbed out of his sickbed. None of the monks had expected the stranger to survive the winter, but the newcomer had regained some of his lost strength and vitality. Now, they watched as he climbed unsteadily to his feet and tottered toward the outstretched arms of Brother Seamy.

"Well done, Brother Balor. Just one more step," Seamy encouraged, half supporting the weakened man, whose muscles had atrophied from lying in his sickbed these past months.

Balor smiled softly but did not speak. He had not spoken to any of the monks since his mysterious arrival.

"You'll be back on your feet in no time," Seamy praised. "One more step, Brother Balor, and we'll call it a day."

Balor was the name that the Monks of Leithban had given to the stranger, as none of them knew his real name. In Pectish it meant simply 'lost'. It seemed appropriate for the man had indeed been lost, hanging at death's door for some time before showing some signs of recovery. Some of his injuries were beyond repair, such as the gaping holes in Balor's face where eyeballs used to be. Abbot Gearoid had decided to cover up the holes, as they had horrified some of the more faint-hearted within the community. As Brother Seamy led Balor back to his sickbed where the steaming broth awaited him, the monk smiled and gave a silent thanks to Deanna, the goddess of life, for his patient's recovery.

Some of the monks had wondered whether Balor would have been better off suckling on the bosom of Macha, such were his injuries when he had first arrived. No one broached the subject openly, of course. They accepted the whims of the Seven Greater Gods as they went about their daily duties and meditations.

Abbot Gearoid signalled his friend aside. "He's recovering well, I see. All credit to you, Seamy."

"Pah!" Seamy rejected, looking over at the man in the cot who was patiently spooning broth into his mouth. "His will to live has healed him far more than I ever could, that and the blessing of the gods."

"True, Seamy, but still you've done well, and you deserve some credit."

"I'm just a humble servant, the same as you, Gearoid," Seamy said with a shrug, though he was pleased by the compliment.

"What about his dreams, Seamy? Are they still as bad?"

"They've eased a little, but still, there are nights when he screams himself awake and shakes with terror. He mumbles strange things and his mind seems filled with horrors. I fear that he might be possessed. We can only hope that, with time, he can heal and find some peace."

Gearoid nodded and said a silent prayer. "He still doesn't speak?"

"He speaks only in his dreams, Gearoid ... only in his dreams."

Abbot Gearoid sighed. "The man is surely a mystery. At times, I wish I could unravel his secrets and understand how he came to be here, but at other times I think that ignorance might be the better option."

Gearoid's memory of how the stranger came to be on their island had blurred with time, and much though he strained for recollection, all that came to him was haunting imagery of a figure in black. The more he tried to delve into his memories, the more the image eluded him, leaving him frustrated and unsettled.

"We'll find out what we need to, given time," Brother Seamy predicted.

Gearoid shrugged. "I always thought that you'd have been much better equipped to take over as our spiritual leader, Seamy," he noted ruefully, placing a hand on the other monk's shoulder. "You have an inner peace, which I can only strive to attain."

Seamy smiled as he explained the ways of the world to Gearoid. "I'm easily contented, and I've never striven for more than that. You, on the other hand, have a need to do better. I think this is why Brother Guerin chose you as his replacement." Seeing Balor's bowl was finished, he moved toward the sick bed.

"Well done, Brother Balor, that's great. Let me tuck you in there, and you can rest for a while."

Balor settled himself down in the cot and nodded, licking the last of the broth from his lips. He was already weary after the small exertion, and his mind was drifting toward sleep.

*****

Maerlin sat up, clutching her face where the raven had pecked out her eyes. All she could see was a blinding light as she sat there panting. Her body was clammy with sweat, and the chill air made her shiver.

"It was only a dream, Maerlin," Nessa's voice assured her.

Maerlin realised that the raven had gone, but her head throbbed, and she still couldn't see.

"Am I blind?"

The magpie gave her a cackling laugh. *"No silly, you're fine. Are your eyes hurting?"*

Maerlin moved her hands away from her eyes and opened her lids again. The pain had lessened slightly, but the world was still much too bright. She could vaguely see the magpie sitting on the end of her cot, but only as a small black-on-white shadow on the wall of light. Turning her head toward the light, she squeezed her eyes shut again. The pain was too much to bear.

"Lie back down, Maerlin, and keep your eyes closed. You're going to have a bad migraine for the next few days. I'll go and fetch the others."

Maerlin snuggled back down and pulled the blanket over her head. The darkness helped, but did not fully alleviate the pain in her head. She heard the magpie take to wing, and then there was silence. Lying curled up in the darkness, her mind drifted to thoughts of Dubhgall the Black. *"Darkness is a mantle I wear well,"* he had said. She wondered why the old wizard haunted her dreams. She would have to ask Nessa about it sometime, or perhaps the High Priestess. She was a Dream-catcher, after all.

*****

Nessa flew out through the open door of the cottage into the clear winter's day. The sun was reflecting brightly off the half-melted snow, and even the magpie had to blink a few times to adjust her vision. Magpies are not the most gracious of flyers and Nessa was new to her form, which made her flight even clumsier, but she managed to make it over to the garden without crashing into anything. Thankfully, there were few objects on the plain to hamper her flight. She flew over the low picket fence, deciding not to risk attempting to land on its turreted top and opting for a softer landing on the ground beyond instead.

Cora and Seabhac were busy digging in the vegetable patch, clearing the snow away from the clamped potatoes, and they had not noticed Nessa's graceless landing. The magpie hopped forward, stopping only once when a particularly fat worm distracted her attention. The worm disappeared quickly as no one had bothered to feed her. She nearly spat the worm out in revulsion, but her bird instincts quickly swallowed the choice morsel before her human spirit could intervene. Her first breakfast was actually quite tasty, as long as she didn't let the human part of her brain think about it.

Nessa hopped closer, but the two women were intent on their work. *"Excuse me,"* Nessa called out, but all that came out was a half-hearted cawing sound, like a cat with a fur ball in its throat. Her efforts were ignored. For some reason, it seemed that no one could hear her, apart from Maerlin. She tried again, more firmly this time *"Hey! Over here!"*

A shrill shriek came from one of the apple trees beyond the garden, a shriek that sent a shiver of instinctive fear through the magpie. Nessa noticed the hen harrier's sharp gaze on her as he shrieked again.

"What?" said Seabhac and looked around and then down at the magpie. "Oh, hello there, little one, didst thou come out to get some fresh air? There are lots of juicy worms around here for thee, if thou art hungry."

Nessa was trying hard to ignore the worms that were wriggling temptingly nearby. Her eyes darted from the grey hawk in the tree to the old woman beside Cora. She hopped closer and tried to speak again.

"Maerlin's awake," Nessa explained *"She needs something for her headache."*

Seabhac smiled down at the magpie. "Aye, it's a lovely day. Don't thou love these clear winter's mornings?" Seabhac reached down to pet the magpie on the head, and Nessa had to fight back the urge to peck at her hand. She sensed that the harrier would not approve of that.

Hopping away from the friendly pat, Nessa took to wing, cawing constantly as she flew around and around the women.

"It certainly seems perky today," Cora commented, dropping potatoes into a bucket.

"Will you stop chattering, and go and see to Maerlin?" Nessa shouted. Her words fell on deaf ears. She found that when she wasn't thinking about it, she could fly an awful lot better. Her bird instincts were able to do the job quite nicely, when her human spirit wasn't interfering. Feeling more confident, she flew a few more times around the women and then headed back toward the cottage door. She landed on the doorstep and turned back to the women. They had stopped their work and were watching her, so she cawed again and danced around on the flagstones.

"Dost thou think that she's trying to tell us something?" Seabhac asked.

"She's a very strange little bird. I don't think I've ever seen a magpie do that before," Cora answered.

They looked at each other, and realisation came to them. "Maerlin!" they exclaimed in unison and hurried out of the garden.

"Finally!" Nessa cawed in relief and flew over to the cot. *"I've brought you some help, dear,"* she assured as they came through the door.

*****

Maerlin peeked out through the covers and shaded her eyes against the bright sunlight.

"You're awake, Maerlin!" Cora cried, rushing over and hugging her.

Maerlin winced. The jostling was not helping her headache.

"Take it easy, Cora," Seabhac warned. "I'm sure she's probably feeling a bit fragile right now."

Fintan followed them into the cottage and resumed his perch in the rafters, as Seabhac closed the door.

"That's better." Maerlin sighed as the light dimmed.

"Head hurting?" Seabhac asked as she inspected her patient.

Maerlin nodded as carefully as she could. Even that little movement caused her to wince.

"I've got just the cure for thee, but thou had better eat something first. It's a little hard on an empty stomach."

Cora stoked up the fire and reheated the broth.

"That's a very clever little bird you have there," Seabhac praised.

Maerlin was about to say that Nessa was not a bird, but the more she looked at the magpie, the more she realised that she would never see the old healer again, apart from inside her head. She was not sure that Seabhac would understand if she tried to explain. It was a long story, and one that she had not really figured out herself yet.

"Canst thou understand it?" Seabhac asked, and Maerlin looked up at her sharply.

"How did you ...?"

"Ah, I thought so," Seabhac beamed "I knew that the magpie was special."

"But how did you ...?" repeated Maerlin.

"Let's just say that Fintan and I have a similar blessing."

Maerlin looked up at the piercing gaze of the old harrier. "He's beautiful."

"He's a crotchety old feather-bag, but we've been together a long time. I've got used to his bad habits."

Fintan screeched and flapped his broad wings in reply.

"See what I mean." Seabhac didn't bother to translate the harrier's rude comment to the girls. "He's not so bad when thou get to know him," she assured. "So has thy little friend got a name?"

"She's called Nessa."

Cora nearly dropped the steaming pot of stew into the fire. "What!"

"She's called Nessa *MacTire*, Earth-sister of the Broce Woods," Maerlin declared, letting her words sink in.

"Nessa?" Cora asked, her eyes brimming with tears.

Maerlin nodded, finding it hard to swallow past the lump in her own throat.

Seabhac looked at them and then at the bird. "Thou art burning the broth, Cora. Give it here!" she said, taking the pot from Cora's hands. Cora stumbled over to the cot, her eyes shifting from Maerlin to the magpie.

Seabhac poured out two bowls of broth and handed them over. "I'll leave thee to chat for a while, shall I? I'd better go finish off the gardening, anyway."

She hurried outside. Fintan followed and returned to sunning himself in the apple tree. "We'd better give them a wee while, Fin. It looks like they have a bit of catching up to do, and they don't need two nosy old goats like us around."

Fintan, being a wise old bird, refrained from comment.

Chapter Eight: The Journey Begins

Vort led the way through the melting snow and over the hills to the shrubby ground at the base of the mountains. As Seabhac had predicted, the snows lessened the farther they travelled, until it disappeared like a bad dream, leaving the browning grassland and hazel coppices in its wake.

Cull followed close behind with Conal and Taliesin bringing up the rear of the group. Conal was pleading with Taliesin to continue the tale of Uiscallan and the Dragon-lord.

"So what happened next?" Conal persisted.

"I've told you already, I don't really know. No one is sure about the next bit of it," Taliesin explained.

"But you must have some idea, Tal."

The bard remained silent for a few moments. "The old *Seanachai* who taught me the harp once told me a wild tale about their adventure, though whether it was true or not, I couldn't say."

Conal's eyes gleamed with curiosity. "... Well?"

Taliesin looked at the young prince and laughed. "It looks like I'll get no peace until I tell it to you."

Taliesin put on his storytelling voice and told what little he could remember.

"It was said that they left the hill fort a few mornings later, after Luigheagh had arranged for his most trusted advisors to protect the Clan in his absence. Many thought that the young prince had been bewitched by Deanna's witch, but whenever they objected to his quest, Luigheagh would listen to their arguments in silence, and then he would walk away and continue his preparations. His clansmen finally accepted his decision.

Selecting his trusty white stallion and a sensible grey palfrey for the priestess, along with two pack horses, Luigheagh readied himself as best he could for the journey ahead. Uiscallan had given him instructions of what would be needed for the journey, and though he questioned her choices, he finally relented to her authority, as his clansmen had done to him.

I'm sure the young prince was apprehensive when the day came to leave, as he had spent his whole life safely cocooned within the community of his Clan. Even on the battlefield, where he had won much honour for bravery, he had always had his trusty clansmen to guard his back and support him.

They rode eastward onto the vast open plain and away from the sheltering mountains to the west and north. Soon the wild Broce Woods disappeared from view, and as they continued east, the gigantic Mountain of the Gods slipped away over the horizon.

At first they travelled through his own lands and then beyond to the lands of the Horse People. Luigheagh's Clan had no fear of the Horse Clan, each respecting the others territory and even assisting each other against their common enemy: the Pects. They received a warm welcome from the neighbouring clan with feasting and a warm bed for the night.

Uiscallan insisted that they continued their eastward journey without delay and they soon reached the Screaming Plains. Here the land grew more rugged, with a vast expanse of limestone rock and sparse shrubbery, instead of the rich grassland of the plains. The wind howled through holes in the rock, making eerie noises and the horses became skittish. They travelled by day, and they were forced to a slow walk, fearful of the horses breaking a leg in the many hidden holes within the rocky landscape..."

*****

The Prince's chin had shadowed with a light curly down of hair during the journey, and much though he scratched and cursed at the newly-growing beard, Uiscallan refused to let him shave.

"Thou wilt need it before too long," she assured him.

"That's easy for you to say. I don't see your face getting bristly. I look like one of the Bear Clan," Luigheagh grumbled.

"I think it looks kind of cute," Uiscallan teased.

"Cute! Oh great, that's all I need ... cute!" Luigheagh cursed in disgust.

Eventually, they came to the edge of the land, and Luigheagh looked out across the Bitter Eastern Sea for the first time. "It's magnificent!"

Uiscallan nodded in agreement.

"It looks angry. Is it always like that?"

Uiscallan studied the grey sea, and at the jagged waves that crashed against the limestone rocks. "Mostly ... this sea has a bad history. She has claimed many lives for Macha and is always hungry for more souls to feed on."

"Is it true that my ancestors crossed it? I see no land on the other side."

Uiscallan looked over at the blonde youth. She was of Pectish blood, the race who had once ruled over the entire island from one coast to the other, and her people were small and dark, unlike the young prince and his warriors. He was a 'Fear Ban', and there was still much animosity between the Pects of the wild northern lands and Luigheagh's people, who now claimed the richer lands to the south as their own.

"Yes, it's true," Uiscallan confirmed. She pointed north-easterly to where dark storm clouds lurked on the horizon. "If thou sailed for half a moon in that direction, thou wouldst meet thy ancestors."

"They travelled over this?" Luigheagh asked, looking dubiously at the angry sea.

Uiscallan smiled. "It takes a brave man to sail the Bitter Eastern Sea, even in summertime, either that or a desperate one."

"Is it dangerous then?"

"Very. Many are the dead who sleep in the cold, dark waters of the Bitter Eastern Sea."

"Then why did they bother?"

"Thy ancestors came from a harsh land, Luigheagh. It's a land that is almost as unforgiving as the seas that surround it. Hunger and poverty *made thy people strong and reckless, and desperation is always a good motivator."*

"So they moved here?" Luigheagh asked.

"Not all of them. Many still live in the Northlands, but as their Clans grew and needed more space, the young and the brave ventured forth seeking glory. Some, like thy Fear Ban ancestors, decided that life was better here, and they never returned to their homelands."

Luigheagh looked into the distance, at the storm clouds. "So where now?"

"We go north, I guess."

"You guess! I thought you knew what you were doing?"

Uiscallan gave the Prince a despairing look. "Luigheagh, we need to find a Dragonship that will take us across the sea to the Northlands. Such ships tend to be owned by pirates and raiders. None of the local fishermen will sail in that direction, even in good weather. They huddle close to the coast, and keep a wary eye out for Reavers."

"So how do we hire a ship?" Luigheagh asked.

"The first part is luck. We will need to walk the coast, and keep an eye out for any square sails to the east. That storm out there might be helpful, as the Dragonships will be racing ahead of it, seeking a safe harbour."

"And the second part ...?"

"Ah! That's a bit more difficult."

"Why's that?"

"When the ship comes to shore, we need to get them to take us on board."

"How much will that cost? You told me not to bring much gold with us."

Uiscallan smiled grimly. "The Reavers would take all the gold in thy Dun and still want more. We will not offer them gold."

Luigheagh looked at his beloved stallion and went pale. "Surely you're not suggesting selling them our horses?"

"No. We'll need to find a safe place to stable our horses before we go any farther, and from there, we will travel on foot."

Luigheagh was confused. He could see little else of value in their packs to trade with.

"What exactly will the Northlanders want, Uiscallan?"

Uiscallan looked away from Luigheagh's piercing blue eyes and decided that it was better not to reveal all of her plans just yet. He would learn about it in time anyway, and he would only fret about it, once he knew all the details. "Don't worry, Luigheagh. I'm sure we'll find something to barter with the Northlanders. Come along. Let's go and find a fishing village to stable the horses"

*****

"Ho! Is that you, Vort?"

Taliesin stopped his tale and looked up to see a man standing nearby. He was dressed similar to Vort, but his hair was pure white, and stood stiffly up from his head. His features were albino.

"Cathal!" Vort greeted "A blessing on your Sett."

"And to yours, cousin," replied the Brocian. "It's been too long since your last visit. Where are Orla and the boys?"

Vort's face darkened at the mention of his family.

Cathal frowned, sensing Vort's discomfort. "I think you'd better come along and speak to the Elders. The place has been buzzing since runners came from Broca. From the look on your face, I think you may be involved."

"Am I safe here?" Vort asked.

"You are my honoured guest, cousin," Cathal replied.

Vort knew that those words meant that Cathal and his Sett would protect him with their lives. They were an offer of sanctuary. He looked at Cull and the others. "These are my friends. What about them?"

"A friend of my cousin is my friend too," Cathal replied with some formality. "They are also my guests. Come along. Let's get into the shade of the woods." Cathal turned away into the thick hazel coppice.

"Is it safe?" Cull asked.

"Cathal's my cousin, and he has made us guests in his Sett. No harm will come to you in the Sett of *Clann Na Broce Snochta*."

Cull nodded, remembering Vort's own invitation as a guest into the Southern Dell Sett.

"What was all that about runners from Broca?" Vort asked when they had caught up to Cathal.

"I don't know the details. I've been out on sentry duty all day. Since the war banners were raised in Broca, we've all been on high alert. We're vulnerable here on the northern tip of the Broce Woods, and being a small Sett, we can't afford to take any chances."

"Have there been any Boarite attacks on your Sett?" Vort asked, with obvious concern.

"No, but we've found some patrols nearby. They were too small to be raiding parties."

"Oh no! That doesn't sound good."

Cathal chuckled. "We can't let you lowlander Setts have all the fun, Vort."

Vort smiled. "Have they been patrolling long? I would've thought that this would be too near the Pectish border for the Boarites."

"Usually it is, but we've had some incursions over the last couple of days."

"Oh, dear!"

"What's the matter, Vort?"

"I'm sorry, Cathal, but we might be the reason for your recent interlopers," Vort admitted. He thought that they had eluded the Boarites in the confusion of the battle, but Lord Boare clearly had not given up his pursuit of the young prince.

"Are they hunting you, Vort?" Cathal asked. "That could explain why they've started sending their Elites out on patrols."

At the mention of the Boarite Elites, Vort's worst fears were confirmed. He nodded grimly in reply.

"Well then, we'll have to arrange a feast for you tonight," Cathal announced cheerfully.

"A feast?" Vort asked.

"We'll have to do something in your honour, Vort. It'd be tardy of us not to show our gratitude. The winters can be very dull up here, you know. You've given us some hope of an exciting winter and many a good tale to tell afterward. It's not every day that *Clann Na Snochta Broce* can show off their prowess," Cathal exclaimed, slapping Vort happily on the back.

"I always said that all that white blood was addling your brain, Cathal. Now I see that your whole Sett has gone mad."

Cathal laughed at the insult. "It's been too long since I heard your sharp wit, Vort, and it's been too long since we drank and wenched together at Broca."

Vort flashed a grin, remembering the wild parties during their time in the city of Broca. "I don't recall that much wenching."

"What! You were the rogue of the city, Vort. Fathers feared for their daughters' chastity. That is, until you got all moony-eyed over that Orla one ..." Cathal teased "Though I grant you, she always was a fine looking woman! You were lucky to catch her eye first, Vort. Had I not been suffering from a hangover that morning, you'd still be a single man."

"Orla wouldn't have been dazzled by those pink eyes of yours, Cathal. You wouldn't have stood a chance," Vort protested, and they both laughed.

They came into a clearing in the dense coppice, and although the woodland around the Sett differed, the layout of round hillocks that were the Brocian underground homes was just the same.

With the coming of evening and the setting sun, other members of *Clann Na Snochta Broce* were stirring.

"Ho, Cathal!" they shouted in greeting as they inspected the new arrivals. Soon word spread, and the whole community gathered around. Young children touched the companions' clothing and ran off giggling. Older Brocians stood a little farther back, apprehensive, but still curious to see why Cathal had brought *Fear Ban* into their Sett.

Cathal stood waiting, with Vort by his side, until all of the small community had gathered. The last to arrive were a bunch of older men and women, who walked regally toward them.

The crowd made room for the Elders, and silence fell on the clearing. Cathal bowed formally to them. "I have brought some guests home for dinner."

One of the Elders, an ancient woman with a long plait of white hair that nearly trailed to the ground, stepped forward. She, like the others, had very pale skin and pink eyes. She squinted as she inspected the visitors, coming close enough to sniff at Cull, Conal, and Taliesin. She stopped before Vort and felt his face for a moment before speaking "Cathal, my son, who do you bring to our Sett?"

"Mother, this is Vort MacAiden Na Broce of the Southern Dell Sett, War Chief of the *Clann Na Broce*."

"Forgive me, Vort, but my old eyes are failing me. It's been too long since you visited us. No doubt, there's a reason why you bring these *Fear Ban* into our Sett? It is a strange wind that brings you to us on this of all days."

Vort frowned at the last comment. "A blessing on your Sett, revered Sionna. My father often praises your wisdom."

A shadow crossed Sionna's face, and her eyes welled up with moisture. "Your father was always a great charmer, and I see that he has passed on the gift. Sadly, it seems that you not have heard the news that flies through the woods, Vort."

"We have travelled across *Magh Dragan*, revered Sionna," Vort replied apprehensively. He wondered if he was now outlawed for his actions during the Blood-truth. "Cathal has offered us sanctuary, but I'll relinquish him of this burden should that be necessary. I wouldn't have your Sett's blood spilt on my behalf."

Sionna absently wiped a tear from her eye. "Have no fear, Vort Na Broce. You and your companions are welcome here, but I thank you for your consideration," she paused in hesitation. "We have much to speak of, and I'm lost as to where to begin. My heart is burdened with a heavy task, and I wish that it were not so, but none of us can ignore our chosen path. Cernunnos has brought this task at my door, and I won't doubt his wisdom."

Vort's hands shook, sensing something was seriously wrong. "What is this news that you speak of?"

"Perhaps you'd better eat and rest first."

"Please ... tell me," Vort insisted.

Sionna bit her lip and tears rolled slowly down her cheeks. Struggling to get the words out, she said. "It's ... your father, Vort. He has passed on to the Hall of Heroes."

"What? No!" Vort gasped. Realisation hit him like a physical blow, and he sank to his knees.

Sionna came forward and enveloped him in her frail arms. "He led the attack against the Boarites in your absence, and he fought like a true hero. After the battle, he set off back to Broca to plead your cause. It was while he was on his way there that he fell. Cernunnos has called him to his side. He will sleep now with your Mother and feast with the other heroes."

Murmurs of agreement came from all around. Aidan, Vort's father was well respected throughout the Broce Woods.

"Come," Sionna urged, pulling Vort gently to his feet. "Let's go inside and speak warmly of your father."

Vort stood and was led to one of the many hillocks that concealed the Setts of *Clann Na Broce Snochta*.

When Cull and the others moved to follow, Cathal stopped them with a firm hand. "Leave him be. It's always hard to lose one so close. He'll need a little time to gather his wits."

"But …" Conal protested.

"No, he's right," Cull agreed.

Cathal showed his relief that Cull understood. "A man must be allowed time to grieve in peace for a while and gather his strength. After that, there will come a time for remembrance and praise of the one who goes to feast in the Hall of Heroes. In the meantime, my Sett isn't far. You can eat and rest there while we wait. Sionna will look after Vort for you, don't worry."

Another man joined them as they headed toward Cathal's Sett. He was darker than the other Brocians.

"Was it you that brought the news, Feilim?" Cathal asked.

"Aye, that and more."

"More?"

"I'll tell you in a bit. I haven't slept in days, and the Elders have had me telling and retelling the news since I first arrived," Feilim grumbled.

Cathal nodded. "Mother can be like that. She always thinks you've forgotten some important part of the message. Come on, let's grab some food, and you can fill me in on all the gossip."

Chapter Nine: The Warrior-shaman

"... And the High Council agreed to this?" Cathal asked, a short time later.

Conal and the others sat quietly, listening as Feilim relayed the news.

"It was unanimous from what I could gather."

"But didn't the shamans object?"

"You forget, Cathal," Feilim explained, "only the High-shaman can speak at a Council meeting. Since Dorcha's disappearance, they have had no representative on the Council to object."

"Has he still not returned?" Cathal asked incredulously. "He's locked himself in his dark tower before, but he's never ignored the summons of the High Council. The man loves to have his bloody hand in things."

"Is this the High-shaman you're talking about?" Taliesin asked.

"Yes," said the Brocians in unison.

"We might be able to help you there. Vort told us that the man we knew as Dubhgall the Black and the one you knew as Dorcha were one and the same."

"What!" Cathal exclaimed.

"That cannot be!" Feilim protested, looking to the others for confirmation.

Cull nodded grimly. "That's what Vort told us. When we saw him at the High Council meeting, we couldn't see his face. He was wearing a dark cowl, but later, on the burial mound, he revealed himself to us. Vort was surprised to see him there, but Dubhgall happily gloated over his duplicity."

"I'll kill that conniving snake," Cathal swore angrily.

"I'm afraid you're too late," Cull informed them. "He's already dead. While the Brocians were fighting on Dragon's Ridge, another battle was taking place at the Twelve Warriors, and Dubhgall lost."

"It seems that the Brocians are indebted to you."

"It wasn't me that killed him. It was a novice of Deanna, Maerlin. She was the girl that was with us at the High Council meeting."

"Where is she now? Did she survive the battle?" Feilim asked.

"Barely. She's recovering at a cottage down on the edge of the plains."

"She's with the Hawk witch?" Cathal asked in surprise. "Is that wise?"

"Why do you say that?" Conal asked, not liking the look on Cathal's face. "She's just an old woman."

"Old! That witch is ancient!" Cathal explained. "She settled there a very long time ago."

"That's no reason to call her a witch," Taliesin objected.

"That familiar she has with her ..." Cathal added. "...He's old, too. Any normal bird would've been dead, years ago. It's not natural for a bird to live that long."

"He does look a bit shabby," Conal conceded.

"That bird is older than my grandmother," Cathal said as if to explain his concerns.

"So, she has a very old bird with her. What of it?" Conal asked.

"You misunderstand me. There's more to it than that. Our Sett has been here for many generations, and this is our land. We do not tolerate trespassers on it, and we take measures to evict any who dare to invade it. In other parts of the Broce Woods, Brocians and non-Brocians may live in peace, but not here. We have previously suffered persecution because of our appearance. Some men call us demons."

"One old lady can't be that much of a threat to your Sett, can she?" Taliesin asked.

"Long ago, when she first came here, we tried to 'discourage her'. She didn't take kindly to our warriors trampling her garden at night and stealing her goats. The witch and her cursed hawk followed the warriors back to our Sett and attacked them with magic. Our shamans were swept aside by the ferocity of her attack. Trees fell, the earth shook, and some of our homes collapsed. We attacked with spears and arrows, but these were swept aside by strong winds. Our arrows turned in mid-flight and came back at our warriors. The very grass fought against us, tangling our feet as we tried to attack. Finally, she left, but not before retrieving her goats."

"So … she's a witch." Conal, by now, was getting used to having witches around. "It seems to me that you have asked for it. Does she still attack you?"

"We've learned to give her and her harrier a wide birth. She comes to the woods to gather herbs every now and then, but she doesn't go near our Sett."

"She seemed fine to me," Cull commented. "Anyway, we had no choice. Maerlin needed somewhere to recover. I'm sure she'll be fine. She has Cora with her, and they're both novices of Deanna. I doubt they'll come to any harm."

Taliesin decided to change the subject. "So tell me, what does this decision by the High Council mean?"

It was Feilim who answered. "The Council has decided to allow the result of the Blood-truth," he explained. "That means that they support Vort's decision to support the *Dragan* heir against *Clann Na Torc*. They will honour the Truce brokered by *Luigheagh*, *Ri Na Dragan,* and pass that peace on to his heir."

"Does that mean that we're not going to be hunted by Brocians?" Cull asked.

"...Far from it. It has been decreed that we should aid you in your quest, wherever possible."

"And what about Vort?" asked Conal. "Is he an outcast?"

"Outcast ... why would he be an outcast?" Feilim asked.

"I don't know. I got the impression that his Form-melding caused quite a stir."

"Oh, it did that," Feilim agreed. "There was a lot of talk about it."

"What was the consensus?"

"A lot hung on the outcome of that discussion, and for a long time, no agreement could be made. When the call to war came, all talk was abandoned until after the battle. As you know, Vort's father, Aidan *Crionna* died soon after the battle, and they brought his body back to the city for burial. Orla, Vort's wife, led the procession through the city, and a magnificent sight she was too. She walked through Broca with her head high, defying any who would speak ill of her husband. Finally, she came to the High Council's chamber and addressed the whole city. I've never seen the chamber so packed. You could hardly move in there. It was tighter than a litter of piglets."

"Did they let her speak?" Taliesin asked.

"She's not an Elder, but she had been elected by the Southern Dell Sett to act on their behalf, and therefore, she had a right to be heard even if she couldn't vote. It was her support for her husband and her praise for her father-in-law that swayed the Council. The first thing to decide was the legitimacy of the Blood-truth. It wasn't long before this was deemed to be within the rules of combat, and the decision went Vort's way. After that, there was the trickier question."

"What question was that?" Taliesin asked.

"It was Vort's status, of course. Vort had been a warrior, but during the Blood-truth he had used magic to defeat his challenger. This made him a shaman."

"The gods above, I don't think Vort will be too happy about that," Cull declared.

"I'm sure he won't," Cathal confirmed. "Our warriors have little time for the ways of the shamans, and they view our warriors with similar dislike. Each has a role to play within our society, but that doesn't mean we have to like each other."

Feilim continued "As you can imagine, there was a lot of heated debate, with the shamans and the warriors contradicting each other and bickering over it. It went on for days, and everyone was getting irritable. No one could decide on Vort's new status within the Clan. None could deny that he was the elected leader of the Southern Dell Sett. As to whether he was now considered a shaman, and therefore, entitled to all the rights and honours accorded to that status, that was another matter. The same difficulty occurred as to whether he was still the Clan Champion and entitled to all the honours and rights of this office. Our Clan is very structured, and there are a lot of complex laws and rituals. They are the pillars to the stability of the Clan," he explained. "One way or another, we had to make a decision on his status. A lot more that Vort's future hung in the balance, you see. The whole strength of the Clan was at stake."

"So does Vort have to give up his warrior status and don the garb of a shaman?" Cathal asked.

Feilim grinned at them all. "Not at all!" he chuckled, slapping his thigh enthusiastically. "That wonderful wife of his had the last word and sorted it all out. It was so obvious. I don't know why someone hadn't come up with the idea sooner. I guess that sometimes, we can't see the woods for the trees."

"Well ..."

"As I was saying, she stood up before the Council and waited for the bickering to die down. You could have heard a pin drop, I swear. Anyway, when everyone was quiet, she addressed the people...

"I wish to speak on behalf of my husband," Orla declared boldly. "I know that this issue concerns all of us, and I respect your opinions on this matter, but my husband's fate, and therefore, the fate of my sons is resting on this issue. I beg you to listen."

The High Councillor agreed to let her speak, and she continued "When I first met my husband, here in Broca, I had already heard the tales of his prowess. I remember looking down at the small man who was trying to charm me with sweet words, and I almost laughed in his face. Surely, I thought, this couldn't be the same warrior who was spoken of with such reverence. I was new to the city, but he was already making a legend of himself in Broca. Even in my small Sett on the edge of the mountains, his name was mentioned with reverence. I don't need to name the many battles that he has fought in. I'm sure they come to your mind as they do to mine. Can anyone doubt that he's earned the right to be called a warrior, or even for that matter, that he earned the right to be honoured as our Champion?"

At this point the room broke into loud applause and cheers of support for her husband. Finally, the Head Councillor resumed order, but Orla was still standing.

"I've not finished yet," she announced. "I beg your patience for just a few moments longer."

Who could refuse her? Certainly not the High Councillor.

"As I was saying, surely my husband has earned the right to be considered a warrior. Nevertheless, a dilemma arises for us all. Although I didn't witness the Blood-truth myself, there are many here who did. They speak of my husband's Form-melding, and so many honoured clansmen and women cannot have imagined it. My father-in-law, Aidan the Wise, also spoke to me of this matter. He told me that this was not the first time that Vort had performed this legendary feat. As a youth, Vort had Form-melded in the heat of combat."

Murmurs echoed through the chamber at this revelation, and Orla waited for silence before continuing "If the Council wishes, I can bring forth a witness to this event: Vort's childhood friend, Liam MacPhelim Broce of the Eastern Dell Sett. He's a respected warrior of the Clan, and he was bitten during the fight. He still wears the scars to this day. He has agreed to come forth and bear witness to the tale given me by Vort's father. This proves that the scene witnessed by so many during the Blood-truth couldn't have been, as some would have us believe, a thing of mass hysteria or hallucination. Vort has been gifted by Cernunnos and has the ability to Form-meld."

Murmurs again filled the room, but Orla continued, raising her voice with ease to be heard above the noise. "I had always thought that tales of shape-changing were mere fairy tales told to children at bedtime..." she joked, and the crowd responded to her wit, "but it seems that I was wrong. I put it to the shamans gathered here today... can any of you work such magic? I, for one, have never seen it done."

The crowd all turned to look at the huddled group of shamans at the front of the assembly, but none of them stepped forward. If anything, they seemed to shrink away from the challenge.

"It seems not,' said Orla dryly. "Then let me ask this of our learned shamans. Are there any of you who would dispute Vort's ability to Form-meld?"

Again the shamans, who had been so loud and argumentative before, remained silent. Those who had witnessed Vort's change would not be told that it was a figment of their imagination, and the shamans knew this. None of the shamans would tell the High Council that they were wrong. Only one amongst them would have been brave enough to challenge the Council, and he was notably absent. Without Dorcha's leadership, they were like lost sheep.

After a moment, Orla nodded and continued with a small smile on her face "It's as I thought. We seem to be in agreement that Vort possesses the ability to Form-meld: a gift thought lost in the distant past, and a gift that clearly defines his magical ability. Correct me if I'm wrong, High Councillor and respected Elders, but I'm sure that our laws and tradition state that anyone who shows magical abilities within the Clan should be deemed a shaman. Furthermore, that all efforts should be made to further enhance and educate that Clan member to the best of their abilities?"

No one needed to discuss this issue for all knew the tenets of the law.

"Then I put it to you, High Councillor, and to all here present, that my husband Vort has earned the right to be classed as a shaman. In fact, let us go further than that. With the absence of our current High-shaman, who seems to have fallen off the face of the earth and left his brethren leaderless, I would go so far as to say that we should elect Vort as the new High-shaman. No one else seems to be blessed with as much magical ability."

At this point, some of the shamans protested, but their protests were drowned out by the cheers and heckle of the crowd.

Finally, the High Councillor called the meeting to order and after some consultation with the other Elders, responded "Your arguments seem to have stirred up the people, Orla. You will make a fine Councillor in the years to come, and there is great wisdom in your words. However, I'm a little confused as to what you're suggesting. Do you wish Vort to be re-elected as the Clan Champion, or as the High-shaman?"

Orla paused and the room fell silent. Most people were holding their breath as they waited for her answer. Finally, she shrugged her delicate shoulders in a matter-of-fact fashion and said "Both, of course."

After that, it didn't take too long to hammer out the details and ratify the decision. After a short time in recess, the High Council came back to the chamber and made an announcement. "People of the Broce, let all here listen and acknowledge the decision of the High Council, and let runners go to the four corners of our lands and share the news with our brethren. Let it be known that from this day forth, all who have shown magical ability should be considered as shamans and that, in the interests of the protection of the Clan, all who show adeptness in weaponry and prowess in battle should be deemed warriors. Furthermore, it has been decided that there is no reasonable argument to suggest that gifted individuals cannot be honoured as being members of both sections of our community. If Cernunnos and Dagda in their wisdom have blessed them with both abilities then the Clan should honour the wishes of the gods. Therefore, they are entitled to stand for, and be elected to, any position of authority". The decision was met with the approval of all the Clan present ..." Feilim concluded, "apart from the shamans."

"So has Vort been elected as the High-shaman now?" Cathal asked.

"Well, he'll need to present himself for the position first," Feilim explained, "but I'd wager my money that he'd get the job if he did, especially in light of the news of Dorcha's recent demise."

"And knowing Orla, she'll talk him into doing just that," Cathal predicted.

Chapter Ten: Meeting the Dragons

Time passed slowly as Cull, Conal, and Taliesin waited for word of Vort. They were treated well by the albino men and women of *Clann Na Broce Snochta,* but still, they chafed at the delay, knowing that they were racing the onrushing winter.

Cull prowled back and forth as his restlessness became too much. "This is taking too long."

"I'm sorry, Cull, but the loss of a loved one is not taken lightly amongst us Pects," Cathal placated. "Such things cannot be rushed."

Cull thought of his own 'father ', Broll the Beggar-lord, who had been lingering at Macha's doorsteps for these past few years. Time was running out for Broll, and Cull was stuck far away from home and in a hurry to head even farther from the old man's deathbed. This decision sat heavily on Cull's shoulders, but he had a job to do and he would see it finished. Too much rested on the success of the young prince's future: the weight of the whole Kingdom in fact. Cull had been given the task of protecting Conal until he came to manhood. Only when the time came for Conal to be declared a man could Cull return to Manquay. "I know, Cathal, and I'm sorry, but we must reach the pass before the snows block it."

"Is that all you're worried about?" Cathal asked. "Have no fear on that score, Cull. It can snow all it wants, but that won't stop *Clann Na Snochta Broce* from passing through the mountains."

"Why's that?" Cull asked. "Surely when the pass is blocked, your clansmen must wait out the winter just like everyone else?"

"We've never had much liking for the border checkpoints, or for the greedy tax collectors of the Pectish High King," Cathal explained. "The tolls charged for goods crossing from Dragania into *Ard Pect* were always exorbitant, but recently, they've become daylight robbery. We were forced to find an alternative solution."

"…An alternative solution. That sounds interesting. Please explain."

"As I said, Cull, it's never stopped *Clann Na Snochta Broce* from passing *through* the mountains."

Cull grinned wickedly. "Are you telling me that there's a way *under* the mountains?"

Cathal nodded. "I'd be happy to guide you, but alas, the time away from home could leave my purse a bit light. I'd be unable to trade my furs at the spring fair. However, perhaps we could discuss some form of compensation."

Cull licked his lips in anticipation. "What did you have in mind?"

The next bell was spent in a heated negotiation between the two, finally ending with a spitting on hands and a firm shake to seal the deal.

It was at this point that Feilim returned. "Cathal, there are some *Fear Ban* camped on our borders," he announced. "Sadly, they don't seem to want a fight. They're holding up a parley banner, so I thought I'd better come and fetch you."

"Boarites?" Cull growled, reaching for his weapons.

Feilim turned to Cull. "No, I don't think so. Maybe you'd better come along too."

They armed themselves and headed into the woods, where a force of Brocian warriors had already gathered. Quickly, they slipped through the trees toward the edge of the plain. At the treeline they halted. Standing on the grasslands was an equally large group of people.

As they watched, a horn blew to announce their presence, and a man stepped forward. He was carrying a flag of parley before him, and he walked alone toward them. He was clearly an experienced warrior though his armour had seen better days, as had his threadbare cloak. Despite his dishevelled apparel, he walked with calm authority toward the warriors of *Clann Na Broce Snochta*.

"I guess we'd better go and say hello," Cathal announced with a grin. "Do you want to come along and see what he wants, Cull?"

Cull nodded, before turning to issue a quick order to Conal and Tal. "Stay here, the pair of you."

"But ..." Conal protested.

Cull glared sharply at the Prince, and with a sigh, Conal added "... I know, I know, just do as I'm told!"

Arguing with Cull was about as much use as fighting the ocean.

Cull and the Brocian pair walked down the hill to meet the *Fear Ban* warrior. They met in the middle

"You seem a little lost, stranger," Cathal greeted amiably, before adding with mild reproach "People could easily mistake your presence in their territory. Such things could quickly turn nasty."

On closer inspection, the warrior before them was a little past his prime, with grey hairs in his drooping moustache and a peppering in his short, blonde hair. His weathered features and piercing grey eyes showed no fear as he smiled softly. "My humblest apologies, friend, we didn't mean to cause alarm to the Badger Clan. We didn't realise that your lands extended quite this far out onto the plain. We were out hunting a mutual enemy, and followed their tracks here."

"These are dangerous times. If a man is to sleep safely in his Sett, he needs to watch beyond his normal peacetime borders. Tell me, who is this enemy that you were tracking?"

"Our scouts spotted a column of Lord Boare's Elites heading this way a few days ago, so we set out to intercept them. They should never have ventured into our lands."

"Your lands ...?" Cull interrupted. "... Who exactly are you?"

The man's gaze flicked from the Brocians to Cull. "I'm the Grand Marshal, Declan Morganson of *Clann Na Dragan*."

"*Clann Na Dragan!*" Cull exclaimed. "I thought all resistance had been wiped out!"

"So Lord Boare would have everyone believe," the Grand Marshal said. "Our forces may be scattered, but we still cause the Usurper-king some sleepless nights. We shelter around the edge of the mountains and sally forth to torment the Boarites whenever we can."

"How many of you are there?" Cull asked in astonishment.

"That's hard to say really. Many of my kinfolk are living amongst the Horse Clan to the east of here. Then, there are those who are lounging in Boarite gaols and work-gangs, but there are still nearly three hundred of us living on the Plains of the Dragon, scattered here and there. Some are us were sheltering in caves on the mountainside, preparing for the winter, but the recent invasion of Boarites has stirred up a hornets nest. We mean to send them packing with their tails between their legs."

Cathal interrupted at this point "I'm afraid you've had a wasted journey, Grand Marshal."

"Oh ... why's that?"

"The *Fear Ban*, the Elites you were hunting ... they foolishly wandered into our territory."

"Ah, I see." Declan waited for further clarification.

"They won't be bothering you again," Cathal confirmed.

The Grand Marshal's face dropped with disappointment. Cull had more news for him. "I wouldn't call it a wasted journey, Cathal. The gods might have guided the Grand Marshal here. If you'll just wait here a moment, I'll be right back."

Cull hurried over to where his companions were waiting with the rest of the Snow Badgers. When he got close enough, he signalled Conal and Taliesin forward. "I think this is going to be an auspicious day, Conal."

"Oh ... why's that?" Conal asked. "Who are these people anyway?"

"You'll see," was all Cull would say as he led them forward.

They got to within a few feet of the Grand Marshal before Declan exclaimed in surprise "Conal!"

Conal stopped in his tracks. "Captain Morganson! I thought you were dead."

"And I thought you were safely hidden away with the priestesses of Deanna. What, in the Nine Hells, are you doing out here?" Declan asked. "It gladdens my heart to see you, Sire ..."

Conal swallowed hard on the lump in his throat. "...And mine too, old friend."

"I gather you two know each other, Grand Marshal?" Cull asked.

"Grand Marshal?" Conal asked.

Declan's face darkened. "Sadly, Sire, I'm the most senior ranking officer left in your depleted army, so I've been left holding the title, though I'll gladly relinquish the task if you wish."

Conal placed his hand on the old soldier's shoulder. "I can't think of a more loyal or capable person for the position," he assured, adding "In fact, perhaps this is a good time to make it official. Summon forth the rest of the Dragons, Declan."

The bedraggled group assembled around the Prince, and after some initial confusion and whispering, they all knelt down before him.

"Clansmen ..." Conal announced with as much authority as he could muster. "I praise you all for your efforts in resisting Lord Boare's tyranny. You do me and the memory of my father a great honour."

He paused, waiting for his words to sink in. "I want to thank you all, and I want to take this opportunity to recognise your efforts. I'm sure that with time, I'll come to pay gratitude to you individually, but today, I want to formally recognise Declan Morganson."

A cheer went up from the assembled Dragons.

"Declan," Conal continued, pulling his cloak aside to grasp the handle of his sword. "I decree upon you the title of Grand Marshal."

With a flourish, Conal pulled *An Fiacail Dragan* out of its sheath and raised it high over his head. The winter sun shone brightly off the blade, making it shimmer. A loud gasp could be heard from those present.

"It's the High King's sword!" people cried.

"It's the Dragontooth!" others declared.

"Is that what I think that is?" Cathal whispered to Cull.

Conal lowered the sword to touch the Grand Marshal's head and shoulders. "By the power vested in me as heir to *Clann Na Dragan*, I declare you our Grand Marshal. Let all acknowledge your position on my right hand. In my absence, let all heed your words. Dragons; rise up and greet your champion!"

The assembled *Clann Na Dragan* rose as one, and their battle-cry rang out across the plains *"Dragan abú! DRAGAN ABÚ!"*

"Nice speech," Taliesin mumbled.

"Aye, the lad's learning," Cull conceded.

It took a while for the celebrations to settle down, but eventually Cathal and Feilim managed to pull Cull aside.

"We'll be heading back to the Sett now ... this sun's a little harsh on our eyes," Cathal explained. "I presume you'll be fine out here? We'll let Vort know where you went, when he emerges from my mother's Sett."

Cull nodded. "It might take a while for all this to get sorted out, so that makes sense. Thank you both for your help. I'd better stick around but we'll still need that expedition through the mountains, if that's okay?"

"Of course!" Cathal assured. "I'm sure I can manage to fit you into my busy schedule ... for a reasonable price."

"I thought we'd already agreed on the price?"

"We did ..." Cathal agreed, "... but that was based on bringing only three of you through our mountain. It could get a whole lot more expensive if I have to bring a small army of *Fear Ban* into *Tir Pect*. I'm sure King *Conchubhar* would find that quite intrusive. Naturally, we'll need to renegotiate the terms."

"Oh no, I'm not planning on bringing this lot with me. The whole point was to sneak into *Ard Pect*, not start a small war. It'll still be just the three of us."

Cathal looked crestfallen but shrugged, good-naturedly.

*****

When Balor awoke, it was with a blood-curdling scream that even the sedatives couldn't quench. His mind had been haunted by strange dreams for many days, dreams that made his heart beat faster and sweat run from his pores. He suffered visions of battle and forbidden magic, of death and sacrifice that would make a hard man weep. His dreams were filled with faces. Some of those faces were children, lying prone on stone altars with terror in their eyes. Others were the faces of warriors, blood lust on their features. Three faces, however, came back again and again to haunt him. The first was a dark-haired woman with eyes like death, skin like alabaster, and lips like blood. He saw within her, the child, the woman, and the hag: the triad of womanhood, yet something shied away from thinking of this woman as a mother, a creator of life. Perhaps it was the dark lifeless pools that bored into his very soul, or could it have been the way that her smile seemed ... carnivorous? An unkindness of ravens flocked around her, and they did little to ease his fears. These 'Dark Angels' had always been associated with war and death. She haunted his dreams in many guises, with many names, but the eyes were always the same. Now, she had come to him as a gigantic raven and stolen away his sight, causing him to scream with abject terror. He trembled as he uttered her name: "Macha!"

The second face that haunted his dreams was also a woman. She too was beautiful in an exotic fashion, and she haunted him in many guises. She also appeared as a crone, a mother, and a child.

Both women exuded power. It seeped from their very spirits to crackle into the world, but there, the comparisons ended. He had watched as this woman had grown in power. He had tricked her, and he had seduced her. He had fought against the awesome power she wielded, and he had lost on not one, but two occasions. Once as a woman and then as a girl ... or perhaps he had that the wrong way around. His mind became confused as memories blurred and mixed and became distorted with time. The medicines in his system were not helping his clarity.

The third face of his dreams was himself, of that he was sure. Or at least as sure as he could be of anything in his drug-induced delirium, but again his dreams were confusing. He was a youth, despised and banished into the wilderness. He became a slave to a half-mad shaman who abused him until the day came when he grew strong enough to murder his master. After that, he spent years in the shaman's cave, reading and learning from ancient scrolls, delving deeper into the forbidden arts that had brought his previous master to the brink of insanity. He became powerful.

Finally, the time came when he could learn no more from the fragile parchments, and he ventured out into the world. His hunger for power made him travel across continents, seeking out hidden treasures. Mysteries, long since buried to keep them away from the eyes of men such as he.

Age took its toll, and his endless search became desperate. There was still so much to learn, and so much to achieve. It was then that he was guided to the Temple of Macha.

Visions blurred, and he was young again, his limbs free from the aches and disabilities that had dogged his quest. Only his eyes reflected the years he had aged during his search. His eyes, the mirrors of his soul, were tainted and corrupted. His dreams went on and on, as he aged and became young again, in a cycle of revitalisation. With each cycle, he became more and more indebted to the one he ultimately served. He again became a servant, just as before he had been the servant of the half-mad shaman. He was treated no better, but he was always granted longevity as long as he was willing to pay the price.

Now, lying blind on his cot, he knew the price he had paid. It was far more than just his eyes that he had lost. His mind teetered on the brink of insanity as he looked back at his unnaturally long life. Only the numbing effects of the potions kept him from seeking the final peace, that and the question that ran through his brain. Was he finally free, or was he still in bondage? Was there more to pay? With a shudder, he wondered if the Dark One would ever release him from service. On that day, so long ago, he had paid the ultimate price for his freedom. He had sold his soul to the darkness.

Waking up with a jolt, his mind still half in his dream, body cringing away from the pain of his dying moments, Balor struggled to flee himself from the raven's claws. Macha's words rang around in his head as she pecked out his remaining eye *"There is a price for life, mortal. There is always a price for worshipping me, manling."*

"He's asphyxiating!"

Balor struggled to break free as he felt hands grappling with him.

"Help me, Fionn!" Brother Seamy called out "Hold him down while I give him something to calm him."

Clarity came to Balor then, as the last of the nightmare disappeared, leaving him in the black emptiness of his own mind. "No!" he protested, "No more! No more!"

Feeling hands pressing down on his chest, Balor struggled against his bonds. The leather bindings were cutting into the half-healed skin as he fought in desperation.

Brother Seamus came to the bedside, holding a vial of rich purple liquid. "Hold his head," he instructed, and Fionn gripped Balor's skull in a vice-like grip.

"No! No more. I need my wits! Let me be!" His body fell limp and he stopped thrashing. Only his jaw remained clenched tight. He must not let them drug him again.

Seamy tried to force his mouth open, but the muscles bunched in Balor's jaw. When Seamy paused and waited a moment, Balor stopped fighting.

The three men paused, catching their breath. Finally, it was Brother Seamus who spoke "Can you hear me?"

Balor nodded, his jaw still clenched tightly as he strained to make out his surroundings with his remaining senses.

"You understand me?" Seamy asked.

Again the bandaged patient nodded, his head looking toward the sound of Seamy's voice, even though he was heavily bandaged above the nose. "I hear you and I understand."

"Good. You need to remain calm. I just want to give you some medicine to help you sleep."

"No," Balor said forcefully. "No more medicine." As an afterthought, he added "please."

"But it'll help with the pain," Seamy protested.

"It addles my brain. No more!"

"You need to sleep and heal."

"No more sleep. The dreams ... they bring me to the brink of madness. Sleep brings me close to insanity. I need to keep my wits about me."

The monks looked at each other. "Fionn, go and fetch Abbot Gearoid."

"But ..."

Seamy gave the younger monk a stern look. "Just do it."

When the two men were alone, Seamy spoke again "If I untie you and let you up, will you behave?"

Balor nodded. "Where am I?"

"You're in the monastery of Leithban Isle, on Crannockmore Lough."

"She brought me to a monastery!" Balor laughed bitterly. "...A monastery! You're a monk then, I take it; you and that bear cub that helps you?"

"Yes, I'm Brother Seamus, and that was Brother Fionn," Seamy explained as he freed Balor's wrists.

"Which god do you worship?"

"All of them," Seamy explained. "It's not wise to ignore a deity, even worse to antagonise them by denying their existence or right to be worshipped."

Balor laughed again, a strange haunting sort of laugh. "How right you are. It's not good to antagonise any of the gods, least of all a goddess. They can be tetchy ... very tetchy indeed, believe me."

"Are you a religious man, then?" Seamy asked.

Balor chuckled. "I suppose you could say that. I certainly have no doubts about the existence of the gods, if that's what you mean. In fact ..." he went on, "...I guess you could say that I was a priest, too."

"Oh, really! Which Order do you come from?"

"You probably wouldn't have heard of it. It's a *very* ancient Order. There are few of us left now to keep the faith alive. How long have I been here?"

"…Most of the winter."

Balor felt the bandages on his face. He winced at the touch, but he continued to probe around the bandage, ignoring the pain. "I've been in the wars, it seems."

"You were in a pretty bad way when you arrived," Brother Seamy agreed. "Can you remember how it happened?"

Balor pulled a face. "I'd rather not. From what little I have seen, it makes me think it wouldn't be worth the effort. Some things are better forgotten."

"Yes, I understand," Seamy replied, but he couldn't hide the disappointment from his voice.

"If I remember anything important, I'll be sure to let you know."

Chapter Eleven: Maerlin's Education

At first, Seabhac had found it hard to acclimatise to her new guests. The cottage felt crowded, and since the winter had set in, it proved harder to spend time outside. However, Seabhac was not averse to cheating every once in a while, when she thought no one was looking. On more than one dreary day, after too long spent in the cramped confined of the cottage, Seabhac would declare that she was going out for a walk. Within a few moments of her leaving, the sun invariably broke through the heavy rain-clouds.

Finally, Maerlin brokered the unspoken subject with Cora. "She's doing that, isn't she?"

"Doing what?" Cora asked, failing miserably to act innocent.

Maerlin pointed at the sun, shining brightly through the cottage windows. "...That, of course! Don't pretend that you haven't noticed. I'm sure you can feel the tingle just as much as I can."

"Tingle?"

"You know something!" Maerlin accused, seeing Cora's eyes flinch.

"I don't ..." Cora denied.

"What's going on?"

"Nothing!" Cora's voice raised an octave in protest.

"Nessa?" Maerlin asked, looking up at the rafters.

"Awwkkkk!"

"Don't pretend that you don't know what I'm talking about," Maerlin accused. "What's going on?"

"I can't say," Cora admitted.

"Awkkk."

"Fine, it's like that, is it? I'll just go and see for myself."

"You can't!" Cora protested.

"I've been lying around here for over a moon," Maerlin complained, throwing back the blankets "...apart from short walks in the orchard or being assisted to the outhouse. I'm not going to fall over, you know."

Swatting away Cora's restraining hand; she grabbed her cloak and headed for the door. "Stay here," she ordered, closing the door firmly behind her.

Cora stamped her foot before turning to the magpie. "You'd better follow her ... just in case."

Nessa shook her feathers with a sigh of resignation. She had been quite happy to stay snug and warm on the rafter. "Awwwkkkk!" With a gentle glide, she slipped through the open window and out into the sunshine. The cold air hit her immediately, despite the sunshine. Ignoring its chill, she peered around and spotted Maerlin, at the edge of the garden. Flitting from tree to tree, Nessa followed.

Maerlin followed her instincts, sensing that she was going in the right direction. She had felt the distinctive gentle tingle of magic, so subtle that it had taken her some time to realise what it was that she was feeling. This time, it had come from behind the small hill to the south of the cottage. Now that she was a little away from the cottage, her pace slowed. After the initial bluster, she could feel her legs weakening and her head swimming from the exertion. She was getting stronger, but it was infuriatingly slow work. Trying to take her mind off her body's protests, she wondered what Conal and the others were up to. She had been furious when she found out that they'd left Cora and her behind, and it had taken days to calm down enough to see the reasoning behind their decision, not that that was going to stop her giving Conal a right earful when she caught up with him. He was not going to get off that lightly.

Only her bedridden condition and Nessa's sternest berating had stopped her from attempting to follow the young prince. Little did she realise that the current wet spell was also a backlash of her deep anger over the incident. Only Seabhac's intervention had prevented a full-blown snowstorm striking the region. It was this intervention that had first alerted Maerlin to the hidden talents of their host.

Maerlin crested the hill and looked down on the undulating countryside. In the distance, the plain flattened out all the way to Dragon's Ridge, but nearer lay the foothills of the mountains, a slow undulating land of small hillocks, as if the ground had wrinkled up in preparation for the towering mountains behind the cottage. Along its edge lay the wild woodlands of *Clann Na Broce Snochta*. It truly was a wonderful site in which to build a cottage. Taking in the view, Maerlin looked around until she spotted Seabhac, standing a little way off. Resting on her shoulder was her ever-present hen harrier, Fintan. The old bird was watching Maerlin silently as she made her way forward.

"Thou shouldn't be out here on thy own, Maerlin," Seabhac declared, not looking round.

Maerlin was surprised that Seabhac knew that she was there, but then she remembered that Seabhac had the same gift with Fintan that she had with Nessa. Maerlin glared at the bird for a moment, but he ignored her.

"Well, art thou going to just stand there?" Seabhac asked "I presume that there's a reason for thou wandering around outside without thy boots on."

Maerlin looked down at her feet, dirty and calloused, as usual, though a bit bluer than normal in the cold. She had been in such a rush to leave the cottage that she had forgotten about her footwear. Having grown up in a rural village and spent her childhood roaming the mountains like a wild goat, she was used to walking around barefoot, but Seabhac did have a point.

"I was getting cabin-fever lying around all day," Maerlin admitted. "And also, I think we need to talk."

"Oh! Why's that?"

"It's about this weather ..." Maerlin broached.

"The weather ...?" Seabhac recovered quickly "Wonderful, isn't it? I do love the winter sunshine. Everything looks so clear and inspiring in this light and the air is quite invigorating."

Maerlin smiled. "It must be nice to get your favourite weather, whenever you feel like it ..."

Seabhac turned sharply toward Maerlin, causing Fintan to flap his wings to steady himself. "What art thou implying?"

"I'm just saying that it must be nice to stop the rain when you feel like it, or move a cloud aside to let the sun shine through and direct it onto your vegetable patch. I notice that it's still growing away healthily, while the prairie grass is scorched with frost. I grew up looking after a garden for my mother, and I know a thing or two about growing plants."

"I see thou art feeling better," Seabhac commented. "The fresh air will do thee good, and a little exercise can strengthen thy muscles."

"Don't change the subject. I've been around too many priestesses to be so easily led astray."

Seabhac frowned. "I hope that there's a point to all this?"

"You have the gift, don't you? You can do Wild-magic?" Maerlin declared. "I feel it when you do it, you know. It's like a tingling in my brain."

"... And what if I do?"

Maerlin paused, almost afraid to say out loud what she had been thinking. "You could teach me," she finally blurted out.

"Teach thee?" Seabhac laughed at the idea "Thou can't be serious."

"I'm bored senseless!" Maerlin begged. "Nessa teaches me some, but if you're an Air-sister, you can help me more. It makes so much sense."

"Perhaps to thee it might, but thou dost not understand what thou art asking. Surely, it'd be better to wait and go back to the Holy Isle. There, thou canst learn all that they have to teach thee. I wouldn't even know where to start."

"Can't you try? Just some little thing to keep me going... like how to move a cloud without getting a headache?"

"Thou haven't inkling ..."

Maerlin sighed and turned away. Seeing the magpie perched on a nearby aspen, she stopped. "A wise woman once told me that Wild-magic was like a muscle. It needed exercise to make it stronger, the same as any other muscle. So I presume to heal it after an injury, you'd need to manipulate it, not let it weaken up from lack of use?"

"Thy reasoning is sound. Some small magic might be beneficial. However, let us leave the clouds alone. Thou dost enough damage in thy sleep as it is, without messing with the poor creatures during daylight. Go and hunt, Fintan, and take that clever little magpie with thee. We'll be back before supper."

Maerlin tried hard to restrain her excitement, but a little squeal of delight still slipped free.

"I wouldn't be so happy if I was thee. Like any muscle, it will ache before it gets stronger," Seabhac warned.

Having already survived Nessa's teachings, Maerlin was well aware of that.

"After sensing thy magical display down on the burial mound..." Seabhac commented with an arched brow, "I presume thou hast managed the stages of control."

Maerlin flushed with embarrassment before nodding.

"Very well then, prepare thy mind and watch what I do. I don't want thee to try this, but I need thee to see it with thy inner eye, so that thou canst fully understand the complexity of the procedure." Placing her staff on the ground, Seabhac drew power from around her. "Come, my sweet Sylphs, come to my aid."

Maerlin closed her eyes and centred herself, before focusing on the Air Elements that were gathering at Seabhac's summoning. The breeze stirred the grass, flowing around Seabhac's robes. She moved her hand until it rested above the staff and made a simple coaxing gesture. The staff quivered and slowly rose from the ground, creeping upwards until it hovered inches away from Seabhac's outstretched hand. Maerlin's inner-senses could see the near-invisible Elementals coiling and slithering along the staff's length. Seabhac pressed her palm down on the well-worn wood, putting more and more pressure on the staff until she was satisfied with its resistance. Then, she hopped up onto the wood. After the slightest of wobbles, the staff maintained her weight, her feet dangling inches off the ground, her upper thighs resting on the floating staff. "Bless thee," she praised and motioned forward with her free hand.

With an eager quiver of enthusiasm, the staff set forth in the indicated direction, carrying Seabhac at a leisurely pace. She floated around in a large circle until she came to a stop before Maerlin and hopped off the staff. Releasing her Elementals, she deftly caught the staff as it dropped toward the ground.

"So, all of those tales about witches riding around on broomsticks is true!" Maerlin exclaimed.

"Certainly not!" Seabhac exclaimed with indignation. "A good stave is much more comfortable on thy posterior."

Maerlin giggled. She had never heard it referred to so politely before.

Seabhac smiled. "Of course, from a distance I guess they'd look similar. Besides, no self-respecting witch would be caught dead lugging around a broom."

"Can I have a go?" Maerlin asked eagerly.

"Oh no, I think not. Before thou can start flying around the place, I think that thou had better learn some of the basics." Seabhac walked over to a nearby alder and snapped off a lightweight branch, about an arm's length and the thickness of her finger. "Here, try this to begin with. Pretend that it's an arrow. When thou hast mastered this, I'll give thee a real arrow to play with. When thou can place ten arrows into the bull's eye from fifty paces, then and only then, wilt thou be ready to try thy hand at flying."

Maerlin was crestfallen, but took the twig and placed it on the ground before her. Summoning an Air Elemental, she tried to replicate what she had seen. Concentrating hard, she managed to move the stick along the ground. After some hard work, she even managed to get one end to rise up, before it wobbled and slipped away. Sighing, she rubbed her aching temples and took a few deep breaths to calm herself.

"Take thy time, Maerlin, there's no rush. Thou art trying too hard," Seabhac instructed. "Relax, and let the Elemental see what it is thou wants it to do."

Maerlin breathed deeply. Focusing on the act of raising the stick off the ground, she released her magical energies in a slow trickle. The Elemental responded, and slowly, inch by inch, the errant stick obeyed her will and began to rise. When it was level with her hand, she willed the stick to hover in place.

"Very good, now lower it again."

Maerlin willed the stick to descend, but it slipped from her mental grasp and dropped to the ground. "By Dagda's plums!" she cursed.

"That wasn't bad for a first attempt," assured Seabhac, "but don't forget that thou art fighting the forces of gravity when thy goes upwards. The same gravity is helping thee along on the way down. Don't forget this lesson when thou start to fly. I don't want to spend all of my time patching thee up! Oh, and please refrain from that uncivil language. It ill befits a servant of Deanna."

"But ..."

Seabhac's hard stare stopped Maerlin from further protest "Yes, Seabhac."

"Now, I believe that it's time for supper. Shall we?"

*****

"I'm getting tired of your draughty fort," Taliesin complained. "You should've taken Vort up on his offer to stay at his Sett until spring and rebuild the damned *Dun* then. It's too cold to sleep rough like this. There's a blizzard outside!"

"There's nothing wrong with my fort," Conal protested, though in truth it was a bit draughty "...At least, there won't be when it's finished." With the building only half-completed, they'd been lucky to get some of the roof on before the snows blanketed the Plains of the Dragon. Now, they were stuck with it half-built until spring.

Conal had been tempted by Vort's offer, but word had soon reached other Clan members of Conal's return. Loyal supporters had begun gathering at the ruins of the old *Dun*. Conal could not have brought his entire retinue into the Broce Woods, and he could hardly leave his supporters behind to endure the harsh winter without him, while he relaxed in the warm comfort of the neighbouring Clan's Sett.

Only one option had been open to Conal, and that was to stay and organise the rebuilding of his ancestral seat of power, *Dun Dragan*. That meant that his guardian, Cull, also had to stay. Taliesin had been seduced by the opportunity of becoming a royal bard and had volunteered to stay, too. It was only later that Taliesin realised that Conal's coffers were limited and that his life of luxury as a royal bard was still some moons, if not years away.

The three companions and over three hundred of Conal's clansmen had worked hard to prepare the fort for the coming winter. Unfortunately, they could not take timber from the nearby forest, which marked the boundary of the Brocian Clan's territory and was bound by the Great Truce. Instead, they had to haul the timbers from the newly-built Boarite forts, scattered across the plains. These forts had recently been built by Conal's arch-enemy, Lord Boare. Now, these had been deserted in the wake of the battle at Dragon's Ridge and Conal was having these forts systematically dismantled and hauling their timbers away to Dragon's Ridge to rebuild his ancestral home: *Dun Dragan*. To make matters worse, the autumn rains were quickly followed by hailstorms and finally snow, snow ... and even more snow.

With the work called off, Cull had again broached the subject of the trip north to see how things were going in *Tir Pect*. It was no secret that Conchubhar, the Pectish High King, looked hungrily across his southern border to the lands of *Clann Na Dragan*. The plain was once owned by his ancestors, and it was rich farmland.

And so it was that Conal, Cull, and Taliesin bade farewell to the Grand Marshal and returned to the Snow Badger Clan. Declan Morganson had not been pleased when he'd been told that Conal was leaving again, but he finally agreed to the necessity of the journey. He watched them ride away, while he continued making *Dun Dragan* defensible before the coming spring. The much-diminished *Clann Na Dragan* was trapped between two powerful enemies, and sooner or later, one of them was going to test the Clan's weakened defences. With enough time and manpower, Declan was sure that he could be ready, but time was something he might not have. This was why he had accepted Cull's decision to visit *Ard Pect* and gather intelligence on at least one of their enemies. Cull had also sent messages south to the Beggar-lord and to the

High Priestess of Deanna, to let them know how things were going and to ask for their help.

Broll the Beggar-lord had already responded. Only the day before, a ragged group of clansmen had arrived from the south, thanks to a cleverly-executed escape from Manquay's gaol. It was through Cull's earlier intelligence and Broll's intervention that the escape had been a success. The Dragon Clan ranks had swelled with the additional fifty warriors. Broll had also sent some much-needed supplies to help feed the clan folk through the harsh northern winter. In addition, Vort's Brocians had donated food and furs to keep them warm, as well as their firm commitment to maintain the peace treaty brokered by *Luigheagh Dragan*: Conal's great-grandfather.

Chapter Twelve: Into the Bowels of Stone

Cathal led the companions deeper into the forest at the foothills of the mountainside. A dozen members of *Clann Na Snochta Broce* had joined them. Each carried a heavy pack of provisions, furs and other items to sell in *Ard Pect*. They climbed high above the tree line on a well-worn path that followed the contours of the mountainside. Soon, Conal was feeling the burn of his leg muscles as the gradient became steeper and their task harder. Finally, they came to a large waterfall, pouring forth out of the side of the mountain, high overhead. Cathal called a brief halt. "We'll grab a bite to eat here before we proceed."

"How long will it take us to reach *Ard Pect*?" Cull asked.

"It'll take about a week or so, maybe longer."

"And how long will we be in the mountain?" Taliesin asked.

"About five days, give or take. Hopefully, we won't run into any trouble."

"Trouble ... such as?"

"*Na Coblinau-Dorcha* raiding parties for the most part, but occasionally, you'll get a hungry *Ciudach* or a giant spider. Nothing that we can't handle," Cathal assured them.

"I've heard that *Ciudach* are dangerous," Taliesin declared.

"They are, but we rarely see them. Usually, it's a rogue that has been kicked out of the tribe."

"What did they do to get kicked out of the tribe?" Conal asked.

"Sun-madness usually does the trick. On rare occasions they can become addicted to Chorthium dust. Sometimes, they've challenged their chief, lost, and somehow managed to escape with their legs still attached ... that sort of thing."

"What's Sun-madness?"

"Conal, did anyone ever tell you that you ask too many questions?"

"Not that I can think of, Cull. I just want to know what I'm getting into. After all, it was you who taught me the three rules of warfare."

"What are those?" Taliesin asked.

Cull groaned.

"The first rule is know thy enemy. The second rule is: know thy friends, and the third rule is: know thy battlefield," Conal recited. "Surely, this is a good time to ask these questions, Cull?"

"Whatever!" Cull grunted. "You might as well tell the lad, Cathal. You'll get no peace until you do."

"Sun-madness is a rare ailment that only occurs in *Ciudach*. Some think it's something to do with having too much quartz in their diet and sleeping out in the sun, but no one's really sure."

"What are the symptoms?" Taliesin asked, ignoring the glare from Cull.

"That'd be frothing around the mouth, a reddening and glazing of the eyes ... oh, and some psychotic tendencies."

"Psychotic tendencies, I thought that all *Ciudach* were psychotic?"

"No Taliesin, that's not true. Usually, *Ciudach* have a healthy respect for their own hides, though they are tough fighters. A *Ciudach* with Sun-madness, however, tends to be downright reckless, almost suicidal even."

"What about the ones with the dust thingy?"

"Let's just hope we don't meet any of them, Conal. That'd tend to ruin our day."

"Why's that?"

"A *Ciudach* that's addicted to Chorthium dust is homicidal *and* suicidal. They are pretty much immune to pain, and once they've started fighting, they won't stop. The only way to stop one is to hack it to pieces and that's easier said than done."

"I really shouldn't have asked, should I?"

Cull refrained from commenting.

Taliesin cleared his throat, hesitantly.

"Whatever it is, Tal, you might as well ask it now?"

"Sorry, Cull, but he mentioned spiders .... I really hate spiders."

Cathal bit back a laugh. "Taliesin, I hate to be the bearer of bad tidings, but there are a lot of spiders in there. There are small ones, big ones, *really* big ones, and on rare occasions, gigantic ones. *Most* of them are relatively harmless."

"Relatively, what's that supposed to mean?"

"It means that they're more dangerous in your head than they are in real-life. Now, can we stop with the questions and get on with it?" Cull grumbled.

After eating, Cathal indicated the handholds to the right of the waterfall. "From here on we have to climb."

"I thought you said we didn't have to go over the mountain?" Cull asked.

"Oh, we don't. We only climb up to where the waterfall flows out. It comes from an underground river. We'll follow it for the next day or so, but there are some things I'll need to explain to you first, as you won't be able to hear me once we get inside. Once we're inside, you'll find a thin ledge running along the side of the river. Please be careful as the river is fast-flowing, and it's a long way down if you get swept away."

He waited until they nodded their understanding before proceeding "You'll go last, just in case there's any trouble ahead. The path is narrow, so once we start it's hard to change your position in the line. My warriors are better able to defend us against any threat in the darkness."

"Darkness, but what about torches or those fungi things you use?"

"Sadly, Cull, you'll have to do without light for a while. The light might help you see a few feet in front of you, but it'll be a beacon for any unpleasantness within the mountain. We'd draw our enemies to us like moths to a flame. We're safer using stealth than having to fight our way through the mountain, which brings me to my final point. Noise must be kept to an absolute minimum. No talking, not even in whispers, unless it's completely necessary. Again, as with the light, noise carries and echoes though the caverns like ripples on a pond. A dropped knife can resonate for days in the darkness and attract the curious onto our trail."

"You're not giving us much confidence, Cathal," Cull complained.

"Don't worry. If you do what I tell you, when I tell you, we'll make it to *Ard Pect* in one piece," Cathal assured with a wicked grin. "Now, let's begin." He signalled to his clansmen, and the scout led the party upward. He was followed moments later by the next man and then the next. Conal watched as they climbed nimbly upwards, despite the heavy packs that each warrior carried.

"Follow my lead, stay close, and do what I do," Cathal advised as he grasped the first foothold and climbed.

"Okay you two, are you sure you're up for this?" Cull asked. "This is your last chance to back out before we go into the darkness. If you want to go back to Dragon's Ridge, now is the time to say so. I'll go on ahead to *Ard Pect* alone. I'm sure you'll be safe with the Grand Marshal."

Conal was looking forward to some adventure after the previous moon or more of tedium and manual labour. "Not on your life, Cull. I'm coming along. I want to see what the fabled city of *Ard Pect* looks like ... and anyway, it's got to be better than sitting around in that leaky half-built *Dun*."

"That's your ancestral home you're talking about," Taliesin teased.

"I know it is. Don't tell Declan I said this, but that doesn't make it any warmer to sleep in. I'm sure when the roof is fixed and the windows are all in, it'll be a lovely place to spend the winter. That, however, isn't going to happen any time soon."

Taliesin had been busy fighting off visions of monster-spiders, but Conal did have a point. Besides, he'd be sure that he'd miss out on some epic tales if he stayed behind. With a heavy sigh, he nodded. "Count me in, too."

Taliesin started to climb. If he was going to have to go, he wanted to be safely nestled between Cathal and Cull, where he was the least likely to get killed. Cull nodded and followed, leaving Conal to bring up the rear.

Conal slung the Dragontooth sword over his shoulder and adjusted his cloak before reaching for the first rung.

The stones were slick with mist, but Conal found that one of the advantages of being last in line was that all the moss and grit had been cleaned out of the handholds. This made it an easier if exerting climb. By the time he reached the top, his legs were quivering with fatigue. Clambering onto the narrow ledge, he looked down at the fast flowing water. Cathal had not been joking when he used the word 'narrow' to describe the ledge. It was barely wide enough to stand sideways on. For Conal to move along the tunnel, he would have to shuffle sideways, step by tiny step. Throwing a piece of moss into the river, he watched as it shot over the edge of the falls. "By the Nine Hells!" he muttered. Cull nudged him, and put a finger to his lip in silent rebuke.

Conal raised a hand in apology and mimed the words "Sorry, I forgot."

Cull nodded and moved off along the narrow footpath. Conal paused to take a last look at the rising sun before following. It did not take long to become immersed in the darkness. The only light was coming from the slowly diminishing circle of sunlight at the entrance. He kept as close to Cull as he could, bumping shoulders lightly with each movement. This contact was his confirmation that he was not alone, that and the breathing of men as they made their way along the passageway. Even this was hard to hear above the gurgling of the water. Occasionally a splash was heard, and all movement stopped as men strained their senses against perceived danger within the pitch-black gloom.

The pinprick of sunlight stayed constant for what seemed like an age of slow shuffling. Their tired legs were forced to continue to toil as there was no place to stop and rest. Then, Conal looked back the way they had come and realised that the light had gone completely. At some point, they must have turned a bend in the tunnel, and it had disappeared. With an inward sigh, Conal bid farewell to it and continued onward, trying not to think of the oppressive weight of stone over his head.

They slogged on and on. Conal occasionally waved a hand before his face in a futile attempt to see something, anything. At times he found it easier to close his eyes and use his other senses. For some reason this seemed to help. It was as if the endless staring at nothingness was straining his eyes or that his ears would work better with his eyes closed. The time passed with painful slowness. There was nothing to measure its passing, but for the dropping of water and his endless thoughts. On more than one occasion the rhythm lulled Conal toward sleep, only to waken with a jolt of surprise when he could not feel Cull's shoulder beside him. On more than one occasion, his foot slipped on the edge of the ledge. Cull had to catch hold of him as he struggled to keep his balance.

It took Conal a while to notice that his eyes could see something again, such was the subtle change in the depth of the darkness. Briefly, he wondered if he had begun to hallucinate from sleep-deprivation before finally accepting that he could indeed see. He could see a subtle blend of shadow on shadows, but even this was an improvement on the mind-numbing emptiness that had existed for so long. Conal realised that it was the same fungus that the Brocians used within their Setts. It lightly coated the walls of the tunnel and as they travelled sleepily onward, occasional blobs of light appeared before them. These were caused by the fungal growths clumping together, before petering out to near blackness again.

Conal stirred from his stupor as Cull grasped his shoulder and guided him backward. Cull backed him into the crevice and around a corner, and then they stopped. Conal heard rummaging and the quality of light intensified until he could see the Brocians gathered before him. They looked as weary as he felt. Quickly, the Brocians spread out within the small cavern and rummaged in their packs for food and bedding.

Cathal motioned the three companions closer before whispering "Grab something to eat and have a rest." Cull organised them with hand signals. In no time at all, a suitable camp was set up. The Brocians had opened vessels containing the glowing fungi and it chased the shadows away. These, they spread around the small cavern. Looking around at the entranceway, Conal noticed that sentries were standing silently beyond the fungal light, guarding the group against any unwelcome intrusion. These men stayed alert while the other clansmen settled down within their furs and slept. Conal followed their example and selected an available space amongst the cramped floor. Wrapping himself in his cloak, and resting his head on his pack, he laid his sword within easy reach. Exhaustion soon claimed him, and it wasn't long before he was deep in sleep.

*****

Maerlin looked around. A massive white structure surrounded her. It reminded her of the feasting hall on the Holy Isle. It was decorated with ornate carvings, strange glyphs, and jagged knot-works. Reaching down, she touched the shiny white floor and flinched at the cold surface. What she had assumed to be marble was in fact, solid ice. The whole structure must have been carved from a huge glacier.

"Do you like my palace?"

She jumped at the sound of the voice behind her. Turning quickly, Maerlin looked upon a face that had haunted her dreams. Here were the same long golden locks that she remembered, the same piercing blue eyes that bored deep into her soul, and the same warm smile that she had dreamed of on the battlefield. "Where am I?" she asked.

"I thought I just told you. You're in my palace."

He was dressed in rich grey furs and plush white velvet, decorated with gold buttons and a heavy gold chain of office rather than the golden armour of her previous dream. She noticed that he still wore the gold circlet around his brow. It was his eyes, however, which captured her attention. The more she looked, the more she became lost in their intensity. Warmth flowed through her body as she was gazing into them. She could feel herself getting lost in those orbs.

"How did I get here?"

He smiled and it lit up his face, even though a missing canine marred its perfection. "I haven't the foggiest idea, but I'm so glad you've finally arrived. I've been waiting for an eternity for you."

Maerlin was confused. "Who ... me?"

"I'd offer you some refreshments, but sadly, the servants have all long since gone. I suppose we could make it ourselves. I'm sure we'll find the right tools for the job down in the kitchen, though I'm not sure how palatable it'd be. I suppose I should've planned this whole thing a bit better. It's not as if I didn't have the time. Come along and we'll see what can be done. We might have to cheat a bit though, if we're going to rustle up a snack for you. I do hope you won't object."

The White Knight of her dreams walked away, and after a moment's hesitation, Maerlin followed. "Sorry, but I'm a bit confused. What am I doing here?"

113

He turned to look back at her in surprise. "Doing here? You've come to live here. Now come along, we've got so many preparations to complete."

"Preparations ..." Maerlin was unable to keep up with either his pace or his conversation "What preparations?"

"...The preparations for the wedding, of course. Tell me, when will the bridesmaids be arriving? I really will have to recruit some servants for the place before then, and maybe get the plumbing inspected. It's been too long since the old place has had any visitors, but there's nothing like a good wedding to shake off the cobwebs."

"What wedding?" Maerlin asked.

"...Our wedding, silly! We can't be expected to save the world without formalising our union, can we? I mean, there are certain protocols that must be followed, by the heavens above!"

"Are you mad?" she demanded. "I'm not marrying you. I don't even know you."

He looked at her with a mixture of shock and embarrassment on his face. "Oh, what must you think of me! You'll have to excuse my poor manners. I'm a bit out of practice at receiving guests."

He made a very formal bow before continuing "Milady, as I no longer have a seneschal to do this for me ... I'm pleased to present ... erm, me, the Royal Highness, King Sygvaldr Frost-Breath, the seventy-sixth ruler of the Icy Wastes and Lord of the Skies, blah, blah, blah!" he announced grandly "So ... now that that's over with, let's get down to business ... I was thinking you could use a mixture of ermine and raw silk for the bridesmaid dresses. That way, it won't get too chilly."

"Wait a moment!" Maerlin protested. "I'm not marrying you ... or anyone else for that matter. I don't even know how I got here. Let's get something sorted out, right here and now. For a start, I don't care how handsome you are or what your fancy titles are, there's no way I'm getting married. Have we got that clear?"

"...You think I'm handsome?" he grinned wolfishly, clearly ignoring the main thrust of her argument.

"Yes ... I mean, no ... urgghhhhh!" Maerlin growled in frustration. "It doesn't matter what I think! I'm not marrying you ... end of story!"

"But it's already been agreed ... that was the deal!"

"Deal ... what deal? I didn't make any deals."

"No, not with you, silly. It was the one I made with your mother. She's the one who proposed this wedding. This was all her idea."

"Well! This is the first time I've heard about it and it's a bit late to check, so you're just going to have to forget about it."

"But ... we had a deal!"

"So you've said! Well ... what can I say? The deal's off."

"Off! It can't be off. This isn't open to negotiation. You've already had the wedding gift for crying out loud, so it's too late to renege on the deal now. That just wouldn't be fair."

"I don't know what you're talking about, but I can tell you this. There's no way I'm getting married. I'm only just getting the hang of my womanhood as it is, and... And... Anyway, I don't even know you."

"Perhaps I'm rushing things a bit. We could wait until spring, if you'd prefer? Spring weddings were all the rage when the rest of my court was alive."

"Spring...!" Maerlin was flabbergasted at his temerity. "Listen! You aren't getting this, are you? There is not ... going to be ... any wedding! Am I making myself clear enough for you?

"Are you telling me that you're calling off our wedding?"

"...Exactly!"

"But ..."

"No wedding!" she affirmed.

"Then ... then you'll have to give it back."

"Sorry?"

"I said that you'll have to give it back. You can't keep the betrothal gift, if you aren't going to be ... well ... betrothed, can you?"

"Sorry?" she repeated.

"If you're not here to get married, then you can tell Uiscallan that the deal is off, and I want it back."

Maerlin woke with a gasp and tried to make sense of the dream. Shaking off the night-time chill, she shook Cora awake.

"Mmm?"

"Wake up!"

"It's the middle of the night ..." Cora tried to pull the blanket back over her shoulders, "Go back to sleep."

Maerlin shuddered. She really didn't want to go back to sleep. She might return to the Ice Palace. "Cora, wake up, I need to talk to you. I've just had the most bizarre dream."

Cora groaned, but finally sat up and pulled a heavy shawl around her to keep her warm. "Were there any nice-looking men in this dream?" she joked sleepily.

"Well, yes there was, but that's not really the point."

Cora snuggled closer. "Okay, I'm awake now. Come on then, tell me all about *him*."

*****

"So let me get this straight. You *think* you tried to murder your own granddaughter. Is that what you're telling me?" Abbot Gearoid asked.

"... Or my great-granddaughter, I'm really not sure which," Balor replied. "I can't see any other explanation. How else could she have got hold of that medallion?"

Gearoid's heart was heavy from listening to Balor's confession. Nevertheless, the patient seemed contrite, so Gearoid continued "Could it have been a similar pendant? Such tokens are common, especially amongst the Hawk Clan."

"You don't understand, Gearoid. I had that piece specially crafted, and it was magically endowed so that I could watch over Uiscallan with it."

Gearoid considered protesting. Much though the rest of the tale was wild, Balor must have been mistaken when he spoke about the mythical figure of Uiscallan the Sorceress? But Balor seemed to have no doubts. The monk gazed at the ragged holes where eyes had once been and wished he could see those missing orbs. He wished to confirm the truth within the windows of Balor's soul. Perhaps not, he thought, given the horrendous tale that he had just heard. He was having bad enough dreams as it was. After listening to today's confession, he was sure that he'd suffer nightmares for the next moon or more. "We are talking about *the* Uiscallan, aren't we?"

"Yes, yes. I've told you ..." Balor confirmed, "Through that pendant I could follow her movements. I'd know where she was. For years she wandered around, but wherever she went, I always knew about it. When she settled down, I knew. All I had to do was scry for the pendant. It was like a beacon, and it always led me to her. It settled for a long time in the wilderness, before moving to Eagles Reach. Again, it settled there for a number of years before travelling to High Peaks, where it finally stopped. For years, I felt nothing, and I'd given up on its usefulness. Besides, she hadn't been a threat for years, so I thought nothing of it. Then suddenly, it started to travel again, and *she* started to come into my dreams."

"Your dreams?" Gearoid prompted.

"Yes, my dreams. The girl has the gift I tell you. Many of Deanna's witches can foretell with Dream-catching, and she must be one of them. She's visited me on a number of occasions in her dreams. The pendant's link must be strong. In my foolishness, when I worked the magic into the metal, I must have created a *two-way* scrying device! That'd explain a lot, but how did she get hold of it, if she wasn't my offspring? It's the only possible solution."

"Do you think the necklace was passed down through the generations? Is that it?"

"What else can it be?"

"But that doesn't mean that she's your progeny, does it?"

"Ah, but you see I tricked Uiscallan into sleeping with me on the night before the Battle of the High Kings. She thought I was the *Dragan*. By the gods, she was such a vixen in the sheets! I tricked her ... I tricked them both. I wanted the Storm-Bringer for my own from the start. Just think of what we could have accomplished if I could have made her mine, but too late I realised that her heart was not going to change. First, it was that stupid Dragon-lord, and then, it was that other prince. I could never get near enough to seduce her without wearing another man's face. Still, at least I ruined her chance at becoming the High Queen."

"But ... why?"

"Why?" Balor snarled, "... because I could, of course!"

"That seems a bit harsh."

"There was another reason also, I guess. There were the prophecies! They foretell something great would come from the union of the Storm-Bringer and the *Dragan*. That union could not be allowed to happen."

"I still don't understand," Gearoid confessed. "How does that make this girl your granddaughter?"

"After the Battle of the High Kings, I disguised myself and hid in the *Dragan's* own household. There was no safer place to hide and see what transpired. I'd been there for some moons, working to undermine the *Dragan* and giving them both doubts. I was able to see the changes in the Storm-Bringer. She was *ripening!*"

"Ripening?"

"Yes, you know, getting fuller of figure. She was getting heavier of breast, and her stomach was starting to swell."

"She was putting on weight?" Gearoid asked, stroking his own paunch

"No, you fool, she was pregnant! I'm pretty sure of it. So I played my hand and got the King to announce his betrothal to that useless milksop of a princess. It was clearly a heavy blow for Uiscallan. The very next day, they found her gone. No one could find her, but I knew where she was. I knew because of the pendant ... don't you see?"

"And ..."

"And I followed her ... I tried to speak to her. I tried to court her. Together we could have ruled the world, but she rejected me ... me! The mightiest wizard in all the world, and she rejected me. Her anger was awesome to behold! She attacked me in a wild rage, and although she couldn't best me, it was a close call. We were both exhausted, and it was only a matter of time before someone made a mistake, and Macha would have her way."

"So what happened next?"

"I flew off. I hadn't come to best her in battle. I went back to Lord Boare. I knew, at least, that she wouldn't interfere with my plans. She wouldn't scurry back to the High King's aid, so I waited and I plotted. It took time, so much time, but eventually I defeated *Clann Na Dragan* and saw Luigheagh's grandson slain in battle."

"So her child was yours?"

"Yes, of course. Who else's could it be?"

"It all seems a little far-fetched for me," Gearoid objected.

"You don't believe me?"

Gearoid sighed, struggling to come to terms with the bizarre tale.

"Watch and believe, Abbot."

Balor's form blurred, and before Abbot Gearoid's astonished eyes, a huge raven appeared on Balor's bed. In truth, it was a rather dishevelled and blind raven, showing half-healed scars and flaking burn marks on its singed wings, but for all of that it was still a fearful apparition. The bird spread its wings and took flight. It was a little ungainly at first, but after a few minor collisions it managed to make it to the window and escaped outside.

"By the Seven!" Gearoid declared. Now he knew how Balor had managed to disappear from his room before. "Seamy!" he called out "Gather the monks together. Balor has escaped again."

Brother Seamus came running into the infirmary with a bewildered look on his face. "How could he have escaped? You were with him the whole time!"

"It's a long story, Seamy. I'm sure you'll find him on the island somewhere, so gather up the lads. Find him before he does any more damage to himself."

With a last look at Gearoid, Seamy headed out to organise the search party.

Chapter Thirteen: *Ciudachbane*

Conal was woken from his restless slumber by a firm shake of his shoulder. He shook off the dreams that had haunted him and rubbed his bleary eyes. Taliesin handed him a hunk of rough bread and a water skin, as if to say 'breakfast is served'. Realisation of where they were washed over Conal while he fought off the last dregs of sleep, and stretched his aching limbs. His body felt a little more rested than his mind, but his empty stomach grumbled, so he bit into the tough bread and chewed hungrily. Washing it down with some of the icy water, he followed Taliesin to the tunnel's entrance. With the all-clear given by the scout, they sidled around the entrance and out onto the ledge, where Conal sighed with relief and vented his bladder into the fast-flowing river. He was as ready as he was ever going to be to face another day in the oppressive darkness.

They quickly packed up their belongings. Soon, they were heading onward, deeper into the incessant gloom. The time passed with tedious shuffling along the ledge before the path started to widen. Their path led them along a dry streambed which headed upwards away from the main river's flow. They followed this new course up a slight, but noticeable, gradient for another indeterminable span of time. Finally, another halt was signalled and food was shared out.

Cathal approached, so he could whisper instructions. "We're approaching the belly of the mountain now, and we must wander through its entrails before we can reach our destination. There are many dangers ahead, so do not stray off the path for any reason. Keep your weapons close to hand, your mouths sealed, and your ears peeled for danger from here on in."

He looked at each of them in turn and waited for their confirming nods before they set off again, still heading gradually upwards. The path widened, but the footing was uneven, making it difficult to walk fast in the darkness, which was only illuminated by the sparse growths of fungi along the way. Where the light allowed, Conal gazed in wonder at all that he saw. The stone floor and ceiling were littered with immense structures, gigantic stalagmites and stalactites. He paused in his walk to touch one of the wonderful formations, only to have the stone disintegrate in his hands. Quickly he scurried back into his place in the line. Despite the immensity of the cavern, the Brocians walked as always in single file. They followed the man in front of them with calm assurance and trusted the scout to lead the way through the maze of dark tunnels and caverns. At times, they climbed upwards. Occasionally, they descended down gullies with the aid of ropes, but they rarely stopped for long in any one place, at least, not until a sound filled the world around Conal and made his bowels quiver with fear.

"What was ...?" Taliesin gasped, before the nearest Brocian slapped a hand over his face. Angry eyes glared at the bard and silenced any further sound. The men crouched and readied for combat. Some of *Clann Na Snochta Broce* drew their three-bladed Brocian daggers: the *Tri-crub*, while others opted for stout fighting spears, but it was clear to Conal that whatever had made the horrendous noise was trouble, and it was not far away.

The sound came again. This time it was nearer, making the walls of the cavern reverberate, and small stones shower down from the ceiling. A stalactite crashed to the ground sending shards of stone flying everywhere.

"More light!" Cathal shouted, and two of the men who had been carrying pots of the glowing fungi, hurled them to the ground. After the long time of darkness, the sudden light dull though it was, made the men squint and shade their eyes. Nevertheless, from its light they were able to see the charging monster.

Three things came to Conal's mind immediately when describing the monstrosity that hurtled toward them. Firstly, it was huge ... really big. Secondly, the thing was seriously ugly in a warped unnatural sort of way. Finally, there were the red, rage-filled eyes that reflected the madness within its brain. It was only later, much later, that Conal had the time to recall the frothing mouth, rotting teeth, claws, and other notable features.

"*Ciudach!*" Cathal yelled as if to confirm Conal's worst fears. Any other enemies in the area would have scurried away on hearing the *Ciudach's* battle-cry, so noise was no longer an issue. This *Ciudach* roared with mindless fury. Few had ever heard such a sound and lived to tell the tale.

The Brocians scattered, hoping to slow down the beast's charge by confusing it with multiple moving targets, but the madness was too deeply embedded into its insane, Chorthium-induced brain. It continued forward, straight toward Conal, who was standing transfixed in abject terror. As an immense arm lashed out, claws extended to rip Conal's head from off his shoulders, Cull dived into the Prince and sent them both crashing into a stalagmite. The ancient edifice shattered on impact.

Rolling to ease the fall, Conal's training kicked in, releasing him from his momentary stupor. Ripping the Dragontooth sword free of its sheath, he roared a defiant challenge and rushed towards the *Ciudach*.

By this time, the warriors of *Clann Na Snochta Broce* had darted forward, slashing at the flanks of the deranged monster with spears and *Tri-crub*. Despite their best efforts, their weapons were making little or no impact on the tough, scaly hide of the beast. They did, however, manage to keep it confused. Each time it tried to close on a target, warriors would dart in at its rear and flanks in an effort to hamstring the *Ciudach*. The warriors danced a deadly dance with the maddened *Ciudach*. Occasionally, one of the men was a fraction too slow and was caught by the flaying claws and flung away into the darkness beyond the glowing fungi. The clansmen were slowly weakening the enraged *Ciudach*, but the task was proving to be monumental. It was like whittling away at a forest with a penknife.

As another Brocian succumbed to the flailing arms, Conal saw his chance. A gap appeared in the right flank, and he ran forward and swung his sword at the back of the *Ciudach's* knee. Having witnessed the limited damage done by the *Tri-crub* and spears, he was expecting to meet similar resistance, but the legendary sword sliced cleanly through the massive leg. Hot grey blood splashed across Conal's face as the monster pitched sideways, almost crushing Conal beneath it as it fell. Dodging aside, Conal struck the sword into the creature's side. Roaring his battle cry *"DRAGAN ABÚ, DRAGAN ABÚ!"* he drove his blade all the way up to the hilt.

Conal didn't hear Taliesin's warning cry, or see the back-sweeping arm that crashed into his skull, but the pain washed over him like a tidal wave. Already unconscious, he sailed through the air and landed in a crumpled heap.

*****

"Let me get this straight," Nessa asked, using her mind-link with Maerlin to communicate. *"The man in your dream, the one you were marrying ..."*

"I wasn't marrying him ... he just assumed I was there to marry him," Maerlin clarified.

"Whatever ... anyway, you described him as blonde, blue-eyed, and very handsome ...in a rugged sort of way. Is that correct?"

"Yes ... and off his rocker ... don't forget that bit."

"How could I? So, to get back to the point, does this sound like anyone you might know?" Nessa prompted.

"No ..."

"Really, are you sure?"

"Why?"

"Well, I'm not an expert on Dream-catching, but I do know the basics. Dreams can be many things from figments of the imagination, and flights of fancy, to visions of the past or even the future."

"Yes, I know all of that, but there's something about this dream. It didn't seem fanciful."

"Okay, so let's look at our options here, shall we? If this was the past, then it must be related to someone else and isn't directly referring to you as the bride."

"That makes sense," Maerlin agreed reluctantly, *"...But what'd be the point?"*

"I'm not sure, so let's continue. If instead, it referred to some future event, what could it refer to?"

"Nessa, you're circling the subject like you're tickling a hornets' nest. What are you thinking?"

The magpie made a strange sighing sound *"Well, it's just ..."*

"Oh, by the Nine Hells, just spit it out."

"If it was in the future rather than the past, based on the description you gave ... could the man in your dreams have been ... well, Conal?"

"Conal!"

"Yes, you know ... the blonde-haired, blue-eyed Prince. How many other Conal's do you know?"

"Don't be silly. It couldn't have been Conal," Maerlin denied, but doubt slipped into her tone. She didn't think of Conal that way. It couldn't be him, but the more she thought about it, the more his facial features, his general mannerisms and his shape blurred with that of the man in her dream. *"No, it wasn't Conal!"*

"You don't sound all that sure."

"Well, it doesn't matter one way or another. I'm not marrying him, whoever he is. He's clearly bonkers, and anyway, he didn't even have the courtesy to ask me properly. I didn't work this hard at learning magic just to give it all up to breed brats for some moronic he-man, king or no-king. He can find himself somebody else to have his babies and darn his socks. It won't be me, I can tell you that!"

"Did he mention anything about darning his socks and having babies?" Nessa asked.

"No, he didn't, but I'm sure that it'll be there, in the small print, someplace."

"Maybe we should put this topic aside for now, before we get another one of your downpours, Maerlin," suggested Nessa. *"How are your exercises coming on?"*

"I can get the arrow lifted okay, but it just sort of collapses when I send it at the target. It just doesn't have sufficient thrust."

"Could you be doing it wrong? Think of it like an arrow in a real bow. When the string is drawn back, the tension increases, the farther it is pulled. The tension between the bending bow and the string creates the thrust as it is released. Can you picture that?"

Maerlin focused her mind and envisaged a yew stave bending under the archer's muscles, the tension on the string increasing until the arm could pull no farther, and the bow was at its maximum stretch. She considered the final release and elasticity of the bow as it sprang back into shape and the pull on the string, thrusting the arrow forward past the archer's thumb and beyond. She replayed the action over and over again in her mind, studying the bow and the arrow from different angles and the forces at play along the bow. She was so engrossed in the motion that the dream slipped from her mind, and she relaxed. *"I think I understand it a bit better now,"* she announced and opened her eyes to look at the arrow on the grass before her.

It rose slowly and swivelled to point toward the makeshift target that Cora had woven. This time, Maerlin divided the Air Elementals she had summoned. She channelled one of the Sylphs to hold the arrow firmly in place, while another she encouraged toward the arrow tip. A third Sylph she coaxed to the feathered end and focused its energy within the knocked end of the arrow. Picturing firmly in her mind the image of the flying arrow and the tension and counter–tensions within the bow, she revealed her will to the Elementals. Holding them firmly in place until she was ready, she refocused her concentration on the red circle that had been painted onto the target. She felt confident that this time it would be right. It was the most complex piece of magic that she had ever attempted. It was a veritable orchestration of concentrated effort. Taking a deep breath, she released her magic and allowed the Air Elementals to follow her wishes. The arrow flew forward, straight and true, to strike into the centre of the target. A sharp 'thunk' sounded as it buried itself into the tightly woven straw where it hummed softly.

"Yes! Yes! Yes!" Maerlin yelled, dancing about in joy.

"Very good," Seabhac congratulated from behind Maerlin, startling her.

Maerlin tried to hide her exuberance, but Seabhac smiled warmly. "Don't be afraid to celebrate thy victories, Maerlin. They are well deserved. There will be many defeats in thy life, and it's important to fully embrace both thy victories and thy defeats."

Maerlin nodded.

"Thou hast done much better than I'd have expected, Maerlin. As I'm sure Nessa will tell thee, many a third-year novice on the Holy Island would have failed at this task. Now that we know thy ability, we'll need to test it further. As I recall thy quote, a muscle needs to be exercised."

"Am I ready for the staff?" Maerlin asked, failing badly to conceal the excitement from her voice.

Seabhac gave a rich, throaty laugh. "No, not quite yet, Maerlin, though I can recall my own excitement at flying. Thou wilt have to wait a little while longer before thou can do that. There's still much to learn before thou can be skimming the clouds."

Maerlin's face fell. She had been itching to try the 'flying broom trick', as Cora had started calling it.

"Thy next step, Maerlin, is to fire more arrows."

"But I've already achieved that."

"Thou hast fired one arrow, at one target ... once, and succeeded. When thou can do it ten times out of ten, we'll begin with ten arrows and then make it ten targets for those arrows. When thou can do twenty arrows at twenty different targets ... at different ranges, then thou will have mastered this particular trick."

"Will I be able to try flying then?" Maerlin asked, knowing there was going to be a catch. There was always a catch.

"That's why I've always been reluctant to become a mentor before. There is always the difficulty of finding a balance between having concern for thy pupil's welfare, and wanting them to grow into all that they can become," Seabhac stated. "It is such a stressful dilemma. Let's just say that thou will be a lot nearer," she relented. "There are still a few other matters to teach thee, but thou will definitely be a lot nearer."

*****

Seabhac turned and walked away, clearly troubled. Until recently, she had been happy to live a life of quiet isolation, but something was growing inside her. She found herself constantly surprised at this feeling, since she had thought it long forgotten.

*****

Fintan watched silently from a nearby tree. He sensed Seabhac's pain as she slipped into memories of a time long-past. His hawk eyes noticed the tears welling in the witch's eyes and fought off the urge to offer comfort. Now was not the time to mind-meld. Lifting his wings into the wind, he took to the air and headed westward. It was time to hunt before the daylight slipped away. The joy of flying always brought him inner peace.

*****

The room was dark, but to Balor, that in itself was irrelevant. However, the silence suggested something else. It must be night, or at least very early in the morning. As the monks of the monastery of Leithban started their day in the pre-dawn and finished well after dusk, there was usually a constant hum of noise to distract the mind, but not now. Now, it was quiet. There was still a gentle breeze blowing outside, and the ever-present noise of waves slapping against the rocks, as well as the creaking of old boards warping in the dampness, but now was as quiet as it ever got on the island.

Silence, like darkness, has many layers that only patience and time can unravel. Balor had both of these in abundance. Strapped securely to his wooden cot, there was little for Balor to do except listen. Despite this, since his recent dalliance into magic, he had found that some of his other magical skills had awoken. Even strapped down as he was, he could allow his mind to roam.

Soon, he could sense the sleeping monks. Curiosity and boredom took over at that point. He delved into their unprotected minds and found many sordid and amusing details. At first, he was happy to skim the sleeping minds, stealing their secrets and doubts, but he soon tired of such simple entertainments. It was not long before he took a more active role. He fed fuel to their weaknesses, encouraged their lusts, greed, fears, and paranoia. He undermined their egos and slipped suggestions into their subconscious. Where he found monks with sexual preferences toward their fellow brothers, he coaxed and cajoled them with subliminal messages and nuances until their vows of chastity fell asunder and debauchery ensued. Others, he fed with the thoughts of slighting and disrespects. Within days of the awakening of his mental powers, the normal order of the peaceful island fell asunder and arguments broke out amongst the normally tight-knit community.

At other times, doubts and guilt washed over Balor like the waters of the Lough washing over the rocks of the island. He tried to undo his earlier machinations, but the mere act of using his powers brought forth his darker side, so that days went by while he fought against his inner-self and the *Darkness* that lurked there.

*****

His confessor, Gearoid, was also wracked with doubts. He was deeply troubled after being told of the evil powers that Balor had wielded in his previous life. Should he exile the ravaged stranger to avoid endangering his small community or should he encourage him toward the light of righteousness? He could not ask the other monks about it, even the senior ones such as Brother Seamy. The act of confession was a sacred thing and not to be shared or gossiped about. Gearoid was forced to seek clarity through prayer, but with each passing day he became more concerned.

Chapter Fourteen: News from Suilequay

Conal opened his eyes, not that it helped much. The world was still just as dark, either way. He waited, listening, and could make out the soft breathing of sleeping men nearby. Raising his head, he saw glow-lamps around the cavern. The fungi within was giving off a soft eerie light. Moving had been a mistake though as pain washed over him, and he groaned. Dizziness enveloped him, and he slipped back into oblivion.

The next time he woke, the light was nearer, and he could make out Cull's face before him. "Water," he croaked. His throat was as dry as an autumn leaf, and his tongue felt swollen in his mouth.

"He's awake," Cull hissed.

"Water," Conal croaked again, wanting to wash away the coppery taste of dried blood from his mouth.

"Yes, of course, hang on a moment, lad," Cull assured. "Bring me that water skin, Tal."

The bard rushed over and beaming down at him, he raised the skin to Conal's lips. "Gently," he advised, as he raised Conal's head to help him drink.

"What happened?" Conal gasped.

"You slew the *Ciudach*," Taliesin declared with a grin.

"Aye, and it nearly killed you in the process," Cull growled.

Conal tried to remember, but it was all still a blur.

"What, by Macha's cold heart, did you think you were doing?" Cull berated. "You're lucky that you're not feasting in the Hall of Heroes."

"What do you mean?" Conal asked. "I killed it, didn't I?"

"Let me help to refresh your memory, shall I?" Cull snarled. "Firstly, you stood there and let the damn thing charge right at you. Have I not told you, over and over again, to avoiding becoming a static target? Footwork, lad, don't forget your footwork! If I hadn't been near to hand, you'd have lost your head before the fight had even started ..."

Some vague memories returned, and Conal groaned.

"... Then, you waded into the thick of it all, and again, you forgot about your footwork. Why, pray tell, do you think the Brocians were dodging around all over the place?" Not waiting for a response, Cull continued his tirade, "not that it helped much. They still lost two good warriors and they have another three that are badly injured, but at least they tried to stay out of its reach. *Ciudach* aren't just strong, they're deceptively quick. You might have noticed that had you been paying attention, but no ... the mighty prince had to go and charge forward with his trusty pig-sticker in hand. It's a bloody good job that your sword is sharper than your wits or you'd have been *Ciudach*-dung by now."

"But I killed it!" Conal objected.

"... Killed it! Oh yes, you did that, alright. You thrust right into its heart with that pig-sticker of yours. You did a fine job of killing it. The problem is that the monster was so strung out on Chorthium dust that it took a while for it to catch on to the fact. Why, by the Nine Hells, didn't you jump back out of the way after you cut its bleeding leg off? That's what I want to know!"

Conal was at a loss for an answer. From Cull's glare, he knew that he was not going to get off that easily. "...It seemed like a good idea at the time," he suggested weakly.

"Aye, I can see it now, written in fancy script on your tomb ... *Here rests Prince Conal, would-be heir to Dragania. He tragically died too young, because of a stupid stunt. Still, it seemed like a good idea at the time* ... Ceila would just love that. She'd chew my head off, and then she'd go on to haunt you in the afterlife."

Conal flushed with embarrassment.

"It was a mighty strike," Taliesin praised.

"Don't you go encouraging him, bard. He doesn't need all your fancy notions of heroism. It's bad enough that the Brocians have started calling him *Ciudachbane.*"

"...They do!" Conal beamed, but his smile faded under Cull's glower of frustration.

"Did it never occur to you that I'm responsible for your well-being until you can take up your kingship? Let's be very clear about this, shall we? If you ever pull a stunt like that again, I'll personally bury you up to your head next to an anthill and pour honey on that dumb noggin of yours. Do I make myself clear?"

Conal nodded weakly.

Cull glared at him for a moment longer. "I'll go and let Cathal know that you've returned from the dead. I'm sure that he'll be tickled pink to hear the good news. In the meantime, Tal, do something useful. You can get his Royal Fecklessness some food, and don't be filling his head full of any of that bardic nonsense while you're at it."

"Yes, Cull." Taliesin nodded with a serious face, before winking at Conal the moment Cull's back was turned. "I'll be right back, Conal."

He returned a moment later. "Your breakfast is served, my Prince. It's all of your favourites. Let's see: five-day-old trail bread, dried apple, horse jerky and a fine vintage of river water to wash it down, though it's been in the water skin for a couple of days now, so it's developing an interesting bouquet."

Conal pulled a face, but his stomach was far too hungry to object to breakfast. At this point, he'd have been quite happy to wolf down a *Ciudach* steak, though he doubted that he would find such a delicacy offered in any of the posh restaurants in Manquay.

When he had eaten his fill, Conal looked around. "Where's my sword, Tal?"

"It's still stuck in the *Ciudach*. The Brocians wouldn't touch it, in case there was some powerful spell warding it. When they asked Cull about it, he merely said 'let the stupid bugger get his own pig-sticker'."

"I really wish he'd stop calling the Dragontooth sword that! It just isn't right," Conal complained. "It lacks respect!"

"Well, it's certainly sharp enough, to have cut through that *Ciudach* so easily. The Brocians were quite impressed when you sliced its leg off, but

Cull, I'm afraid he's a lost cause. To be fair to him though, he was very worried about you. No one knew whether you'd wake up or not, but he insisted on waiting, rather than moving on. He said that moving you might cause further damage. After the fight, the Brocians agreed to give it a few days, despite our supplies running low."

"What about the dangers?"

"Cathal said we'd be fine for a couple of days. Any Goblins in the area would've scarpered after hearing the *Ciudach's* bellow. Either the *Ciudach* would survive the battle, or whatever it was attacking would. Anything that can survive a *Ciudach,* whacked out on Chorthium dust, was going to be far too dangerous for a raiding party of *Na Coblinau-Dorcha*. He figured we'd be safe for about three days. After that, we'd have to high-tail it to the surface before curiosity got the better of them. You've been out for two days now, so we were planning on leaving in the morning. Now that you're awake, it'll save us having to carry you."

Taliesin remembered something else and added excitedly "Oh, and another thing. Cathal thought it might be worth skinning the *Ciudach* and taking the hide with us. When it's cured, it makes extremely tough armour. It'd be lighter than chain mail, but tougher than normal leather armour. There are armourers in *Ard Pect* that are skilled enough to work the hide and discreet enough not to make a song-and-dance about it. Cull was concerned about drawing attention to ourselves, but Cathal assured him that he would get the armour made and bring it back to his Sett for safe keeping. When we come back for the Gathering of the Clans, we can stop off at the Sett and pick it up. They've even offered to escort you to the fair as an honour guard."

"They did?" Conal asked in surprise. Although the Great Truce of Conal's great-grandfather had brought peace between the *Fear Ban* and their Pectish neighbours, for them to offer themselves as an honour guard was an unheard-of step between the two tribes.

"With the warriors of *Clann Na Dragan* and the Brocians at your back when you ride to the gathering, even Lord Boare would be foolish to interfere. Once you get to the Gathering, the Brehon laws can protect you. You'll be safe to compete in your Rites of Manhood with the other young men. After that, you can ask the Brehons to acknowledge you as the leader of *Clann Na Dragan.*

Conal was pleased with the way things had turned out, despite the various aches and pains he was suffering. "Help me up, Tal. I think it's time I got my sword back."

*****

Maerlin found herself on a shadowy balcony, overlooking a massive chamber. Although she had never been here before, she knew where she was. Behind a large gilded throne hung a red banner, from floor to ceiling, and covering most of the wall. The banner depicted iconography of a black boar. It was the same emblem that could be found on the front of any Boarite soldier's tabard. She was in Lord Boare's throne room in Suilequay. Judging by the crowd gathered below, court was in session.

The room below was filled with the same red-garbed soldiers, lining the walls and armed with wickedly-sharp glaives. Richly-dressed sycophants clustered on either side of the blood-red carpet which ran from the double doors to the throne. Sitting on the throne in his finest apparel was the Usurper-king himself: Lord Boare. His fleshy, mottled face was creased with worry lines, and his bloodshot eyes were circled from lack of sleep. Veins stood out on his forehead as he struggled to control his temper. Suffering the full glare of his wrath was a man in crisp military attire. Maerlin could not see his features, but his posture was proudly erect, despite the circumstances that found him facing his king's wrath.

"I can't believe my ears, General. Are you telling me that we've lost over three hundred men during the campaign in the north, and you know nothing of our enemy's losses?"

The General cleared his throat. "Your Highness, please understand me. These Brocian dogs always attacked during the darkest part of the night. The cowards refused to stand and fight."

"But surely you killed some of them?"

"We certainly did, Your Highness, but they take their dead and wounded away with them when they flee. The only evidence of battle would be the occasional mark of blood or splattered gore on the grass. They're like will-o-the-wisps, Sire. They appear without warning and attack with reckless ferocity, and then, as quick as they've come they're gone again, with little or no trace of them by the time the sun rises. We're fighting ghosts, Sire! I did warn you about invading the Broce Woods."

Lord Boare snarled, and his beady, bloodshot eyes were nearly falling out of his head with frustration. "I was following Dubhgall's advice when I built those forts, General, but like the Badger Clan, the black-hearted Mage has disappeared. None of his lackeys can locate him. What news do you have of him, dare I ask?"

"As you know, Sire, only one of our Elites' survived the mission that the Dark Mage had procured them for. We've rung all that we could out of the man, but all that he could be sure about was that the girl had somehow managed to free her bonds and kill the sorcerer."

"That's not good enough, General. Have the man tortured until he gives up all that he knows."

"I personally oversaw his interrogation, Sire. We used your best torturers to question him. They worked in shifts, so that the poor wretch had no time to recover his wits. They were very thorough and kept him alive for as long as possible. After four days of torment, the man's heart finally gave out, and he could tell us no more. By that time, he was telling us so much that it was useless, Sire. He was saying anything and everything to stop the pain, and it was hard to differentiate truth from fiction. One thing he was sure about though, and that was the death of the Dark Mage."

"Damn Dubhgall to the Nine Hells! He's left my Kingdom in tatters," Boare cursed. "What about the girl, General? What happened to her and her companions? Surely, they didn't just vanish into thin air, too?"

The General shuffled his feet nervously. "Our scouts found tracks leading north toward the Pectish Mountains, Sire. We sent a platoon of our Elites in pursuit."

"And ...?"

"As yet, they've not returned, Sire."

"What do you mean, not returned?" Lord Boare demanded, gripping the edge of his throne, ready to pounce on the beleaguered General.

"None of the men came back, Sire, and every scout that we've sent after them has likewise disappeared. That area has always been wild and unruly. It was for this very reason the Dragon-lord signed the Great Truce with the damned Brocians in the first place. Even Luigheagh Dragan struggled to govern that area. Between Pectish raiders and the

Brocians, no one was safe there. It's only since the Great Truce that we've seen any semblance of peace in that area."

Lord Boare rose slowly to his feet. "Do not mention that traitor's name in my court!"

The General took an involuntary step backward before his dignity stopped him, and he faced the Usurper-king. "My apologies, Sire, I was merely trying to explain ..."

"...I don't need a history lesson, General. What I need are results and you've failed to give me any." Lord Boare stalked closer, hand on the hilt of his sword.

The room fell silent as the Boarite sycophants and soldiers waited expectantly.

"So tell me what you've done, General?" The hush in Boare's voice was more deadly than his early ranting.

"We've managed to find some intelligence on the mysterious girl who killed the Dark Mage, Sire. We now know three important things about her. She's believed to be a novice of Deanna and has been seen on more than one occasion in the presence of the Dragan Prince. We also believe that she came out of the mountains to the west of Manquay, at some time last year."

"Are you telling me that a mere novice managed to kill the most powerful sorcerer ever known? Is this what you're suggesting, General Secston? Do I look like a complete idiot?"

"It's true, Sire! People are saying that she's Uiscallan reincarnated."

Lord Boare grasped the General's tunic and pulled him forward. "Tell me some good news, General, and be quick about it. Your life is hanging by a thread."

"Sire, I've sent a platoon into the mountains. I've even sent the three torturers along with them to make sure the job gets done to your satisfaction. They've been instructed to find out all that they can about the girl and then raze the mountain villages to the ground. Wagons full of wood are following the troops, so that they can crucify the villagers after the torturers have completed their work. That will leave a strong message *to all who consider defying your will, Sire. I assure you, we will know everything we need to, and soon."*

Maerlin reeled at the news. Her father was in danger. Even the thought that the other villagers would be tortured and murdered, worried her. She would not wish such a fate on anyone.

Boare released him. "That's the first good thing you've said all day, and it shall earn you a suitable reward, General."

"Thank you, your Highness."

"You've been given a demotion, General. From now on you'll be known as Private First-Class Secston!"

"But, Sire ..."

Turning to the nearest of his guards, Lord Boare commanded "Take this useless bag of pigs-dung away and have it flogged. Perhaps next time, he'll follow my orders with more vigour. Failure is unacceptable."

"Have mercy, your Highness!" Private Secston pleaded.

Turning to him with baleful eyes, Lord Boare growled "Be thankful for my generosity, Private. I was this close to having you hanged, drawn, and quartered for your incompetence. You're lucky that you did at least one thing right to save your sorry hide. Your death would have been quickly forgotten, but that would have been a waste of a valuable asset. Your continued existence as a flayed and demoted conscript on the other hand, will be a constant reminder for others to work harder to obey my orders."

Lord Boare flicked his wrist and the guards dragged the blubbering private through the crowd and away.

Maerlin had heard enough and began to draw on her inner powers. She would summon Elementals to smite Lord Boare into oblivion. "Come, I need you," she pleaded. Images of pulling the hall down around the head of the King and his sycophants filled her mind. "Come," she urged, feeling her power swell within her.

"Wake up, Maerlin!" Seabhac commanded sharply, shaking her urgently to wake her from her dream.

Maerlin blinked and opened her eyes. Her head was still buzzing with all the magical energy she had drawn forth to do her bidding. "No, don't!" she protested, wanting to get back into the dream and release her magic on the Boarite court.

"Stop it!" Seabhac commanded, bringing Maerlin fully awake.

Tingling all over with pent-up fury, Maerlin gazed through flinty eyes at the old witch.

"Look at me!" Seabhac demanded, her voice keeping Maerlin focused. "Look into my eyes, and listen to me very carefully, Maerlin. I need thou to hold all that magic bottled up inside thee for just a few moments longer. If thou release it here, we'll all be sleeping under the stars."

She waited for Maerlin to understand, their eyes locked. "Good girl, now, take a few deep breaths and get dressed. We'll head out into the field behind the orchard," she instructed, handing Maerlin her clothes.

The pressure inside Maerlin's head was intense. She was fit to burst with magical power, but she gritted her teeth and obeyed. Slipping into her boots, she walked to the door. Seabhac was at her elbow the whole time. Nessa hopped onto Cora's shoulder and they followed them out of the cottage.

"Thou art doing great; just hold it in for a few moments longer," Seabhac encourage as she guided Maerlin out into the paddock. It was approximately an acre of rich grassland with a post and rail fence protecting it. Seabhac led her through the five-bar gate and stopped. "Now try and keep thy anger inside the fence if thou can, Maerlin. If thou break my fences, it'll be thee that'll be fixing them. Start releasing thy magic a little at a time. Let it come out slowly, if thou can."

"What?"

"Let it rip ... go for it ... blast away." Seeing Maerlin's confusion, Seabhac released some of her own magic. The pained look on Maerlin's face as she woke had fuelled Seabhac's own anger. "Here, like this!" With only the slightest murmur on release, Seabhac flicked a bolt of white lightning across the field, leaving a burned strip of ground in its wake.

Thunder clashed overhead in response, and Maerlin flinched. Looking from the scorched earth to Seabhac, she nodded, and with a roar of pure rage Maerlin released a small portion of her magical energy. The grass flattened across the paddock, and a couple of the rails on the far side flew off into the distance.

"Very good, Maerlin, but try and keep it inside the paddock," Seabhac reminded.

Maerlin cleared her mind, preparing herself. Her anger simmered like molten lava, fuelled by the helpless rage she felt.

"I've always found fire to be good at times like this," Nessa prompted mentally.

"Fire," Maerlin nodded, and then with more force she yelled "FIRE!"

The back-blast of heat singed eyebrows, as Maerlin released some of the gathered Elementals, and a rolling ball of flame advanced across the field, burning the dead winter grass before it. Maerlin focused on the flame and controlled it, until only scorched earth remained inside the wooden posts. The posts themselves, although blackened, remained intact.

"Awesome!" Cora cooed, patting her burned eyelashes.

"A shower might help about now, to put out the flames," Seabhac suggested, "We don't want the whole plain going up in smoke."

Maerlin looked up at the gathered clouds and released some of the Water and Air Elementals she had summoned. With another peal of thunder, the clouds burst open, and a downpour smothered the flames.

"Excellent!" Seabhac encouraged. "That will do for now. Thou wilt never get it ploughed over if the sod is too drenched."

"Ploughed ...?" Maerlin was calmer now that she had released some of the magic that had been threatening to burst out of her head.

"Why dost thou think I brought thee into my best paddock rather than onto the plain? It'd be a crying shame to let all of that magic go to waste, wouldn't it? Now, if thou can focus thy remaining magic on turning over the sod, it'd be a great help. I've been putting off this job for over a moon now. We'll need to get the winter oats sowed before the last of the frosts."

"But..."

"We'll talk about thy dream afterwards. First, let's finish the task at hand while thou still hast thy strength. Perhaps Cora can help thee."

Cora blinked in surprise, "Who ... me?"

"Well, it's no use me spending all of this time teaching Maerlin how to use her Wild-magic, while thou does the house-cleaning, is there? Thou dost want to learn, I presume?"

Cora beamed and nodded eagerly.

"That's sorted, then." Seabhac turned to look directly at the magpie on Cora's shoulder. "I believe that thou wast an Earth-sister, Nessa. Can I trust thee to make sure the field is ploughed properly?"

Nessa cawed and shook her wings.

"I'll take that as a yes," Seabhac declared, before marching off to get their breakfast ready. Since they were all up, they might as well embrace the morning.

"Sometimes that one really gets my feathers ruffled," Nessa grumbled.

Maerlin giggled, and some of the remaining anger left her.

"I don't know what's so funny, Maerlin. I'm not the one who's still got a paddock to plough."

"It's just ... " Maerlin began, trying to control her smirking face.

"Shall we get on with it, or do you want to try this without my help? I'm sure there is plenty of worms around for my breakfast, now that you've made it rain. I can think of better things to do, if you want to giggle all day."

"Sorry, Ness," Maerlin apologised. Nessa had always been at the top of any pecking order, up until now. Even the High Priestess deferred to Nessa, but she had finally found someone even bossier.

The beady eyes of the magpie bore into Maerlin, waiting for another smirk to cross her face, but Maerlin had got herself under control.

141

"Are you up to this?" Nessa finally asked.

Maerlin mentally assessed herself and knew that she still had too much magical energy bottled up inside. *"I'm fine, Ness. My hands are still tingling and my head's buzzing, so let's get this ploughing over and done with before it dissipates."*

"Well, there's no shortage of Gnomes in this ground to work with. That garden of Seabhac is positively crawling with them."

"Is that why it's always looking good?"

"Oh yes. She's constantly cheating. She does things with magic that I wouldn't even dream of. The sooner we get you two out of here, the better. You're learning far too many bad habits from that one."

Maerlin recalled Nessa's early lessons about the etiquette for magic use and her general secretiveness, whenever she did use her gift.

"I suppose we'd better get this over with ..." Nessa grumbled, *"Though I'd rather you use a horse and plough, personally. This is such a misuse of Deanna's gift."*

"Where do we start?" Maerlin asked, speaking out loud for Cora's benefit.

Though Nessa was clearly unhappy at the concept of using magic to plough a field, she showed her. Maerlin relayed the information on to Cora. It was slow work, and soon Nessa stopped them. *"This won't work at all. It's taking far too long. Have Cora clear her mind and picture your white room. If we can get her to mind-link with us, the job will get done a lot quicker."*

After some trial and error, Nessa had the two novices working in unison, steadily turning over the burned stubble into neat rows.

"Not so fast, Cora ... less haste, less waste. You need to keep the depth even as you go along, or the sod won't turn over correctly. You see where the grass is showing through there? That's where you lost concentration and the cut was too shallow. Here, you've gone too deep, Maerlin, and it became all clotted. Don't forget to keep your breathing even, girls, or you'll end up fainting for lack of oxygen."

Maerlin smiled. She was glad to hear Nessa back to her usual demonstrative self, despite having shrunk considerably from her previous incarnation.

"That's better. You're both getting the hang of it. Now, you need to start doubling up or we'll be here all morning. You should be able to plough at least eight rows apiece, but start with two, and then double up again once you're sure of yourselves."

"I thought we could eat breakfast out here, seeing that it's such a lovely morning." Seabhac was carrying out a tray of warm scones, and a steaming jug of rose-hip tea. "I see the work is coming along nicely."

"No thanks to you!" Nessa grumbled, and the two novices started to giggle again.

*****

Gearoid led Balor out into the sunlight, hoping to speak privately to the convalescing patient. He was confident that he could nurture the goodness he had glimpsed within him. "Can you feel the sunshine, Balor? It's a fine winter's day."

Balor stopped and took a deep breath, letting his remaining senses take in the world around him. He turned his ravaged face up to let the sun's rays warm his scarred cheeks and the holes where his eyes had once been.

"I sense a battle going on inside you, Balor, a battle that I can barely imagine," Gearoid began. "I have to wonder if there's anything we can do to help you to find some inner peace, but with the blessings of the gods, you may yet find salvation."

Balor shook his head.

"Do you not believe in the gods, Balor?"

A raspy and bitter laugh came from the blind monk. "Abbot Gearoid. I have no doubts about the existence of gods. Perhaps it is the gods themselves that wage this war within me? One thing I'm sure about though and it's that praying isn't going to save me. My soul is as black as the abyss, and I'm forever lost."

"No, that's not so!" Gearoid protested. "While there's breath in your body, there is always hope of redeeming yourself for your past transgressions. We all hold sins within us ..."

Balor laughed again, and it was a hauntingly bitter sound. "Sins ... you know nothing of sins, Abbot. I've seen your dreams and I know this. Even amongst this community, you are the most holy of men. Sin is such a small word, and it is ill-equipped to grasp the terrible things that I've done. It would take lifetimes to cleanse the darkness from within me, and this is time I just don't have. I'm an old man; older than the yew trees in the cemetery, and my age is part of my dark past. Believe me when I tell you this, your efforts to save me are wasted. I thank you for trying, but you'd do better off finding a more worthy cause."

"I can't believe that. You've confessed grave evils to me, and I can only believe that by doing so, you've taken the first steps toward healing your soul."

"No, Brother. There's too much evil within me to be washed away by a few mumbled apologies and some half-hearted chanting."

"Then perhaps words are only the start of your journey and that actions are needed to complete it."

Balor slumped into silence, considering the Abbot's words.

Gearoid waited patiently. He was content to spend some time in quiet contemplation under the winter sky.

Finally, Balor signalled that it was time to continue their walk. "Can we go through the orchard, Brother?"

"Of course! You always seem to like it there."

"It's the bees, Gearoid."

"...The bees?"

Balor chuckled. "Yes, the bees."

"What about them?"

"It's a little hard to explain," Balor said. "Since I lost my eyes, my other senses have sharpened considerably. My mind was always sharp, due to the rigorous training exercises I was forced to go through while learning the dark arts, but now ... now it's become more so."

Gearoid guided him along the path, stopping at the wooden gate that protected the orchard from the pigs and goats that roamed freely on the island. Opening the gate, he led them along the path until they could see the woven baskets that held the monastery's bees.

"I have always been able to tap into people's minds while they slept, even from a great distance. I could manipulate the unprotected sleeper and learn their innermost secrets," Balor explained. "Now, however, my powers have grown stronger, and I can sense people's thoughts, even when they are awake. It's not as easy as when they sleep, but it's still possible."

"You mean that you can read my thoughts?"

"How can I explain it ...?" Balor pondered, "Ah yes, if you're reading a scroll, you study each word and sense the meaning hidden by the individual letters, or at least you strive to, though some scrolls are easier to understand than others."

"Yes ..."

"When someone sleeps, I can read them like you would read a scroll, except there is no reference guide and the images within the scroll are a little jumbled. However, when someone is awake, it's like skimming the book and just letting the odd sentence jump out at you. Does that make any sense?"

"I think so, but what does this have to do with the bees?"

"Imagine the headache you'd get trying to read ten scrolls at once ... or a hundred scrolls? That's what my head is like during the day, and it's even worse at night. It's hard to hear myself think for the constant barrage of other peoples inane thoughts."

"...And the bees ...?"

"Mankind is filled with egos and individualities. We've long since lost our pack mentality, though occasionally, in times of great stress, we find it again. If you take a herd of goats for example, each has its own individual characteristics, and yet there is wholeness within the herd, a pack mentality if you will."

"I'm sorry, but I still don't understand where the bees come into this."

"Bees have the perfect mind. They are truly at one with their universe. A bee can fly for miles from the hive, right across the Lough. He can drink from the nectar of a flower in the royal gardens of *Ard Pect*, and yet he is still at one with the hive. What he sees, feels, and tastes, the whole hive sees, feels, and tastes. He, in turn, is linked to the rest of the hive through the controlling power of the queen and the hive-mind." Balor became animated as he spoke. "They are the ultimate mind. If mankind could harness this ability, he would become godlike!"

"I still don't understand, Balor. How does this help you?"

They stopped before the hives, watching the sluggish worker-bees milling around in the winter sunshine. "The hive-minds are powerful things so near to their queens. They are the cortex of their hives. Here, the constant irritating chatter of the monastery is silenced, and I am finally at peace."

"Ah, I see." Gearoid smiled.

"No. I'm afraid you don't ... but I do. Sadly, it's winter, so the bees don't venture far from the safety of the hive. In the springtime, however, if I were to stand here, I'd be able to see for miles."

"I don't understand."

"If I focus my mind on a queen bee, I can see all that she sees. There must be nearly fifty hives here, so that means fifty queens to mind-meld with. Come summertime that means tens of thousands of eyes that I can look out of."

"You can do that?"

Balor smiled and ushered the Abbot away. "You might want to put a little distance between us, or the bees might attack you."

Gearoid backed away until he was at the edge of the trees, and he watched from there.

Balor took a deep breath and summoned forth his magic. The buzzing within the clearing rose in volume from the low murmur to a loud droning. Gearoid sensed the irritation within it. Balor had woken the bees up from their winter slumber. They poured out from their entrances and gathered in angry swarms.

Balor opened his arms and welcomed the irate bees into his embrace, and they descended on him, en masse. He stood calmly and allowed the bees to envelop him until only a shadowy outline remained to confirm that a man still stood before the hives.

Gearoid started forward, but was pulled up by a sharp mental command *"Stay where you are!"*

"Balor, are you alright?"

The bee-man turned to face the Abbot. *"I have never been better."*

"But ...?"

"They will not sting me, Gearoid, I'm quite safe. I've become part of the hive-mind so I am in no danger. You, however, are, so I suggest that you come no closer."

"But why did you do this?"

"Gearoid, I can see through the eyes of the bees ... now ... it is time for you to leave."

"What?"

"I said leave, Druid!" Balor ordered sharply. His voice had suddenly become harsher. *"Leave, while you still can."*

Sensing a change in Balor's personality, Gearoid hesitated. "You need to fight it, Balor. Don't let this *Diabhal* endanger your soul."

"Silence, you fool!" the Darkness within Balor growled. *"Be gone!"*

With a wave of his hand, Balor sent a cloud of the angry bees hurtling toward the Abbot. Gearoid hesitated for only a moment, but by then the first of the bees was already upon him. They embedded their stings into his unprotected face, hands, and feet. Crying out, Gearoid turned and fled with the cloud of angry bees following in his wake like an extra shadow. Swatting the bees aside as he ran through the orchard, he leapt the gate in his rush to be free of his tormentors and raced toward the pier. Bellowing in fear, he hurtled down the rickety jetty and dived into the Lough. Splashing to the surface, he gasped at the bitter cold of the waters, but the bees were close at hand and renewed their attack. Taking a hurried breath, he sank beneath the waves.

Swimming underwater, he tried to put as much distance as he could between himself and the swarm, only surfacing when his lungs screamed for air. Bursting forth from the depths, he choked and gasped as he turned back toward the island. The bees had lost sight of him, but he waited, remaining a safe distance out in the Lough. He needed to be sure that the bees had given up on all thoughts of pursuit, before swimming ashore.

Finally, after what seemed like an age in the freezing water, the bees gave up and flew back to their hives. Only then did he drag his exhausted body onto the rocks. Slowly, he crawled toward the monastery gates and reached for the bell with swollen hands. Hanging onto the bell rope for dear life, he rang it again and again.

By the time help arrived, his eyes were swollen shut, and his face was almost unrecognisable, so much had it swelled with poisonous stings.

"It's alright, we have you," Brother Seamy assured as he gently prised the swollen fingers from the rope. Catching Gearoid as he fell, he motioned the other monks to carry him inside. "How, in the Nine Hells, did you get into such a state?" he asked, but Gearoid had already slipped into unconsciousness.

Chapter Fifteen: Into the Light

Even from a distance, the light of the entrance looked painfully bright, burning into Conal's retinas as he walked forward. Taliesin remained at his shoulder in case his steps faltered. In truth, Conal's legs were still a little rubbery, and his head swam after any sudden movement, but Cathal had set an easy pace, mindful of Conal and the other injured men. His pace had slowed even more as they turned the final corner and saw the beacon of light ahead. They all needed time to allow their eyes to adjust to the brightness, and so, they meandered their way forward. Finally, Cathal called a halt. They stopped fifty paces from the opening and sat down in the passageway. After speaking to his scout, Cathal made his way over to the companions and squatted down on his haunches. "We'll wait here until nightfall. *Ard Pect* is only a short walk down the mountainside from this entrance, but we'll need the darkest part of the night to slip within its walls undetected."

"You can get us all the way inside the city?" Cull asked with surprise. That would make his task easier by far.

"My friend, I can take you into the very palace itself, nay, into the very boudoir of the insatiable Queen Medb, if that is your heart's desire," Cathal boasted.

"I think we'll forgo that particular pleasure," Cull said. "Getting into the city and finding a suitably tavern would be more than enough. From there, we can make our own way around, but thank you for the offer. I thought we'd have to wait until morning, when the gates opened."

Cathal nodded. "It's true that the Pectish monarchs take their security very seriously, and that there is only one gateway into the city. It opens each morning at dawn and shuts firmly with the setting of the sun. Nevertheless, we Brocians are a curious people and blessed with good night-vision. We've found an alternative entranceway for those brave enough to venture it."

"I'm intrigued."

"As with the Great Pectish Mountains, so too, is the great city of *Ard Pect*. Everything must be expelled in one way or another. All of the rich food eaten by the noblemen and merchants of *Ard Pect* must find a way out of the city. It would be most unpleasant for visitors to have this effluence running down the city streets and out of the portcullis, would it not?"

"Are you telling me that there's a sewer?"

"There's a whole warren of sewers, Cull. They go from the highest part of the palace, all the way down to the poorer sections besides the wharf. From there it flows out into the Lough, and eventually into the sea."

"Isn't it guarded?"

"...By both man and beast, but that doesn't mean it's inaccessible."

"Isn't it going to smell?" Taliesin asked, looking down at his once fine, but now travel-stained clothes.

"Have no worries, bard. You'll come out of it smelling like roses, I promise you."

"You said something about beasts?"

Cathal smiled at Conal. "I'm sure it's nothing that the great Conal *Ciudachbane* couldn't best. There are giant leeches and some ravenous rats to contend with, nothing more. The City Watch patrols the walkways, but they'll be of little concern to us if we keep quiet. Then, there are the denizens of the underworld: the thieves, the assassins, and the smugglers, to name but a few."

"It all sounds rather crowded down there. Are there any stalls selling titbits, in case we get peckish?" Cull joked.

Cathal smiled and shook his head. "The Watch makes a lot of noise whenever they patrol. This discourages confrontation, either by the rats or by anything else. Most of the other inhabitants tend to keep to themselves, although there are a few adventurous souls who might seek out confrontation for a quick profit."

"Cutthroats, you mean?"

"That sort of thing, yes, though few would be foolhardy enough to risk an all-out battle in the darkness, especially with a group as large as this one. I'm sure we'll be fine."

Cull nodded. "Lead on, Cathal, whenever you're ready."

As the light dwindled to a reddish glow, they prepared to leave for the final part of their journey.

*****

It was late afternoon when Maerlin and Cora finally finished the field. They had not only ploughed it, but sowed and harrowed it as well, all with the use of magic, much to Nessa's disapproval. Maerlin had been kept so busy that she hadn't had any time to stew over her dream until now. Finally, as they sat in the winter's dusk and gazed out over the day's work, she was able to focus on her dream.

"I need to go to High Peaks," Maerlin announced.

"What?" the others chorused in unison.

"I said that I need to go to High Peaks. I'll be leaving first thing in the morning."

"Whatever for...?" Nessa demanded. *"It's still winter, for Deanna's sake. Imbolc isn't for another two days. The mountains will still be covered in snow."*

"I don't care ... I have to leave immediately."

"I'm coming with you," Cora announced.

"No, Cora ... you're not," Maerlin declared. *"It's far too dangerous."*

Seabhac cleared her throat. "Dost thou know that it's bad manners to whisper? That includes mind-whispering."

"But you do it all the time," Maerlin protested. "You and Fintan are always chattering away to each other. I can tell by the way your eyebrows wriggle."

Seabhac had to concede the point there. "Thou hast to understand, Fintan and I have lived quite happily in isolation for many years, so it's become a bit of a habit. Anyway, some conversations are private, but I think this one isn't."

"Sorry, Seabhac, we've been mind-melding all day. Nessa can't talk any other way."

"Has she even tried?" Seabhac replied somewhat tartly.

"Has she even tried?" Nessa parroted. *"I'm a bird, for Deanna's sake."*

"Actually, she has a point," Cora interjected. *"On the islands we have a multitude of birds, crows that can mimic speech. Many of our shamans use them to carry messages."*

Nessa was about to object, but then she sighed and relented. *"Okay, you make a valid point. I remembered Bess once had a pet jackdaw, although he was obsessed with the word 'bloomers' for some reason. However, I'll need some time to practice, so for now, Maerlin, you'll have to translate to 'she who must be obeyed'..."*

"Are we doing it again?" Seabhac asked.

"Sorry, we were just considering your idea. Nessa says that she'll need a bit of practice so, in the meantime, I'm going to translate for her."

"Very well ... what exactly is the problem, Maerlin?"

"I need to go to High Peaks because my village is in danger. The villagers are going to be tortured and killed."

"Sorry, but we seem to be missing something here. How exactly dost thou know this?"

"It was the dream I had last night. I was in the court of Lord Boare, in Suilequay. His General told him that he'd sent a force into the mountains. This was just before Lord Boare had the man flogged."

Seabhac sighed. "It might be easier if thou started at the beginning. That way, we'll have all the facts before anyone goes rushing off into a blizzard."

Maerlin gathered herself and relayed her Dream-catching. Then, she answered questions from both Seabhac and Nessa. They finally fell silent to ponder the varied ramifications.

"It's getting chilly out here," Seabhac finally declared. "Let's head inside and settle down by the fire. We can continue this conversation within the comforts of the cottage. My posterior was not designed for sitting on fences."

Maerlin noticed that the sun had slipped away while she had been talking and that the crispness of the evening had quickly followed. Rubbing her arms to ward off the chill, she followed the others inside.

*****

After settling before a burning fire, they resumed their conversation.

"Are we all in agreement that this particular Dream-catching is neither historical, nor based at some distant point in the future?" Seabhac asked with a sense of foreboding.

The others all agreed.

"Very well then, I suppose we can assume that the soldiers won't have the courtesy to wait until spring before obeying their orders."

"Not if they want to see another Beltane."

"Thank thee, Cora, exactly my point," Seabhac continued. She briefly glared accusingly up at Fintan in the rafters. *This is entirely thy fault! It was thee that got me into this. We could've been having a nice quiet winter, but for thy insistence on interfering."*

"Admit it, you haven't had this much fun in years, so don't come the all high and mighty with me. It just won't cut it! I know you too well. You're just getting cranky ... or should that be crankier, in your old age?"

"Old age! What dost thou mean, old age?"

"Whatever," Fintan declared. *"You forget that I have hawk eyes and I fly quietly. I see you inspecting your wrinkles when you think I'm not around. There really isn't any need, you know. You've always been beautiful to me, mo croi."*

"Thou hast been spying on me?"

The hen harrier groomed his tail feathers, refraining from further comment, which only vexed Seabhac further.

Maerlin coughed and when Seabhac looked around, she commented "Your eyebrows were wriggling again. Are we missing something?"

"Oh, nothing, sorry, I got a little sidetracked there." Throwing Fintan a final dirty look, Seabhac continued "So where were we? Oh yes, the Boarites. I guess we're in agreement then that they'll brave the elements and to make matters worse for the fools, they're bringing a wagon load of timber with them into the mountains. At least that's a bit of good news for us."

"Why's that good news?" Maerlin protested. "They're planning to crucify the villagers!"

"I'm quite aware of that, Maerlin. Please calm thyself. It is good news for us because it'll take them a considerable amount of time to get to their destination, and if we're really lucky, they'll all die of exposure on the way."

"Can we help it along?" Maerlin asked, wiggling her fingers suggestively.

"If thou art suggesting what I think thou art suggesting, then the answer is no. We're too far away to focus the amount of energies needed. Anyway, no one could make the whole mountainside into a snowstorm. It's just too big of an area. Even the concerted efforts of all the priestesses of Deanna couldn't achieve that."

"There's nothing else for it then. I'll set off in the morning," Maerlin declared.

"Was she always this impetuous?" Seabhac asked.

"Awwwkkk!" *"You have no idea!"*

"Hey, that's not fair. No ganging up on me!"

"Very well then, Maerlin, let's look at thy suggestion, shall we? Although the snow has blessed us by not falling near the cottage, by now the Plains of the Dragon will be knee deep in the stuff and travel will have ground to a halt." Seabhac uncurled one of her gnarled old fingers to emphasise the point. "Then, we have the fact that thou hast no horse to ride." A second gnarly digit followed the first. "Shall we add the lack of suitable clothing, provisions, and a guide who knows the terrain ...?" Further digits followed in rapid succession.

"I can't just leave them all to die," Maerlin protested.

"Did anyone suggest that? I was merely pointing out the obstacles that we must overcome."

"What do you mean, we?"

"Thou can't possibly think that I'd let thee leave in the middle of winter on thy own? I wouldn't be able to sleep at night. If nothing else, I'd be tormented by that misbegotten excuse for a hawk and his 'know-it-all' eyes."

"You mean you'll help?"

"I can't see that I've got much choice in the matter."

Maerlin pounced on the old witch. "Oh, thank you, Seabhac, thank you so much."

After a moment of surprised hesitation, Seabhac patted Maerlin's back. "Don't get thy hopes up too high, Maerlin. We still have an awful lot to do. Even if we can get there on time, it's still going to be a huge task."

"How're we going to get to Manquay?" Cora asked.

"We won't be going to Manquay," Seabhac advised. "We'll head for Eagles Reach, and from there we'll go over the mountain to High Peaks. That way, we'll get there ahead of the soldiers, and we can hunt them down as they make their way up the mountain passes."

"And how are we supposed to do that? Even with horses, we still couldn't get over the mountain," Maerlin translated Nessa's question to Seabhac.

"We fly, of course."

"What ... in broad daylight! People might see us." Nessa was shocked at the idea.

"The priestesses of Deanna have always been overly secretive about their magic, I could never understand why. I mean ... everyone knows that they do it, so why bother trying to hide the fact?"

"It just isn't done," Nessa objected indignantly.

"Such piffle! I could understand thy objecting, if there was a need for some secrecy, though I might not agree with thy reasoning. However, time is of the essence here, so tradition can go and take a running jump. I say we fly there. It's faster, easier, and a lot less dangerous than walking."

"I think she has a point, Ness," Maerlin concurred.

"I warned you about her bad influence," Nessa complained with a hint of resignation. From her tone, Maerlin knew that she had agreed to the plan, too.

"You mean I get to learn to fly?"

Nessa's groan was audible, even to Seabhac.

"I haven't decided on that yet. Let me iron out the details overnight. In the meantime, thou hast both had a long day so I think it's time for bed."

"Awww!" the novices protested in unison, despite their exhaustion.

"Listen girls, if thou want my help on this little adventure, thou wilt have to do what I say, and no arguments."

"Chance'd be a fine thing," Nessa muttered.

With dejected faces, the novices prepared for sleep. As they snuggled into the warm blankets and relaxed, the toils of the day overtook their fertile imaginations, and they slipped into sleep.

*****

Conal followed the Snow Badger clansmen carefully down the mountain. The path was far from straight, possibly having been first created by a drunken mountain goat. He stumbled more than once, but Taliesin was always beside him to offer support. They moved silently, or at least as silent as men could move when descending a mountainside in near-complete darkness. It wasn't long before they came to a cobbled highway, big enough for two war-chariots to pass each other at speed, and their journey became easier. Ever downwards they went, and soon, Conal could hear the lapping of waves on a shoreline to his left. They had reached Crannockmore Lough, and looking ahead, Conal could see the dark shadowy outline of the impenetrable fortress: *Ard Pect*. It was outlined in the torches that had been lit all along its parapets.

Cathal signalled a halt and the warriors paused, remaining in their habitual line. Conal had to admire the discipline of the Brocians. They moved like a well-greased trebuchet, silent and deadly and without the need for barked orders. Each of these warriors knew what was expected of them and none shirked in their duty. How different they were from the Boarite conscripts that Conal had seen around Manquay.

At a silent signal from the scout, the Brocians slipped off the road, taking cover amongst the rocks of the shoreline. Conal and the companions quickly followed, and not a moment too soon. He had just enough time to slip behind a boulder when they heard a distinctive rumbling from up on the road. Two horses passed, their riders holding torches high overhead to light their way. Next came four of the formidable Pectish war-chariots, rattling noisily down the road on their iron-rimmed wheels. In the torchlight, Conal could see the sharpened blades attached to the wheels as they sped past.

"That was close," Cull whispered in his ear.

"Too close!" Conal agreed.

"What are they doing out on the road at this time of night?" Taliesin whispered.

"I haven't the foggiest idea," Cull replied, "...But I'm damned well going to find out."

"Those chariots are far too expensive to risk driving around at night without a reason."

"Exactly, Tal, exactly!"

Cathal slipped in beside them. "I think it's time we took to the water."

"Water ... but I thought you said the water was full of leeches and rats?"

"Once we get into the sewer it is, bard. The Lough, however, is perfectly safe as the seawater is too salty for the leeches, and the rats stay within the safety of their sewer."

"I can't go for another swim," Taliesin protested. "It took days for Aoife to dry out properly the last time. I can hardly entertain the city folk, if she can't hold a tune."

"This is our best chance of getting Conal into the city unnoticed, Taliesin," urged Cull

"I know that, Cull, but I'm not going swimming with my harp, and I'm certainly not going to leave Aoife behind."

Reluctantly, Cull conceded to Tal's point. "So what do you suggest, Taliesin?"

"You'll have to go on without me. We can meet up again in the city tomorrow."

"Tal!" Conal protested.

"No, Conal, he's right. He'll be safe enough if he stays out of sight until dawn. Once the sun rises, he can stroll up to the gate and no one will bat an eyelid. Despite his travel-weary appearance, he's still a bard, and no harm will come to him ... as long as he doesn't get himself run over by a chariot, that is."

Taliesin nodded and gripped Conal's shoulder. "I'll be fine, don't worry."

Cathal gripped the bard's arm silently in farewell. "You'll find us in the Queen's Bedchamber."

"Pardon me?" Taliesin asked, sure that he'd misheard the Brocian.

"I said that we'll be in 'The Queen's Bedchamber': It's just off the market area, on the way down to the docks. Just ask anyone for directions."

"Oh ... I see! It's the name of a tavern. For a moment there, I thought you meant the *actual* Queen's bedchamber. Fair enough then, I'll see you all there on the morrow. Keep safe in the meantime, Conal."

Gripping the bard's wrist firmly, Conal replied "You too, Taliesin."

*****

It was almost dark before Brother Seamy realised that Balor was missing, and he sent out a search party to find their wandering patient. They found him curled up but unharmed next to the beehives. He was weeping softly.

"I'm sorry, Seamy, I'm sorry. It wasn't me. I tried to stop him, but he wouldn't listen," Balor repeated over and over again as they helped him into his cot. The monks could get nothing more out of him, so they fed him some warm broth and gave him a mild sleeping draught to calm him down.

Brother Seamy then headed back to Gearoid's cell to check how his poultices were doing. He found the Abbot sleeping quietly and already looking a little better. He decided to stay by the bedside during the night, in case the poisons in Gearoid's system caused a relapse.

Prostrating himself on the stone floor, Seamy began his prayers to the deities. The ritualistic chanting eased his own concerns and slipped into Gearoid's subconscious, giving his patient some comfort. A bell passed and the frown on Gearoid's swollen face eased a little, and he was able to slip into a deeper sleep.

Chapter Sixteen: Flying Witches

They gathered for breakfast the following morning and started the packing of essential foodstuffs and clothing. While the others prepared, Seabhac wandered around gathering assorted implements.

"What's she doing?" Nessa asked, as they watched Seabhac dragging an old hoe, a hay rake, and a scythe out into the garden, only to disappear back into the cottage with the scythe.

"That's never going to work," Seabhac muttered, placing the scythe back in the rafters where it had been quietly rusting away for the past number of years. Seabhac hadn't realised until now just how much useless clutter could be stored in one small cottage, or for that matter, how much she had grown accustomed to using magic for just about everything. Many of the utensils were beyond repair, full of woodworm or dry rot. Some had been gnawed at by the family of mice that had somehow taken up residence without her realising.

Marching back out into the garden, she looked down at the implements that she had laid out on the grass. Her staff lay there. It was made of well-worn oak, strong and reliable. Maerlin's quarterstaff was also made of seasoned oak and iron-shod on each end. Though it was slightly shorter than Seabhac's staff, it was more than adequate for Maerlin. The only other usable item was a rather gnawed besom. The birch twigs knotted around its base looked rather sad, but the ash handle was still sound.

With these items, Maerlin, Cora, and Seabhac could fly, but Nessa might not be up to such a long journey using wing-power alone. She doubted that the diminutive magpie could survive the bitter cold of the high mountains at this time of year without assistance. That meant that she would have to find another way to get them to High Peaks. No matter how much she thought about it, flying seemed the best solution, but the 'brooms' would not carry all of their baggage. Maerlin could tuck Nessa into her cloak to keep the magpie warm, but what about Fintan? He was far too dignified, as well as too big, for pocket-snuggling.

She looked over at the harrier, who was perched in the rafters watching silently. *"Couldn't thou just ..."*

"Forget it, mo croi! I'm too old to change my ways now. I'm happy just the way I am."

"I love thee just the way thou art too, but that isn't helping."

"Even if I changed, what would I use to fly on ... the scythe?"

"Mmm, thou might have a point there." Seabhac stomped back inside and took the vase of flowers off the table. Then she removed the fine linen tablecloth to reveal the battered pine table beneath.

"Tell me that you're not thinking what I think you're thinking?" Fintan asked.

"No, it's too small. It just wouldn't work, but wait a moment, perhaps we do have something." Speaking aloud, she called to the novices "Cora, Maerlin, take this table out into the garden, will you?"

"What ... now?" Cora asked.

"Well, thou canst wait until the spring fair if thou wish, but I thought we were in a bit of a hurry ... so yes, now would be good."

"You're getting tetchy. You always resort to sarcasm when things aren't going your way."

"How wouldst thou like me to pluck some of thy tail feathers out, Fintan? I need some new quills."

"You wouldn't dare!"

"Don't tempt me." Seabhac waited impatiently while the novices manoeuvred the bulky table into the garden.

"Where do you want it?" Maerlin asked, puffing with the exertion.

"Anywhere will do."

Seabhac inspected the worn rug that covered the stone floor of the cottage. "Thou canst fetch this rug out, too."

"What are you doing, mo croi?"

Seabhac shot a warning glance at the harrier, and he fell silent.

She followed the girls outside and ordered them to hang the bedraggled rug over the washing line. "Now, I think it'd be a good idea if thou banged the dust and mouse droppings off it first, don't thee?"

"Seabhac, why are we spring cleaning?" Maerlin asked. "I mean, it's not even spring yet, and we are in a sort of rush, you know?"

"Then the sooner thou get the rug cleaned, the sooner we'll be off, won't we?" Seabhac answered primly.

"See what I mean ... sarcastic ... it happens every time."

"Dost thou girls know the art of calligraphy? I'm sure Fintan can donate us a few tail feathers if thou would want to start learning."

Fintan ruffled his wings in protest. *"I'm just pointing out some of the bad habits that you've picked up over the years. If we're going to start mixing in polite company again, it'd be better if we worked on some of them."*

"Oh really! Are we going to work on thy habit of regurgitating mice while we're at it? Some people might find some of thy lovable traits a little offensive, especially when they find them on their carpets."

"It was only the once!" Fintan protested *"I told you before; it got caught in my throat."*

"That's what happens when thou gobble thy food."

"Seabhac, you're doing that eyebrow wriggling thing again," Maerlin pointed out.

"Sorry, Maerlin, I thought that thou would be too busy beating the rug to notice. For some reason, thou hast not even started yet. Were thou waiting for something?

Maerlin flushed and quickly picked up her quarterstaff. Cora was also quick to take the hint and selected the besom. Soon, the air was filled with dust, discarded feathers, and mice droppings, as they beat energetically at the rug.

"That'll have to do or thou wilt knock the very lifeblood out of the poor thing. It's seen better days as it is," Seabhac said. "Now, lay it down out on the grass and we'll see what we have to work with."

No one ventured to ask any more questions, as Seabhac's tongue had become quite sharp. Carrying it over to the front of the cottage, they spread the old rug out, "How's that?"

"It'll have to do. It's all we've got to work with. Now gather up thy packs and place them on the rug."

Maerlin and Cora looked down at the rug and then over at Seabhac.

"Come along! We haven't got all day."

"Have you noticed that it always seems to be us doing all the work?" Maerlin grumbled to Cora as they hurried into the now bare-looking cottage and grabbed their belongings.

"Don't forget thy staff, Maerlin. Oh, and bring that besom, too. Cora's going to need it later."

"Oh, great ..." Cora muttered, "...more housework!"

Seabhac wandered off to have one final look at her home. It was with a heavy heart that she walked the garden and orchard, knowing how soon all of her care and attention would run wild. Finally she stepped into the small cottage, built by her own hands ... with a small amount of magical help here and there. She had lived here for a long time; too long, Fintan would say. Within its simple walls, she had found happiness and some well-earned peace. She had watched her daughter grow here, and she had learned to live with the storm clouds that lurked within her soul. Here, she had made peace with her goddess, and with her own destiny. Here, she had believed that she would spend her final days. That was before Fintan nagged her into becoming embroiled in other people's business again. No, she realised, to be fair it was her own unfinished business calling out to her. You can only hide from your destiny for so long before it catches up with you. Wiping a tear from her eyes, she stroked her well-worn door, her chest of drawers, and her bed.

"We're leaving a fine home to the mice."

She looked up at Fintan, sitting quietly in the rafters. *"So thou didst know about the damned mice!"*

Fintan gave a birdlike shrug of his wings. *"It seemed a shame to kick them out. They weren't doing any harm ... and anyway, a few snacks*

164

hanging around might have been handy, if the snow kept me from hunting."

"There are a lot of memories within these walls."

"Aye, a lot of good memories, mo croi, some really great memories."

"Come along, Fintan. The longer I stay here, the harder this is going to be."

With one final look, Seabhac turned and left the cottage, allowing Fintan to glide outside before firmly tying the door shut with a bit of old twine. It wasn't much in the way of security. It was more symbolic than anything else.

Lifting her staff up off the ground, she headed over to where the others were waiting. "Climb aboard, everyone."

"What?"

Seabhac sighed. "Get on the blasted rug."

"Oh, right!"

"Try to stay in the middle; I don't want to have to catch anyone, if they fall off," she advised as she drew forth her magical power. "Come, my blessed Sylphs. Our need is great."

The air ruffled, and the well-worn rug shuddered and gave a sudden lurch.

"Are you sure that this is a good idea?" Maerlin asked nervously.

"I can't think of a better one, can thee? The principle is sound, at least in theory. Anyway, I can't see any reason why it won't work."

"You mean you haven't done this before?"

"For some reason the idea of flying around on a battered old rug has never been on my to-do list, but needs must. Now, canst thou all keep quiet and let me concentrate?"

"It's always best to stay quiet when she gets this tetchy," Fintan advised to no one in particular, especially since Seabhac was the only one who could hear him.

"That includes thee, Fintan."

"Yes, dear ... of course, mo croi."

Giving the old raptor a flinty look, Seabhac tried again to raise the rug off the ground. It proved to be much harder than her staff, as it lacked any rigidity. With some perseverance and experimentation, she finally got it hovering. She then willed it slowly forward. She took it slowly at first, going no more than walking pace, but gradually as she gained confidence, she increased the speed. As they neared the Broce Woods, she focused on height, and the ragged old carpet rose into the morning sky and sailed over the trees.

"Awesome!" Cora cooed. Maerlin just grinned.

"Mind the baggage, girls. I'm going to change direction," Seabhac warned, and the mouldy rug tilted in its ascent and banked until it was flying due south toward the distant mountain peak.

*****

The Lough was bitterly cold, and the short swim had sucked all of the energy out of Conal's body. Gasping and staggering into the outlet pipe, he was glad to be back on dry land. Shivering and with rattling teeth, he quickly squeezed as much water as he could out of his clothing. At least his hair was still short and didn't hold the water the way the clansmen's did.

In the near darkness, Conal could vaguely make out the brickwork within the tubular structure of the pipe on which they stood, feet wide apart to allow the slurry unhindered passage into the Lough. The rank smell was a mixture of rotting fish and human waste, allowed to ferment in the sluggish water of the sewer until its ripeness reached a peak of rancidity that watered the eyes and gagged the throat, but something within the smell called out to the young prince. This foetid odour was the universal smell of a city, and Conal loved cities. Within these city walls lay bountiful opportunities for wealth and gain, at least for those brave enough to risk all for the coin. Having spent a number of years in the city of Manquay, where he had learned to steal and collected a fair amount in ill-gotten gains, Conal's palms itched at the potential for adventure ahead. He had spent too long roaming the open countryside and hungered for the thrill of the burglary, or the sleight of hand of the pickpocket. That was, of course, if he could get away from Cull's sharp eyes for long enough to have a little fun.

"Quit ya daydreaming," Cull grunted, shoving him roughly in the back to get him moving down the outlet and deeper into the dark sewer beyond. Conal considered protesting, but he had long since learned not to cross the sharp-tongued beggar. Saving his breath, he followed the warriors of *Clann Na Snochta Broce* as they moved silently forward. Once they had travelled a short distance from the opening, Cathal called for light and a number of the glowing fungal jars were opened. The soft greenish glow made it easier for Conal to see the features of those around him.

"It'll be better if we can see where we are going from here on in," Cathal advised. "Stay out of the water at all costs."

Thinking of the swarms of hungry leeches that infested the swampy waters around the Holy Isle, Conal was only too aware of the threat of these bloodsuckers. He had once witnessed a cow fall into the Great Marsh and watched her futile struggle as she was rapidly drained of blood. The farmer, although distraught at the loss of such a precious commodity, was wise enough to stand and watch from the bank, knowing that from the moment the cow hit the water, her fate was sealed.

They crept silently forward, led by the trusty scout. The warriors' hands never strayed far from their *Tri-crub*: the distinctive three-tined daggers associated with the Brocian clansmen.

Loosening the Dragontooth sword in its sheath, Conal followed. He was glad of the movement to warm his body after the recent soaking. They crept along the confusing maze of passageways, traversed narrow walkways and crossed small, stone bridges across the slow-moving slurry, as it oozed its way toward the Lough. Occasionally, at a signal from the scout, they stopped and all light was extinguished. There, they waited in utter silence, not daring to move in the blackness lest they put a foot wrong and end up in the water. Moments would tick by while Conal and the others wondered what the scout had heard that had caused him to call the halt. No one questioned his decisions. He was well respected for his abilities, and the clansmen accepted his guidance without hesitation.

A silent signal was passed down the lines and tension eased from weary shoulders, the light was released from the glowing jars, and the warriors moved their hands fractionally away from the hilts of their weapons. Onward, ever slowly onward, they journeyed. Sometimes, they climbed rusty iron ladders that looked like horseshoes embedded into the brickwork while the sluggish water gurgled down from above beside them. They saw rats aplenty, but none of the large packs of rodents attacked the group. Eventually, they halted and Cathal spoke "We're here."

Conal looked at the dead end passageway they had entered. "Where is here exactly?"

"Give it a moment and you'll see, *Ciudachbane*," Cathal assured, signalling for the scout to continue.

The scout scraped moss off the wall beside him and drew forth his *Tri-crub*, which gleamed in the greenish light of a nearby pot. Carefully, he inserted the three razor-sharp prongs horizontally into the wall until the hilt sat flush with the stonework. Twisting the hilt slowly in a clockwise direction, he moved the dagger into a vertical position, and an audible click was heard. The scout then pushed the hilt into the wall until his forearm disappeared into a hole. He continued to push until another click sounded, and a low rumbling could be heard overhead. Conal watched the stone roof overhead as a small section of the ceiling slid aside, giving them access to the room above.

"Neat, very neat," Cull grunted in admiration. "But how do we get up there?"

Cathal smiled and cleared more moss off another section of the brickwork. Then, pulling his own *Tri-crub* from its sheath, he slid its tines into slits in the wall at knee height. Other clansmen came forward, and soon a makeshift ladder of *Tri-crub* hilts extended upwards. Cathal was the first to climb. "Well, what are you waiting for? Your baths are waiting."

Cull looked at Conal in surprise. "Did he just say baths?"

"I think so."

Cull shrugged and started to climb. "This I've got to see."

The scout waited until last and scampered nimbly up the makeshift ladder, reaching down to remove the daggers as he climbed and handing them up to their owners. When everyone was out of the sewer, Cathal pulled a lever that had been discreetly hidden in an alcove, and the trap door slid neatly back into place. Once it was settled, it looked the same as the other flagstones on the floor.

"Follow me," Cathal directed as he led them up a staircase and through a small door.

Conal gazed in wonder at the room beyond. It was richly decorated with ornate tiles, depicting mythical sea creatures in green against an azure backdrop. Wooden benches lined the walls, with pegs for hanging clothing above.

"That door over there leads directly to the baths," Cathal instructed with a sly grin. "Your valuables will be quite safe here. Only the richest and most powerful men and women of the city have access to this particular bathhouse. Your clothes will be laundered while you luxuriate in the curative waters of the various pools, and they'll be dry by the time you've enjoyed the pleasures of the steam rooms and its masseurs."

"Masseurs, you've got to be kidding me!" Cull gasped.

"I promised you'd come out of the sewers smelling of roses, didn't I?"

"You did indeed, but I thought you were speaking metaphorically."

"All part of the service. It's hard to sneak into the city at night if you stink like a cesspool."

"This must have cost a small fortune to set up. It seems like an awful lot of trouble to go to just to smuggle a few furs into *Ard Pect*."

Cathal's smile faltered for a brief moment before he gave a casual shrug of his shoulders. "I didn't mention what we were smuggling into the city, did I?"

Conal looked around at the baggage that the clansmen had carried with them from their homeland; his eyes twinkling with curiosity. "I suppose it would be impolite to ask what else is in there ..."

Cathal grinned at him. "It might be better not to know. Now, the baths are waiting. I don't know about you, but I'll be glad to get out of these smelly clothes ..."

The naked men were soon walking out into the steaming chamber beyond. Conal was awed by the opulence of the bathhouse. The men headed for a large pool nearby and dived into the deep water.

Conal paused for a moment, looking around at the scantily-dressed girls who were handing out towels to the bathers as they climbed out of the water. Other girls stood waist deep in the shallower part of the pool, lathering and shampooing the men and women who relaxed there. Older bathers were being guided along as they shuffled toward the massage tables and steam rooms beyond.

"Not too shabby, eh?" Cull asked.

"It's wonderful!" Conal gasped. Already, he was wondering how he could build such a bathhouse on Dragon's Ridge. Someday, he promised, he would make his ancestral home worthy of such a bathhouse, but he still had a long way to go before *Dun Dragan* would be even half this opulent. Remembering the leaky roofs and fallen walls of the current fortress, he shuddered.

"Last one in is a big girl's blouse!" he challenged and shouldered Cull to unbalance him as they raced for the water. Diving head first into the steamy water, he rose to the surface and whooped with joy. As the warmth seeped into his aching bones, he relaxed further and floated in the pool.

Sometime later, Cull paddled over with his face flushed red from the heat. "You'll look like a winter apple if you stay in here much longer. I don't know about you, but I'm starving. Cathal tells me that there's a restaurant on the next floor up. Are you coming?"

Conal was so relaxed that his muscles felt like jelly, and he wasn't sure if he could climb out of the pool. Shaking off his lethargy, he waded into the shallow end of the pool and clambered out. Collecting a towel from one of the nearby girls, he began to rub himself down.

"Do you need a helping hand, Sire?" the girl asked. Her coy smile warmed Conal's cheeks as she appraised his muscular body.

"Erm ... no thanks, I'll be fine," Conal blustered and hurried away. Covering his nakedness, he headed for the changing rooms.

"I think she's taken quite a shine to you, lad," Cull commented from behind him, which only added to his embarrassment.

Not rising to the bait, Conal hurried on.

"I'm sure that for a good tip, she could help you lose some of that shyness."

"Drop it, Cull."

"What! I was just trying to help."

"Just forget it!"

"If you insist ..."

"Anyway, I thought you were hungry?"

"I am, but I can always eat alone if you've got something better to do ..."

"I'm fine, Cull. Let's just get dressed and find some food."

"If you say so ..."

Conal glared at Cull, knowing that he was winding him up. Grabbing his freshly-laundered tunic, he wrestled his way into it to hide his blushing cheeks. Soon, they were heading up the nearest staircase, searching for the restaurant. They found Cathal and the other clansmen eating at a large banquet table. A rich feast adorned the table before them, and they were attacking it with as the same gusto that they attacked their enemies.

"Cull! Conal! I thought you'd both got lost," Cathal greeted them. One hand clasped a tankard of mead, while the other clutched a turkey leg.

"Conal was charming the ladies below," Cull replied with a grin. "I had to peel them off him."

"Ah!" Cathal laughed. "The *Ciudachbane* has recovered his strength, I see. I told you that the waters of this bathhouse have regenerative powers."

*****

Abbot Gearoid woke suddenly and gasped for air, his dream thankfully forgotten.

"Easy there! You're alright now."

Gearoid felt reassuring hands on his shoulders and recognised Brother Seamy's soothing tones. "I can't see!"

"You're fine," assured Seamy. "I've put some bandages over your face. There's a poultice on them that'll draw out the poison and reduce the swelling."

Gearoid remembered. "...The bees!"

"Yes, you were badly stung. What, in the Nine Hells, happened?"

"Balor, is he alright?"

"He's fine, Gearoid. He's sleeping in his room. I gave him a draught to help him as he was distraught when we found him."

Gearoid relaxed a little.

"How did you get in such a state? I've never seen so many stings before. You're lucky to be alive. The shock alone could have killed you, to say nothing of pneumonia."

"The bees ... they attacked me, Seamy. I had to dive into the Lough to escape them."

"...But it's the middle of winter! Our bees aren't usually that aggressive ... even in the summer!"

"Something in Balor stirred them up ... with magic."

"I told you that no good would come of that man. You should have sent him to *Ard Pect,* and let the priestesses of Deanna deal with him."

"No, Seamy, it wasn't Balor's fault. It was the other one ... the *Diabhal* within him. *He* was the one who set the bees on me."

"What other one? I don't know what you're talking about."

"It's hard to explain. It's like there is someone lurking in the shadows of his soul and that one is evil! *He* is the one who is causing all the trouble."

"Gearoid, you're not making sense. Are you saying that Balor is possessed?"

Abbot Gearoid sighed, not sure if he could explain the change that he had witnessed when Balor used magic. "I'm not sure if it's a *Deamhan*. That's not what I mean, though perhaps that would be easier to justify. It's ... it's like there are two men in the same body. One of them is Balor, and I know in my heart that he's a good man. He feels remorse for his past life and there's hope of redemption for his soul, but then ... then there's *something else* within the same body. This thing is so steeped in evil that it has become a corrupting force. It was *this thing* that I glimpsed, just for a moment, before the bees attacked me. I encouraged Balor to fight it, but it was no good. *Its* hold was too strong."

"Like I said, we should ship him off to the priestesses of Deanna, and let them figure it out."

"Have you forgotten your vows, Seamy? We cannot turn away from one of our brothers in his time of need, whatever his previous life might have been."

Brother Seamus frowned, knowing that the Abbot was right. "I'm sorry, Gearoid, I'm just worried about the others. Strange things have been happening around the island, things I've never seen before and hope never to see again. I had to break up a fight earlier between Brother Fionn and Brother Tomas. They were wielding knives, for crying out loud. They've known each other since childhood and are usually the closest of friends, and yet, they were quite willing to spill each other's blood ... over nothing. When I asked them what they'd been fighting about, neither of them could remember. I don't even think that there was a reason."

"*He* is the reason. *He* emanates evil, I tell you. It seeps from his pores and contaminates those in his vicinity."

"What about an exorcism?"

"Don't be daft, Seamy. Exorcisms are for demons."

"It's got to be worth a try," Seamy argued. "What have we got to lose?"

Gearoid considered the suggestion. "I wouldn't know where to begin ... would you?"

"No," Seamy admitted, "but I'm sure there's something in the library about it. Brother Leonard might be able to help. That old coot never leaves the place apart from to eat. He hasn't slept in his cell for the past twenty years. I'm sure by now he's forgotten where it is!"

"I'm still not convinced, Seamy, but I guess there's no harm in trying, is there?"

Seamy beamed. "Here, let me remove those bandages, and then I'll go and speak with him. I'll see what he has to say."

"...Seamy?"

"Yes?"

"Keep this to yourself, will you. Try and be discreet with your investigations. We don't want to start a panic."

"...Of course, Gearoid."

Chapter Seventeen: Visiting *Ard Pect*

"I woke up on one freezing night and went for a pee without a light.

I stumbled forward, half-sleep, and I hoped I didn't splash the seat.

As I staggered back toward my bed, grunting in my sleep-filled head,

I stumped my toe upon the door and cried aloud and cursed galore.

I finally fell upon the bed and hit the bedpost with my head.

And so I lay there, dizzy and shocked, blood, oozing from my sock,

And from my head it too did weep as I slipped back into restless sleep."

Taliesin finished his jaunty tale to the raucous laughter of the crowd. Coins landed on the stage in acknowledgement of the entertainer's skill. He had been cultivating the audience for some time with some songs, a little music, the odd stories and his current ditty to finish off his witty repertoire.

He quickly bowed. "Thank you, thank you," he murmured as he quickly collected his earnings. When he was finished, he headed over to the table at the far end of the tavern, where his companions sat waiting.

"You did well, Tal," Cull complimented, his face shaded behind his wide-brimmed hat.

"Aye, Cull. They certainly look after their entertainers in *Tir Pect*. I could make a tidy living here."

"Are you planning to give up your job as my Royal Bard then, Taliesin?" Conal joked. His face was similarly hidden behind a broad-brimmed hat.

"Nay, Conal, but you'll have to get around to paying my wages sometime soon, before my boots wear any thinner."

Conal's face dropped. "It's costing me a fortune to rebuild that *Dun*. I can't afford to spend money on luxuries right now, Tal. If you want regular wages then I'd suggest you try the Pectish High King. I hear that he has a great respect for bards. He might even offer you a place at court."

"That'd be a good idea, Conal, but I can see a problem with it. Much though his Lordship loves the sound of a well-played harp, I hear his wife loves her bards even more. In fact, if the local gossip is anything to believe, she's a great fondness for men in general. She's rumoured to consume whole regiments of them for breakfast. I grant you, it'd be a blissful way to pass into the Otherworld, but I think I'll wait a while longer before venturing near to the palace. Medb *Ni Béar* is a ferocious warrioress, but it's her tally of men *off* the battlefield that has me worried."

"I guess that means that you'll have to wait a while on your wages, Tal. There aren't many other kings with enough interest in music to pay for your skills," Cull chuckled. "From what I hear, Lord Boare is tone-deaf."

"Mmm, you might have a point." Taliesin turned to Conal. "Well, it looks like I'm still at your services. That is, if you'll have me?"

"I haven't had any better offers recently, so I guess I'll keep you in my retinue ... for now," Conal answered with an evil grin.

"Oh, that's below the belt, Conal!"

"Tell me, Cull," Conal asked. "Why are we in *Ard Pect*, anyway?"

"I need to catch up on some things. One of Broll's best operators is based here, and I need to speak to her."

"Her .... Is she a female beggar, then? I haven't seen many female beggars. For some reason, they're mostly old men and young children."

"Who said she was a beggar, Taliesin? She works ... in a different trade, but she's at least as effective as any beggar in the city. She has an excellent network of spies and the sharpest ears on the island," Cull explained. "That's why we've come to *Ard Pect* in the middle of winter. If you want to know what's happening in *Tir Pect*, and believe me Conal, you do. She's the only person worth asking."

"So why haven't we been introduced?"

Cull cleared his throat while he tried to find a diplomatic way to tell Conal. "Let's just say that you're a bit young to meet *this* particular woman."

"What do you mean, Cull? My Rites of Manhood are only a few moons away, and I've already proved myself on the battlefield. Surely, I'm old enough to meet her?"

"I don't think the High Priestess would approve if I brought you to the Pink Rose, Conal. In fact, she's likely to have a serious hissing fit about the whole thing," Cull grunted. "Let's just save ourselves the trouble and forget all about it, shall we?"

"Who is this woman, Cull? She's not one of the foul-mouthed harlots from down by the dockside, is she?" Conal asked. He had spent much of his young life living in the streets of Manquay. He was, as princes went, quite streetwise.

"Why is it that you never just let something drop, Conal? You've a bad habit of gnawing away at a subject in the vain hope that I'll change my mind. Have you ever known me to do that?"

"What can I say, Cull, I'm an optimist."

"If your Highness will forgive my frankness, you can forget about it right now. I've told you, I'm going to meet her alone, and you and the bard will have to wait here."

"Surely, *I* can meet this secretive woman?" Taliesin objected.

"Bah!" Cull exclaimed. "You're nearly as bad as he is. Who's going to keep an eye on him while I'm gone? If I left him on his own, he'd be slinking across the rooftops before I'd got halfway down the street. The answer was no ... so let's just drop the subject. Are we clear?"

The two younger men nodded reluctantly, knowing how stubborn Cull could be. That didn't stop them thinking of alternative ways to get around the situation as their eyes met across the table in silent agreement.

"Don't even think about it," Cull warned. "If I spot either of you trying to follow me, I'll beat the pair of you senseless. If I catch a whiff of you near the Pink Rose, you'll wish you were never born."

Conal pressed on, his inquisitive nature never giving up "What exactly is this Pink Rose, Cull?"

"You're not going to let this drop, are you, Conal?" Cull remarked. "Very well, as long as you both promise not to try and follow me, I'll tell you some of it ... but not all. The Pink Rose is a high-class house of pleasure. Many of the lords and barons frequent it, as well as *Tir Pects* generals, and the captains of the Royal Guard. Even the Pectish High Queen is reputed to visit the place."

"It's a brothel, then." Conal summarised.

Cull sighed at the young man's ignorance. The Pink Rose was far more than a mere brothel. It covered all the pleasures of the wealthy and not just those of a sexual nature. The rich and powerful had many tastes, from the eccentric to the downright bizarre. Knowing that the Prince would have another hundred questions, Cull opted for the easy solution. "Well, I suppose you could call it that."

"I've seen whores before, Cull, so why can't I go to this brothel?"

"...Because I said so! I'm your guardian until you can officially call yourself a man, and if I say you can't go, you can't go. Let's just leave it at that, shall we?"

"That's not fair, Cull!"

"Life's not fair, Conal, as I'm sure you've found out by now. It's time you built a bridge and got over it. Let's just drop the subject. Your whinging is giving me a headache."

Conal didn't drop the subject, he merely changed tack. "So, this woman that you are meeting is a whore?"

"I didn't say that, did I?" Cull answered reluctantly. "I just said I was meeting her at the Pink Rose."

"Is she a client ...?"Conal coaxed "Is that what you're saying?"

"...She could be a cleaning girl," suggested Taliesin.

"Drop it, the pair of you," Cull commanded, getting to his feet.

"Awww, but Cull!" Conal grinned.

Cull downed his drink swiftly and looked at his companions. "Right, I'm off. Taliesin, keep an eye on him. I want you both to stay here, even if you have to tie Conal to his bed. Do you understand me?"

"You're no fun at all, Cull," Conal objected.

"I don't care. I've been given the task of protecting you, and you'll not end up in Conchubhar's gaol ... not on my watch. I'm sure her Majesty would entertain you, but that's not the point. We're here to find out information, and I don't need you attracting undue attention to yourself. So that means staying in the room and keeping your sticky hands to yourself. If I find out that you've been picking pockets while I'm gone, I'm going to break a few of those royal fingers. Are we clear?" Cull growled.

"I'll keep an eye on him, Cull."

"Aye, but who is going to keep an eye on you, Tal? That's what I'd like to know! I'm warning you; behave yourselves, the pair of you. I'll be back within the bell if all goes well. Just sit tight and wait for my return. Even if I'm delayed, I want you both to stay in the room and out of sight."

With his final warnings uttered, Cull headed for the rear door of the tavern and made a discreet exit.

Conal sat silently for a few moments longer, looking glumly into his drink. "We aren't really going to spend the whole evening in our room, are we Taliesin?"

"Conal, he'll string the pair of us up if he finds out we've been up to anything," Taliesin warned. He was rightly wary of Cull's wrath.

"Aw! Come on Tal! What he doesn't know won't hurt him. He won't be back for ages. Would you be, if you were going to a fancy whorehouse?"

"He said he'd only be a bell!" Taliesin objected, valiantly trying to maintain control.

"He always says that. Haven't you realised that by now? He's usually gone for half the night when he's out somewhere. We'll have a couple of bells to play with, at the least," Conal wheedled, his eyes sparkling with mischief.

"I don't know, Conal ..."

"What do you fancy, Tal? We could go and find ourselves a couple of floozies down by the wharf ... or would you prefer a game of dice?" He knew that Taliesin had a soft spot for gambling, and he saw the bard's eyes light up at the prospect of a game of dice.

Taliesin tried once more time to discourage Conal. "No, we'd better just drink up and get an early night."

"Awww ... Tal. I'm sure we can find a lucrative card game or a game of Toss around here? It's been a long winter, surely a little fun wouldn't hurt?"

"Well ... I guess ... if it's only for one bell."

"That's settled then. Where should we go? ... I know ... what about the palace? I bet there is a good game going on up there. We could win some real money. The goddess knows that I could do with recouping some of my losses."

"No way, Conal .... Absolutely not! We're going nowhere near the palace. That'll be too near to where the Pink Rose. We'd better stay near to the dockside."

Conal grinned and drained his tankard, having forced the harpist's hand. He might not be able to get near the Pink Rose, but at least he wouldn't be chained up in his room. "Well, what are we waiting for? Let's go find a game then."

Taliesin still looked apprehensive, but he reluctantly drained his tankard of ale and followed Conal out into the wintry night.

*****

Seabhac called a halt for lunch at the foothills of the mountains, where the trees of the Broce Woods thinned out and fields of limestone shale took over. Quickly building a fire, they warmed themselves and made a hot broth. It was bitterly cold, flying so high up. Here, the wind was unhindered by any break in the landscape, and they were all glad of the fire's heat. After eating, Seabhac handed Cora and Maerlin their bedrolls. "Come along."

They looked at each other, curious and wondered why they had been handed their bedding so early in the day. However, when Seabhac gave them an instruction, they had learned to follow it, and quickly. The old witch had a sharp tongue. She led them a little way away from the campfire and directed them to stand a few yards apart.

"That'll do nicely. Now, it's time for thee to learn some more magic."

"We aren't going to bed then, I take it?" Maerlin asked. She was always the bravest of the pair.

"Certainly not, Maerlin, dost thou remember when I taught thee how to use a staff to fly?"

"Yes."

"As thou may have noticed, I used a different method for getting the rug airborne. As thou would see with a staff, or a broom, or even with an arrow, thou must wrap the Elemental around the object to give it support and direction. Sadly, the rug proved to be useless using this method. It was like a ship without ballast, directionless and unstable. So I had to do something different. Instead, I created a cushion of air for the rug to sit on, and then I used other Sylphs to push it along."

The novices nodded, having spent a good part of the morning trying to figure out exactly how Seabhac was making the rug fly.

"A cushion of air is a very handy tool to use, and I will teach it to thee. If nothing else, it could come in handy if thou should be stupid enough to fall off the rug, as it will ease thy fall. Moreover, if needs must, it can be used to protect thee from attack. I have found it most useful to stop charging horses, for example. A word of caution at this point, do not attempt to use it against the likes of spears or arrows, for the shape of the attacking force will cause it to merely slow down, rather than stop. This would be fine if thou were wearing full armour, but I doubt that thou would be doing that, so be forewarned. Instead, thou would need to direct thy magical energies toward diverting the flying missile away from thee, but I digress. Summon up thy magic, and I wilt show thee how to make a cushion of air."

Maerlin and Cora soon realised why they had been given the bed rolls to carry for after some brisk instructions, Seabhac headed back to the warmth of the fire and a well-earned cup of tea, leaving them to practice what they had been taught. Taking it in turns, they flung the bedrolls at each other, one using only their magical skills to guide the bedding toward the other, while the other tried to stop the attack with a similar cushion of air.

Sweat was soon pouring off their bodies, despite the bitter mountain chill. As they became more proficient, their attacks became more devious, with the bedroll swerving and dodging to strike from unexpected angles.

Maerlin finally won the day with a clever double-strike. Firing the first of the bedding rolls using brute speed, Cora easily rebuffed the attack and sent it rolling away behind her. Then, Maerlin lifted the second roll and sent it forward. This time, it veered left and right, keeping Cora guessing as to the point of the attack. Finally, it rushed forward, and Cora moved her invisible cushion of air to counter. It was at this point that the forgotten bedroll behind Cora whacked her in the back. Cora's concentration collapsed and her defences disintegrated, leaving the second bedroll unimpeded to also strike the novice.

"I win!" Maerlin yelled, jumping up and down with joy.

"You cheated!" Cora accused, trying not to laugh.

"Did not!"

"Did, too!"

"No one said I couldn't use the two bedrolls in unison, did they?"

Cora stuck out her tongue and sat down on the rocks to catch her breath. "Okay, I'm too tired to argue. You win."

Maerlin grinned and came over to sit beside her. "That was fun though, wasn't it?"

"It was until you cheated," Cora argued with a grin, slapping Maerlin playfully on the shoulder.

They sat side-by-side, enjoying the warmth of the sun and catching their breath before Maerlin nudged her friend. "Looks like it's time to go."

Seabhac was waving them over, ready for the second part of their journey. They hoped to arrive at Eagles Reach before nightfall.

Maerlin was eager, and at the same time a little nervous, about going to Eagles Reach. It was her mother's birthplace. It was the unknown part of her heritage. Maerlin was unique in many ways, not least of them being that she was the only person who had ties on both sides of the mountain peak. Her father was the blacksmith at High Peaks. It was here that Maerlin had grown up. Her mother was from Eagles Reach, and although her mother had taught her some of the old tongue that was still spoken by her mother's people, she knew very little else about them and had never visited the place.

Standing between the two isolated communities was the peak known as the Mountain of the Gods. They might as well have been worlds apart, for although as the crow flies they were fairly close, the mountain peak that divided them was formidable.

Only the very bravest dared climb through the thin air to cross its unforgiving slopes, and even then, only in the best of weather. Many a soul had died trying to defeat the silent menace of *Sliamh Na Dia*.

She wondered how her father had been brave enough to cross the mountain and win her mother's heart. After all, he was such a silent and unobtrusive man. Maerlin didn't know the details because they had never told her.

Chapter Eighteen: The Pink Rose

As her name would suggest, *Sile Ceathrar-Cioch* had been blessed at birth with not two, but four breasts. This gave her a remarkable and unique beauty, which was only one of her many gifts.

Being from a poor family her career options had always been limited, but Cliodhna, the goddess of love, had seen something in the young girl. She had chosen Sile for her service when Sile had fled her abusive stepfather for a better life in the big city. As she wandered into *Ard Pect* on that first night, Cliodhna had intervened and led her to her present occupation.

The first proposition had come from a young merchant that was too deep in his cups. He had shocked and frightened the young Sile. The second proposition had caused a similar reaction, but when a Street-walker noticed the lost-looking girl, the goddess of love could again have been said to give Sile a guiding hand. Sile had accepted the shelter and guidance offered by the older woman. Her first night in the big city had, so far, made her question the decision to run away from home. Even the terror of her licentious stepfather might have been better than this, but the lessons taught to her by the older woman had changed all that. And so it was that Sile learned about the novelty factor of her breasts, or rather, the value that could be accrued from them.

Another one of her gifts was her charm, whether dealing with a poor baker's apprentice or a rich lord; she left them all feeling special. Her reputation quickly grew within her chosen trade, and it gained her rich and powerful clients. Here, a further gift came to the fore as she was careful with her newly-found wealth and diligently saved her hard-earned gold. By the time she had reached the age of twenty-one, she had bought her first brothel, and over the next few years, she had built it up into the best and most luxurious establishment in the city of *Ard Pect*. By the time she reached her thirtieth year, she had become the second wealthiest woman on the continent, only bested by the High Queen herself. Sile had established salons in every major city within *Tir Pect*, but *Ard Pect* had become her home, and here she resided.

Her astute nature led her into the intriguing world of politics. Many state secrets were revealed by those inebriated and relaxing with a fine concubine, and she had trained her staff to listen carefully to the idle boastings of their clientele. Sile taught them to have a sympathetic ear and a soft bosom to cry on. This was as much a part of their profession as the act of intercourse itself. This special treatment she gave to her clientele was the difference between a high-class, high-paying trade and the work done by the 'doxies' on the street-corners. In fact, many of her clients declined sexual gratification completely, merely visiting her establishment for the pampering and care given to them by her carefully selected staff.

Knowledge has always been power, and Sile was one of the most knowledgeable people in *Tir Pect*. A dear friend had started her on this road to knowledge. He had recruited her into the field of intelligence when she was only starting out in her profession and had helped her to establish her first brothel. As her business grew and her clients became more powerful, the bond between her and her business partner grew stronger. They had a common purpose. Each had come from the dregs of humanity and each had a mission to improve the lot of the common people by subtle manipulation of the system from within.

They were the two sides to a blade, each complementing the other. With their shared resources and knowledge, they could manipulate kings and guild masters, exerting their will upon the world around them with invisible hands. Neither sought acknowledgment for their work. Such recognition would only endanger their influence. What they wanted was something else, a far greater reward than infamy.

Now, her partner was sick and close to Macha's bosom. He no longer played the game of power directly. For some time now, he had left such tasks in the capable hands of his heir. It was for a meeting with this heir that she prepared herself this evening.

Her scent was a subtle nuance, which though expensive beyond imagination, left both the wearer and any within its range feeling euphoric with anticipation of the charms of the flesh. She was careful in her application, wanting just a subtle amount of enticement in the air. Theirs was an old game since they had known each other for some time, and on many levels. Seduction was no longer the main objective, but still, Sile enjoyed the game of allurement and provocation. It was the sweetest of elixirs to her, even after all these years of working in her trade. She loved her work, not in a nymphomaniac sort of way, but rather for the game of cat and mouse which proceeded, and on a good night continued, long after the act of coitus. She viewed her work as an artist would view his finest painting. She was never satisfied and was always striving for greater creativity and accomplishment.

The gossamer gown she wore hid as much as it revealed, enticing in its shades of black, the soft alabaster of the bare flesh beneath. As she moved before the mirror, twisting to be sure of the overall effect, she smiled in satisfaction. It complemented her raven locks to perfection and hung snugly around her waist, leaving her buttocks and thighs clinging to the material, causing it to become almost, but not quite, transparent. When she had finished brushing the glossy strands of her long tresses, she turned to the balcony doors and opened the windows, letting in the cool of the evening. A large fire battled against the wintry breeze coming off the Lough as she stood and watched the city below. Physically, she was as prepared as she ever would be, but she stood for a few moments longer, waiting for her mind to relax. Finally, she turned toward the warm glow of the room and walked over to the chaise lounge.

There was a discreet knock on the door, and her handmaiden entered.

"The gentleman has arrived, Ma'am." The girl's country accent was still thick, despite three years in the big city.

"Thank you, Charlene. Send him in, and then you may go for the evening. I won't need you any further."

Charlene returned moments later with a well-dressed lord, wearing a broad-brimmed hat. Curtsying silently to her mistress, she left them alone.

"Sile, were you expecting someone else?" Cull quipped. A smirk was clearly visible on his face.

Sile smiled inwardly, noting how his eyes roamed over her luscious curves while his face feigned disinterest. She knew how to play this game just as well as he did and retorted with "... Oh! It's you, Cull. I must've got my appointments mixed up."

She reached down to lift her silk dressing gown from the chaise lounge, revealing more of her double cleavage as she stooped.

The smirk grew on her companion's face. "I can come back another time if you'd like ..." he offered, half way through removing his cloak. The serge suit beneath bulged with his muscular frame "...But give me a moment first to warm my old bones by your fire. That night's getting bitter. I don't know why you insist on living in this cold northern climate, Sile."

Sile sighed loudly. "Since you're here, Cull, and since my strapping young masseur is absent, perhaps you could be useful. We can discuss whatever mundane reason you have for disturbing me while you replace his services. ... You can manage that, I presume?" She strolled boldly toward him as she wrapped the belt around her slim waist. "You *can* serve and pamper, can't you?" Her tone relayed a certain amount of doubt.

Cull gave a delicate cough as he suppressed a laugh.

"ONE BELL TO MIDNIGHT AND ALL'S WELL!" the crier called from outside, momentarily breaking the mood in the room

"Perhaps we should stick to business, Sile. My time in *Ard Pect* is short," Cull suggested with a look of regret.

"...Ach! All business and no pleasure, as usual, Cull. You still have the driving force of a dozen men, I see. When will you ever stop and watch the world go by?"

"I watch it go by quite often, Sile," Cull objected with a grin. "I just study it closely as it passes. You can learn an awful lot if you pay attention to the details, as you well know. Tell me, Sile, what do you know about life in the castle? Is Conchubhar still lounging contentedly in the Royal Palace, or has he ambitions for expansion? As I'm sure you know, I've been asked to baby-sit the Dragonson and see him safely to his throne. I need to know if Conchubhar and his rapacious wife are planning any expeditions southward."

Sile raised a perfectly groomed eyebrow in surprise. "You must indeed be in a rush, Cull, to be so succinct ... even to me. Come, sit beside me and we'll talk. Even these walls have ears."

She took Cull's hand and led him over to the chaise lounge, a wicked glint in her eyes. She had not yet given up on the possibility of some playtime after their discussion was over, but she knew that she would have to help Cull unwind first.

The musky scent of her perfume filled his nostrils as he sat, feeling the warmth of her thighs against his own. As she filled him in on all that she knew, she massaged his broad shoulders and neck, rubbing away the tension that lurked there. Slowly, her subtle ministrations and the heady scent of her perfume relaxed him as she assured him that all was well in the palace. The fire was warming the room, and Cull allowed himself to be undressed further while she filled him in on the gossip of *Ard Pect* and the kingdom of *Tir Pect* beyond.

"Sile!" he protested, fighting off his arousal "I can't stay. Conal Dragonson is waiting in 'The Queen's Bedchamber', and I told him that I'd return within the bell."

"Are you mad, Cull? You've brought the *Dragan* Prince into *Tir Pect* ... into *Ard Pect*?" She was so surprised that for a moment she forgot all about her plans for seduction.

"Don't worry, Sile. No one will recognise him," Cull assured. "His own mother wouldn't recognise him, apart from those *Dragan* eyes of his. He's been well disguised."

"Still, it's a great risk to take, Cull."

"He's in safe hands. I'm sure he won't get into any trouble. Believe me."

Sile smiled like a cat with a bowl full of cream. "Well, if he's so safe ... there's no need for you to rush off, is there?" she purred, standing up and slipping out of her gown. As the soft silk slid down her arms and pooled around her feet, she leaned forward and kissed Cull passionately on the mouth. Leaning into the kiss, she pressed him back into the soft couch.

He tried to speak, but her soft lips cut off any protests as she pressed her naked body against his chest. Cull resisted for only a few moments more, knowing that it was futile, but enjoying making Sile work for her satisfaction. Finally, with a soft moan, he relented and allowed her to undress him. "You're incorrigible, Sile," Cull gasped, as her lips roamed down his neck and along his naked chest.

"You can encourage me anytime, *Cuilithe*," Sile purred, using Cull's secret name.

*****

The cockerels had already started crowing around the city when the Mistress of the Pink Rose finally allowed him to leave. Sated, they kissed before Cull slipped out of the back door and down the nearest alleyway. He headed quickly toward 'The Queen's Bedchamber'.

When he arrived at their rooms, he found the beds empty and unused. "Damn you, Conal, and damn you too, Tal! Can't you do anything right?"

He slammed the door and headed back down the staircase.

Seeing the landlord asleep on one of the trestle tables, Cull shook the man roughly. "Wake up!"

"Mmm ... what?" The man rubbed sleep from his eyes and stared in disbelief at his irate guest. "Whatisit? Whatsthematter?"

"Have you seen my companions?" Cull growled.

"Huh? Err ... oh yes, they were asking about a game of Toss. I sent them down to the Crooked Kingpin," the still-sleepy barkeeper murmured, turning over and hoping to slip back into slumber. His efforts were again disrupted when Cull shook him and dragged him roughly off the table by his collar. "Where do I find it?"

The man tried futilely to free himself. Finally, in an effort to rid himself of his tormentor, he pointed down the street. "It's down on the quayside. You can't miss it!"

Cull released him and marched from the room, cursing under his breath as he headed down the hill to the docks. It didn't take him long to find the Crooked Kingpin, a ratty-looking rundown inn. "I'm looking for two young men," he growled at the obese man who was cleaning the bar. He absently noted the fresh bruising on the barman's face. He had been in a brawl recently.

"I don't care," grunted the barman. "Are ye drinkin' or leavin'?"

Cull looked around the dark tavern, where drunken sailors lay comatose on benches. Some others still drank at this early bell of the morning. "I don't need a drink," he protested "I'm just looking for my friends. I was told that they were here last night."

The barman belched loudly with indifference. "Order a drink or get out. De choice is yours."

Cull clenched his fists as anger brewed up inside him, but he swallowed the curse that crept to his lips and eyed the barman. "Give me a shot of rum," he finally conceded, not wishing to try the local hooch in such a dubious establishment. Fishing into his pouch, Cull pulled out a copper farthing and slapped it on grimy counter.

The barman nodded absently and pulled down a small wooden beaker, into which he poured a shot of dark liquid. He wiped the bar down with a grease-stained cloth and with a well-practised move; he presented the drink to Cull and slipped the coin beneath the counter.

"I'm looking for two men. They came in here last night, sometime after midnight. One is a young lad with blue eyes, and the other is a tall, gangly harper. Have you seen them?" Cull asked, more softly this time. He was hoping to avoid confrontation with the surly barman. To emphasise his need, he slid another coin across the counter. This one was a silver shilling piece.

For a moment the barman ignored the question and the shilling, but eventually greed overcame his taciturn nature. "Dey ain't 'ere," he grunted and reached for the coin.

Cull swiftly clamped his hand over the barman's wrist. A short, silent wrestle began as the man tried to pull his arm free, but Cull's grip was stronger and he held the wrist in place.

The barman sighed. "Ya young friend's a poor bleedin' excuse for a thief. He tried to pick some of me regulars' pouches, while da tall one was distractin' dem wiv 'is stories, but he got 'imself nabbed, didn'he! Dey got into a fight and ended up busting up some of me tables and stuff." The barman tried again to pull his wrist free.

Cull released the hand and nodded, allowing him to retrieve the shilling.

"Where are they now?"

The barman scowled silently, forcing Cull to hold his fraying temper in check. When the man finally spoke, it wasn't much help to Cull. "It'll cost me more'n a silver coin to repair da damage dat dey done."

Cull cursed and drained the bitter-tasting rum as he fished again in his pouch. "How much are we talking about?"

"I'd say it'd cost me five silver bits, at the very least." The barman clearly sensed an opportunity to swindle some coin out of the well-dressed gentleman before him.

"You've got to be joking!" Cull protested. "I could build this hovel for less than that."

The barman shrugged and continued to spread the grease around the counter with the grimy cloth.

Knowing that an argument would get him nowhere, Cull dug out the coins and slapped them onto the counter, one at a time. Keeping his hand firmly on the four silver pieces, he demanded "Where are they now?"

The barman licked his lips, clearly wondering if there was more to be gained, but the hard look on Cull's face tempered his avarice. "Last time I saw dem, dey was bein' 'auled outta 'ere by da Watch. If I were ye, I'd look for 'em up in da gaol'ouse. Dat's da big red buildin' right next to da palace."

Cull left the silver coins on the counter and marched back up the hill. His thoughts were on a suitable punishment for the two mischievous companions.

*****

Snow whisked by underneath when Maerlin peered over the edge of the musty rug. The frozen ground rushed by a few feet below them. They had descended to a lower altitude to reduce the effects of the buffeting winds. Seabhac had advised them that flying any lower than this would risk them crashing to the ground, if they ran into any turbulence. The shadows grew as the sun fell toward the mountain, but Seabhac assured them that they would reach Eagles Reach before nightfall.

Maerlin fought off the shivering and clenched her teeth to stop them rattling. Cora, if anything, was even worse. Her skin had turned a shade of pale blue from the biting cold. They huddled together, sharing their warmth with Nessa, who huddled deep inside Maerlin's cloak. "Are we nearly there yet?" Maerlin asked for the umpteenth time.

"It's over yonder ridge," Seabhac assured them "...and it won't get any nearer, no matter how many times thou asketh me. I can't go any faster. Thou might survive the crash, but my old bones are too brittle for such an adventure. Thou wilt just have to be patient. We're nearly there now."

Finally, they crested the elusive ridge. Below them they found a small valley, and hidden within its shelter, was a cluster of huts very similar to those found at High Peaks, where Maerlin had grown up. Smoke rose from the chimney holes in the top of each thatched roof and children played in the slushy snow.

A shout went up as they were spotted, and soon, the whole village gathered to greet them. Some of the men held bows and spears, wary of visitors to their isolated community. They relaxed, however, when Fintan took to wing and raced ahead with a loud screech of pure joy.

Seabhac laughed and waved to the villagers, and her gesture was reciprocated. Seeing the hen harrier flying overhead was, for the people of Eagles Reach, a good omen. They were the Clan of the Hawks, and the sight of Fintan flying before the rug boded well in their eyes. By the time the rug had settled on the ground in front of the Chief's hut, the atmosphere within the community was almost carnival. Children mimicked Fintan's cries as he circled overhead. Their imitations were strikingly close to the original.

The Chief emerged from his hut, dressed in a lavish feather cloak. With arms wide in welcome, he marched forward. "The blessings of Imbolc upon thee. May the Earth-mother sing her joy at your coming during this auspicious time," he greeted them in the old tongue of the Pectish Clans.

Seabhac responded in the same language, and thankfully, due to her insistence that Maerlin practice the old tongue with Cora, Maerlin was able to keep up with the conversation. Cora and Nessa had both grown up amongst Pectish Clans, and they had no trouble understanding. Maerlin, however, had grown up in High Peaks amongst the *Fear Ban*: her father's people. She had only learned the basics from her mother.

"Iolar-Mara, it warms my heart to see thee again."

"It's been too long, Mother, since you honoured us with a visit. It's good to see you and Father again. We had feared that you had both left us to fly in the Otherworld. It has been too long since you shared our hearth."

"Truly, time has passed. I see its passing on thy face and in the windows of thy soul ..."

"..And yet you are as ageless as the mountain."

Seabhac smiled at the compliment. "Even I have suffered the weathers of time, Iolar-Mara, despite my curse."

Iolar-Mara looked skyward to where Fintan hovered on the breeze. A deep sadness fell across his face. "He still flies amongst the eagles, Mother? Has he forgotten that his feet once brushed the dust of this mountain?"

Seabhac's tone showed her pain. "Iolar-Mara, if thou had the gift of wings, would thou bother with such mundane tasks as tending thy crops? Someday, he might release his wings and we might both see his face again, but I for one would not begrudge him his blessing. He has always been the rock that supported me in my time of need. Hear him cry out, Iolar-Mara! His heart soars, knowing that he is back amongst his people. He has not forgotten who he once was. He has not forgotten his beloved children."

The old Chief nodded, and a smile returned to his weather-beaten face. "Come, let us seek out the warmth of my hearth and feast. I'm sure that you're all cold and hungry after your journey, but first, who are these guests that you bring to my home?"

"Ah! The world is changing despite my unwillingness to go along with the idea. Deanna, it seems, has decreed that she has further need of me and won't let me live out my final years in peace. She sent these lost souls to my door in the heart of winter, and I'm still learning the full extent of their tale, but I digress ..."

Leading the old Chief forward, she introduced Cora "This is Cora of the Isles. She's a princess amongst the People of the Seals and a Water-sister of the Order of Deanna. Cora, this is Chief Iolar-Mara."

"You honour me, daughter of Mannaman. Please give my warm wishes to your father when next you see him. His wisdom is legendary." Turning to Seabhac, he mock-scolded "...You should have warned me before bringing such an honoured guest into our home. I could have made the place more presentable."

"Thy house is in the same state in which they found my own. However, there are more surprises yet to come. Thou may be more familiar with thy next guest than I was." Turning to Maerlin, Seabhac carefully pulled back her cloak and lifted the magpie from the warmth of her bosom. "Iolar-Mara, let me introduce thee to Nessa of *Clann Na MacTire*, Earth-sister of the Order of Deanna."

A confused look crossed the Chief's face as he looked at the magpie. "There must be some mistake ..."

"There isn't, believe me. It's a long story and one that I've yet to fully fathom, but I am assured that this is indeed the famed healer of the Broce Woods."

Iolar-Mara bowed formally to Nessa, though his eyes glittered with curiosity. "My house is truly blessed this day."

"And finally, Iolar-Mara, let me introduce you to Maerlin of High Peaks. Maerlin, this is my son, the Sea Eagle: Iolar-Mara."

Maerlin bowed formally before the elderly chief, a little confused that Seabhac referred to him as her son. The man looked old enough to be a grandfather.

As Maerlin raised her head, the evening sun glanced off the silver pendant that she always wore. Iolar-Mara let out a gasp. Raising a shaky hand, he pointed at the silver bird that hung around Maerlin's neck. "Sweet Deanna! Where did you get that?"

"Ah! I see that thy sight has not failed thee yet, Iolar-Mara," Seabhac responded. "It is indeed the same amulet."

"But ... I thought that was forever lost!"

"As did I. It seems that the damned thing is set to haunt me for all of my days."

Shaking his head, Iolar-Mara apologised "Forgive me my outburst, child, but have you any idea what that is?"

Maerlin looked surprised and clasped the amulet protectively. "It's a merlin ... a little hawk."

"It is indeed, but it's so much more than that. If you'll forgive an old man's impertinence, pray tell me, how did you come by this?"

"Nessa gave it to me when I came into my womanhood. It belonged to my mother," Maerlin explained.

"Dagda's divine blessing!" Iolar-Mara exclaimed. He looked toward Seabhac for confirmation. The old witch nodded in response.

"Where is your mother now?"

Tears welled up in Maerlin's eyes, and she was unable to answer.

Seeing her reaction, dread filled Iolar-Mara's heart as he tried to confirm the meaning of the pendant. "My humblest apologies, but ... what was she called?"

"Aiteann," Maerlin mumbled, hardly able to speak it aloud.

"Say that again!"

"Aiteann," Maerlin replied. Her voice was stronger this time.

"So it's true then! Oh, Deanna, what hast thou done?" Seabhac gasped, gripping her staff to stop herself from falling.

"Uiscallan, what does this mean?" Iolar-Mara demanded.

Seabhac's face was as ashen as his own.

"Uiscallan!" Cora and Maerlin blurted out in unison.

"...As in *the* Uiscallan?" Maerlin added, looking sharply at Seabhac.

"No wonder that old windbag has such a superior air about her!" Nessa exclaimed.

"I just knew that this was going to be a bad day," Seabhac murmured. Glaring up toward the hen harrier, she commanded *"Come down here, right now, Fintan MacIolar-Mara. It was thee and thy meddling that got me into this."*

*****

Abbot Gearoid led the monks into the sickroom.

"What's happening?" Balor asked, sensing something amiss.

"Please remain calm, Brother. We're just going to try something and see if it's any help to you," Gearoid assured, signalling four of the strongest monks forward. "There's no cause for alarm. We're just going to move your cot into the middle of the room."

"Whatever for? I told you, Gearoid, I'm sorry about your accident. I couldn't help it."

"There's no need to apologise, Brother. I have no anger for you in my heart, only love. Please ... be at peace. It is important that you remain calm."

The four monks lifted the bed and placed it in the centre of the small infirmary, allowing the others to encircle it. Brother Seamy stepped forward and placed his hand over the centre of the cot. From his fingers hung a long piece of twine, and attached to the twine was a nub of charcoal. Keeping his hand centred, he passed the charcoal to Gearoid, who started to draw a circle between the cot and the encircling monks.

Balor listened, straining to decipher the noises he was hearing. He was becoming more fearful with each passing moment. "What are you doing?"

The monks lit candles and placed them equidistantly around the marked circle. Slowly and with great care, Gearoid inscribed various symbols within the circle, at each of the four compass points. He carefully copied the strange arcane symbols, with the help of the tome that they had found in the library. Signalling to Seamy that they were ready to proceed, they stepped out of the circle, careful not to break the line or knock over any of the candles. Thankfully, Balor was, as usual, strapped firmly to his cot. Gearoid had briefly considered gagging him, but the archaic tome had mentioned on a number of occasions the risk of vomiting. Gearoid was worried about the danger of Balor drowning on his own sick during the ritual, and so he had opted against a gag.

"Lie back and relax, Balor. We're going to say some prayers over you and seek the assistance of the gods in curing you."

Balor became frantic. "Wait, no! Stop what you're doing." He fought against the restraints that were holding him to the cot.

"Hush now. It'll be alright," Gearoid assured, looking down at the heavy tome in his hand. "Lady Deanna, we beseech thee as your humble servants to aid us in our time of need."

The monks of the Order repeated his words, raising their voices in unison and chanted the words with their deep, masculine voices.

Gearoid prepared himself and sang the next line strongly. "Lord Dagda, we beseech thee to come to the aid of your humble servant."

Again, the monks took up the prayer, filling the room with their chant.

Gearoid steadily went through each of the Seven Greater Gods, finishing with Lady Macha, for the goddess of life and the goddess of death should always be opposites. Thus is ever the circle of life, death, and rebirth: the Sacred Triad. When each of the Greater Gods had been beseeched, ensuring impartiality in accordance with the doctrine of the monastery, Gearoid nodded his head. Seamy took over the chanting, and they began again, but this time with more complexity and variation.

This chanting was the strength that bound the community together, and it reverberated around the monastery every day in their prayers and their celebration of life. As the prayer continued, some monks took the deeper bass phrases, while others responded with the baritone, tenor, and even falsetto phrases. Soon, the room was filled with glorious homage to the Greater Gods, and the monks swayed in time with their hymn, becoming lost in the wonder of its sound. The room began to fill with magical power. As the priestesses of Deanna created a blank canvas within their minds, upon which they created their magic, thus it was with the monks. However, their meditative state was created through sound and repetition, bringing their combined minds to a higher order and allowing their magical will to come forth.

As the power grew, Gearoid noticed that the words on the tome before him had begun to glow. Sensing that the time was right, for the monks had never before performed this particular spell, he raised his voice and shouted out firmly. "Dark Spirit, leave our Brother be! By the powers vested in me, I command thee, be gone from this sacred place!"

Balor strained against his bindings, and his face became a rictus of pain. "Stop this ... please!"

"I speak to the Dark One within. Leave this man at once! Get thee back unto thy Underworld. Thou art an abomination and not worthy to bask in Lugh's glorious sun! Thou dost not belong to this fair land. Get thee back to the Nine Hells from whence thy came!"

"Gearoid ... stop this before it's too late!" Balor pleaded. The wooden cot creaked loudly as the leather straps binding him strained against his rigid body.

"Demon-spawn! Get thee away into the dark hole from whence thy came. I command thee in the name of the Seven Greater Gods! Leave, and do not stain this land with your presence ever again!"

Balor screamed a blood-curdling scream of raw terror and anguish as the bed rose off the ground.

Desperately, Gearoid repeated the words of the exorcism, louder and louder, until his throat burned with the effort. Still the cot hovered in the air, turning slowly in a widdershins direction.

"NOOOOOOOOOOOOOOOoooooooooooooovvvoo!" Balor roared. The tendons in his neck stood out as taut as harp strings.

A dark malevolence filled the room, bringing with it an evil stench of corruption, and a deep sound of mocking laughter could be heard coming from the bed.

The malice within that laugh caused Gearoid to stop. Terror ran up his spine as he looked at the ravaged face that once was Brother Balor. At the best of times the face was horrible to behold, but now... now, the evil creature within was clearly revealed for all to see. Gearoid gagged at the nightmare before him, turning away to emptying his stomach in revulsion.

"FOOLISH DRUIDS! YOU FEED ME WITH YOUR POWER, AND THEN YOU EXPECT ME TO SCAMPER AWAY LIKE SOME ... IMP!"

"Be gone!" Gearoid shouted, with desperation in his voice. The other monks had all fallen silent.

Again, the mocking laughter filled the room, and one by one, the leather straps snapped. Balor was released from his bindings.

"I AM NOT A FLY TO BE SWATTED AWAY! I AM THY WORST NIGHTMARE! WHO DOST THOU THINK THOU ART, MORTAL, TO MAKE DEMANDS OF ME?"

The cot landed with a resounding crash, shattering into pieces, and the candles flickered and went out.

The mocking face of the *Diabhal* gripped Gearoid's mind, and his eyes moved to the charcoal line before him as if of their own volition.

"THOU SHOULD HAVE AT LEAST DRAWN A PENTAGRAM, FOOLISH DRUID! THIS IS NOT STRONG ENOUGH TO CONTAIN ME!"

Gearoid reached out a hand to wipe away the line. Much though he fought against his own body's actions, he could not stop his hand from breaking the magical circle. All the time, the mocking laughter echoed around inside his terror-filled brain.

"ATTACK!"

As one, the gathered monks jumped into the melee, punching and kicking at each other, jumping on their fellow brothers and biting into their soft flesh. Gearoid watched in frozen horror as the monks' bludgeoned each other with berserk rage, but what terrified Gearoid the most was the looks of confusion upon the faces of his brothers. Although their bodies fought like the demons of the Nine Hells, the men were mere puppets being played by invisible strings, and all the time, the puppeteer lay on the broken cot, laughing manically.

Suddenly, a blow struck Gearoid on the side of the head, knocking him off his feet and making his head spin. He turned around and saw Brother Seamy, his oldest friend, wielding a cot leg as a makeshift club and swinging with all his might toward his head. Too late to move, even if he could control his limbs, all Gearoid could do was watch as the blow struck. Pain exploded in his head a moment before oblivion overtook him.

Chapter Nineteen: Cull's Wrath

Conal woke up feeling nauseated. A pounding headache tormented him, and his jaw ached. Trying to draw spittle into his sticky mouth, he tasted the sweet metallic taste of blood and the residue of vomit. Bleary-eyed, he shuddered and strained to rise from the cold stone floor. The pain and wooziness washed over him in waves. A groan slipped from his broken lips and he paused, while his body re-orientated to the world spinning around him. His tongue trailed around his sticky mouth until pain shot through his head. Conal had found a lose molar that was sensitive to the touch. He fought briefly against the urge to probe at it, knowing that the pain would come again, but still ... the urge was great.

Where was he? How had he got here? Where were Cull and Tal? Questions flitted through Conal's brain as he strained to remember. Giving up, he sighed and tried to open his swollen eyes. They were glued together, so he used his fingers to pry the lids apart, which brought a fresh bout of pain to his tormented brain. Blinking away the dried blood and tears, Conal attempted to focus. Colours and forms blurred and took shape as he stared at the ground beneath him. What he saw made his stomach lurch. The scent of last night's regurgitated residue filled his nostrils. His stomach lurched as he gasped for clean air, but none was to be found in his current environment. Rolling over to move away from the gross remains of his night's drinking, Conal groaned loudly. Vague recollections of the evening before returned, only confirmed by the dark ceiling and barred doorway of the cell in which he now found himself.

"Hold ya whisht!" a guttural, whisper warned. "Ye'll bring da Nobblers down on our 'eads!"

Conal wiped his mouth on his grimy sleeve and struggled into a sitting position, which caused another bout of torture from his tormented body. He ached from parts of his body that until now, he hadn't even known existed. "By the Seven, what happened?"

"It must've been a grand night, lad," wheezed another voice. "It looks like it ended on a sour note though, eh, young 'un? You were well and truly knobbled by their Majesties' finest. They gave ye a right going over."

"I need a drink!" Conal croaked. He had never suffered so much from the ill-effects of a night's excessive drinking.

"Don't ya think ya had enough of it last night, lad? The Dagda knows, you must be a glutton for punishment," wheezed the second voice, and then it cackled with manic laughter.

"Keep it down or ye'll bring da Nobblers down on our 'eads," the first voice warned again.

"What're the Nobblers?" Conal asked, clasping his head to ease the pounding.

"You're not from dese parts, I take it?" wheezed the second voice. "Da Nobblers are the local gaolers. It's an affectionate term," he laughed at his own joke. "T'was dem dat gave ye de hammering I'd bet, or at least t'was dem dat finished ya off."

Flashes of the night before came back and a sudden realisation hit him. Cull was bound to find out about this, and he was going to throw a serious wobbler. "By all the gods, I'm dead meat!" Conal hung his head between his knees, wanting to curl up and die.

"Ye just feel that way. Remember lad, if ye can feel da pain then you're still in the land of the living. Even Macha wouldn't be cruel enough to make ye suffer. Only Deanna gives us that sweet blessin'," the second voice blasphemed from the darkness.

"Where's Tal?" Conal groaned. "Have you seen my friend?"

"KEEP THA' NOISE DOWN!" The yell came from outside of the cell. "IF WE 'AVE TA COME IN DER, YE'LL ALL REGRET IT!"

Conal flinched, as the shout echoed through his overburdened skull like a canyon wall.

One of the other occupants of the cell shuffled closer, and Conal looked over at him. The small, skinny man wheezed through a grin full of rotting teeth. "Would ye be looking for yon lanky-legged fella with da fancy clothin'? He's lying over yonder in dat corner, but he's still out for da count." The man pointed over toward the darkest shadows.

"Hold ya whisht or ye'll get us all mangled."

The skinny man placed his finger to his lips and motioned Conal away from the cell door, leading him farther into the cavernous dungeon, to where Taliesin lay in a heap.

Nodding his thanks, Conal inspected his friend before shaking him awake. "Tal!" he hissed. "Tal, wake up!"

Taliesin's groan was quickly stifled by Conal's hand.

"Shush, Tal, keep it down!"

A few moments later, they heard the sound of hobnailed boots from beyond the barred door. From the sound of it, a number of heavyset men were moving toward the dungeon.

"Oh! Cack in me kilt, we're in for it now!" The skinny man looked around nervously for a hiding place. There was no such place within the cell. They froze like rabbits in the torchlight as keys rattled in the cell door.

The skinny man let out a low whimper when the iron door clanged open with a loud shriek, causing Conal to wince again. The first of the Nobblers marched into the room, holding his torch high before him. He was heavily built, stubble-chinned and dressed in grease-smeared studded leather armour and an iron pot-helmet. His mean, beady eyes searched the prisoners with a threatening glare, before he moved aside to let his companions enter. One hand held a torch high, while his other held a long blackjack, which he swung back and forth like a pendulum to intimidate the prisoners.

"Which one of ye cretins is Tal?" the Nobbler demanded.

Conal flinched when he heard Taliesin's name. He looked from the gaoler to his semi-conscious friend. Realising that subterfuge would get him nowhere, he hoped for the best. "He's over here, sir, though he's a bit groggy."

"Ye must be da other wee dross bag we wuz lookin' fur, da Connor one?" the Nobbler grunted.

For a moment Conal nearly corrected the gaoler, before slowly nodding.

The Nobbler signalled his partner forward. Another stood in the doorway, his features hidden in the shadows. The torchbearer looked briefly over at the shadowy figure and received a nod of assent.

"Right, ye two, on ya feet!" he growled. The other Nobbler poked Conal hard in the ribs, motivating him into action. Taliesin needed assistance to stand and wobbled precariously as they followed the torchbearer out of the cell. The other Nobbler locked the cell and followed along behind, prodding the prisoners in the back to goad them along the passageway.

Only at the end of the corridor, where the passageway ended in a wide room, did Conal finally see the features of the shadowy figure. His heart dropped as his gaze met Cull's furious eyes.

"You're lucky I didn't leave you in there to rot," Cull growled.

The Nobbler laid his truncheon on the scarred table. "Are dese da ones ya wur lookin' fur, Sire?"

"Aye," Cull replied, handing over a heavy purse. "I hope this donation to the retirement fund settles matters, Sergeant."

The Nobbler hefted the purse and smiled through dirty teeth. "Dat oughtta do it." His partner unlocked the outer door of the prison. "Tis bin a pleasure doin' bus'ness wiff ya, Milordship," he said with a slight doffing of his helmet.

Cull grunted and walked out, leaving Conal and Taliesin standing in the room.

"Well?" the Sergeant prompted. "What're ya waitin' fur? Are you goin', or do'ya wanna stick around fur breakfast?" His tone suggested that breakfast was not an especially pleasant experience.

Half-carrying the bard, Conal hurried through the open door before the Nobblers changed their minds. They blinked as the bright morning sunshine hit their faces and tried to shade their eyes from the light.

"Cull, wait up!" he yelled to the disappearing back of the beggar. Even from behind, the Prince could see the anger in Cull's shoulders as he stomped away. Conal hefted Taliesin a little higher, and the two of them shuffled along after him.

Taliesin was slowly recovering, and by the time they reached the tavern, he could walk unassisted. They reached the sleeping quarters and found Cull angrily stuffing clothing into his travel bags.

Conal felt that something needed to be said "Cull, I ..."

Cull interrupted him with a glare that would curdle milk. "Whatever it is your about to say, lad, save your breathe. I don't want to hear it. Now, get your things together. We're leaving."

Taliesin groaned at the prospect of riding, but refrained from protests, knowing that it would only make matters worse. Conal nodded and moved to his bunk. As he packed his belongings, he wondered how long he would have to wait before Cull started shouting. He was fairly sure that shouting would be inevitable at some point in the near future, but the waiting was getting on his nerves. Much though the thought of Cull's angry yelling caused the youth to shudder, the silence was even worse. It was like waiting for a storm to break. The tension in the air was oppressive, and he knew that it would only get worse before the first clash of thunder erupted.

They stomped down the stairs in silence, Cull leading the way with resolute strides that just bellowed his fury, much more so than words ever could. Within moments, they were trotting through the streets of *Ard Pect*, the horses' hooves echoing loudly off the cobbles.

Cull kept up the bone-jarring pace for most of the morning, the pace only heightening the effects of his silent torture. Finally, he slowed to a walk, though Conal was sure that this was more for the benefit of the horses than out of sympathy for either Taliesin or himself.

Conal shivered, gritting his teeth against the biting wind as they headed into the mountains. This time they used the King's Highway, occasionally stepping off the road to allow charioteers to pass. The loud rattle of their iron-shod wheels left a dull ache in Conal's head.

Thirsty and aching all over, he grimly followed Cull, hoping that eventually he would get it out of his system. He hoped it wouldn't take too long, but Cull didn't speak for the rest of the day. The next day was just the same. Cull continued the gruelling pace through the mountain pass toward the border. Cull spoke quietly to the border guards, before slipping them a fat purse. Passing from *Tir Pect* into Dragania was of little concern to the border patrols. They were there to keep invaders from entering *Tir Pect*. In reality, even this was improbable, given the small size of the unit stationed on the border. Mainly, they collected the King's taxes from those entering *Tir Pect*. Still, there were always awkward questions that could have been asked. It would be better to grease the wheels of bureaucracy and avoid unnecessary delays.

They slept that evening, huddled in their cloaks against the bitter wind that swept up through the mountain pass from the plains below. Cull remained sullenly silent as he had been throughout. Even when they had crossed into Dragania, Cull's only words were brief taciturn commands. During the entire journey, Cull had hardly spoken more than a dozen words and his oppressive presence kept Conal's and Taliesin's nerves on edge.

When they finally reached the road leading toward Dragon's Ridge, Cull reined in his horse. They were all weary from their journey, and Conal was looking forward to the relative comfort of his half-built *Dun*, so he was surprised that Cull had stopped.

"I'm leaving you here, Conal ..." Cull declared wearily. "With a bit of luck, you'll live long enough to learn some cop-on, but I'm tired of being your wetnurse. I've got better things to do."

"Cull ..." Conal began, hoping to talk him round, but Cull raised a hand.

"Don't bother, Conal. I can't blame you for wanting a little fun and I know it hasn't been easy for you. It was stupid of me to leave you to your own devices, but I can't deny that I'm disappointed," Cull sighed. "Anyhow, it doesn't matter. You don't need me anymore. Lord Boare's too busy licking his wounds, Dubhgall the Black is dead, and King Conchubhar is content in *Ard Pect*, so there's no real danger to you. Another moon or so and the snows will thaw. You'll be able to ride south to the Gathering of the Clans and participate in your Rites of Manhood. After that, you'll officially be a man. By Brehon law, you can be declared the Lord of the Dragons. In the meantime, you've a fort to build and I'm sure that the Grand Marshal can keep you safe. He seems more than capable. Go with the blessing of the Seven. I've business elsewhere that I've been putting it off for far too long."

Cull turned his horse toward the road, intending to be beyond the Broce Woods before nightfall.

"Where are you going, Cull?" Conal asked.

"...Manquay, of course. Broll is dying, and I should be by his side."

"But I need you, Cull!"

Cull stopped and turned to face the youth. "No ... you don't. You need to grow up and shoulder your responsibilities. One day, you'll be a king. You'll blunder along, make some mistakes and hopefully you'll learn to fill your father's boots. Don't worry about it. We all make a few mistakes along the way. Just try not to start any wars if you can."

"Cull, wait!"

"I'll see you at the spring fair, Conal. Take care of him, Taliesin." Cull didn't look back when he kicked his horse into a trot and rode south.

Conal watched Cull disappear in sullen silence.

"We really let him down this time, didn't we?" Taliesin murmured.

Conal sighed, a grim look on his face. "Let's go find some dry clothing and a warm meal."

"That sounds good to me," Taliesin agreed. He was relieved to see that Conal was taking it so well.

Conal kicked his weary horse into motion. The sooner they got out of this wind, the better.

*****

A conference was called within Maerlin's mind, and Cora and Nessa were in attendance. They sat in the white room that Maerlin had created there. Some improvements had been made since Nessa had originally helped her construct it. It now had a pretty red door and some windows, which were decorated with floral curtains, not to mention the roaring fire in the hearth and the comfortable chairs that she had installed. Maerlin reasoned that if she was going to have a room in her head, then the least she could do was make it comfortable.

"...But it can't be the real Uiscallan," Cora objected. *"Uiscallan must be dead by now. By all the gods, she was around at the time of Conal's great-grandfather! She was already a well-respected Priestess of Deanna*

at that time. That'd make her at least eighty, more likely a full century in years! She can't be that. The Chief looks older than she is."

"You forget, Cora," advised Nessa. *"Those blessed by the goddess of life, Deanna, live longer than other people. Had I chosen to have children, they might all have passed to the Otherworld by now. Some say that it was for this bitter irony that her sister, Macha, allowed the blessing in the first place. Macha was always the patient one. She knows that we all go to her bosom in the end. Thus it was with my reincarnation, Macha was willing to agree to Deanna's wish and grant me an extension of my life, but there's always a cost for such things. Macha always gets what she wants eventually and by granting her sister's boon, she's gained my service in this life, too."*

Maerlin looked over at Nessa, and for the first time she noticed a change in her. She had become used to looking at Nessa as a magpie, so she hadn't noticed the change in her human form until now. With this talk of the goddesses doing a deal over her life, Maerlin finally noticed the change in her mentor. Where before, Nessa's hair had been grey-white with age, it was now more like her magpie self: piebald. The grey had turned snow-white with a raven-black patch flowing down her back from temple to temple. This was not the time to discuss the change in her mentor's appearance, however. *"So you think that Seabhac really is Uiscallan ... as in the Storm-Bringer, Uiscallan?"*

"It makes sense, Maerlin. Take, for example, her magical prowess. No normal Hedge-witch could ever reach such a level of proficiency without the proper training, and there's only one place she could have got that: the Holy Isle. Think about the things that she's taught you, Maerlin. They've been mainly dealing with Air Elementals. In fact, all the magic she's used has been Wild-magic, in one form or another. Damn it all! I should have seen this sooner. It's so obvious now!"

"She was the one who stopped the snowstorm ..." Cora admitted.

"What snowstorm?" Maerlin asked.

"The one you made as we were travelling north. You were having another one of your nightmares and we got smothered in a blizzard. Seabhac turned up and the snow stopped. I guessed at the time that she had something to do with it. I mean, she radiates power, doesn't she? I asked her about it and she told me to keep it to myself. So I never mentioned it."

"You kept something like that from me?" Maerlin demanded.

Cora shrugged. *"It all got kind of hectic! What with Conal leaving and then the magical training and stuff ... Sorry, Maerl, I just forgot."*

"Anyway, what's done is done. Do we all agree that from the look of it, Seabhac really is Uiscallan?" Nessa asked.

The novices nodded in agreement.

"So what's all this about your pendant?" Cora asked. *"The whole village seems to be a-buzz about it. I can't make any sense of it."*

"I honestly don't know, Cora. All I know is that it was my mother's most cherished possession. She wore it all the time. After the accident, my father hid it away, along with the rest of her stuff. He was grieving so much, that he probably didn't want to see it. Perhaps, he figured by hiding it, he would be saving me some of the loss too. I'd forgotten all about it until Nessa found it. Whatever the reason, they're not having it back. It's mine. It's all I have left of my mother."

"I don't think they intend to take it from you, Maerlin," Nessa assured. *"There's certainly more to this than meets the eye. The whole thing is one big mystery, but I'm sure we'll get to the bottom of it."*

"We haven't got time to waste on mysteries, Nessa. We need to find a way over the mountain and save my village. Whatever else, that comes first."

"Don't worry, Maerlin. I'm sure we'll get there in time to save it. A day or two isn't going to matter. It might even be of help. For one thing, we need to know exactly how Uiscallan is tied up in all this."

"Why didn't Ceila say anything to us?"

"I don't think that the priestesses even knew. They were as baffled by Uiscallan's disappearance as everyone else. One day, she was overlooking the coronation of the new High King, Luigheagh An Dragan, and the next; she'd disappeared off the face of Dragania. Many thought that she'd gone back over the sea to the Icy Wastes. Others thought that she had been slain by the Dark Mage. No one would've believed that she was living in a small cottage, just a few days ride from Dragon's Ridge."

"I'm going to ask her," Maerlin declared. *"I've had enough of all this secrecy. I think it's time that someone had it out with her."*

"Do you think that's wise?" Cora asked nervously.

"Cora has a point there," Nessa agreed.

"Well, she's coming over, and I'm not waiting any longer." Maerlin slipped out of her mental hidey-hole just in time.

"Not interrupting anything, am I?"

"No, Seabhac ... I mean Uiscallan, far from it. I was just coming to find you."

"...Really?"

"Yes. I think we need to talk. Don't you?"

Seabhac/Uiscallan sighed. "I guess so. I might as well be hung for a sheep as a lamb. Let's go find somewhere quiet." Uiscallan indicated one of the guest rooms that they could use.

Raising her head high and determined not to show her anxiety, Maerlin followed. She dreaded the coming meeting, but she didn't realise that the legendary Uiscallan dreaded it even more.

*****

It was hard for Abbot Gearoid to know at what point he woke up. The pain had been there even in his sleep, so that in itself was not an indicator of consciousness. It could have been the point at which he acknowledged the existence of pain, and groaned loudly, but maybe not? The groan, however, started the inevitable process toward consciousness, so it was as good a point as any.

Prising his one good eye open, he looked around. The other eye was swollen shut and marked with all the colours of the rainbow. The lurid bruise covered most of his face. Gearoid let out a second groan. Taking deep breaths to fight off the dizziness that threatened to send him back into the abyss, he gingerly sat up.

The infirmary was a mess. Bits of broken furniture lay scattered around the room. Some of the monks were gradually regaining consciousness, but he could see that some of his brothers were beyond hope. It was obvious, for example, that Brother Mihael had passed on to the Otherworld. The shattered bed-leg that was embedded into the socket of his eye, deep into his skull, was a clear enough indicator without seeing the death mask or smelling his soiled sackcloth. Gearoid felt the heavy burden of responsibility as he took stock of the room's inhabitants. Brother Seamy was lying unconscious with a large egg-shaped lump on his forehead and a split lip. Brother Ciaran lay beside him. His neck was twisted at an unnatural angle, and Gearoid feared the worst. Brother Niall and Brother Tomas were tangled together as if they had still been fighting when they had passed out. Both looked the worse for wear, but none of their injuries looked fatal. He thanked the gods that no sharp implements had been kept in the infirmary or there would have been more fatalities. As it was, they may get away with only the two deaths and some bruising and concussions. Brother Leonard was getting shakily to his feet at the far side of the room. Dried blood covered his face and his nose was badly broken, but such minor injuries could wait. That left only two monks unaccounted for: Brother Fionn, the youngest of the monks on the island, and Balor.

Getting slowly to his feet and supporting himself against the wall, Gearoid looked around frantically. "Fionn!" he called. No answer came from outside the room.

"Balor!" Still there was no response. *"Why did I agree to an exorcism?"* he thought. Just then, realisation dawned on him. *"Magic, of course, it was the damned magic. That was the key that unlocked the Darkness within Balor!"* Whenever Balor used magic, he had opened the door to the *Deamhan* within him, and they had tried to use magic to banish it. Instead, they had made it stronger!

"Stupid ... I've been so stupid!" He now realised that avoiding magic would have been the answer, but it was too late for that now. He must find Balor before any more deaths weighed down his soul, but where was young Brother Fionn?

"Brother Leonard," he commanded, shaking the other monk out of his stupor. "See what you can do about Seamy and the others. I need to look for Fionn and Balor. Oh, and get Seamy to fix that nose of yours, as soon as he's able. The longer it stays off-kilter, the worse it'll be." Gearoid hurried from the room, calling loudly as he went "Brother Fionn, Brother Balor."

Chapter Twenty: Family Ties

"Sit down, Maerlin. Hovering about like a demented robin isn't helping."

"What exactly am I supposed to call you?"

"Seabhac has worked just fine up until now. I don't see any reason to change that."

"But Iolar-Mara called you Uiscallan. Is he mistaken? He also called you his mother. What was that all about?"

"They're all just names, Maerlin, but I'd prefer to keep the name Uiscallan low-key, if that's at all possible."

"So you are Uiscallan then ... as in ... *The Uiscallan*, the legendary Storm-Bringer. Is that correct?"

"Legends are often so overrated as thou wilt soon learn."

"Stop avoiding the subject! I've been around priestesses of Deanna for long enough to not see when someone is avoiding an issue. A simple yes or no will suffice."

Seabhac's eyes sharpened with annoyance, but she reined in her temper. "Very well then, if it's such a big deal, the answer is yes ... I am."

"Damn it all to the Nine Hells!" Maerlin cursed. "Do you know what this means?"

"Watch thy language, Maerlin! It ill-becomes thee ..."

"Ill-becomes me! Have you any idea of the trouble I've been through this last year? Have you any idea of the dreams I've had concerning you? There's so much that I could have asked you about, had I known."

"Perhaps ... hindsight is all well and good, Maerlin, but I'm afraid thou art not seeing the full picture."

"You've got that right. There's a whole lot of this picture that I don't see."

Seabhac frowned, but Maerlin was too annoyed to notice.

"Thou must understand, Maerlin, that I've spent most of my life avoiding things. Had it not been for Fintan, I probably would have ignored thy storm, despite the damage it was doing to my garden. I've strived for a long time to ignore the world. Perhaps it would have been better for all concerned had I continued to do so."

"But we'd have been buried in a snowdrift!"

Seabhac paused, wisely refraining from the reply that sprouted to her lips. Instead, she asked "What is it exactly that thou would like to know, Maerlin? I shall do my best to enlighten thee, but I warn thee, knowledge comes at a cost."

A hundred different questions came into Maerlin's mind: mysteries about the Dragontooth, the expedition into the Icy Wastes, Dubhgall the Black, and *Clann Na Dragan*, but one thing was much closer to her heart. "Tell me about my pendant?"

Seabhac's lips tightened. "I knew from the first how sharp thy perception was. Thou hast asked the question which causes me the most pain."

"Where did it come from, and how did my mother get it?"

Seabhac held up her hand to hold off further questions. "Please, give me a moment. I'm not trying to avoid thy question, just collecting my thoughts. Very well! We'll start at the end of the tale rather than at its root, if that is thy wish. As thou said, the pendant came to thee from thy mother, and she in turn was given it by her own mother. Thus, it has been passed down through the generations. It is a family heirloom."

"...But what has that to do with Iolar-Mara?"

Again, Seabhac paused, composing herself for what was to come. "Thy mother was of the Hawk People. She was born in this very *Dun*. Iolar-Mara was married to thy mother's mother."

"What?"

"Did I not make that clear enough to thee? I said that he was married to thy grandmother ... thy mother's mother."

"Hang on a moment. He said that he was your son?"

"My son-in-law to be accurate, but yes ... he is."

"So ..."

"It's not that complicated, Maerlin. I'm sure that thou can work it out."

"So he's my grandfather ... is that what you're telling me?"

Seabhac gave a slight nod of her head.

"If he's my grandfather ... then that means ... by Dagda's sweet chestnuts!"

"Please try to keep the conversation polite, Macrlin. Thou hast been hanging around with the wrong sort for far too long."

"Sorry, but this is a lot to take in. Let me get this straight. That means that you're ... that I'm ..."

"Yes, Maerlin, I did warn thee that knowledge has a price. It was a shock to me too. It was far more of a shock than thou might realise."

"You mean that there's more?"

"Sadly, yes ... but that can wait for another day. I think we've both had enough surprises for the one day, don't thee?"

Maerlin was tempted to ask more, but the shock of what she had just learned had left her reeling. *I am the great-granddaughter of Uiscallan the Storm-Bringer,* she thought. *No wonder I've had so much trouble with storms! Not to mention all those damned dreams about Uiscallan. Just wait until I tell Cora about this.*

*****

Cull rode into Manquay as the sun was setting. He was soaked to the bone and aching all over from his long ride. His horse was in an even worse condition, and he would be lucky if its wind wasn't broken from the exertion, but he was finally home. Dropping the horse off at a stable, Cull walked the last mile. He needed to shake off the stiffness in his limbs and get a feel for the city again before seeing Broll.

He needed time to become reacquainted with the city, familiarise himself with the subtle changes since his departure, and slip back into his persona as Cull the Beggar. He had been away for far too long, and despite the grime and the winter dreariness, he had missed Manquay.

He noticed that the Boarites had become more frequent, and the city's Watch were less predominant. Lord Boare had obviously consolidated his position in the second largest city in Dragania since Cull's departure. Rather than bringing his troops all the way home to Suilequay after his incursion into the lands of *Clann Na Dragan*, Lord Boare had left a formidable force behind in Manquay. The recent breakouts from the gaol had obviously caused repercussions.

Cull shambled along the cluttered streets, slowly morphing into a beggar despite the lordly clothing he still wore. Granted, his clothing was not at its finest after so long in the saddle, but it was more than just this. It was Cull's ability to blend into the foreground. His gait subtly altered as he walked, changing from the businesslike, purposeful strides of a gentleman of the city into the shambling movements of a beggar. This slowly changed during the time it took to walk one mile. His shoulders slumped, and his face took on a dejected, disinterested air that made him all but invisible within the bustle of the city.

By the time he reached his destination, a nondescript dead-end alley, passers-by would not have recognised him as the same man who had dismounted his horse a short while earlier.

He shuffled along, occasionally stopping to rifle through the debris in the gutter, as if in no particular hurry. Finally, he reached the opening that led into the inner sanctum and stopped, slipping into the concealing shadows and waiting. Time passed. Only when he was satisfied that no one was watching him did he activate the secret door and slip into the darkness beyond.

Finding the peephole, he slid the clasp aside and peered out, waiting another few moments. When he was sure that the coast was really clear, Cull searched his pockets and struck a match against the rough stone wall. He released the peephole and turned slowly around.

In the sudden flare of light, he grinned at the assassins that he knew would be waiting. So silent had they been that he had not even heard them breathe, but they had been expected, and he showed no concern over the naked blades they clasped. Cull carefully removed his broad-brimmed hat, so that his features were clearly visible in the light of the match. This was not a time for mistaken identities.

"Welcome home, Cull. It's been too long."

As the match burned down, Cull dropped it, pitching the room into darkness. "Tell me about it."

One of the Black Daggers opened a lantern to light the way, and Cull followed the assassin down a long passage. Two more of the shadowy assassins dropped from the rafters as they came to a pair of double doors. Again, Cull cautiously removed his hat until all were satisfied with his identity, before being admitted. He admired the quiet efficiency of Manquay's Assassins' Guild.

Leaving his hat off, he waited, allowing the Black Daggers to slip back into the shadows while Cull was left holding the lantern. Then, he knocked on the door.

Stepping back two paces he waited, holding the lantern high to reveal his features. Again he waited, while he was scrutinised and examined, and then the double doors clicked open and he was allowed to enter. He stepped into a small antechamber, where another set of doors stood closed, opposite the first set. The room was lit with sconces, but otherwise it was bare. Cull knew about the hidden dangers within the room, and again he waited. Finally, the doors shut behind him. This was the signal to proceed to the inner sanctum. As he neared the opposite doors, they opened to admit him into a well-lit room with a large table surrounded by chairs. Unusually, he found the room was silent and deserted. None of the Beggar-lord's minions were in attendance.

Cull placed his hat back on his head and walked through the room, relaxing now that he was within the inner sanctum. The varied masks and subterfuges slipped away. Here was the one place he could be himself. Stepping onto the slightly raised dais at the end of the room, he reached a small door and knocked softly, before entering the chamber beyond.

Although he had been expecting the worse, the smell that assailed him as he entered the bedchamber still shocked him. The room was filled with the stench of disease, and death lurked near to hand. The room was dimly lit by candlelight. Incense burned on the table nearby, but it failed to deal with the cloying reek of sickness. Lying as if already dead, was a reed-thin figure, outlined within the heavy quilting on the bed.

"Is that really you, Cuilithe?" Broll wheezed. His voice had become weaker since they had last spoke.

Tears welled up in Cull's eyes. "Aye, it's me, Broll. You look like shite!"

A raspy chuckle came from the emaciated man, followed by a hacking cough. Cull hurried over to help him sit up and reached for the spittoon. He could feel the bones sticking through Broll's skin, where once there had been thick cords of muscle. Looking at the blood-filled phlegm only confirmed his worst fears.

"You always did have a way with words, Cuilithe. It's good to see you again. I wasn't expecting you back until springtime. What happened? Did your mission fail?"

"Don't worry, Broll, the lad's in safe hands. He has a small army at his beck and call, and the Brocians standing between him and Lord Boare. He'll come to no harm during what's left of the winter. Your promise to his father will be kept."

"So what brings you back?"

"Let's call it intuition, that and a little frustration, perhaps. I sensed things were not going well here, and clearly I was right. Why didn't you send me a message?"

"To say what exactly, Cuilithe, come home and watch me die?" Broll growled. "No one should have to go through what I'm going through, but it's even worse to sit helplessly by and watch another going through it. I wouldn't wish that on any man." Another coughing fit attacked him, and their conversation lapsed into silence while he fought his way through it. Finally, he sighed and lay back against his pillows. "So tell me all about it. Your reports have been succinct to say the least."

"I'm sure you know most of it already without me having to fill you in. You do have the best spy network in Dragania, not to mention the network that Sile has in *Tir Pect*. Surely you don't need a blow by blow account from me?"

"Does it look like I'm busy doing something else, Cuilithe?"

Cull looked around the deserted bedroom and remembered the empty antechamber beyond. "Now that you mention it, no, I guess not. Where is everyone anyway?"

"I've sent them away. They were wrecking me head!"

"Why, by the Nine Hells, did you do that?"

"I couldn't even die in peace with that racket going on," Broll grumbled. "It was like a bleedin' circus out there. That's to say nothing of all the well-wishers. I was sorely tempted to let the Black Daggers loose on the lot of them."

"So who's running things now?"

"No one in particular, I guess. They can manage their own districts without much interference from me, as you well know. They've done so for years, so there really isn't a problem. Once a week, I call a meeting and they prattle on for a few bells, while I sleep on my throne. Then, they potter off back to their homes. If there's something that needs to be done, I pass a message on and make sure it gets done. Other than that, I leave them to it."

Cull nodded.

"Oh, don't worry, Cuilithe. I've a heap of reports to fill you in, a bleedin' room full of the damn things to be accurate. You're not missing anything. If you ever get the time to read them all, that is. So now that you've finished changing the subject ... are you going to tell me about your little adventure or what?"

Cull smiled. He was glad to see that Broll still had a sharp tongue, despite his sickness. His mind was still as sharp as ever. "Where do you want me to start?"

"I've always liked the beginning for some reason, call me old fashioned. It's not as if I've somewhere else to be. Think of it as a bedtime story."

"Very well then, if you insist ..."

*****

Conal was rudely awoken by a foot in the ribs. Bleary-eyed, he looked up and scowled at Taliesin. "Remind me to fire you later!"

"You'd have to start paying me first, your Highness. That's usually part of the agreement. You hire someone to do some work for you, and then, you pay them their wages so that they can feed themselves and buy stuff that may or may not be useful to them. If you get fed up with them, then and only then, do you fire them. You've missed a few steps along the way, Conal."

"I was just saving time and skipping to the best bit," Conal declared, before pulling the covers back over his head.

The boot in the ribs was firmer this time.

"Ouch! What was that for? If I had an executioner, you'd be walking on thin ice right now."

"You'd have to pay him first. Should I just go out and cut my own head off? I could send you the bill afterwards."

Resigning himself to being awake, Conal looked balefully at Taliesin. "Was there a point to this conversation?"

"There are two, actually."

Conal waited. Clearly, Taliesin was out to annoy him this morning. "And what would they be ...?"

"The first is to make sure that you're fully awake as I know that you'd turn over and go back to sleep if we didn't have this little chat ..."

"... And the second?"

"Ah, yes ... the second. Well, seeing as Cull isn't here any longer to look out for you ..."

"You mean pester, nag, and generally bully me into doing things that he wants me to do ..."

"Exactly! Well, seeing as he isn't here to pester, nag, and generally bully you into doing things that should be done, then I figured somebody else has to ..."

"Someone else has to what exactly?"

"...Get you to do what needs to be done, of course. Let's face it, there isn't anyone else around here that'll do it, is there? They're all too pleased to have their beloved *Dragan* Prince back. None of them want to rock the boat ... but Cull was right. You need to start facing up to your responsibilities, and since it's partly my fault that Cull left, I feel that it's up to me to take up the slack."

"Tal ... Did somebody hit you on the head?"

"No ... why?"

"I can arrange it if you'd like? I'm pretty sure I can do that."

"Not until you start paying them their wages, you can't."

"You're getting an awful fixation on money, you know. It can't be good for your health."

"Ah, you see! That's the sort of thing I'm talking about. If you're going to rebuild this sorry excuse for a fortress, then you're going to need to start thinking about commerce and all of that. Those sorts of things don't handle themselves you know, and I'm sure that someone, somewhere, is making a tidy profit from your ignorance. For instance, let's take all the horses out in the paddocks, and the sheep and cattle for that matter... have you looked into what they've earned you yet? Before the spring fair, you'll need to have all of that sorted out. Once you get to the fair, you'll be far too busy to handle those details yourself, which brings me to another point, and the real reason why I got you up so early."

"Finally ... we get to the point. I'm all ears."

"Well ... you've been lolling around here for over a week now. As you know, I've never been one for physical exercise, but I'm not the one who has my Rites of Manhood coming up. To put it bluntly, you'll need to put on a good show at the trials if you're going to drum up support for your kingship, and you aren't going to do that if you're huffing and puffing after the first mile of the big run."

"Taliesin, I'm the only heir. It's not as if I'm going to have a younger brother come along and boot me off my throne."

"Conal! As your friend, let me just say ... don't be such a cloth-eared, spawny-eyed prat. You know full well what I mean. It's not *Clann Na Dragan* that I'm worried about. It's the throne of the High King. You'll need powerful friends to keep Lord Boare at bay while you rebuild your kingdom. Otherwise, come springtime, this place will be swarming with Boarites again. You can't rely on the Brocians to keep them away. You need to win the respect of the other Clans."

Conal blinked in surprise. He had never heard Taliesin say anything like this before. The bard was usually too busy composing sonnets to worry about his next meal. With a sigh, he threw back the covers and started searching under the bed.

"What *are* you doing?" Taliesin asked, after watching him for a few moments.

"I'm looking for my socks. I had them on last night."

"Why don't you wear a clean pair?"

Conal's hand came up with a threadbare blue patterned sock. "It's alright, I've found one!" A further rummage found another sock. This one was red and rather longer than the first.

"Conal, your chambermaid puts your laundered socks in that small cupboard over there."

"She does! Since when?" Conal got up and flipped open the cupboard. "That's a stupid place to put them!"

Taliesin shook his head. "As opposed to storing them with your bellybutton fluff collection under your bed, is that it? Conal, you really need to get your act together. Get some socks on, and we'll go and see Declan. I'm sure he can arrange a suitable training regime to get you fit."

Conal sighed and silently relinquished his life of luxury. Taliesin seemed determined to make up for Cull's departure, and knowing Declan, he'd be only too happy to oblige.

Chapter Twenty-One: The Seven Greater Gods

"We've searched everywhere, and there's no sign of them, Gearoid. With the currach missing, we can only assume that they've left the island. It's no use, Gearoid, they've gone," Brother Seamus reported.

"Then we'll have to follow them ..."

"But they could be anywhere! How are we going to find them? Anyway, they've stolen our only boat."

"Then we'll just have to make a raft, won't we? I'm sure we could use some of the empty mead barrels and remove a couple of doors to make a suitable raft. We can't just let them go! They need our help."

"Gearoid, this is a fool's mission," Seamy protested.

"Seamy, our brothers are in trouble. Would you leave them in peril? I know you think Brother Balor is responsible for this, but he's not to blame. He begged us to stop that exorcism, and we ignored him. We fed fuel to the *Darkness* within his soul, and we: you and me, Seamy, and we cannot deny our responsibility for this. As for Brother Fionn, he was always the most sheltered of our flock. We can't just leave them in the hands of this *Deamhan.*"

"But we don't even know where they've gone ..."

"Power is always attracted to power, Brother Seamy. You should know that. He'll head for *Ard Pect*. It's the most logical choice. That's where I'll find them."

Seamy nodded.

"Someone will need to watch over our monastery while I'm gone. Brother Leonard is far too old to go on this expedition. I'm going to take Brother Niall and Brother Tomas with me, and we'll row across to the mainland. We'll return as soon as we've retrieved our lost sheep. In the meantime, Seamy, I'm leaving you in charge."

"What! You can't leave me here to look after Brother Leonard. I should come with you."

"Seamy, you're my second in command, so please obey me in this. I have to go, but we cannot leave Brother Leonard here alone. Someone has to tend to the animals or they'll all starve. You know as well as I do that he'll get lost in his books. He forgets to eat if he's left to his own devices!"

"There has to be another way?"

Clasping his friend's shoulder, Gearoid looked him in the eyes. "There isn't, Seamy, believe me. This is the only way, but first, we need to lay Brother Ciaran and Brother Mihael to rest. Come, we have graves to dig, and the day isn't getting any longer. Have Brother Niall and Brother Tomas start work on the raft while we dig. When we've finished, we'll ring the bell to call the others together and I'll speak to them all. Together, we'll say our final farewells to our lost brothers, and after supper, we can pack a few supplies and be ready to leave at first light."

*****

It took a long time for Maerlin to fall asleep as she was restless from all that she had learned. Eventually exhaustion overtook her, and she slipped into sleep.

She awoke in a darkened bedchamber lit by a single candle that flickered softly. In the bed lay the ravaged body of an old man. His face was a ragged mask of pain, and he was fighting for every breath. Sleeping in a chair beside the bed was another man. His face was hidden by a broad-brimmed hat that Maerlin knew well. She gasped with surprise. "Cull?"

He slept on. He was too exhausted from the long days of travelling to wake.

The man in the bed opened his eyes and stared directly at Maerlin. "Ah, finally, you've come at last."

"Excuse me?"

"I said you've come at last ... though I must say that you're a little younger than I'd have expected. Anyway, it doesn't matter. I'm ready whenever you are ... as ready as anyone has ever been."

"You can see me?"

"Of course I can see you, though frankly, you don't live up to my expectations. I was imagining someone a little ... bigger ... scarier perhaps. Still, I guess when you've gone through as much as I have, even death holds no fear. I can't help saying though ... I'm a little disappointed."

"Disappointed? Sorry, I'm confused."

"Well, I mean... I'm a humble man, despite all that I've achieved, but I'd have thought you could have put a bit more effort into it. Forgive my bluntness, but hey ... what are you going to do, kill me?"

"What are you talking about?" Maerlin demanded.

The old man waved a hand in Maerlin's general direction to indicate his distaste. "This ... the whole ensemble, the innocent little girl look, you know! Personally, I think it's in poor taste. I mean, I might not have been the best person in the world and I certainly did some bad things in my time, but hey, what choice did I have? I had to do the best I could with my limited resources. Nevertheless, I would've thought that I'd deserve at least some effort on your part, given my standing in the community. I never forgot to pay you proper respect in my prayers, and I never showed any preference toward the others. Each to their own was what I always said. Better to be neutral and give each, his or her due. So, although I'm not surprised to see you here, nay, in fact I'm more than ready to go ... still, I would've expected a bit more effort!"

Maerlin felt a cool breeze behind her and a sense of power filled the room, but she was too distracted by the sick man's ramblings. "What are you babbling on about?"

His face paled even more, if such a thing was possible. His eyes widened. "Oh, by the Holies!"

Maerlin realised that he was no longer looking at her, but rather, he was looking beyond her, to something behind her. She turned around and blinked in surprise. Standing there were two women. Their faces were so similar that they must have been related. They looked like sisters. There, however, the similarity ended. One was blonde while the other's hair was raven-black. Their long flowing robes reflected their appearance. One was dressed in satin robes of alabaster, while the other was wrapped in the shadows of midnight.

225

"It's time, Sister," declared the fairer one. "I bequeath him to thy bosom. May he find peace in the Hall of Heroes for he was truly a king amongst men." Stepping forward, the lady kissed the old man's forehead and spoke to him "Thou hast served me well, Broll, Lord of the Beggars, may thou find succour within my sister's arms."

She turned to Maerlin and smiled warmly. "Maerlin, thou must remain strong in the times ahead. Do not get lost in the past, but look instead toward thy future, for here lays thy fate." With a slight popping sound, Deanna disappeared.

The darker sister stepped forward and took the sick man's hand. "It is time," she declared softly, and a gentle smile lit up Broll's face.

"A blessing upon thee, Macha."

The goddess gently helped Broll rise from the bed, and for a moment, Maerlin saw double. One Broll was lying peacefully on the bed with a soft smile on his lips while his twin was standing beside the goddess of death. Then with a soft popping sound, Macha and the shade of Broll disappeared.

*****

Blessed by Deanna, Maerlin's worries and unanswered questions slipped away, and she slept soundly for the rest of the night. When she awoke, feeling revitalised, she reached out to Nessa with her mind, a task that was now as familiar as normal speech.

"Ness?"

"Mmm, yes dear. What is it?"

"I saw the goddesses last night."

"What?" Nessa coughed up the dried blackberry that she had been eating, trying not to choke. *"What did you just say?"*

"I said that I saw the goddesses last night: Deanna and Macha. They were in my dream."

"Tell me all about it. It sounds important."

Maerlin told her about her dream.

"So Broll has finally passed away," Nessa murmured. *"I'm sure it'll be hard on Cull, but it's for the best. The poor man has suffered a lot over the last few years. May he be well feasted in the Hall of Heroes."*

"The thing is, Ness, I'm a little confused."

"What about...?"

"I'd always pictured Macha as evil, but she seemed quite nice, in a dark sort of way. So I thought I'd better ask you about it. I'm still a bit confused. How is it that you can serve two goddesses?"

Nessa smiled. *"I sometimes forget that with your isolated upbringing, your knowledge of the Gods is as limited as your knowledge of the country's politics. Let me explain. There are Seven Greater Gods, Maerlin, and most people worship all of them equally. Think of them as seven faces on a jewel. Each is a part of the whole, but their true strength lies in the complete jewel. Each of the Seven has their own strengths and weaknesses. Deanna, the goddess of life, is naturally held in high esteem. Mankind has a strong urge to live, but even life can sometimes be a two-edged sword. Take Broll for example. He lived a long and fruitful life, but over the last few years he's been in a lot of pain as his body slowly wasted away. Death might have been a kinder option for him. Deanna still had need of him, so Macha agreed to wait. Such things, however, always come at a price or we'd all live to a great age. Macha is the goddess of death. Most people fear death, and therefore, she sometimes gets misrepresented, but in nature, life, death, and rebirth are all part of a natural cycle. If we take winter for example, it's a classic example of death within nature, but this death is essential for the rebirth in springtime. It is for this reason that we celebrate Imbolc. This is when the first signs of life emerge, after the death we suffered in winter. The first shoots of grass pop up and the spring flowers emerge. The ewes start to wax and produce milk in readiness for the first lambs of the season. If we examine a compost heap, it is filled with death and with rotting things, and yet from it, we obtain healthy, vibrant soil. It is full of the essentials of life ... as well as some juicy worms for me to eat."*

"So Macha isn't evil?"

"No more than the mountain wolves are evil, or the cunning fox. When a pack of wolves attacks a herd, they look for weakness within it and cull it

out, enabling the strength of the herd to prosper. The death they wield brings strength to the herd. To the farmer who has lost a lamb, this might seem a little harsh, but it's just part of the laws of nature. It helps to maintain the balance. No, Macha is not evil, far from it. Her gift is essential, and she, like Deanna, does what needs to be done, but we are mere mortals and sometimes we fail to see the bigger picture. Who are we to judge the gods?"

"Then why do the priestesses of the Holy Isle only worship Deanna?"

"We honour and respect all of the Seven, Maerlin, but we have chosen to be servants of Deana. Some of us have been given a special blessing from Deanna, in order to aid her in our service. We are blessed by her. That doesn't mean that we dislike the other gods. It merely means that we are the tools of Deanna's will. Each of the gods has servants to do their will, as well as those who dedicate their lives to all the gods equally, the Seven Greater Gods and the many minor deities."

"You mean there are others?"

"Of course there are! The very mountain that stands before us is a god, but its influence is limited and, therefore, so too is its worship."

"But that's silly! It's just a mountain, Nessa."

Nessa sighed. "Have you forgotten the first lesson that I taught you?"

Maerlin bit her lip. "No, Ness, 'What we see isn't always there and what we can't see, still exists'... but it's still just a big lump of rock, isn't it?"

"Maerlin, I remember you saying the same thing about a certain tree. Can you remember that?"

"Yes, Nessa."

"And was I right when I told you that it was much more than a mere tree?"

"You were," Maerlin admitted.

"Then believe me when I tell you this. The mountain which dominates the skyline and stands as king of the world is much more than a mere lump of rock. As an Earth-sister, I can feel its presence, in the same way as you *and Seabhac can sense the coming of a hurricane. It is an immense power and not to be trifled with. Should it fully awaken from its slumber, the earth would tremble and shake as it stirred. We'd be knocked about like autumn leaves in a storm. I can sense, deep within its belly, a rage so fearsome that it makes me weak just to think about it. It is not content to sit quietly and be forgotten! Should it ever break free of its bondage, the very sky would darken like an eclipse as it belched flames and noxious gases into the sky. Day would turn to night and liquid fire would burst forth. It would rain fire across the land for miles around. Liquefied rock would flow down from its mighty shoulders and engulf not only the villages of High Peaks and Eagles Reach, but much, much more! It would decimate every living thing on the mountain, and the fire would reach as far as Dragon's Ridge. The Broce Woods would burn to cinders and disappear. Believe me, Maerlin, when I tell you this. That mountain is no minor deity to be dismissed as a mere lump of rock! There is real power within it!"*

Maerlin was astonished by the passionate outburst, and she nodded her head in acceptance. *"I'm sorry, Nessa."*

"There's nothing to apologise for, Maerlin, but please remember this as your own power grows. It's always important to understand the repercussions of your actions and be aware that although you may hold immense power, you must be careful in its use. Seabhac's philosophy of using magic willy-nilly can sometimes lead to a lack of caution and errors of judgement can be made. As I have said on more than one occasion, there's always a price to pay for the use of power. Sometimes, we don't see the price until it is far too late. Now, I don't know about you, but I want to see the rest of this village while we're here. I'll need you along to ask questions for me."

"While we're on the subject ... how is your speech coming along?" Maerlin asked. She had spotted Nessa practising when she thought that no one was looking.

The magpie glared pointedly at her before admitting *"Not very well, since you insist on bringing it up."*

"Could the healers on the Holy Isle help? Have you spoken to Ceila?"

"Maerlin, we aren't all gifted with Dream-catcher abilities. Some of us have to use more traditional methods of communication, and the nearest of the Order's dovecotes is in either Manquay or Ard Pect. So no,

Maerlin, I haven't, but it's a good idea. However, that was part of the reason for taking a walk around the village this morning. I've heard that the Hawk Clan keep a wide variety of birds as pets, so with luck, we can garner some knowledge nearer to hand?"

"That sounds great. Let's go!"

*****

The chariot bounced wildly about as it raced across the open plain. The two stocky mares pulling it chewed on their bits in their eagerness to run. All Conal could do was hang on to the light wickerwork frame and keep from falling under the war-ponies' hooves. A sharp jolt buckled his knees and sent him reeling backward, only his tight grip on the reins stopped him from leaving the chariot altogether. In an attempt to slow down the frisky young mares, Conal pulled hard on one of the reins, pulling the chariot around in a tight arc. This manoeuvre created its own challenges, however, as the turn proved to be too sharp. Although the mares slowed, their momentum caused one of the wheels to lift precariously off the ground.

Quickly, Conal leapt to the side of the chariot, adding extra weight there to prevent the unruly vehicle from flipping over and crushing him underneath. The wheel refused to stay grounded and continued to spin freely as the chariot turned. Conal leaned as far out as he dared, until his face hovered inches above the iron-shod wheel. The whistling of the scythe-blades made him gulp as they whisked past his nostrils. Finally, the wheel thumped back to earth and the chariot righted itself with a bone-shaking shudder.

Before him, half a mile away, was the ancient hill known as Dragon's Ridge upon which sat his ancestral home. The still dilapidated fort, or *Dun,* was well on its way to being repaired. The mares, as if smelling the bucket of oats and fresh hay in their stables, picked up speed again and hurtled toward *Dun Dragan.* Conal hung on for dear life, knees bent to absorb as much of the shock as possible and to help maintain his balance. He hoped that he looked sufficiently regal as he approached the hill road up to the *Dun.* Thankfully, the steep ascent slowed the frolicsome horses down enough for him to regain his composure, and he was able to drive through the oaken gates with a small amount of dignity, at least, if you ignored the angry protests from the startled chickens.

When the world settled enough for Conal to step shakily down from the driving boards, his ears rang with the sound of laughter. Blushing furiously, he noticed that Taliesin and Declan were lounging against the paddock fence, grinning.

"I thought you said these ponies were broken?" Conal accused.

"No. Actually, what I said was that they were trained. I've never believed in breaking a horse. They need to keep their spirit if they're going to pull a war-chariot. You don't want them to be too timid," Declan corrected.

"No fear of that," assured Conal. "They're wilder than a couple of wolves. They wouldn't do anything that they were told!"

"It's all a matter of confidence. Horses can sense that sort of thing. They can feel it in the reins. I'm sure you'll get the hang of it, Sire."

"Are you sure there aren't a couple of quieter ones around that I could use ... at least to start with?"

"Taliesin said that you wanted the best. Those two are bred from King Conchubhar's own personal stables, and I'd wager that they're the fastest ponies in Dragania. If you're going to win the chariot race, believe me... it'll be with these beauties."

"That's if they don't kill me first!"

"If you train with them for two or three bells every day, you'll be ready by the time we get you to the spring fair. Give them another week and we'll start training you to throw javelins."

"I already know how to throw a javelin."

"Not while going flat out on the back of a bouncing chariot you don't."

"It'll take me at least a moon or more to learn that!"

"You haven't got that long, Sire, so you'd better learn fast. Should we aim for six bells of chariot work each day?" Declan suggested.

"How am I going to fit in everything else if I do that?"

"Less sleep ..." Taliesin answered, "... a lot less sleep. Speaking of which, you're late for your archery lessons."

Conal groaned and jogged off to where they had set up the targets, knowing that the Weapons-master hated tardiness. He was aching all over, and the sun had hardly reached its zenith. Taliesin had awoken him in the pre-dawn bells to ensure that Conal was ready for the first of the day's five-mile runs before having breakfast, and following that was two bells with the demented duo and the chariot. He still had to fit in a session of archery, sword, and spear work, before his evening run. Then he could grab something more substantial to eat and begin the arduous task of examining the taxation documents, which he had requested from Declan. He would be lucky if he managed to get his bed warmed before the bard woke him up again for tomorrow morning's run.

To make matters worse, he knew full well that Taliesin was slipping quietly back to bed to catch some more sleep, while Conal ran around Dragon's Ridge. At least Cull had the decency to run with him around the Holy Isle and Maerlin had joined them also, to make it more competitive. Running for miles alone in the bitter wind, while half-asleep, was not the most fun thing to do, but much though Conal was tempted to slink off and catch some shut-eye in an outhouse, he knew that Taliesin was right. He needed to work harder to prepare for the Gathering. So Conal stuck at it despite his weary muscles. He would not be the laughing stock of the Rites of Manhood.

The Rites of Manhood consisted of a number of arduous tasks, and each candidate elected to do as many, or as few, as he saw fit. However, the eyes of his peers, his Clan, and the rest of the spring fair, were watching and would judge his worthiness during these contests.

Some of the tasks relied on the candidate's strength, such as rock and caber tossing, while others involved stamina or skill, such as the Great Race and the archery bouts. There were also tests for the mental prowess of the candidates with cryptic puzzles, quizzes, and board games. Every possible aspect of a youth's character was examined during the Rites of Manhood, in an effort to truly gauge the young man's worth.

No candidate could compete in all the tasks. There simply wasn't the time, but the more tasks that a candidate completed successfully, or better still excelled in, the more respect he could earn amongst his peers.

Many of the legendary warriors of the land had first come to renown during their Rites of Manhood.

Because of the importance of the trials for Conal's future kingship, Taliesin and Declan had recruited a number of experts to train him during the remaining days of winter. Once the snows melted, it would be time to head south to Manquay. Due to its central location, Manquay always hosted the spring and autumn fairs on the large open plain to the east of the city.

Over the last number of years, Conal had been forced to watch the event from high on the city walls, hiding away from the many Boarites that attended the event. This would be the first year since his father's death that Conal would be able to attend the Gathering, but even within the fair there would be risks. Despite the strict Brehon laws that maintained the peace of the Gathering, there was always the risk of an assassin's blade in the dark of night. Hopefully, the combined force of *Clann Na Dragan* and *Clann Na Snochta Broce* would ensure Conal's safety during the journey and at the fair. Nevertheless, gaining the goodwill and respect of the other Clan leaders would be vital for Conal's future.

Chapter Twenty-Two: The King Is Dead, Long Live the King

Maerlin walked out of the guest quarters. Nessa was perched on her shoulder, and Cora followed in their wake as they greeted the first day of spring. It was still bitterly cold this high in the mountains, but the sun shone brightly as it crested over the shoulder of the immense mountain upon which the village stood. It reminded Maerlin of the morning prayers on the Holy Isle, and she stopped and raised her hands high in greeting to the sun god, Lugh, and to Deanna, the goddess of life.

Inspired by the bright morning, she began to sing, letting the joy of the occasion fill her.

"Come forth, father Sun. Bring light into the dark,

Cast away all shadows from the spirit and the heart.

Let your warmth and radiance bring a new and joyful day,

Where new life is everywhere and children laugh and play."

Nessa and Cora joined in, creating a harmony as they added their voices to hers.

"A Blessing to the goddess, Creator of the Earth,

Giver of all life and love, and everything of worth.

We sing the Song of Morning in praise for all you give,

Your blessing on our children and on the life we live.

The sun will rise each morning with you to guide his way,

Your hand will touch each petalled flower and show them the new day.

The fox beneath the hillside, will curl up, fast asleep,

Safe in the knowledge that the world is in your keep.

Birds awake and sing thy praise, in the glory of the dawn,

They sing in joyous thankfulness of the gift of a new morn."

The villagers had come out of their huts to hear the novices sing, and striding through them like a queen, was Seabhac. Fintan rode majestically on her shoulder. Her face glowed with joy as she joined them in the final verse.

"Each morning as the day breaks and the sun comes from the east

We praise the glory of thy gift and break our morning feast.

So it was in childhood and to this very day,

And will be forever. This, we hope and pray."

As the last echoes of the 'Dawn Chorus' drifted across the mountainside, the birds began to sing. Seabhac wiped tears from her eyes and embraced Maerlin. "Thank thee, daughter of my blood, for this unexpected gift. It has been far too long since I heard that song. I hadn't realised how much I had missed it. It's such a wondrous gift. I feel ashamed that I have nothing to give thee in return. Thank thee too, Cora and Nessa. I wish thee all a joyous Imbolc."

Maerlin had forgotten that today was Imbolc, and she remembered fondly the celebrations in her own village at the first signs of spring. "Seabhac, you've already given me so much. Don't you realise that?"

"I have?"

"You've given me a treasure beyond counting," Maerlin assured, looking around at the faces of the Hawk Clan. Their features were a reflection of her own face and that of her mother's. So much so that it hurt to look at them, and yet, it also gave her immense joy. "You've given me back a piece of my mother. I'd always wondered who she was, and where she came from, and you've given this to me. All through my childhood, I'd stood out. I felt like I didn't belong. I was different from the other children in High Peaks. I was shorter and darker than them. I never understood why. Now, I look around at the little boys and girls, playing in the snow, and I see myself in them and know that I finally belong. The blood of the Hawk People is strong in my veins. The blood of the Pects: my mother's blood, your blood, and maybe it took a vision of Deanna and Macha for me to see this, but I see it now. You've played no small part in this, Seabhac. My thanks to you also, Fintan, for being the guiding hand that brought us together. You are the grandparents that I never had."

Seabhac winced at being called a grandparent, but still the thought brought tears to her eyes and a lump to her throat. Sniffing to regain her composure, she said "Yes, well, enough of that! Today's a day of celebration, and Iolar-Mara insists that we honour the first day of spring here."

Maerlin looked at the formidable mountain that they needed to cross to reach her father's village. She felt an urgency to get there, but this urgency fought against her hunger to learn more about her mother's people. Hoping that High Peaks would be safe for one more day, Maerlin nodded her acceptance of the invitation.

Seeing her nod, the people of the village broke into celebrations. Soon, Maerlin and Cora were inundated with warm winter clothing and pieces of beautiful jewellery, each depicting some image of birds. Nessa was not forgotten either and soon complained of a swollen stomach from too many rich treats.

*****

A large crowd had gathered in the far corner of the cemetery despite the bitter wind that blew up from the river. Hundreds of raggedy-looking vagabonds of all shapes and sizes had come to the Pauper's Plot. They had come to pay their respects to a fallen hero. Many had walked for miles, as Manquay was a large city. No one would have stayed away if at all possible. These were the poor down-trodden masses that eked a living out of the city. They were the slum-dwellers, the sewer-men, harlots, beggars, rag-and-bone-men, and other lowlifes. They were the gel that bound this city together and greased the wheels of commerce. Even prominent members of the underworld attended. The heads of such guilds as the thieves, forgers, assassins, smugglers and so forth stood silently alongside the rest of the congregation, as a short prayer was said by Madame Dunne.

Cull and the other district leaders stood beside the small oblong hole that had been cut out of the near-frozen ground and looked down silently. The remains of Broll the Beggar-lord were wrapped in a simple canvas shroud, as befitted his station. No fancy coffin or headstone would mark his passing into the Otherworld. Such wrappings of power would not have been to Broll's taste. He had grown up amongst the slums, and his people were the poor who lived and died in them. Much though he had attained great power, he had always been a man of the people. His wealth was not to be spent on such trivia as an oaken casket, brass fittings, or a lump of engraved rock. It was to be used for a much greater purpose. Some of his garnered wealth trickled back down into the slums. Though the poor were not noticeably richer since he had established the Beggar's Guild, their mortality rate had significantly improved. Much more of his accumulated wealth had been used in his subtle control of the status quo.

Recently, he had been undermining Lord Boare's efforts at taking control of the High Kingship. For Broll had learned the lessons of history. When the Boarites had last controlled the Kingdom, mass poverty, wars, and pestilence had been rife. Millions had died, neglected and abused by their High King, while the then Lord Boare and his sycophants debauched themselves. Only the intervention of a young northern prince and a headstrong Priestess of Deanna had saved the Kingdom. The priestess had forced changes in the policies of her Order, allowing them to take a more direct role in the politics of the world. With Luigheagh's help, she had put a stop to the excesses of the High King. Luigheagh had become the next High King, and with the help of Uiscallan the Storm-Bringer, he had saved the land from disaster.

It was Broll's intention to maintain the Dragon dynasty and the status quo that had alleviated the suffering of the poor within Dragania. The benevolent effects of the Dragon reign had been far reaching, even as far as *Tir Pect*. By maintaining a strong leadership, they discouraged rash acts of war by the High King and Queen in *Tir Pect*. The old enmity of the *Fear Bans* still burned strongly within the people of *Tir Pect*, and should they invade the southern realm, many of the population of Dragania would suffer. In the southern cities and the rich plains of Dragania, the *Fear Bans* and their Pectish neighbours had merged and prospered over the past century. Even the border Clans, who still kept to the old ways of the *Pect*, accepted their independence from *Tir Pect*. They had thrived under the rule of the *Dragan*. The Great Truce protected their Clan lands and allowed them to prosper. Even the twice-yearly Gathering of the Clans, established by *Luigheagh An Dragan* and controlled by the ancient laws of the Brehon, had ensured peace and prosperity between the *Fear Ban* and the Pects. It brought wealth and trading opportunities for all. Much to the chagrin of the palace at *Ard Pect*, many Pectish clansmen came to the fairs to trade, thus avoiding the heavy tariffs of King Conchubhar. His patrols could not control the epic amount of smuggling and bribery that went on, and his tax collectors bemoaned their lost revenue. Comical anecdotes of smuggling regularly filled the taverns of *Ard Pect* with laughter.

With this in mind, Broll had pulled the strings of disruption on Lord Boare's power struggle. The recent breakouts from Manquay goal had been carefully planned and executed by the Beggar-lord. It had been an expensive venture, involving many bribes of officials, as well as coercion, and a number of assassinations, to achieve. It was important that not only was such a deed successful, but also that the source of the action could not be traced back to the Beggars Guild. Lord Boare needed to think that the very gods were against him. Much of the power of the Beggars Guild lay in their invisibility, and should Lord Boare ever find out about the duplicity right under his very nose, thousands would die. Such was the burden of responsibility that Broll had carried. With his passing, that responsibility had fallen on the shoulders of his heir: Cull.

Although Cull had never sought the title or the responsibility, he reluctantly acknowledged that of all the good men and women who stood beside him, he was the best suited for the task. Broll, as usual, had shown wisdom when he selected a starving boy from the quayside district as his apprentice and eventual successor. To this day, Cull wondered what Broll had seen in him. He had taken the shivering orphan under his wing, and Cull would be eternally grateful to the man. Broll became the father that he had never known. When the pox had killed his estranged mother, Cuilithe had been evicted from their small hovel and left to the mercies of the city. His life would have been short and brutal had he not met Broll. At first, he had been wary of the man because his time on the streets had taught him some hard lessons. He had learned about the perversity of some men and their tastes for young boys. Therefore, his hand had never strayed far from the sharpened shard of metal he used as a shank. Gradually, over time, he had learned to trust the beggar. Broll had never asked for anything from the boy and had shared all that they had earned together, as equals. He had taught him the art of begging. He had shown Cull all of the subtle nuances that would make him successful. They worked well together and made a good team.

As Cull grew, Broll spoke to him of his vision for the future. At first, Cull could not understand the bizarre philosophy that Broll preached, but over time he learned to understand the driving force behind the plan. Over the last forty years, that vision of a future had grown, and Broll had gathered together a group of like-minded individuals to put his plan into motion. Now, these men and women huddled together to pay their last respects to the visionary.

Looking around at the haggard faces of those beside him, Cull could see the loss in their eyes. It was the same loss that must have been reflected in his own eyes. Gazing out across the bleak landscape of the Paupers Plot, his eyes glistened at the mass of people who had come to pay their final respects. So many people had been affected by such a simple idea. So great had Broll's influence been that a veritable nation now stood in quiet homage of the man who had improved their lot and given them hope for a brighter future. "I won't let you down, Broll," he murmured. He repeated it again with more conviction.

As they lowered Broll's remains into the hole for his final journey, Cull removed his hat and pronounced loudly "Rest in peace, ya' auld bollix. I'll see ya again the next time round."

The others nodded and similar dark farewells were uttered. Some even went as far as to draw forth phlegm and spit into the grave.

Stepping forward, Cull kicked at the dirt that bordered the hole, sending a clump of the half-frozen clay down on top of the body. Placing his weather-worn hat back on his head, he walked off. His ears rang with the sound of dirt landing on the corpse, as others kicked dirt into the hole. He walked through the gathered crowd with his eyes fixed on the middle-distance. Many nodded their head in respect. By now, word had gone out that there was a new Beggar-lord. The man who had always walked in Broll's shadows had taken up his mantle.

Hearing footsteps beside him, Cull acknowledged the others for the first time. "Pass the word around. There'll be a wake this evening at the disused tannery sheds. We'll have a feast and a wee dram in his memory and sit by the warmth of a bonfire for a sing-along. It's Imbolc, after all. It's the way he would've wanted it. Call a meeting for the day after tomorrow and we'll discuss the future of the Guild. By then, we'll all have clearer heads."

"Aye, Cull. We'll see that it's done."

*****

Conal had only just fallen asleep when a boot poked him in his ribs. Looking up at Taliesin's sleepy face, he protested "It can't be dawn already. I've only just closed my eyes!"

"It's not ... but you need to get up anyway."

"What! I need is some sleep, Tal ..." he pleaded, "...just for a few bells!"

"I'm sorry, Conal, but you've got visitors ..."

"...At this time of night! Who, in the Nine Hells, comes visiting at this time of night?"

The answer flashed into Conal's sleepy brain as Taliesin answered "The Brocians, of course!"

"What do they want? Can't this wait until morning?"

"The sooner you get up, the sooner you can ask them."

Grumbling in a most un-regal fashion, Conal climbed out of his warm bed and flung on his clothes. The days were getting warmer, but the nights were still bitterly cold, and the wind seemed to find every crack and crevice within the half-built fortress. Wrapping up in a thick cloak, he hurried after Taliesin, heading for the meeting hall. This was one of the only rooms that were fully repaired, and it had become a temporary sleeping quarters for many of the Clan. Suitable housing was still being built for his ever-growing followers.

They heard the hushed grumbling from within the hall, even before they had opened the door. Conal, it seemed, wasn't the only person rudely awoken by their nocturnal guests. As he entered, the enormity of his midnight visitors came to him. A large band of Brocians stood waiting in the centre of the hall. He could see that they were a mixed bunch. Mainly, they consisted of Snow Badgers, but the different coloured garb indicated that warriors from other Brocian Setts were also present. He estimated that over fifty Brocians stood waiting. Normally, such visits consisted of only a handful of the fearsome Pectish warriors.

The Dragons had surrounded the Brocians. Thankfully, Declan had followed Conal's explicit orders to treat the Brocians as honoured guests, but even so, such a large force of heavily-armed men would surely have made the Grand Marshal apprehensive.

Declan was the first to notice Conal's approach and grunted an audible, "humph," to signal his soldiers to attention. The slap of war spears as they rapped them against their shields brought the room to silence. All eyes turned to the sleepy-eyed Prince.

241

By then, Conal had started to recognise some of his guests. "Cathal! Vort! Welcome to my humble abode."

Vort grasped Conal and Taliesin's forearms in the greeting of warriors. "It's great to see you alive and well, Conal. I hope we didn't disturb you."

Conal beamed warmly at Vort. "I was just catching up on a bit of shut-eye. Believe it or not, it's sort of a habit around here to sleep during the hours of darkness whenever we can, though that shouldn't darken my welcome to the warriors of *Clann Na Broce*. Declan, you can send the men back to their posts, and let's see if we can rustle up some food for our guests?"

With a firm nod from the Grand Marshal, the Dragons headed off, some to their beds and others for sentry duty.

"It looks like you've gathered quite an army since last I saw you, Conal. "

Conal smiled. "Yes, there are more clansmen coming in every day. After meeting Declan's force on the edge of the mountains, word has got out. First, the men and women who were sheltering in the caves along the border came down to join us, and they've been joined by those sheltering in the villages on the edge of the Broce Woods and others who were taking shelter with the Horse Clan. More are still coming north from Manquay and beyond. For some unexplainable reason, Lord Boare has suffered a large number of breakouts from his gaols and work-mines lately. Whole quarries have been emptied as prisoners escaped en masse, and he's been unable to apprehend his missing slaves."

"Such news gladdens my heart, Conal. I'm sure that'll hamper his war effort."

"Great minds think alike! So, what brings such a large group of Brocians to my door? I think you've given the Grand Marshal a sleepless night."

"After you left, I headed to Broca to face the High Council. Thanks to my wife's bullying, it seems that things aren't as bad as I'd initially feared. So when I'd finally dealt with my affairs, I thought it prudent to take a tour of the other Setts as the newly-reappointed High-shaman. That way I could strengthen ties with the other Setts and at the same time keep an eye on their shamans. I needed to know if there was a move afoot to undermine my title."

"Oh yes, I'd forgotten about that! How's that going?"

"Actually ... it's quite good! It turns out that there were many other Brocian warriors with hidden talents. I've opened the floodgates. Since the High Council's decree, many warriors have come forward to learn how to use their natural abilities. I now have a strong group of Warrior-mages from across the Setts to call upon. Any potential revolt by Dorcha's old regime has been thoroughly squashed. Anyone foolish enough to think that they could challenge me for the position has scurried back into the shadows rather than face a full cohort of magic-wielding warriors. I was just finishing up my tour with our northern cousins, the *Snochta Broce*, when I bumped into Cathal. He told me of your exploits with a *Ciudach* and of his plan to come visit you this Imbolc. He suggested that my Warrior-mages might want to tag along. You seem to have won the hearts of *Clann Na Snochta Broce* with your bravery, and they've offered to act as your honour guard when you ride south

"They have indeed, and I'm very honoured by their offer. Would that cause a problem for the other Brocians?"

"Normally the High Council would be apoplectic."

"Oh, dear!"

"I said normally ... but these are far from normal times. I firmly believe that the future of my people is entwined with your own, so I've supported the *Snochta Broce* in their gesture. I've sent runners to each of the Setts, expressing my wish for solidarity. It is my intention that representatives from all of the Setts should ride south with you."

"By the Seven!" Taliesin exclaimed.

"How many of your clansmen normally attend the spring fair, Vort?"

"Mmm, let me see, it could be three or four hundred, all told. It's a mixture of craftsmen, shamans, warriors, and around forty boys that have come of age, along with their families."

"That's a formidable force. I'd be greatly honoured to have your clansmen at my side."

"Due to the occasion, you may find that there's a slightly higher number this year."

Conal was overwhelmed. Counting his own soldiers and the force of Brocians, Conal would be marching to the Gathering of the Clans with a small army at his back.

"That is, of course, if you don't have any objections?"

"…Objections! Why on earth would I have any objections?"

"That's settled, then," Vort declared, slapping Conal on the back. "We'll meet you by the Mage's Tower, just to the south of my own Sett. Manquay is only a few days walk from there. Now ... Cathal's itching to speak to you so I better put him out of his misery."

Cathal grinned at Vort and waved forward some of the *Snochta Broce*. Each carried a bulky package. "Greetings, *Ciudachbane*!"

"Well met, Cathal, and a blessing on *Clann Na Snochta Broce* on behalf of all at *Clann Na Dragan*. Your Sett will always be in my heart."

"May our Clans always fight as blood-brothers," Cathal declared, "and to acknowledge this bond between our Clans, I wish to present you with a small gift." Cathal took a large sack from one of his Clansmen and presented it to Conal.

The Prince quickly untied the bindings. Conal gasped aloud as the sacking opened to reveal the gift within. "Bring me some more light!"

Lifting the leather breastplate out of its wrappings, he raised it up to the torch light to inspect the craftsmanship. It was made from greenish-grey leather. Though slightly thicker than normal, it was still light and pliable. The leather had been finely tooled with knotwork engravings. Carefully embedded into the workmanship were also several magical runes. Wonderfully-crafted silver buckles and clasps adorned the breastplate, depicting dragons in flight. Conal was too overwhelmed to speak.

Thankfully, Taliesin expressed his feelings for him. "That craftsmanship is superb, Cathal! Conchubhar will be piddling himself for a moon when he finds out that this has escaped his greedy mitts."

"Cathal!" Conal's eyes showed his pleasure far more than mere words.

Cathal's grin grew wider as he held up a hand. "There's more ..." He waved Feilim forward with the next package.

Laying the ornate breastplate carefully aside, Conal accepted the second parcel. "Thank you, Feilim," he mumbled, as he struggled with the twine that held the sack closed.

By this time, not a sound could be heard within the Hall. Even the wolfhounds that constantly fought over scraps had fallen silent. Finally, the string fell away, and a leather helmet was revealed. It was made of the same green-grey leather with silver buckling, and it had a richly-embossed white horsehair ridge cresting down the centre of the helm. Conal's fingers brushed along the densely packed furrow of hair, feeling it ruffle under his fingers. The helmet was perfect, with deep chin-guards, and a silver embossed nose plate to protect the face, while leaving his vision unimpeded.

"Well? Don't just stand there ..." Taliesin urged, "try it on!"

With an eager smile, Conal slipped on the helm and fastened it into place. "It fits like a glove, Cathal. Thank you ... but this must have cost a small fortune?"

Cathal grinned wickedly.

"What have you been up to this time, Cathal?" Vort demanded, recognising the glint in the other man's eyes.

"Actually, it didn't cost me anything ... not a penny," Cathal declared.

"What do you mean? The armourers of *Ard Pect* are notoriously greedy. They wouldn't have parted with the likes of this for anything less than a king's ransom!"

"Ah! That's just it! I told them that it was a gift for the King."

"...And?"

"...I just didn't tell them which King I was talking about. They were so eager to out-do each other that they didn't even bother to ask. They were too busy thinking about the fat commission that the High King would reward them with, once the armour was presented at the palace."

"You do realise that they'll put a bounty out on your head, don't you?"

"Of course, Vort, but it was worth it. I've been waiting for a chance to get one over on those armourers for years. If I can rub Conchubhar's nose in it at the same time, then so much the better. As it is, I've got a priceless piece of armour from each and every one of the greedy pox-riddled flea-bags, and they've worked like dogs to out-do each other."

"You mean there's more?" Taliesin asked.

"Of course, bard. There's a full suit of armour here. We've even got a sheath for *An Fiacail Dragan*."

"In that case, Declan, break out the mead! I think we'll start the Imbolc feast a little early this year, in honour of our guests."

"Now that sounds more like the welcome I was hoping for," Cathal declared.

*****

Imbolc celebrations were in full swing in *Ard Pect* as the two monks walked through the city. The festival had encouraged the revellers out onto the streets. There, they watched the jugglers, fire-eaters, and other entertainers, despite the bitter wind that blew off the Lough. Multi-coloured bunting decorated the main road leading up to the castle, and traffic was at its densest here. Slowly, the monks made their way through the crowded thoroughfare.

The younger of the monk's face was almost catatonic, with drool dribbling down from the side of his mouth. His face held a constant blank expression. He seemed oblivious to the swirling chaos going on around him and plodded steadily forward toward the Royal Palace. He was leading his more diminutive partner and using his formidable strength to shoulder his way through the crowd. His eyes were the only animated part of his face, always searching out any potential danger.

The second monk's features could not be seen. His face was hidden within the deep cowl of his hood. His hand gripped the shoulder of the younger monk, ensuring they stayed bound together amidst the mayhem. His hood never rose to take in the sights and sounds around them, or to check on their progress. It remained tilted ever downward towards the cobbled street as they walked.

Finally, they broke free of the celebrants and stopped before the raised portcullis of the palace gates. Two guards barred their way with wicked-looking pikes.

"I'm sorry, Druids, but there's no entry into the castle without an appointment," the senior guard declared with a bored expression.

"We're here to see the King. Step aside," Balor hissed from within his cowl.

"You'll need an appointment for that, and I know for a fact that there are no appointments tonight. Now be off with ya." The guard's irritation flared up as he added, "bugger off, and give me some peace, will ya? Come back in the morning and speak to the administrator, if you need to see the King that badly. He's kind of busy right now, and the Queen will flip her lid if they get interrupted. None of us would want that!"

"Get out of my way, you fool! I need to see the King right now. Tell him that Dubhgall the Black is waiting at the gates."

"Dubhgall the Black, eh ... aye and I'm the king of the *Draoidín*. You must've been sampling too much of ya home-brew, Druid. Now, be on ya way before ya get a swift kick up the arse." The guard placed a gauntleted hand on Balor's shoulder and shoved him backward.

Balor staggered slightly, barely managing to maintain his grip on Fionn's shoulder. "You really shouldn't have done that," he hissed. Pulling back his hood so the guard could see his ravaged face, he uttered a single word of command "Burn!"

Fire burst from his outstretched hand and exploded in a rolling wall of flames. It washed over the two guards before passing into the yard beyond. In that instant, the heat melted their exposed flesh and boiled them alive in their armour. Their screams were short lived, but loud enough to stop the revelry in the street below and alert the nearby guards.

Alarm bells had started to ring within the keep before the first of the men collapsed onto the cobbles. As they fell, the sounds of running feet could be heard, drawing closer. Despite the festivities, the High King maintained rigid discipline within his guards, and it wasn't long before the gateway was barred by a dozen pikes. Balor waited calmly, reserving his strength. It had been too long since he had exerted this much power. The simple act of maintaining control over Brother Fionn's mind for this long was already taking its toll on his weakened body. He could ill-afford to battle his way though these soldiers to reach the King. He needed a show of strength to work for him. Let doubt creep into their minds and fear eke into their souls. He waited, indifferent to the threat of the soldiers' weapons.

The soldiers, who couldn't fail to notice the burned carcasses of their fellows, had also opted to wait for instruction from someone more superior.

It didn't take long for someone of a higher rank to appear, hurriedly buckling on his breastplate. He was clearly unhappy at the interruption to his night's festivities. "What, by the Seven, is going on here?" he demanded as he marched forward. When no one answered him, he glared at the intruders. "What is the meaning of ...?" He had finally spotted the dead guardsmen.

"As I told your men ... I'm here to see the King," Balor declared calmly. "They were foolish enough to question my credentials. I do hope you're a little smarter, Captain, or there'll be an awful mess for someone to clean up on the morrow. Now, go and fetch me your King. It's cold out here, and that's making me irritable."

"Who, in the Nine Hells, do you think you are?"

Balor hoped that he wouldn't have to incinerate the rest of the King's soldiers. He was sure that it wouldn't help to encourage a good working relationship with the Pectish monarchs. "I'm the man who turned your gatekeepers into charcoal. Does it really matter? If I told you who I was, you probably wouldn't believe me, and then they'd need to find another fool to take your place, so why don't you just save us both the trouble and run along and get your boss? Or better still, save us even more time and go and fetch the bloody King?"

"Seize them!" the officer ordered. When the soldiers hesitated, he added "Seize them or I'll have you all be doing border patrols along the Bitter Eastern Sea, you mangy sewer-rats."

Winters were cold in *Ard Pect*, but they were used to that. The Bitter Eastern Sea, however, was a notoriously bad place to get sent, even in midsummer. Men had been found frozen into blocks of ice after a night's sentry duty. The men moved reluctantly forward. Each of them hoped that

248

someone else would charge first and suffer the brunt of whatever was going to happen next.

Balor shrugged his shoulders and decided to use force this time, rather than fire. With a flick of his wrist and a guttural command, he released his spell. The Dark Mage sagged perceptibly afterwards.

Fortunately, the captain and his men were too busy to notice. They had been sent flying backward when an invisible wall crashed into them.

Balor gripped Fionn's shoulder firmly and marched forward. The Captain was vainly trying to stand when Balor walked passed, but the Mage's eyeless gaze stopped any further movement. "Don't bother getting up, Captain. I'll find him myself."

Chapter Twenty-Three: Flying to *Sliamh Na Dia*

The previous day of merriment had gone well, but Maerlin knew that the longer she stayed in Eagles Reach, the harder it would be to leave. Today they would depart, she decided. It was time to face *Sliamh Na Dia*. After waking the others, they hurried outside to sing the 'Dawn Chorus' together. Singing it yesterday had felt so right that she had decided to continue the practice.

"As the most senior priestess here, I think it only fitting that you should start it, Seabhac," Maerlin declared.

"Me? This was thy idea. I'm a bit rusty at this."

"Cora and I are both novices, so it really shouldn't be us, and Nessa is still trying to find her voice, so you're the obvious choice."

Seabhac pursed her lips for a moment before nodding. Raising her arms to the glowing skyline, she sang out the first verse just as the sun was breaking over the horizon.

When they had finished, the gathered villagers burst forth with imitation birdsong. The many birds that lived in the community joined in.

"Didst thou have any luck finding a way to help Nessa?" Seabhac asked as they headed for breakfast.

"Not really. Many of the villagers believe that the trick is to splice the bird's tongue. They say that this will help her to pronounce the words better, but that seems a little barbaric. Also, we've come across quite a few birds here that didn't have this operation done, and yet they still speak. Of course, most birds wouldn't have the vocabulary that Nessa has. She never lost her memories when she was reincarnated. What about Fintan? Does he speak?"

Seabhac smiled warmly. "Fintan, like Nessa, is quite unique, but no ... he doesn't speak. He has no need to. We know each other too well."

"He was human once though, wasn't he?" Maerlin asked. Her curiosity was piqued about her mysterious great-grandfather."

"I'm sorry, Maerlin, but that isn't my story to tell. Fintan will have to tell thee about that himself, if and when he wants to. I promised thee not to hide *my* secrets from thee anymore, but this one's not up to me."

Maerlin nodded.

"Before we leave today, I'm going to teach Cora and thee to fly. It's no use putting this off any longer and thou might need it once we get over the mountain. We may need to split up then to find the Boarites. We'll have a lot of the mountain to cover, after all."

"Really?"

Seabhac looked at Maerlin's beaming smile and broke into a chuckle. "Yes really, but I pray that thou doesn't fall off and break thy neck. There'll be hell to pay if thou do."

Seabhac was well aware that Maerlin and Cora had been practising together when they thought that they were not being watched. They had not, however, allowed for the farsightedness of the hen harrier. Fintan had been given specific orders to keep an eye on the novices and keep them out of danger.

After breakfast, they headed out to the edge of the village. The villagers followed along, eager for a little entertainment during this quiet season. With the snow still on the ground and any repairs completed during the long winter, life on the mountain in early spring was a time to relax. Having spectators did little to boost the novices' confidence as Seabhac came forward. Handing Maerlin her quarterstaff and Cora the besom, she placed her own staff on the ground.

"This broom will have to suffice for now, Cora, but thou might want to get thyself a staff, if thou wish to fly in the future. In the meantime, I'd suggest tying a stout cushion to the handle. It may ease the discomfort on thy posterior, much though it's got more padding on it than Maerlin's has."

It was too close to call as to which of the novices was more embarrassed by the comment. Although Maerlin had fleshed out over the last year as she grew more into her womanhood, she was always going to be petite whereas Cora was a little more on the shapely side.

"Let's begin. Place thy staffs on the ground and centre thy minds, and then we'll summon forth some assistance."

The air ruffled as the novices summoned Air Elementals.

"One at a time, raise thy staffs off the ground. Thou can go first, Maerlin, as thou hast more of a gift for this particular Elemental."

Cora was clearly relieved to be going second.

"While Maerlin is flying, Cora, I want thee to focus on the air shield, just in case it should be needed. There'll be no resting on thy laurels in my class," Seabhac instructed.

"Raise thy staff, Maerlin. That's it ... all the way up ... thou art doing excellent! Now, place thy posterior on the centre of the staff and let it take thy weight. Please! Canst thou stop all that childish giggling? Thy staff is wobbling all over the place!"

Maerlin tried to control the smirk that covered her face. Seabhac's quaint phrases had become something of a private joke between the two novices.

"Posterior! Posterior! Posterior! Should we spend the next while repeating it together and forgo thy flying lessons?" Seabhac asked primly.

"No, Seabhac! We're fine ... honest." Maerlin maintained a poker face with some difficulty.

"Then please control thy staff and prepare to mount."

Maerlin got a firm grip of both herself and the Elemental that was controlling her quarterstaff, and the quivering ceased. Deftly, she mounted the staff for the first time and let it take her weight.

"Thou might find it a bit easier if thou tilt the front of thy staff upwards by a hand's breadth."

Maerlin followed the instructions. It did indeed give her more stability.

"Excellent! Now, Maerlin, I have a firm hand on the back of thy staff, so thou won't fall off, have no fear."

Maerlin hovered nervously.

"We'll start forward at a nice steady pace. Remember to keep that cushion of air ready, Cora, just in case Maerlin should need it ... aaaannd ... ready ... we're off!"

Maerlin willed the Elemental forward, trying to keep her pace steady as she heard Seabhac's footsteps in the snow behind her. It was a little wobbly at first, but she was quickly gaining confidence.

"Good ... good ... yes, excellent. Now that thou hast got the hang of it ... we'll pick up the pace a little. I'm sure that thou can risk it."

Maerlin picked up speed, her staff steadying itself as her pace increased.

"Now, lean over slightly to bank to the right."

Maerlin did as she was told, and the quarterstaff turned as instructed. It was only then that she realised that Seabhac's voice was not on her shoulder. Looking quickly around, her concentration slipped, and the staff lurched and dipped. Before Maerlin could right herself, she had crashed, face-first, into a snowdrift.

Spitting snow out of her mouth, Maerlin shook off as much snow as she could and blinked.

"Are you alright?" Cora asked when she had run over. She was trying not to laugh at Maerlin, caked in snow.

"What happened to the air cushion?"

"Sorry, Maerl, I forgot! Here, let me help you up." Cora brushed the remaining snow off Maerlin's clothing. "Anyway, it looks like you found a soft enough landing without my help."

"No thanks to you!" Maerlin retorted, but she couldn't help smiling. Pulling her staff out of the snow bank, she heard Seabhac's panting as she approached.

"Excellent start, Maerlin, but try to maintain thy concentration."

"You let go! I thought you said you were holding onto the back of the staff, in case I fell?"

"Do I look like I can run around the mountain after thee? Of course, I let go. Anyway, there's nothing like a few harmless crashes to focus the mind. Now, I think it is Cora's turn, don't thee?"

"Me?" Cora asked.

"Yes, Cora ... thee. I've the greatest confidence in thee. Let's see if thou canst out-do Maerlin and do the full circle without nose-diving thyself into a snowdrift, shall we? Maerlin, thou art on protection duty. Hopefully, thou can do a better job of it than Cora did. Chop-chop! We haven't got all day."

By the end of the lesson, Seabhac had declared them proficient enough at flying to continue on their staffs, while she carried the baggage with her on the dishevelled rug. After some heartfelt farewells, they headed farther up the mountain.

The Great Pectish Mountains ranged from the northern edge of the land at the Bitter Eastern Sea, right across to the Sea of Hunger, before petering out in the archipelagos of the Western Isles. It created a natural boundary between the lush plains of the south where the *Fear Ban* settled over two centuries earlier, and the lands still owned by the Pectish Clans of *Tir Pect*. The mountains curled down the western coast, before dwindling to foothills near the city of Manquay.

One peak, however, towered above its smaller cousins. It was known as *Sliamh Na Dia*: the Mountain of the Gods. Legends said that the Seven Greater Gods once fought against the Elder God, *Crom Cruach* and defeated him here. As everyone knows, gods are immortal, and even the mighty power of the Seven could not slay him. Instead, they captured the Elder God and entombed him in molten rock for eternity, which was how the Mountain of the Gods was created. Over the centuries, the molten rock cooled to form a gigantic stone peak. This divided the mountain range of *Tir Pect* from the smaller range that lay between the Broce Woods and the Sea of Hunger.

On the northern face of *Sliamh Na Dia*, Eagles Reach was situated, while on its southern side of the great mountain sat the village of High Peaks. Few people had ever survived the journey over the peak that separated these two villages, though some foolhardy adventurers had tried.

Even during midsummer, the head and shoulders of this mighty edifice were shrouded in snow and ice. That is, on the few days when the clouds cover rose high enough to reveal its lofty peak. Giant Eagles nested on the shoulders of the mountain where few enemies could threaten them. Even the wolves and bears that roamed freely on the higher parts of the mountain avoided the frozen peak. Here, the air was so thin that any movement was exhausting, and the urge to lie down and die could be stronger than the will to live. It is to this icy wasteland that the priestesses now flew.

Seabhac called a halt when they reached the shoulders of the mountain, where the last of the stunted conifers and rocky hillside finally gave way to solid ice. Before them, there stood a bank of dense, impenetrable fog. Though the sun glistened off the icy ground, vision was limited. Here, they ate a quick lunch. Seabhac knew that they must consume plenty of food in order to maintain their body heat against the blistering cold. They were bundled tightly into as much of their clothing as possible, but despite the extra layers of wool and fur, the cold seeped into their bones and leached away their strength. After everyone had eaten as much of the rich, high-energy food as they could, she handed each of the girls a scarf.

"Cover thy faces with these. There are eye holes in them. They will reduce the risk of thy noses and lips getting frostbite and help thee avoid snow-blindness."

They followed her example and covered their faces securely with the thick cloth.

"Pack thy staffs away on the rug. From here on up, we'll fly together." Holding a hand up to stem their disappointment, she added "I will need thee both to help me, if we are to survive this mountain. Apart from the added warmth when we huddle together, I will need thee to help me to see where we are going. This fog will only get thicker, and I cannot fly and move the fog out of the way at the same time."

"Couldn't you rustle up a wind and push it away?" Cora asked.

"That's a good question, Cora, so let me explain. If I asked thee to hold back the tide of the ocean, could thou do it? Thou could not, because the weight of it is just too vast, the area it covers too great. It's the same with this fog. It extends for miles and I'd be exhausted without reward. If all the Air-sisters of Deanna were to stand here, we could not dissipate this cloud of fog, no more than we could move the mountain itself. Instead, what we need to do is create a more localised breeze, directly in front of us and stretching for no more than say ten spans across. This would be sufficient for us to see by, without overexerting ourselves. That's what I need thee to do while I control the rug. Dost thou understand?

"How do we do that?"

"Remember the air shield that we were using earlier? What I want thee to do is use an air shield as a wall, moving before us. It will work twofold. Firstly, it will stop us running headlong into any large boulders that may stand in our way, and secondly, it will push the cloud of fog before it, forcing a pocket of clearer air for me to fly in. The momentum of our flying will send the barrier forward, all that thou wilt have to do is maintain the shield. It will be hard work, so I want thee to take turns at it. Thou must switch over regularly and rest. Listen to me now for this is important. Do not overexert thyself in this task, for we are all dependant on thee. Our forward pace will depend solely on thy ability to maintain this barrier, so do not try to push it too far ahead. The farther it is from thee, the harder it'll be to control."

She waited, looking sternly at the novices before continuing. "Very well, then. Huddle around the centre of the rug, and we will cover ourselves with our bedding, too. Once we enter the fog, the temperature will drop severely. Although thou might not realise it, the sun here is giving us some warmth, but it rarely manages to break through this fog."

*****

Balor awoke in darkness, but after the last six moons of blindness, that in itself was no great surprise. The soft bed he was lying on and the lack of restraints were the first clues to his whereabouts. It all came flooding back to him. He recalled the exorcism, his escape, the trip to *Ard Pect*, and finally bursting into the bedchamber to disturb the King and Queen's Imbolc orgy.

The Queen had been furious at his interruption and was only placated when Balor agreed to release Fionn from his mental bondage to take the King's place, while Conchubhar and Balor discussed affairs of state.

Guilt washed over Balor in waves at the further tarnishing of his soul. He recalled his manic laughter and the deaths of his brother-monks during the failed exorcism. The kidnapping of Brother Fionn weighed heavily upon him. To make matters worse, he had handed Fionn over as a plaything to Queen Medb's debauchery. Even in his half-conscious state, he could feel the waves of horror coming from the young monk as he was subjected to lurid acts of fornication far beyond his wildest nightmares... and yet, deep within Fionn, there was a part of him that revelled in the excesses. Fionn's pure soul was being tainted by this new world he had been dragged into. In an effort to save the young monk's sanity, Balor would be forced to yield his will to the *Darkness* that lurked within his own soul. *He* would need the monk's eyes to see the world around him, a world which Balor had been content to leave behind. Much though Balor hated yielding control to his darker self, he felt that he owed it to Fionn. Balor focused some magical energy and could already feel the *Darkness* taking control before he released the spell.

With a sigh, Dubhgall reached out and gripped Fionn's mind and clamped down firmly on the monk's will. Having had a firm grip on Fionn's mind for these last few days, the task was simple enough. He chuckled at the Queen's howl of frustration, when her new plaything was taken away from her, mid-coitus.

Fionn climbed out of the massive bed, shedding the Queen's other playthings without regard. Pushing aside any who stood in his way with his powerful arms, he headed for the door, ignoring Medb's colourful curses. One of her paramour's foolishly tried to detain him and was flung across the room into a priceless piece of furniture. Oblivious of his own nakedness, he opened the door to the Queen's bedchamber and walked away without a backward glance. He took to the corridors like a sleepwalker, heedless of the world around him and the chaos he produced. His only objective was to get to where Dubhgall waited. Nothing and no one could hinder him in his forward progress. Despite the Queen's wrath, Fionn marched purposefully onward until he reached the Mage's bedchamber.

Dubhgall gripped the young man's shoulder and looked down at the fine black gown he had been given to wear, though Fionn's eyes. "Come. Let's find some breakfast. I'm famished."

They headed down the long spiral staircase to the ground floor and into the banquet hall, ignoring the occasional scorch mark that marred the resplendent flooring and fine furnishings. It had taken some time to find the King the previous evening, and his guards had proved to be persistent, if impotent.

Conchubhar was sitting at the head of a long table, eating heartily. "Good morning to you, Mage. I figured that you might be awake. That'd explain the disturbance on the second floor. I think you've managed to upset my wife ... again! There are not many men who can boast that."

"I'm sure she'll get over it, your Highness, but I needed my 'eyes' back. She'd had them for long enough, and I was getting hungry."

The High King chuckled and waved a hand generously at the wealth of food on the table. "Please, help yourselves. My house is yours."

Dubhgall nodded and took a seat. He selected choice morsels to satisfy his appetite. "It's good to see real food again. You have no idea of the pig-swill that they fed me in that monastery. They insisted on eating porridge for breakfast ... every morning! The heavens forbid that I could have some honey to sweeten the blasted stuff! I'll refrain from going into the detail of the broth they insisted on serving for dinner. The sooner that place is forgotten, the better! The only saving grace they had on the island was their mead ... but I got little enough of that."

Conchubhar cleared his throat and broached a delicate subject "Could I ask you a small boon?"

"Certainly, your Majesty, I'll do my best. What is it?"

"It's about your manservant ... I wonder if he could take a seat. Looking at the man's genitalia while I'm trying to eat is putting me off my breakfast, especially since he's hung like a horse. Much though I like to see my wife content ... even I have my limits!"

Dubhgall quickly assessed the situation. "I see your point." He relaxed the hold on Fionn's mind enough to allow the monk to sit and eat. "I'll find a suitable robe for him after breakfast."

"Excellent. Do try the venison sausages. They're the cook's secret recipe and they go particularly well with the duck egg omelette."

*****

Conal was rudely awoken and feeling the worse for wear. He swore, not for the first time in his short life, that he would abstain from drinking in the future. For some reason, he didn't have the constitution for the stuff the way the Brocians did. A foot poked him again in the ribs, and he grunted to acknowledge that he was awake. "This is getting to be a bad habit, Tal!"

"It's nearly dawn, and traditionally that's the time we get up. Who am I to go against tradition? As you passed out so early yesterday evening, it's not as if you didn't get enough sleep."

"I think I preferred Cull! Can I have him back now?"

"Ah! You must be awake to come up with that one. Sadly, Cull is far away, and I'm the only one around here who has a free licence to torment you. That is, at least, until you start paying me some wages."

Conal groaned. "Not that again!"

"Sorry! Did I touch a tender nerve there? How are your studies on the royal treasury going, by the way?"

"Not too good. I've tried to do the accounts a dozen times, but they always turn up with the same answer ... I'm broke."

"I thought that might be the case. You can't go gallivanting around the countryside for a few years and expect your affairs to look after themselves while you're gone. Someone was bound to see all that money gathering dust and find a better use for it."

"You'll have to wait a while for your wages, Taliesin. That is, unless you've got a better idea."

"Well, now that you come to mention it, actually I do! Or rather ... I know a couple of fellows who do. While you were busy dancing on tables yesterday and flirting with the serving girls, I was talking to a couple of visiting merchants. It seems that lowland wool is fetching an exceptionally high price in *Ard Pect* at this time of year."

Conal's brain was struggling to keep up with Taliesin's conversation. "Sorry, Taliesin, you've lost me. What has that to do with me getting rich?"

"Conal, what is your kingdom famous for?"

"I don't know, grass, I guess. It's got lots of grass. Then, I suppose there are the cows ... the horses ... oh, and the sheep."

"Sheep, yes sheep, exactly! But not just any old sheep, oh no! You've got one of the finest flocks of Jacob sheep, this side of Suilequay. Not the course black-faced mountain sheep of *Ard Pect*, but fine lowland sheep with lovely soft fleeces."

"Sorry... I still don't understand. I'm not a farmer, but even I know that sheep get sheared in early summer, and it's barely even spring. We don't have any of last year's wool left. From what I could tell, it was all sold off at the autumn fair."

"Ah! That's where my idea comes in. All we have to do is shear them early."

"Taliesin, it's freezing out there in case you haven't noticed! You can't shear sheep before they've lambed. They'll freeze to death out there on the plains. Anyway, by the time we've paid the taxes to haul them over the border to *Ard Pect*, it wouldn't be worth the effort."

"You're not looking at the bigger picture, Conal."

"Really! Maybe that's because I've just woken up ... oh, and the fact that I'm still hung over. Please ... enlighten me."

"Very well then, here's my plan. Firstly, we shear the sheep ..."

"Yeah, I figured that would be in there somewhere."

Taliesin gave the Prince a flinty look and waited.

"Sorry, I won't interrupt again, I promise!"

"Very well then, where was I? Oh yes. So ... we shear the sheep, and then we herd them into the Broce Woods. That way, they get the benefit of the shelter there."

"Hang on a moment, Tal! Won't the Brocians object to a load of sheep roaming around in their woods?"

"I thought you said you wouldn't interrupt?"

"Sorry, sorry!"

"I've spoken with Vort, and he's agreed to the venture ... for a suitable compensation."

"Compensation? Spit it out, Taliesin. How much will it cost me?"

"Vort's agreed to wait for payment until the autumn, so it won't be too bad. We've agreed a price of five fattened lambs for every fifty ewes we shear."

"Five... that doesn't seem too bad."

"And then there is another five for the cost of smuggling the fleeces across the border. This would go directly to *Clann Na Broce Snochta*. Plus a ten per cent merchant fee for the goods, at point of sale."

"Let me get this right. If we're lucky, we'll get an average of one and a half lambs per ewe. That would be seventy-five lambs' tops for every fifty ewes. Of this, the Brocians will get ten of them *plus* a commission?"

"I know that sounds steep, but if you take into account the fact that we lose a similar percentage every year ... then it's a bargain!"

"Sorry, you've lost me again there, Tal."

"Each year we lose a portion of our ewes and lambs."

"You mean to wolves, and foxes, and the likes ..."

"Yes... but mainly to the Brocians."

"What! Are you telling me that they've been stealing my livestock?" Conal demanded. "How long has this been going on?"

"Conal! They are warriors of the old ways. Stealing livestock is part of their heritage. Your father and your grandfather knew all about it. They were content to ignore it as long as it didn't get out of hand. That's the genius part of this whole plan. Vort has agreed to take a share of your flock in exchange for his Clan looking after them. Therefore, you won't need to worry about foxes or wolves. They don't venture into the Brocians' woods. The Brocians will watch over your flocks for you, and they'll still only take what they need come the autumn. It's a win-win situation. Vort gets to help you out and at the same time, it costs you next to nothing. As to the price charged by Cathal for the fleeces, it's still less than you'd be charged if they went across the border legally. King Conchubhar would charge you fifteen per cent, at least. Probably more, if he finds out that you stole his new armour."

"I didn't steal it!"

"Conchubhar might disagree, but let's get back to the wool. The price is currently high due to the shortage of supply. Once the spring fair begins, the price will plummet. The southern merchants already have wagons packed and ready to drive north, just as soon as the weather clears. This way, we get to make a killing while the price is still at its best. That'll have a double benefit to you."

"Sorry, you've lost me again, Tal. Maybe I should hire you as my treasurer instead of my bard?"

Taliesin sighed and explained the basics of commerce to the Prince. "Okay, the price is currently high due to the shortage of good quality, lowland wool. We come along and flood the market prior to the spring fair. Once that happens, the price will drop as there will no longer be such a high demand. Are you with me so far?"

"I'm not stupid, Tal."

Taliesin refrained from comment on that and proceeded with his explanation "So ... the southern merchants will arrive at the spring fair, after hauling wagon loads of worthless wool north, hoping to meet a demand that no longer exists. They'll be forced to sell the wool at a loss in order to recoup their expenses. They'll need to buy something else at the fair to take home with them and make some profit on the return journey to at least break even. As Lord Boare owns most of the southern wool and pays the merchants to trade for him, he'll be seriously impacted by the loss."

"That's brilliant!"

"Well, yes, it is ... but I haven't finished yet! What's really brilliant is the next part. From the profits we make from our initial investment, we buy the southern wool at rock bottom prices."

"Why, by Macha's blessed paps, would we want to do that?"

"So that we can store it and wait for the market price to rise again. If we hold onto the stuff until just before the autumn fair, the price will have increased enough for us to do the whole thing all over again. This time, we'll be selling Lord Boare's wool to King Conchubhar, and we'll make another tidy profit."

"How, by the Seven, did you come up with such a scheme?"

"Have you any idea of the amount of conversations I've overheard about the cost of wool, or beef for that matter, or some other commodity? I've just never had the wherewithal before to act on the knowledge. Of course, I shall expect a small commission as your broker."

"That seems fair. What were you thinking of?"

"Ten per cent seems fair."

"...Ten per cent! That's daylight robbery. How about five?"

"Why, you cheapskate, Conal *MacDragan*. You'd still be broke if it wasn't for my idea."

"I guess I could stretch to seven, but that's still robbery."

"Eight ... and not a farthing less."

"Done! Now, hand me my tunic. My bladder's fit to burst."

Chapter Twenty-Four: The Prodigal Daughter's Return

Time eked slowly by, like a dripping tap filling a bath. They drifted through the noiseless, directionless, nothingness of the mountain mist. Maerlin and Cora rotated regularly to maintain their strength as they pushed the fog before them. By trial and error they found that creating a curved wall of force rather that a flat one needed less effort to cut through the dense fog, and therefore, they could push the force wall farther out and increase their speed, but it was still slow and tedious work. The highlight of a bell's work would be startling one of the snow-white rabbits that inhabited the mountain.

"How do we know which way we're going? We could be going around in a big circle," Maerlin asked despondently. The boredom was getting on her nerves.

"We're going upwards, Maerlin, ever upwards."

"How do you know that, Seabhac?"

Seabhac considered her answer. "Instinct, I guess, and also a sense of balance. Here, I'll show thee." Seabhac reached into one of the bags and pulled out one of the dried apples. Placing it on the rug before her, they watched as it slowly rolled into her lap. "See! The front of the rug is still higher than the back."

"But how far have we gone, and how far do we still have to go before we reach the top?"

Seabhac looked pointedly at Maerlin. "Hast thou ever heard the anecdote about the length of a piece of string?"

"That means she doesn't know. Though to be fair, she does have a point, Maerlin. Stop whining and quit fidgeting. It's stuffy enough in this cloak already without you twitching about like a flea-bitten mongrel."

"I'm not twitching, Ness. I'm just bored."

"Maerlin, when you're my size, believe me, you're twitching."

"Shush, I'm trying to concentrate," Cora demanded.

"Do you want me to take over? Are you getting tired?"

"You asked me that a few moments ago, Maerl. I'm fine, and Nessa's right. You fidget when you get antsy."

"I see, so it's pick on Maerlin day, is it?"

"Oh, for the love of Deanna ... here! Take over if you're that bored. Listening to you whine is giving me a headache."

"Thanks, Cora." Maerlin quickly set up her shield behind Cora's and nodded to signal that she was ready to take over.

"Hast thou switched again? I would have thought that thou would have had more stamina, Cora?"

"I'm fine, Seabhac, but Maerlin was getting antsy."

"I was not!"

"Oh yes you were. Fine, I'll have my turn back then."

"You will not!"

"See what I mean, Seabhac?"

Maerlin stuck her tongue out. The gesture, however, was wasted as she got a tongue full of the woollen scarf that covering her face. She then tried spitting out the bits of wool that had stuck to her tongue, but this was also futile. Still ... it broke the monotony.

"Is it just me, or is the fog getting thinner?"

"Well spotted, Cora. I think we're nearly through."

As Seabhac said this the fog disappeared altogether, and they found themselves in brilliant sunshine.

Shading her eyes against the midday sun, Maerlin looked around. In front of them, they saw the tip of the mountain peak. It was clear of ice and revealed the volcanic rock beneath. Other than that, there were just bright blue skies, blistering sun, and a carpet of billowy clouds beneath them. "What a sight!"

"Yes, we are seeing something that very few have ever seen - apart from the gods that is."

"Let me out of this cloak, Maerlin. If I miss one of the great wonders of the world, I'll never speak to you again!"

"Sorry, Ness, I forgot all about you." Maerlin carefully unfolded the blanket and fur cloak so that Nessa's head could peek out, without letting too much of the cold air in.

"By the Seven, that's indeed a wonder to behold. It'd bring a tear to the eye of a dragon."

Cora wasn't looking at the majestic vista of clouds that covered the land below them. Instead, she was looking at the rock wall of the peak. "Seabhac, can you bring us a little higher? I want to check something out."

"I guess so, why?"

"I'll let you know when I'm sure. It might just be a trick of the light, but I thought I saw something." Under Cora's directions, Seabhac raised them higher so that they were farther away from the rocky peak, and Cora could see it better.

"What is it, Cora?"

"Hang on, Maerlin. Just another few feet ... yes, that'll do. Hold it there. Now ... what do you see?"

Maerlin looked around, but she saw nothing out of the ordinary. Nothing moved on the mountainside, even when she used her inner eye. "It's just a mountain top?"

"No ... look closer! There." Cora pointed.

"Oh that! It's a couple of small caves." Maerlin's tone indicated her lack of excitement.

"Not caves, Maerlin, they're nostrils. Can't you see them?"

Maerlin looked again. "Are you saying that that's supposed to be a nose?"

"She might have a point there. It does look kind of like a face, if you squint when you look at it."

Maerlin squinted and had to agree. The whole side of the mountain had been carved into a gigantic face. "It's a damned ugly face, if you ask me."

"It might be better to keep that opinion to thyself, Maerlin. At least until we get off this mountain. Thou never know who might be listening."

Maerlin looked at Seabhac and then back at the face carved into the stone. "You don't mean ... no! It can't be. Someone must've carved it into the rock as a practical joke."

"Bit of a stupid joke, if you ask me. No one will ever get to see it." Cora pointed out.

"But still ... it can't be!"

"What we see isn't always there ..." Nessa began.

"...And what we can't see still exists. I haven't forgotten, but even so ... you're suggesting that we're looking at the face of a god: the Elder God, frozen in time?"

"It's at least as probable as a drunken dwarf climbing all the way up here, and freezing his cherries off, just to carve a face into the side of the mountain," Cora argued. "That doesn't sound like a very good practical joke to me, but if you feel more comfortable with your theory, Maerl, I won't argue with you. I guess it'll just one of life's mysteries."

"But you think it's really *him*, don't you, Cora?"

Cora shrugged, but her eyes glittered with excitement.

"Well, fascinating as this may be, I think we need to get over the peak and start heading down. I don't know about thee, but I'd like to get below that fog before nightfall."

Smiling, Maerlin reset her force shield and nodded to Seabhac. "Ready whenever you are, Grandma."

Seabhac scowled and started the rug forward. "I think we'd better hurry. This thin air seems to be afflicting Maerlin. At least it better be the air. If she calls me Grandma one more time, she may live to regret it."

"Would Granny be better, or to be more accurate, Great-granny?"

"Maerlin, hast thou ever wondered why in fairy tales the handsome prince gets turned into a frog? Believe me when I tell thee this, thou wouldst not like being a frog. After the fifth or sixth fly got stuck in thy throat, the novelty would wear thin."

"Ouch! That told you."

Maerlin pouted, good-naturedly. "See, I told you! It's pick on Maerlin day."

Seabhac smiled innocently. "Thou did start it! It's always good to know thy limitations."

*****

Conal felt the shift of air, but kept his eyes closed and his posture relaxed, listening as the footsteps came closer. Grasping his pillow, he waited for them to stop. He sensed someone beside the bed, and turning quickly around, he hurled the pillow into Taliesin's startled face, catching the sleepy bard completely by surprise.

"Conal, you scared the life out of me!"

"Morning, Tal. What torture have you got lined up for me today?"

Taliesin threw the pillow back at the Prince as he listed off the day's schedule. Conal nodded and occasionally groaned, while preparing for his morning run.

"Oh, I nearly forgot. Declan suggested doing riddles with you, so here's one to think about while you're running."

"I hate riddles, Tal. Do I have to?"

"That's why they're important to practise. We don't want the fair to think we've elected a stupid king now, do we? Anyway, here goes: I'm a giant, and I can fly while standing on my own two feet. I'm blessed by the Seven, but hold within me: envy, cowardice, and rage. What am I?"

"I'm never going to get that!"

"Just think about it. I'll meet you at the stables afterwards, and we'll see how you've got on. Declan wants you to begin with the javelins today so bring your armour."

"What do I need my armour for if I'm throwing javelins?"

"In case you fall off the chariot, of course. Getting run over can be a bit painful, to say nothing of the scythe-blades."

"Is that really necessary when I'm training?"

"Declan's a firm believer in 'start as you mean to go on'. It's no use you getting into a comfort zone. The blades will keep you focused on your balance while you throw."

"Fine! If you insist, I'll wear my armour."

*****

They slipped quietly through the fog, making their way down the far side of the mountain. Maerlin had mixed feelings about going home. Much though she missed the quiet solidity of her father, she had few happy memories there, at least since her mother's death. She had always been different from the taller fair-haired children of the village, and until recently, she hadn't even known why that was. Now, she knew that the reason behind these differences lay in her mother's ancestry. It was in the blood that ran strongly through Maerlin's veins: Pectish blood. But it was more than that. It was Maerlin's magical abilities, the unique combination of her abilities as a Dream-catcher and an Air-sister. These powers had set her apart from the other villagers and alienated her. They had feared her, and eventually, they had forced her father to abandon her.

Hindsight, however, had given her a different viewpoint. They had set her free and given her the opportunity to find her destiny. Had the villagers not sent for the healer to cure her, she would never have met Nessa. She would not have had the opportunity to learn about the Order of Deanna and of the blessings that she had been given. The villagers were simple, superstitious people, with little knowledge of the world beyond their mountain. This didn't make them evil or even stupid for that matter. They had no need of the knowledge of magic before Maerlin had come along. Realising this, Maerlin also knew that it was time for her to put aside her childish anger at the people of High Peaks and accept them for what they were.

As they broke through the dense fog and flew down into the high pastures where the cattle grazed during the summer moons, Maerlin called a halt. They stopped outside the small cave that she had so often used as a shelter. With tear-filled eyes, she walked into the cave and sat down. So much had happened since the last time she had taken shelter here. That was the day that she had become a woman and suffered her first moon-bleed, frightened and alone. Not even a full year had passed since that day, but for Maerlin, a whole lifetime had come and gone.

"Are you okay, Maerl? They're getting worried."

"I'm fine, Cora. I'm just reminiscing, that's all. This is where I used to hide out when the world got too much for me."

"I used to have a place like that, too. It was high up in a beech tree where no one could ever find me."

Maerlin smiled and grabbed Cora's hand. "You've no idea how much your friendship means to me, Cora. I'd be lost without you."

Cora squeezed Maerlin's hand. "I think I do, Maerl. You're the best friend anyone could ask for. Now, let's get out of this smelly old cave and go somewhere warm ... pleeeeeaaase!"

"Okay, we'll go and meet the villagers ..." Maerlin agreed, "...but on one condition."

"What's that?"

"We'll go there in style! I'm not riding to High Peaks on that dusty old rug. If I'm going to have to face my past, I'm doing it with some panache. I'm going to fly there under my own powers. Do you want to join me?"

"Just you try and stop me."

It took some persuading, especially with Nessa, who was always reluctant about the misuse of magic and was abhorred the idea of using the goddess's blessings for showmanship, but eventually Ness agreed that under the circumstances it was probably for the best. She felt that Deanna would understand.

And so it was that Maerlin Smith of High Peaks returned to the village of her birth on the second day of spring. She flew in on her quarterstaff and led the others into the village square. Stopping before her father's smithy, she waved nonchalantly to the villagers, before racing into her father's surprised arms.

"What in the blazes ...?"

"Hi, Poppa, the blessings of Imbolc upon you."

"Maerlin, I hardly recognise you. By the gods, you've grown!" Holding Maerlin at arm's length, he inspected her closely through the tears that welled up in his eyes. "You look so much like your mother, it hurts me to look at ya, but it's great to see you all the same. I didn't think you'd ever come back here once you'd seen a bit of the world."

Guilt washed over Maerlin. In truth, she wouldn't have come back and faced her inner fears, had it not been for the danger that the village faced.

"I've got lots to tell you, Poppa, but first I want you to meet some people." Maerlin dragged him out into the sunshine and over to where the others waited.

"This is my friend, Cora. She's a Water-sister of the Order of Deanna. Oh, and she's also a princess of the Western Isles, by the way."

Maerlin's father gently took Cora's hand and shook it. "I'm very pleased to meet you, ya Majesty."

"I'm pleased to meet you too, but please call me Cora. Everyone else does. That whole thing about my father being the King is so overrated."

"Cora! Your father is King Mannaman the Wise: the legendary ruler of the Clan of the Seals. Not everyone can say that!"

"Ach! He's just a big, old cuddly bear really ... but you do get invited to some great parties."

Maerlin's father smiled nervously as he was led over to where Seabhac stood. "Poppa, this is Seabhac: Air-sister of the Order of Deanna ... oh, and by the way, she's your grandmother."

"What was that?"

"I said that she's your grandmother. I assume you haven't met before. Momma was the daughter of Iolar-Mara: Lord of the Hawk People, and this is Iolar-Mara's mother: Aiteann's grandmother."

"I do wish thou would stop bringing that up, Maerlin. It's hardly necessary."

"But I've never had a grandmother before. Well, not one that I knew, anyway. Let alone a great-grandmother. Maybe I'll get tired of the novelty ... eventually."

Seabhac shot Maerlin a flinty look before smiling a greeting at her new grandson. "It's a pleasure to meet thee, good sir."

"I'm honoured," he replied, still reeling from the shock. "Please, call me Eoghan."

"And this is Fintan, her ... well let's just keep it simple and say that this is Fintan."

Eoghan bowed to the hen harrier, though his face showed confusion as he added "I'm pleased to meet you, too."

"Are you going to let me out of here any time soon? It's getting kind of stuffy in here, and all this jostling is doing nothing for my tail feathers."

"Oh sorry, Nessa, I forgot all about you."

"So I gathered!"

Maerlin quickly opened her fur cloak and carefully set the magpie on her shoulder. "And of course, Poppa, you've met Nessa *MacTire."* She indicated the magpie.

"Erm ..."

"Yes, I know, Poppa it's complicated. We've got a lot to talk about. How are things here?"

"Oh, you know ... just fine. It's the same old place. Nothing has changed really, but we've all heard the stories about you defeating whole armies of evil magicians and rampaging around the country. Are they all true?"

"Hardly!" Maerlin assured, "You really shouldn't believe everything you've been told."

"But you ..." Eoghan stopped and indicated the quarterstaff, which was still obediently hovering a few feet above the ground.

"Oops!" Maerlin released the Sylph with a silent thank you, and the staff clattered to the ground. "Let's just say that I've learned a few things, and we'll leave it at that, shall we?"

"The villagers are boasting all over the mountain about how one of their own has become the next Uiscallan."

"One of their own, eh? Mmm, anyway, much though I'm honoured to finally be accepted around here, there're more pressing matters that need to be discussed. Poppa, you're about to be invaded, so we need to get everyone together and find a way to put a stop to it."

"Invaded? Maerlin, don't be silly. We live at the top of a mountain. Who'd want to invade us?"

The concerned look on Maerlin's face erased his smile. "You're serious, aren't you?"

"Sadly, yes, I am. That's why I came back."

"I'll go and get everyone together."

Maerlin watched her father march purposefully away, chewing nervously on his lip. He was not a man who took surprises well, and she was sure that she'd brought a whole bucketful of them with her for him to chew over. "Come on. We'll head to the tavern. It's the only place big enough to fit everyone in, and even then it'll be a tight squeeze. At least it'll be warm, and we'll be able to get something to eat and a place to sleep. I don't think we'd all fit in Poppa's hut."

*****

When Gearoid and the monks arrived at the docks of *Ard Pect*, they found the monastery's currach already tied there. "It looks like we've come to the right place," he said. "Could you two find us some lodgings for the evening and take our stuff ashore? I'll take a walk around the city and see if anyone has spotted them."

"Shouldn't we come with you, Abbot?" Brother Niall asked, as Tomas steered the raft alongside the currach.

"It might be dangerous, Niall. I can't risk that. The monastery has lost enough good men already ..."

"But, are we not brothers, Abbot? Are we not supposed to look out for each other?"

Gearoid could not argue against Niall's logic. It was for this very reason that he felt the need to rescue Brother Balor and Brother Fionn. With a sigh he relented, "Very well then, but please be careful and do exactly what I tell you. I couldn't live with myself if you two got hurt, as well. We'll find some lodgings for the night, and then we'll head on up to the palace."

"Why the palace...?"

"...Because it's the obvious place for *him* to go, Tomas."

"There's a tavern over there at the end of the docks," Niall pointed out.

"I don't think that'd be a good choice, Brother. It might be wiser to visit the Sisterhood of Deanna and seek more suitable hospitality. They may have heard something about the others, too. Grab our bags, Brothers; it's not far from here."

Chapter Twenty-Five: Cliodhna's Kiss

"Stop fidgeting!" Cora hissed, as they waited for the last of the villagers to arrive.

"That's easy for you to say. You're not the one who's going to have to speak to them. Is it hot in here?"

"It's fine! Just take a few deep breaths. I'm sure you'll be great. That must be the last of them now. I see your father closing the doors."

"Well, it looks like it's time for me to make a fool of myself," Maerlin grumbled, as she rose nervously to her feet. She looked around at the waiting faces. The whole village was there. Even Duncan Gammit and his cronies had come along. She could see them whispering together in the back seats.

Straightening her spine and lifting her head, she looked toward the back wall rather than into individual faces. She focused on a picture that was hanging there and spoke to it. At least it wouldn't pull faces at her while she was going through this ordeal.

"I've come to speak to you on a matter of grave importance," she began. Breathe, she thought, just breathe. "Your lives are all in danger, and we've come to offer our help."

"How do ya know this, Maerlin?" a voice interrupted Maerlin, pulling her vision away from the safety of the picture and into the crowd. The voice belonged to Auntie Millie, who was a distant cousin of her father's. Everyone in the village was someone's cousin, or an uncle twice-removed. Such was the nature of small communities. If they weren't a blood relative, then they were married to one.

Clearing her throat, Maerlin smiled. "Well Millie ... it's like this. I dreamed it, just the same as I dreamed the storm that killed my mother." There it was ... out in the open. They would just have to deal with it.

A low murmur of conversation broke out and Maerlin waited, allowing it to ebb and flow. She kept her eyes fixed on Millie, fighting the urge to run away. Finally, she raised her hands above her head for silence.

"When I left here, I visited a place called the Holy Isle. It's in the Great Marsh, far to the south of the mountains. There, I met the High Priestess of the Order of Deanna, who is a renowned Dream-catcher. She told me that I also have this gift. With it, one can see the past, the present and even glimpses of the future. I was told that I'm also gifted with the powers of an Air-sister. That means that I can do a very special type of magic. They told me that I've the potential to become a Storm-Bringer, which is why I have such an affinity for storms. Before coming here, I spoke to my fellow priestesses." Maerlin indicated her companions, sitting silently behind her. "And we all agreed that this particular vision was a real threat, and that it was likely to happen soon. Too much of the dream was accurate, and pertinent to what is happening now, to make us think otherwise. That's why we made the perilous trip over the Mountain of the Gods. Even for priestesses of Deanna, such a feat is not without danger."

Again the room broke out into murmured discussions, and she waited, though her legs felt like jelly. The villagers would need time to digest all that she had told them.

"You're doing great," Nessa assured her silently. *"Remember to show confidence. If you show any doubt, they'll sense it. You need to be strong for their sakes."*

"Tell us more about this dream, Maerlin," Auntie Millie asked. Her reassuring smile gave Maerlin some strength, so with a nod Maerlin began. She told them everything that she could remember, branching off occasionally to explain briefly about certain characters in the dream, or to put a comment into context.

"So, thishhh Lord Boare isshhh sending troopshhh into our mountainshh becaushhh of you?" Uncle Joe asked, his question whistling past his one remaining tooth.

Maerlin bowed her head. The accusation was true, and there was no use denying it.

Before she could respond, Millie answered for her "Ach! Joe, ya auld windbag! Ya can't be layin' dis at the wee lassie's door. From the sound of it, he was a rotten kettle of fish to begin with. If it wasn't for Maerlin and this prince-fella, we'd all be up to our necks in the privy. If not this year, then they'd have come next year, or the one after. Cut the wee lassie some slack, will ya? She didn't need to come here and offer us any help.

It's not like we've been all that good to her lately, though it shames me to admit it."

Maerlin could see others nodding in agreement. She tried to speak, but the lump in her throat had become too big to swallow.

"Be brave, Maerlin."

Quickly wiping her eyes and fighting back her emotions, Maerlin smiled at Millie. "Thank you, Millie, but Joe's right. They're coming here for me, or for those that mean anything to me. I'm sorry, honesty I am, but there's nothing I can do about that. I didn't ask to be given these powers, and no matter what I do, it seems I'm destined to be embroiled in this whole mess ... but yes, the blame lies with me. Nevertheless, we still need to deal with it. I'll go out and I'll hunt down this particular band of killers, and I'll stop them from hurting you. Believe me, when I tell you this. There will also be a reckoning with Lord Boare over this, but that doesn't stop the risk to you and yours. I can't be here all the time. I can't always be at Twin Falls, Gorse Meadow, Sally Tops, or the other villages on the mountain, either. So it's important that you know about this danger and that you do what you can to defend yourselves. Prince Conal and many others are fighting to prevent Lord Boare from becoming the next High King, but if they fail, as Millie pointed out, the world beyond these mountains will drag you into its politics just like it did to me. We cannot hide in these mountains and hope that the world goes away!" Maerlin's temper had flared, and she finished with passion in her voice and a soft rumble of thunder outside.

"Take a deep breath, Maerlin. You're doing great, but we don't want to scare them by blowing the roof off the tavern now, do we?"

"I'm sorry Maerlin! I washhn't trying to get at ye," Joe wheezed in apology. "I washh just tryin' ta figure it all out, thatshh all. I know ya could've left ushh be, but ya took da time ta come 'ere 'n' talk to ushh, and I'm sure we all want to thank ye for dat. Twashh a bad day when we sent ya away like that, and many of ushh burned with the shame of it. By the time we copped on, it washh too late to do anythin' about it. You'd already gone, but it warmed our heartshh to hear dat ya were doing great thingshh in da world. We were mighty proud to hear that it was one of our kith and kin!"

The rumble of agreement was louder this time. Tears rolled silently down Maerlin's cheeks.

Finally, it was Eoghan who broke the silence. He was always known as a silent man, not one who spoke out at meetings, let alone in front of the whole village, and even more so when he was sober. "What do you suggest we do, Maerlin? We aren't warriors. We've nowhere to run to, and we aren't trained to fight either."

Maerlin didn't have an answer to that.

Cora rose to her feet and walked over to Maerlin's side. "I come from the Western Isles, and we, like you, live in isolation from the rest of Dragania. For many years we suffered from Reaver raids, from the pirates and slavers of the Icy Wastes. My father, King Mannaman, finally united the island Clans, knowing that there was strength in numbers. He made an agreement with the other Clan Lords. He made them understand that when one Clan was threatened, then we were all threatened. Watchtowers and signal fires were set up from one end of the archipelagos to the other, and whenever the fires were lit, the war boats of all the Isles took to the sea to challenge the Reavers. Ferocious sea battles ensued, but finally, we broke the backs of the raiders. They have learned to avoid our waters. Occasionally they still test our defences, but we are ever-vigilant, and we haven't lost a single Clansman to the Reavers in almost two decades. If you and the other villages do the same thing, together you can defend each other. Your mountains are like our islands, small and isolated, with the usual standoffish mentality, but believe me, there is strength in unity."

"Aye, an' if we put towers on the tops of the peaks, we'd be able to see for miles. It'd be hard for anyone to sneak up on us, if we did that!" Duncan Gammit blurted out.

"But you'd have to get the other villageshh to agree?" Joe argued.

"Maerlin will have to speak to them, just like she spoke to us. I'm sure she can make them see sense," Duncan declared, surprising Maerlin with his support.

"There's no one on this mountain that's not related to someone here," Eoghan added. "We're all in this together, whether we like it or not. When Maerlin and her friends are out looking for these Boarites, she can speak to the other villagers. If some of us go along, we can add our weight to her words."

*****

Conal looked blankly at Declan. "Isn't that a bit dangerous?"

"...Only if you miss. As long as your feet land perfectly on the shaft, you'll be fine. It really is the best place to cast a javelin from. There's less movement there than anywhere else on the chariot."

"But what if I miss?"

"I wouldn't recommend that if I were you. It's likely to hurt a lot ... even if it doesn't kill you."

"Isn't there another way?"

"Not if you want to hit the targets, there isn't."

"Let me get this straight. You want me to jump off the back of a fast-moving chariot, land on the thin shaft that runs between the ponies as they are galloping along, balance there, and then throw a javelin at the target. Is that all?"

"Yep, that's about it. Don't forget the part about jumping back onto the driving board afterwards though. You'll need to get the next javelin. Oh ... and avoid the scythe-blades whatever you do. You'll be given five javelins to throw on each round of the trial, and the points you score on each cast accumulate as you proceed toward the final. That's if you get that far."

"I see! I'm glad we've got all that straightened out. Now ...there's just one more thing. Why is the chariot standing on blocks?"

"We thought we'd give you a few tries without the horses first... so you can build up your confidence."

"Believe me when I tell you this, *nothing* is going to build up my confidence about this. I guess we might as well give it a go."

"Look on the bright side, Conal," Taliesin added, from the edge of the paddock. "The other contestants have only had a year to train for this, so they won't be too far ahead of you."

Conal gave the bard a dirty look and began to strap on his armour. "There's always a smart-mouth sitting in the cheap seats, isn't there?"

"I'm just trying to help."

"Maybe you ought to shear some sheep instead."

"I'm sorry, Conal, but I can't do that. My dad always said that I wasn't cut out for manual labour."

"It's a good job you can hold a tune, then, isn't it?"

"By the way, did you manage to answer the riddle I set you?"

"No, not yet, but don't tell me. I still haven't given up on it."

"Let me know when you do. Now, get on the chariot and we'll see what your javelin throwing is like."

*****

Maerlin slipped into her dreams....

She thought she was back on the mountaintop, wandering through dense fog with no clue of her direction or destination.

"Hello? Is anyone there?"

At first there was no response, but eventually she heard an answer. "Maerlin, is that thee?"

"Ceila?"

"Thank the goddess. I thought I'd never find thee. What on earth is going on? Where hast thou been?"

"Sorry, Ceila, but I've been a bit busy."

"Thou hast been gone for moons. I finally got word from Cull yesterday. Art thou with him or art thou with Conal? I gather that he left the Prince at Dragon's Ridge, but that doesn't make any sense."

"What exactly did the message say?"

"It said that Conal was safe, and that he was rebuilding Dun Dragan. Cull was in Manquay, sorting out the Beggars' Guild after Broll's passing. He said that he'd meet me at the Gathering of the Clans and fill

me in on the details there. That was about it. There is only so much that he could fit on a note for the dove to carry."

"Wow! That's a lot of news to cover. I haven't seen Conal or Cull since before the first snows of winter. They left us behind when they went to Ard Pect."

"Ard Pect? Why would Cull take Conal to Ard Pect?"

"Cull took Conal and Taliesin there when he went to spy on King Conchubhar."

"Who's Taliesin? Why were they spying on the King of Tir Pect? No, forget that. More importantly, did they leave thee behind on thy own?"

"No, I've got Nessa and Cora with me."

"Hang on! I thought Nessa was dead!"

"She is ... well, was ... it's a bit complicated, and I haven't figured it all out myself yet."

"I'm clearly going to need to sit down and interrogate someone for a few days before I can make sense of all this."

"Listen, Ceila, we're all fine, and I'm sure if Cull left Conal behind, it was for a good reason."

"Let's start with something easier, shall we? Where art thee now?"

"We're in High Peaks."

"What, by Deanna's sweet grace, art thou doing in High Peaks? Is there something wrong with thy father?"

"No, he's fine, but Lord Boare plans to slaughter everyone here, so I've come to stop him."

"That sounds dangerous. I hope Nessa is looking after thee."

"Erm ... about Nessa. There's a bit of a problem there."

"Is something wrong with Nessa? Is she sick?"

"No, no! She's perfectly healthy. It's just ... well ... it's just ..." Maerlin sighed. "It's just that Nessa's a magpie."

"Pardon?"

"You know... a magpie. It's a small black and white bird, kind of like a crow."

"I know what a magpie is, Maerlin, but did thou just say ..."

"Yes. Nessa's a magpie, but other than that she's as fit as a fiddle."

Maerlin could sense Ceila's frustration. "Maerlin, speak slowly, and tell me exactly why Nessa is a magpie?"

"It was part of the deal that Deanna made with Macha. Nessa was reincarnated, but now she has to serve both goddesses."

"I knew that I shouldn't have asked! So basically, Cora and thee are alone on the top of a mountain, and thou art about to pick a fight with some Boarite soldiers. Is that it?"

"Oh no, Ceila. We have Seabhac and Fintan with us."

"Who exactly are Seabhac and Fintan?"

"Seabhac is my great-grandmother, Uiscallan the Storm-Bringer, and Fintan is ..."

"Stop! Stop! I don't think I want to know. My head's hurting enough already. Every question I ask, gives me three more riddles to unravel. Perhaps ignorance is the better option. I shall ponder all that thou hast told me and speak with the other Dream-catchers..."

The mists swirled, and Maerlin sensed that she was alone again.

She slipped back into restless sleep, but it wasn't long before she found herself again in the land of her Dream-catching.

A beautiful woman walked calmly down a passageway and into a walled garden. It was at the rear of a palatial building, and here, she prepared for some arcane ritual. She looked up at the pinkening sky and smiled. The sun would soon be up, and it would burn away the last of the pre-dawn mist.

Tying her hair back into a bun, she shed her silken gown, letting it slide gracefully off her body and pool around her feet.

Maerlin immediately noticed something unusual about the naked woman. It was hard to miss the four breasts that protruded from her naked chest.

The woman crouched down and uncovered a large jar, and then proceeded to smother her nakedness in the honey. When she was fully immersed in the warm, gooey substance she walked slowly forward, heading for the beehives nearby. There she stopped, arms and legs akimbo in supplication, facing the newly-rising sun. The goddess star, Venus, so long associated with love and beauty, nestled close to the sun as it crested the horizon and filled the garden with the light and warmth of spring.

The woman began to sing, a low, humming song filled with droning chants. Standing splayed and open to the elements, she worked her magical arts and called the bees forth from their hives. Slowly at first, the sluggish insects stirred, flew up, and settled upon her honey-encrusted body.

The humming buzz of the swarms, and the woman's song rose together in sweet harmony, and soon she disappeared under the tide of yellow and black bodies, each suckling upon her nakedness.

The woman quivered, for even within her trance-like state, the pleasure was intense. Her quivering caused a few of the bees to panic and sting her, but this only seemed to heighten her pleasure. As they feasted on the honey-drenched skin, they cleaned her body and rejuvenating her flesh. Her body shook in orgasm from the bees kisses. Finally, the bees were sated and began to drift away, one by one, in search of the first pollen of the season.

The woman remained standing, muscles quivering slightly with the effort, until the last of the bees left her. Her eyes remained closed as she finished her spell and became quiet. With a sigh, she relaxed her strained muscles. "Blessed be Cliodhna, goddess of beauty and love!" she exclaimed, looking up at the bright star.

Maerlin awoke with a startled cry, her own body shaking with her first orgasm. It shook her to the very core and left her sweaty and flushed in the pre-dawn chill. Still only half-awake, she felt Cora's arms enfold her, caressing her over-sensitive skin. The scent of Cora's sweet perfume filled her nostrils.

"Hush, Maerlin, it's alright. It was only a bad dream," Cora assured, misunderstanding the passion that still coursed through Maerlin's panting body.

The arcane ritual of the goddess of love had yet to fully release her from its grip. Shakily, Maerlin clung to Cora, gasping as she tried to gain control.

Cora kissed her neck gently, murmuring "It's alright, Maerlin. I'm here for you." She continued to stroke and comfort Maerlin.

Maerlin turned to look at Cora intensely, their faces close together, and then their lips met. Maerlin couldn't be sure who had kissed who, but enveloped in the soft cocoon of passion her body moaned in hunger, and her kisses became more urgent. The magical glow that was boiling up inside her quickly transferred to Cora, and they were swept away by their desires.

*****

Shaking off the last of her sensual tingling, Sile proceeded with her morning ritual, for beauty and youth needed more than just the regenerative spell of the honeybees. It also needed hard work. She lifted two razor-sharp stilettos and stretched her muscles. Chanting softly, she danced, twisting and thrusting with the blades as she went through her daily routine. She pranced and twirled until her body dripped sweat like raindrops, and her mind glowed with heated blood. Finally, she spiralled down to a stop and relaxed. Standing still, she clenched and unclenched each muscle in turn, tensing and relaxing herself from head to foot.

Once the knives were put aside, she walked over to the spring-fed pool in the corner of the garden. There she braced herself and with a sudden whoosh and a whoop of joy, she dove feet-first into the icy water. Although the pool was not large, it was deep - a full seven feet in depth - and she sank fully into the pool. Surfacing with a spluttered laugh, she shuddered and began to wash, letting the icy water seal her pores as she bathed.

Her morning ritual completed, she pulled herself out onto the rocks and lay there, letting Lugh, the sun god dry her well-formed body. This was one of the secrets of her long-lasting beauty. These morning rituals contained some of the magical enhancements that kept her looking so young and fresh. The magical arts had taken years of study to master, for it was no simple incantation to summon forth the swarms, nor was it an easy task to stay perfectly still while they cleaned the honey and dead skin from the body. The Dance of Blades was likewise not mastered without constant training, but within these rituals the secrets of Sile's youthful complexion were hidden.

When she had dried off completely, she headed back into the Pink Rose to start another day. Firstly, she had to organise the cleaning staff and review the previous evening's business, and then she would collect and sort the snippets of information which each of the staff had gathered during their work.

Most of this information would seem inconsequential or useless, but when filed and sorted a veritable pool of knowledge could be garnered. The working girls and boys would be sleeping soundly by now, after a hard night's activities, but others would be waking and starting their day. These she would have to oversee before she could seek out her own bed.

She headed down a dusty staircase into the wine cellar beneath the house, and from there she went down ill-lit passageways until she reached a solid brick wall of weathered stone.

She paused, selecting a particular stone and pressed it firmly. Again, she paused, counting in her head, and then she selected another stone, farther down. She waited and counted, and a third stone in the sequence was pressed. With a grating sound, the wall moved aside as a final stone was triggered, revealing a passageway into the darkness beyond. Raising her candlestick high, she stepped through the opening.

A farther hundred yards down the passageway was another wall and another mechanism, which she methodically opened to reveal a well-lit room.

Here, her retired girls and boys worked when their work above had ended. Sile's trade was mostly a trade of youth. Here, in the depths of the Pink Rose, she had established a secondary employment for the loyal staff who had for years been gleaning the gossip of the day. Here, they now worked on the snippets of information, sorting, collating, and filing them away in precise order.

Sile handed over the night's pickings to a wrinkle-faced old lady and wandered through the crowd of silent people, busy shuffling parchments.

She loved to come here before sleeping. The knowledge garnered here gave her comfort and soothed her mind. Within this chamber lay her life's work.

Sile read the data, which had been compiled as it made its way down the row of tables, memorising the relevant details. She never took a single parchment out of this room, memorising the details before leaving in case the secrets were compromised. When she had finished, she finally sought out her bed. She would sleep on the newly-gained knowledge and allow it to sink into her brain and mingle with the other secrets, great and small, that were hidden there.

*****

Maerlin woke up as the first rays of the pre-dawn sun broke through the window, and she realised what time it was. Unwrapping herself from Cora's arms, she shook her urgently. "Hurry, we're going to be late!" she urged, as she quickly dressed.

Cora struggled awake and reached for her own robe. Together they rushed from their room, bumping into Seabhac in the doorway, where she was standing with a fist raised, about to knock.

"Sorry, we overslept!" Maerlin mumbled as they rushed past on their way outside.

Maerlin's mind was far from the 'Dawn Chorus' as they sang together. Doubts and concerns interrupted on her thoughts. When the song had finished, they headed back inside to break their fast.

"Art thou feeling well, Maerlin? Thou seemeth a bit 'out of sorts' this morning," Seabhac asked.

"Oh, I'm fine. I just had a strange dream, that's all."

"A dream, eh. Dost thou want to talk about it?"

Maerlin flushed and hurried on. "No, I'm fine. I'm just a bit groggy this morning, that's all."

"Cora seems to be in a world of her own, too. Maybe thou should speak to each other about thy dreams and compare them? When thou art ready, we can discuss our plan of action."

"Good idea. I'll let Cora know."

Hurrying inside, Maerlin grabbed a few handfuls of biscuit and a pot of yoghurt and motioned Cora into their bedroom. There, they could talk in private. Dropping the food on the bed, Maerlin blurted out "Cora, I'm sorry! I don't know what came over me."

"What?"

"About last night ... I think it was the dream."

"What are you talking about, Maerl?

"You know ... the kissing and stuff." Maerlin flushed and was at a loss for words.

"Didn't you like it?" Cora's face was a mask of concern.

"Well, yes, but ..."

Cora came over and stroked her cheek. "Maerlin, there's no need to be sorry. What we shared last night was something wonderful, and there's no need to worry about it ... unless of course I did something wrong?"

"No, no ... it's just ... I've never done that before. I ... I don't know what came over me."

Cora kissed her lightly on the neck, bringing back warm memories and sending a shudder down her back. "Hush Maerlin, you've nothing to worry about. The priestesses often share their love for one another. It gets lonely on the Isle, away from our families and friends. Many of the novices do it too."

"You mean you've..."

"Once or twice, just to see what it was like, but what we did last night meant more ... at least to me. However, if you didn't like it, we never need to speak of it again."

Maerlin slid her hand into Cora's. "I didn't say that! It's just ... well ... can we keep this just between the two of us? I'm not sure if I'm up to kissing in public yet, if you know what I mean." Her eyes implored Cora to understand, and she was relieved to see Cora's impish smile.

"I guess so ... but you'll have to make it up to me when we're alone."

A weight of worry lifted from Maerlin's shoulders. "That'll have to wait for now. Firstly, we need to eat. I don't know about you, but I'm starving. Then, Seabhac wants us outside. I think she has a plan that she wants to discuss."

Cora gave a mock pout of disappointment before biting into a biscuit. "Very well then, if you insist."

Chapter Twenty-Six: Trading Places

Dubhgall stood on a raised platform before the palace's training ground, beside the King and Queen. He maintained firm control over Fionn with his physical and mental grasp. "Are these the best of your magicians? They're a sorry bunch, if ever I saw them!"

Studying them as they displayed their battle skills left Dubhgall with a bitter taste in his mouth. Compared to the trained sorcerers he had previously had at his disposal, the rabble before him were a poor lot. Individually, they were competent enough, but they had never been coordinated before into a united fighting force. "This could take many moons to bear fruit ... years even."

"We haven't got years, Mage. Our spies have confirmed our earlier intelligence. Now is the time to strike, while the *Fear Ban* are in disarray."

"What about your soldiers? I hope they're better trained."

"Don't worry about the warriors of *Tir Pect*, Mage. They are ferocious and hungry for this fight. Our magicians, however, have never been able to get their own egos to work cohesively. I can see an improvement already, and I'm sure they'll quickly develop under your guiding hand, but are you sure about the wisdom of this morning's executions?"

Dubhgall swivelled Fionn's eyes to take in the burned remains that lay nearby. "An example needed to be made, Sire."

"But they were the best we had!"

"Exactly, and that's why I chose them. Fear is a great motivator as I'm sure you know. The others will work twice as hard, knowing that death is only moments away. The risk of dissension in the ranks is diminished significantly with the loss of those three cretins. Believe me, they weren't that good really. They were all show and no substance. They were little more than Hedge-wizards."

"Can you work with what's left?"

"I'll have to, but as I said, it'll take a little time. Don't expect miracles overnight."

"Time is something we haven't got. Lord Boare is in disarray, and the young *Dragan* has yet to come into his own. The only other strong leader in Dragania is on the Western Isles, so now is the time to strike."

"What about this young Storm-Bringer we've heard about? She's not to be underestimated," Medb asked sullenly. "I thought you said that you could defeat her?"

"I can. She caught me by surprise last time. Next time, I'll be ready for her."

"I see no problems, then. We'll begin preparations straight away. I'll issue orders to the generals to assemble our forces. Within a moon, they'll be ready to march. You've got one full cycle of the moon to sort that motley crew out there into something worthwhile."

Dubhgall nodded, biting back a response. It seemed his only option was to succeed.

A page rushed over and spoke briefly to the King in a hushed whisper. Conchubhar looked over at Dubhgall, asking "Were you expecting company?"

"Sire?"

"It seems we have some Druids at the front gates. They're demanding an audience."

"Then I suggest you have them flogged and hanged for their impertinence."

"I'm not sure that our citizens would approve of hanging Druids. Shouldn't we see what they want before we discuss their possible demise?" Queen Medb suggested. She was clearly still vexed that her new plaything had been taken away from her.

*****

They left the tavern after breakfast and found that the villagers were already busy. The men folk had left at dawn, tools in hand, heading for the high pastures. There they were building the first watchtower. The community was comfortable working together. They would commonly work together when bringing in the harvests, shearing the mountain sheep, as well as communally building any houses needed. By midday, the wooden structure was well on its way, while the younger boys scoured the mountainside gathering a huge pile of gorse to build into a signal fire. Such a fire would light easily and burn brightly, leaving a good smoke trail that could be seen for miles. Gorse was in plentiful supply on the mountainside and ideal for the job.

The women surprised Maerlin even more. They all wanted to help with the search, and the prospect of flying on the flimsy-looking rug seemed not to deter them in the slightest. In fact, tempers began to rise when it became clear that Seabhac could not carry them all.

Nessa finally came up with the solution. *"Maerlin, Cora. Do you think you could raise more than one staff and still fly safely? If we're going to be so blatant about using magic, then we might as well have as many eyes out there as possible. After all, we have a lot of mountain range to comb."*

"Ladies, your attention please!" Maerlin shouted over the bickering. "Go and fetch your brooms."

As it turned out, Cora was strong enough to manage three brooms comfortably, while Maerlin could manage five and was considering adding another before Seabhac stopped her. "Five will suffice, Maerlin. They'll all have to be near enough to thee to maintain control, anyway. More than that would be pointless. I can take four safely on the rug and another two on brooms. If we can't spot them with that many people searching, then we're in trouble. They didn't come here to hide under rocks."

"Ladies, the rest of you will have to wait until tomorrow," Maerlin declared. Quickly, she got the selected villagers mounted on their brooms. With some reluctance, the rest went back to their chores, leaving the lucky ones to silently gloat.

"Okay, ladies, listen up! We're going to split up and search the mountain passes. We'll head toward the other villages. When we reach a village, we'll stop for long enough to speak to them. We'll meet back here before dusk, so please give plenty of time to get back. Night-flying is not recommended. Fintan, canst Nessa and thee handle the other passes, to make sure that they are covered? Maerlin, thou canst take thy crew to Twin Falls. Cora, thou canst head for Gorse Meadow, and I shall proceed to Sally Tops," Seabhac instructed, pointing in the three different directions. Maerlin would head due south, while Cora headed west, toward the sea, and Seabhac would fly east toward the Broce Woods. "Fintan, take the south-west, and Ness, thou canst take the south-easterly direction. Alright, the morning is slipping past us ... let's fly!"

"She makes it sound so blasé!" Nessa grumbled, still unhappy about such flagrant use of magic.

"If anyone spots the enemy, please do not engage them. I'm sure that they'll be well armed. I want thee to head back here and light the signal fire. If thou see the fire burning, thou wilt know to head home at once. Does everyone understand?" Seabhac asked, before signalling her ladies onto the rug. "Remember ladies; keep thy posteriors firmly on the rug at all times. Sit back to back so that thou canst look in all directions."

And so, the search for the invaders began. The first day was unsuccessful, as was the second. They did, however, get the cooperation of the nearby villages. Each agreed to build watchtowers and signal fires. Soon, the mountainside was a-buzz with busy people.

Each evening they flew home, too exhausted and broom-sore to do anything but sleep. The novices grew accustomed to falling sleepily in each other's arms after silently shuffling their cots together and waking up still entangled. Each morning, they quietly separated the beds before anyone came into their room.

There was one unusual occurrence on the third day. It was nearly dark, with the last rays of the sun slipping over the mountains, when not one but two magpies were spotted flying home.

"Where've you been all this time?" Maerlin demanded as Nessa settled onto her shoulder.

"I was a bit busy!" Nessa replied, a little peevishly.

"I see that you've brought a guest home for dinner."

"Tell me about it! I've been trying to shake him off all day. The poor blighter just won't take no for an answer."

"You mean you've got a boyfriend?" Cora teased.

"How would you like me to take a dump on your head, Cora?" Nessa warned testily.

"Oh, nasty! So you didn't invite him ... is that what you are saying?"

"Invite him! I nearly pecked his love-smitten eyes out, but the silly clod seemed to think it was some sort of foreplay. He's too young to know any better, I suppose."

"Ah, young love!" Cora cooed.

"Listen, Cora. You might be able to fool these villagers with your sneaking about in the night, but I wasn't reborn yesterday."

Maerlin flushed bright red, and even Cora looked a little surprised by Nessa's comment and stopped making fun of her.

"What are we going to do about him? He looks exhausted," Maerlin asked.

"Bring him in and feed him, I guess," Nessa conceded, somewhat reluctantly. *"I'll talk to him later and try to make him see reason."*

"So you can speak to him then?"

"Duh! Maerlin, I'm a magpie. It'd be logical that I'd be able to speak to other magpies, though he's not the brightest spark in the fire."

"Have you spoken to Fintan?"

"We have, once or twice. We speak when there's something important to say. He tends to be the strong, silent type. He's very polite, though."

"Has he told you anything about Seabhac ... about their past?"

"Not really. As I said he's a quiet one, but there's certainly a story to be told between those two."

"Is everything alright with Nessa?" Seabhac asked, making Maerlin jump. She hadn't heard her approaching.

"What! Oh, yes, she's just fine. She was just telling me that she'd invited a guest for supper. Speaking of which, I don't know about you lot, but I'm starving."

*****

Maerlin slipped into an exhausted sleep and woke to find a world of mists again.

She heard screaming and hurried toward the sound, racing through the mists until she broke free. She found herself in an isolated mountain valley. Below her she saw a solitary oak tree standing tall in the moonlight amidst a lush meadow. In the distance lay a silvery lake. The screams were coming from across the water. A village stood on the far side. Maerlin knew immediately where she was. She recognised the tree and the lake. It was here that Nessa had first taught her about magic, using the oak to help Maerlin see that which was before her eyes and yet unseen. They had stopped in the village for supplies, and Nessa had helped the local midwife with a difficult birthing.

Another blood-curdling scream filled the air, and Maerlin raced down the hill. On and on she ran, her breath burning in her lungs as she hurried around the lake. She was desperate to get to the other side and stop the awful screaming that echoed across the landscape.

The sky flared into brightness, and Maerlin looked around for the cause. Flames leapt skyward, as one after another, the thatches on the huts of the village caught fire. In the bright light she could clearly see the crosses and the silhouettes tied to them. They writhed as the flames rose higher and eventually engulfed them.

Maerlin yelled in rage and frustration. Tears streamed down her face. She was desperate to help, but unable to reach the far shore. One by one, the crucified figures collapsed into the inferno. As the last one slipped sideways into the hungry flames, sparks flew skyward, and Maerlin cried out in pure rage.

Seabhac burst into the bedroom, lantern in hand and stopped. Cora was trying desperately to console Maerlin. "What, by the Seven ..." Taking in the scene, she quickly slammed the door shut behind her, aware that the Tavern-keep and his wife were also stirring. She could hear them rushing down the stairs. "Art thou okay?" she asked softly, keeping her back firmly pressed against the door to prevent intrusion.

"She's awake now, at least. I couldn't get her to wake up at first," Cora replied, clearly shaken.

Seabhac nodded. "I'll be right back. I'd better go and calm the household before all hell breaks loose!" She left quickly, closing the door firmly behind her, and she could be heard speaking outside, confident and authoritative. Soon, order was resumed and with a soft knock on the door, Seabhac returned. Nessa was perched on her shoulder. No one, not even Seabhac, was going to stop Nessa from entering, even if she had to peck the door down.

They waited, sitting silent and helpless, until Maerlin was finally able to speak "I know where they are. I saw them, and saw what they were doing." Anger flashed in Maerlin's red-rimmed eyes. "They'll not leave this mountain alive!" she declared with venom.

"Dost thou want to talk about it?" Seabhac asked softly.

Maerlin shuddered, reliving her dream for a moment. "You really don't want to know the details. Tomorrow, I shall go and kill them ... every last one of them!"

"Maerlin, I know you're angry ..." Nessa placated.

"Angry ... Nessa, I'm bloody furious! They can't be allowed to get away with this! They came here looking for me. Well, tomorrow, they shall find what they came for." Rage rolled off Maerlin in waves.

"Maerl, whatever tomorrow brings, we should face it together," Cora assured.

"No! This is my fight."

"Don't be silly, Maerlin," Seabhac objected. "We didn't come all the way here to let thee face this danger alone."

"I'll be fine. You don't need to worry about me."

"Maerlin, anger is not the way. Revenge is not the way. Have I taught you nothing?"

Maerlin wiped her eyes and looked at Nessa. "They can't be allowed to do that ... ever again. Those villagers were innocent. What they did to them was ... evil."

"Maerlin, I understand your anger. It's not them that I'm worried about. It's you. If you use your powers for slaughter, it'll tarnish your soul. There is a price to pay for wanton destruction, and I fear for you. Some of those men are conscripts, caught up in something beyond their control. If you slaughter them, you'll be no better than Dubhgall the Black."

"But you didn't see it!"

"Maerlin, I've seen enough horrors in my life to make you weep for a year, but revenge is not the answer, believe me."

Maerlin stared off into the distance, lost in her own thoughts. Finally she nodded. "Very well, we'll go together, and we'll take as many of the ladies with us as possible."

"Whatever for?" Seabhac asked.

"I want a show of strength. I want Lord Boare to be so afraid of coming into these mountains that he won't send his troops here ever again."

"What's that got to do with the ladies? They can't do magic," Cora asked.

Maerlin smiled for the first time, an evil glint in her eye. "*I* know that. *You* know that, but he doesn't know that! Lord Boare has been looking for *one* witch in the mountains, but he's about to find far more than he expected. Seabhac, we'll take to the brooms tomorrow, as many as we can lift. Right now, I need to get dressed."

"But it's the middle of the night!"

"After what I just dreamed, I don't think I'll be able to sleep for a week! So who's for an early breakfast?"

*****

Abbot Gearoid led the others through the palace. They were escorted by a phalanx of guards. They had been forced to wait at the gates for most of the day, but eventually, they had been granted an audience. He regretted taking the young monks with him. They were bound to see things that would endanger their souls within the infamous palace. Neither of the young monks was prepared for the task ahead, but they had refused to stay behind.

"Remember, keep your eyes on the floor and your hoods up," he repeated for the third time. Brother Tomas had been entranced by the world around them. The opulence of the palace was bad enough, but it was nothing to the sordid tales of debauchery within its walls. Queen *Medb Ni Béar*, in particular, was renowned for her sexual hungers and sought out new conquests at every opportunity.

Double doors opened ahead of them, leading them into the massive throne room itself. Here, the twin-thrones of *Tir Pect* sat at the end of a rich purple carpet. Gearoid was sure that the cost of the carpet alone would feed the city for a year. Sitting on the thrones were the High King and High Queen of *Tir Pect*. To the King's right stood Brother Balor, with a firm grip on Fionn's shoulder. Fionn's blank expressionless face caused Gearoid's heart to skip a beat. Drool dribbled from his lips and ran down his bare chest. Queen Medb had refused to relinquish the monk's robe and had provided Fionn with a skimpy pair of leather shorts instead. They clung to his muscular thighs and barely covered his manhood, but it was his catatonic expression that pained Gearoid the most. Only the eyes moved, swivelling to follow the procession as they came nearer. On the Queen's left stood a stocky midget, dressed in motley clothing and wielding an inflated pigs-bladder on a stick. As Gearoid neared the dais, the fool scampered forward and pranced around the monks, occasionally swatting a buttock or chest with his balloon and giggling inanely.

Gearoid bowed deeply, ignoring the jester's antics.

"Your Royal Majesties, this is Gearoid Brightstar, the newly-appointed Head Monk of Leithban Monastery," the Captain of the Royal Guard announced.

"Head monk ... head drunk ... on sweet elixir ... we get the picture!" the jester prattled as he frolicked around.

Conchubhar looked up with a bored expression on his weathered face. "So this is the simpleton who *demands* an audience with the High Monarchs?"

Gearoid raised his head slightly from the bow. "Begging your humble apologies, Sire, but your guards refused us entry."

"Only your sackcloth has so far saved you from a public flogging, Druid," Conchubhar growled.

"Flay their skin ... on a whim ... branding iron ... will have 'em crying!"

"That's enough, Malachi, unless you want to test the heat of those irons on your own pox-riddled buttocks," Medb commanded, dismissing the fool.

The jester bowed deeply, touching his forehead to the floor in his obeisance. "My humblest apologies, my voracious Queen. You may do unspeakable things to me later for my impertinence. I am forever at your disposal for a sound thrashing."

Medb chuckled. "You'd enjoy it too much, Malachi. Now, be off with you, you cheeky imp!"

Gearoid waited for the chance to press his case.

"So, Druid, what have you to say for yourself?" Medb demanded.

Gearoid looked more closely at the infamous, High Queen. Both of the regents were big-boned and well-muscled for Pects, Conchubhar being the equal in height of any of the *Fear Ban*. The Queen, though slightly shorter in stature, was still a tall woman and nearly as broad of shoulder. Her voluptuous curves were hard to miss as she lounged on her throne. Her face would not be considered pretty. Her lips were a fraction too thin, and her nose had clearly suffered previous breaks. The smouldering power within her eyes, however, would make a poet swoon. He could well believe her reputation for ferocity: on and off the battlefield. She was acclaimed to be a holy terror on her war-chariot, with madness in her eyes and her long red tresses flowing behind her like a cape of fire. This was a woman who could test any man's vow of celibacy.

"Please, let me offer my apologies for any misunderstanding, your Majesties. I had requested an audience with my fellow monks. It was not my intention to disturb you."

"The Mage and his 'eyes' were busy doing the King's bidding, and therefore, you did in fact intrude on royal business," Medb advised, though she seemed more amused than annoyed.

"I say again, my apologies. As the leader of our Order, it falls upon me to protect my flock. Those men who stand beside you are in grave need of my help."

Conchubhar glanced over at Dubhgall's sneering face and at his drooling sidekick.

"I can understand your concern for the younger Druid. The one we have come to refer to as the 'Mage's Eyes', but the Mage himself doesn't appear to need your aid."

"Your Majesties, Brother Fionn is an innocent. He is inexperienced in the ways of the world and ill-suited to the machinations of the High Court. I beg you to release him from his bondage. Such treatment could permanently damage his tender mind. As for the one you refer to as the Mage, he is but one side of a coin and our Brother Balor is the other. It is for Brother Balor's sake that I have come. He is seriously ill and in need of special care, which only our monastery can provide. His inner-struggle against the *Darkness* within him is tantamount to his recovery. The longer that *Darkness* holds his soul within its grasp, the more peril to his soul. Let me take this opportunity to warn you both. There is a great evil hiding within the shadow of the Mage. It must not be allowed to gain ascendancy."

The King and Queen spoke in hushed tones for a moment before reaching a decision.

"Druid, sadly we cannot grant your request, much though we can understand your situation. We have need of the Mage, despite the risk that you speak of. It seems that Dubhgall's mind is the more dominant of the two. However, we appreciate your making us aware of his inner struggle. Much though the Royal Court respects all of the religious Orders, and we do our best to appease the gods and their servants, our need is great. Therefore, your wish is declined."

"What about Brother Fionn? Surely you have no need for him? Another could take his place ... that prancing fool, perhaps?"

This time, Conchubhar conferred with the Dark Mage. Dubhgall was clearly unhappy with the way the conversation was going, but finally nodded agreement.

"We have a dilemma here," Conchubhar announced. "Dubhgall has need of eyes in order to see the world. However, slavery has long since been outlawed within the kingdom of *Tir Pect*. I cannot order another to take the young Druid's place, but neither can I release him and leave the Mage handicapped. He is too valuable to our current objectives."

"Then let me be those eyes!" Gearoid offered, stepping forward. "That way, I can help Brother Balor, and my brothers can take Fionn home."

The room fell silent as his offer was considered. "Are you sure about this, Druid?"

Gearoid didn't hesitate for a moment. "I am."

"Then, let it be so!" Conchubhar declared, ordering the Dark Mage to release Fionn.

With some reluctance, Dubhgall moved forward. Placing his free hand on Gearoid's shoulder, he murmured "This is a stupid idea, Druid. Your friend is already lost to you. He's safely locked away, and I'll never let him out of his cage."

"I can only pray that he finds a way to escape your grasp, and when he does ... I'll be there to make sure that you never again see the light of day. I'll send you back to whatever Hell-pit you crawled out of."

"You'll be waiting a long time, Druid. Now, relax. You won't feel a thing." Dubhgall slipped easily past Gearoid's feeble defences, and Gearoid slumped as his face slackened. Releasing the other monk, Dubhgall allowed Fionn to collapse to the floor. "It's done, Sire," Dubhgall announced as he marched his new 'eyes' from the room.

Conchubhar stood and addressed the younger monks for the first time, "Take this young man home with my blessing, and let it be known that Abbot Gearoid volunteered for this new role of his own free will. Now be gone, before my wife finds a better use for you all."

Chapter Twenty-Seven: The Retribution

They left the village as the skies began to lighten. The clouds were heavy, reflecting Maerlin's mood. They had decided to forgo the Dawn Chorus prayer this morning. Today was not a day to sing their praises to Deanna. There was little joy in their hearts.

Led by Fintan and the magpies, a flying squadron of fifteen brooms took to the skies. Maerlin directed the procession south.

Knowing their destination made it easier, as they could fly at full speed. They did not need to scour the ground as they went. By mid-morning, they had covered many miles of mountainside. In the distance, they could now see smoke rising from the burned-out village and adjusting course slightly, they headed in that direction. It wasn't long before they circled over the dwellings, and all could see the remains of the previous night's horrors. The Boarites had already left.

"We'll need to split up and find them," Maerlin shouted.

"That won't be necessary," Seabhac assured, pointing skyward to where Fintan was soaring on the updraft. "Nothing will escape his hawk eyes."

A moment later, he screeched and dipped his wings, heading northeast. "Ah! He's found them. Let's go."

They followed the harrier, quickly covering the ground as they headed into one of the mountain passes. "Don't bunch up too much. We don't want to make an easy target for their archers," Seabhac warned, making sure that her own flyers were spread out.

The wagons came into view first, making slow going over the rough ground. The ladies flew low and fast over the Boarites. They flew so silently that they were already overhead before the first sounds of alarm came from the soldiers below.

"Bloomers! Bloomers!" Nessa cawed loudly, and Maerlin felt the venom in her voice, despite the innocuous insult.

"Pork-droppings! Pig-fondlers!" Auntie Millie berated. Soon the whole group were venting their hatred while they flew overhead.

Maerlin channelled her own building anger in a different way. Thunder rolled overhead, breaking in waves, and the ground shuddered in response. Suddenly, a sharp crack rumbled across the skies. For a moment everything went quiet, and then the rumbling increased. The snow-filled banks of the mountain began to slide down into the valley, picking up speed as it hurtled into the narrow pass.

It was a small avalanche, all things considered, but no less deadly for that. It crashed down into the tightly-packed ranks of Boarites with all the ferocity and power of a Snow Giant's fist.

"Ooooops!" Maerlin's tone showed little remorse.

"I thought thou said that thou wast going to ask them to leave. That *was* the plan, wasn't it?" Seabhac asked.

"I was just trying to get their attention, that's all. I didn't think it'd cause an avalanche."

"That's what happens when you use magic willy-nilly. You don't think things through first," Nessa scolded.

"Bloomers, Nessa ... really? Is that the best you could come up with?"

"It was the first thing that came into my head!"

"Well, at least you've found your voice," Cora pointed out, trying to put a positive spin on things.

"Fintan tells me that there's movement back there. It looks like thou didn't kill them all, Maerlin," Seabhac reported.

"Good. Let's drop the ladies off somewhere safe and head back. I'll need to speak to the survivors." Maerlin led them to the top of the ridge, now relatively free of snow, and safe for the villagers to stand on. "We'll be right back, ladies. In the meantime, I want you silhouetted against the skyline. You're well out of bow range so there's no danger. That's it, spread out and hold the brooms aloft so that they think you're about to fly down at a moment's notice."

Maerlin signalled to Cora and Seabhac, and the three of them glided down to where the Boarites were busy digging survivors out of the snow.

"Let's be careful. Have thy shields ready and remember to deflect any arrows rather than trying to stop them," Seabhac warned.

The Boarites noticed their approach and some drew bows, but the volley when it came, was half-hearted at best and far from coordinated. Maerlin deflected most of the incoming missiles, but her anger had not yet dissipated. In a fit of pique, she sent the last few arrows back toward the archers. After that, the bows were thrown down, and hands were quickly raised in surrender. The conscripts had little eagerness for the fight.

Three men, however, drew swords. These were dressed in black leather aprons and matching hoods covered their faces. These, Maerlin assumed, were Lord Boare's torturers. These were the men who had been responsible for the previous night's slaughter. Maerlin felt her anger rising again as she stared at the faceless murderers.

They stopped a few feet away, and Maerlin stepped off her quarterstaff and released the Sylph holding it. "Are you looking for me?"

"Are you the witch they call Maerlin Storm-Bringer?"

"Is that what they're calling me these days? I hadn't heard that one. I'm Maerlin of High Peaks, Air-sister of the Order of Deanna, and *you* are trespassing."

"Drop the staff and come quietly. You're under arrest for high treason, by the orders of Lord Boare."

Maerlin growled at the fool's stubbornness. "Let's get something straight, shall we? Firstly, you're on *my* mountain, and this isn't within the jurisdiction of Lord Boare. Secondly, the only ones under arrest around here are you three clowns. I intend to have the three of you up before a mountain court for your actions last night. You're wanted for murder. Now, I'm in no mood to get wet feet in this snow, so I suggest you come quietly before I lose my temper. You really don't want to see me when I do that."

The men tensed.

"Drop the bloody weapons, NOW!"

The conscripts were already backing away but the three torturers stood their ground.

"Very well, I tried to be nice," Maerlin said. "I asked them nicely, didn't I Cora?"

"Well ... sort of. Certainly better than scum like that deserve."

Maerlin beckoned forth an Air Elemental and showed it her will, which it eagerly put into action. The foremost torturer's sword jerked skywards, nearly wrenching his shoulder out of its socket as it was torn from his grasp. He yelped with pain and tried to reach for the sword, which danced tantalisingly, just out of reach.

"Here... let me help," Maerlin growled. With a flick of her fingers, the man was lifted into the air by invisible hands, his sword staying just ahead of him as he rose higher and higher. He screamed in fright as he grew smaller and became a dot in the sky.

Maerlin turned to look at the other two torturers. "You're still carrying swords. Why is that?" A dangerously soft tone had crept into her voice.

Their swords fell from their hands as if they were red-hot.

"You lot!" Maerlin ordered, pointing to the conscripts. "I want these murderers trussed up tighter than a drum, and be quick about it. I haven't got all day!"

The conscripts leapt to the task, roughly manhandling the torturers into irons, and then they used a rope to lash them firmly together.

Cora stepped forward and removed their hoods. "There, that's better. You shouldn't be able to hide your crimes behind a cloak of anonymity."

"Good idea," Nessa agreed.

Maerlin turned to the Boarite conscripts. "Who's in charge?"

The men looked around seeking a leader and eventually one of them stepped hesitantly forward. "I guess that'd be me, Ma'am. The Cap'n and the Sarge are both buried under that snow somewhere. As far as I'm concerned, they can stay there." The others nodded their agreement.

"I've a bit of a problem with you lot. You see, I've been told that you're conscripts and that you were just following orders, but what happened last night was unforgivable. Someone should have stepped in to stop that

306

sort of nonsense, but you let it happen, and to me, that makes you little more than spineless cowards. Nevertheless, I've been told to show you some mercy. So let me make this quite clear to you. The temptation to blast you all to smithereens is *really* strong right now, but I'm giving you one chance to redeem yourselves. This is your only warning. Should we ever meet again, you will die."

She looked each of them in the eye, remembering their faces. "I want you to turn around and leave my mountain and never come back. Having seen firsthand Lord Boare's punishment of those who fail him, I suggest you avoid Suilequay. Here are some options for you. If you think you can hide from his wrath, then I suggest you go and seek out some sewer to slither into. If not, then you might want to try one of the monasteries that scatter the countryside. They may take you in and offer you sanctuary. You can spend the rest of your lives praying for forgiveness. I hope you pray very hard, because the stain of last night's deed will take a lot to wash away."

She paused, looking harshly at them. "There is one other option ..."

"What's that?" the young corporal asked.

"Prince Conal of *Clann Na Dragan* is gathering a force on the Plains of the Dragon. I know him, and I believe that he'll make a good king, a worthy king, a king that men will follow." She paused, letting her words sink in "Maybe ... if you're lucky, he'll accept you into his service. You'll be able to fight to overthrow the man who forced you to take up arms. Conal doesn't want conscripts, however, only free men fight under his banner, so the choice is yours. If you choose this one, then tell him that I sent you. It might help to overcome his natural aversion to all things Boarite. Now, get off my mountain before I change my mind."

She watched as they gathered what possessions they could from the snow and hurried southwards. Finally, she turned to her companions.

"You did well, dear. Thank you," Nessa murmured, pleased that Maerlin had held her rage in check and not abused her powers.

"I hope I don't regret this, but we'll have to wait and see. Shall we go?" Maerlin hopped onto her staff and hovered there a moment as she focused on her two prisoners. Soon, they were hovering beside her, and she started forward.

"Hang on, Maerlin. I think thou hast forgotten something?" Seabhac announced, pointing upwards.

Maerlin glanced skyward for a moment confused, and then it dawned on her. "Oh, yes. I'd forgotten about him!" With a sigh, she released the Sylph, high overhead. "Okay, that's done."

As Maerlin moved on, the others could clearly hear the torturer's screams, getting louder, as he plummeted toward the ground.

His sword came first, shattering on impact. Seabhac cursed, "Damn it!"

The torturer came next, still screaming in terror.

Maerlin refused to look back, having braced herself for the sound of breaking bones, or at least a loud splat. Much though she disliked the thought of murder, she felt that the souls of the dead villagers deserved some retribution. She had hardened her heart and allowed the man to fall to his death, but somehow, she had been circumvented. The man floated there, inches above the ground.

"He has a strong heart, that one. Most people would've died of shock, long before hitting the ground," Nessa commented absently.

Cora wrinkled her nose. "It's unfortunate that his bowels aren't so strong ... and we're downwind."

"Which one of you did that?" Maerlin demanded, glaring at her companions. It had taken all of her willpower not to stop his fall, but someone had interfered.

"Sorry, Maerlin, I couldn't let you do that. I know how much it would have cost you," Cora apologised.

"No, Cora. It was me," Nessa admitted.

"Actually... it was neither of thee. Thou can't stop something going that fast with a force block. Thou hast to slow it down first!" Seabhac instructed, showing no remorse.

"All of you!" Maerlin exclaimed in exasperation. After a moment, she added "Thank you."

The torturer was still screaming, so Maerlin flew over and tapped him on the shoulder. He ignored her. He was too consumed in his own terror, so she reached out and pulled his hood off. He stopped screaming for long enough to open his eyes and look around. Seeing Maerlin in front of him made him start screaming again.

"Oh, stop that!" she demanded. Realising that he was beyond reason, she placed a hand over his mouth to silence him. His eyes were wild with fear as he looked at her. Placing a finger to her lips, she signalled for him to be quiet. Only when his muffled cries became whimpers, did she release her hand. "I have a special task for you. Are you paying attention?"

He nodded briefly.

"Good. I want you to deliver a message for me to Lord Boare."

The man shook all over, hearing his death sentence being pronounced. Either way, he was a dead man. It was just a matter of time. He could refuse and die now, or agree and die at the hands of Lord Boare. Hope is always a heady elixir, and he chose to die later.

"Tell him that this is *my* mountain, and any Boarite who steps foot on it is sentenced to death from this day forth. Oh, and tell him that I will come for him. The murder of those villagers will be laid at his door. There *will* be a reckoning for last night. Have you got all that?"

He nodded, his eyes still wide with terror.

"Good ... do not fail me on this. Now get off my mountain."

The Elementals holding him up were released, and he fell to the ground with a soft thud. By the time he looked up, Maerlin and the others were already flying away.

*****

Gearoid awoke. He was lying on a narrow cot in a richly-decorated bedroom. He tried to rise before he noticed the heavy straps across his limbs, restraining him. He could, however, move his head freely and raising it, he saw that Brother Balor was similarly restrained in the four-poster bed that dominated the room.

"Balor!" he hissed. "Balor, wake up!"

Balor stirred. "Is that you, Gearoid?"

"Yes, it's me."

"Where are we?" Balor started to rise from the bed. "I'm stuck. I can't get up. What's happening?"

Vague memories swirled in Gearoid's mind of how they had got here, and why they were strapped to the beds. "It's *him!* It's *his* doing. *He* had the guards secure us so that *he* could get some sleep. *He* gave very concise instructions that we were not to be disturbed."

"Who are you talking about?"

"*Him* ... the *Diabhal* who steals your soul and takes over your body: your other self."

"But why would I do that?"

"That's what I realised when we did the exorcism. I learned the key, the catalyst! It's magic. When magic is used, it releases the *Deamhan* within you. Every time magic has been used, *he* has emerged. It's the one common denominator."

"So, we are left here to rot until I use magic to release us, but by doing that, I release my other half. Is that it?"

"Exactly! We are doomed, either way."

"What are we to do?"

"I don't know. We wait, I guess. At some point *he* will make a mistake. Until then, there's nothing much we can do. In the meantime, we must act like obedient puppets to his mad scheme."

"You should've let me die, Gearoid, when you had the chance. I've caused too much death and suffering in this world already. I told you before, I am beyond redemption."

"No one is beyond hope, Balor. There is always hope. Now, let us pray."

"You want me to pray? The gods won't listen to me. Don't you understand? I was dedicated to Macha, and even she has abandoned me."

"Perhaps not ... let me get this straight. *He* dedicated you to the goddess of death in order to extend *his* life. Is that correct?"

"Yes, at the cost of many innocent lives."

"In our teachings, Macha is no more evil than any of the other Seven. Life, death, and rebirth are the natural order of things. She is merely doing her part in the Circle of Life."

"What are you saying, Gearoid?"

"You say that the other gods will not listen to your prayers, that your soul has been dedicated to Macha. Is that correct?"

"Yes."

"Then we will pray to Macha."

"Am I to pray for our deaths, Gearoid? How will that help? I'll not have your death on my conscience, too. I can't do that."

"I didn't ask you to do that. I merely asked you to send your prayers to Macha. She might aid us in another way, but if we are destined to die, then such is the will of the gods. Come, Brother, pray with me and we will ask Macha for her guidance."

"Very well then, if you think it'll help."

"Have faith, Brother. It is the path to redemption. Now close your eyes and repeat after me..." Abbot Gearoid closed his own eyes, hoping that it would ease his troubled mind. "Blessed Macha, goddess of death and rebirth, mistress of the long winter, and queen of the darkest night, we beseech thee. Hear our humble prayers ..."

*****

Conal was wolfing down a second bowl of porridge when Taliesin entered the hall. The bard was looking sleepy. He had clearly slipped back into bed after waking Conal for his early-morning run.

"Did you sleep well, Tal?" Conal teased.

"Not bad, thanks, but this getting up early is really exhausting."

"I've told you before that you don't need to get me up. It isn't necessary."

"It's the least I can do. We all have to make sacrifices."

"Hah! My heart bleeds for you! It's tipping it down out there, in case you didn't notice," Conal informed the bard. "Oh, and that reminds me ... it's a rainbow."

"Sorry, what is?"

"A rainbow, you know ... a flying giant who stands on his own two feet, the one blessed by the Seven, but holding within him envy, cowardice, and rage. It's a rainbow."

"Oh, that! I'd given up on you getting that, ages ago. How did you finally figure it out?" Taliesin asked, dipping a crusty roll into the porridge pot.

"I just told you. It's raining cats and dogs out there, possibly a couple of horses, and the odd sheep too from the look of it. I got soaked through and had to seek shelter in one of the shearing pens until the worst of it passed over. Last time I saw a sky like that, Maerlin was having a hissing fit over something. I hope she isn't in any trouble. Anyway, when the rain stopped, the sun came out, and I saw it, big and bright, flying across the sky."

"Are you telling me that if you hadn't been soaked with rain, you'd never have got the puzzle?"

"You could put it that way. I told you I'm useless at these things. I'm better at board games if that's any help."

"It looks like you'll have to be, if you want any chance of gaining credit in the mental challenges. Well, I guess we can't all be geniuses."

"Wow, thanks, Tal!"

*****

Sile sat watching the debauchery through a peephole. It had been a long evening, and dawn was not far off. Despite the best efforts of her most experienced courtesans, the General's lips remained firmly sealed on the reason for the additional troops that had arrived in the city. The expensive wine and heady incense had done little to unleash his secrets, despite the cost. Still, he was paying for the pleasures, and the girls would be well rewarded for their efforts. Sile hoped that the others would be more successful with the visiting military leaders. Surely, one of them would let something useful slip.

Finally Sile gave up. Her back was aching from sitting for so long, so she slipped out of the hidden passageway. It was nearly time for her morning ritual to the goddess, Cliodhna, and she needed time to prepare, mentally and physically, for the rituals.

Stepping into her bedroom, she was surprised to find her personal aide waiting. "What is it, Charlene?"

"Everything is prepared for you, Mistress, but I thought I should let you know straight away ... under the circumstances."

"Spit it out, Charlene. I'm tired."

"It's that stupid pigmy, Mistress. He's been waiting to see you." Charlene's face said more than her tone about her opinions of the client. "I told him that you were busy, but he stubbornly refused to leave. You know how obnoxious the little pig's-pizzle can be, when he's deep in his cups."

"I don't know why you let him get under your skin, Charlene. You're playing into his hands when he gets you rattled. Ignoring his little pranks is the best way to defeat him. Well, at least his sessions are short ... a bit like his stature."

Charlene's face finally broke into a smile. "If that is your wish, Mistress. I could always get the bouncers to oust him, if you'd prefer?"

"No, Charlene. He's an important client, even though he can be an obnoxious one. Give me a few moments, and then you can send him in. Serve him some of our best claret while he's waiting, and maybe he'll pass out and save us both the trouble."

Sile shook off her tiredness along with her robe. This may be her final chance to find out what was going on, and she couldn't afford to waste it. Throwing her expensive robe in the closet, she selected a dark green deerskin bodice with a matching kilt. The armoured bodice had cost a small fortune to create by one of the local armourers. Not only did it afford adequate protection, but it looked damn sexy too. It was an exact replica of another infamous bodice, but this one was even more unusual, which was why it had cost Sile so much. This bodice, by some clever artifice, merged Sile's double breasts into one pair of very voluptuous ones. Pulling the side cords as tight as she could, she checked herself in the mirror.

Next, she selected a wig. It was one of many such wigs that sat on wooden stands in her expansive closet. This one had been specially made to order and shone like living fire as she covered her own hair with it. Carefully, she brushed out any tangles and splayed it around her body. The effect was already remarkable, but with some careful make-up, it could be made even more so. Sile opted to leave off the false nose for this evening's work, hoping that the overall effect would be sufficient for the inebriated fool. Finally, she pulled on her 'killer heels' with the matching belts and greaves. These were all made from the same green deerskin, but were decorated with sharp silver studding. Pulling the final boot up her calf, she admired herself in the full-length mirror and smiled. It wasn't perfect, but her client was probably far too drunk to notice. She was ready and just in time. With a gentle knock, the door opened to her private chambers.

"Your Mad-jestery ..." Malachi tried again, taking a deep breath to get the words out before his tongue-tied drunken mouth failed him. "Your Madjesty."

"Come in, Malachi! What've I told you about lurking in doorways?"

"Yeshh, your Bountifulness. My apologieshh ..."

Sile strutted into view, all confidence and swagger. Holding her head high, she glared imperiously down at the jester. "You're late ... again. Have you been drinking, Malachi?"

"But, your Madjeshhty! They had me waiting outside for ages!" Malachi protested.

Sile selected a short riding crop from the rack beside the bed and marched forward. "There's always an excuse with you, isn't there, runt? There's always someone else to blame." Flicking her hand around quickly, she raked his cheek with the edge of the whip, leaving a red welt.

He staggered backward, but failed to hide a small smile. "Begging your humble pardons, your Voraciousness."

"Do something useful for once," she ordered. "The bedpan is under the bed. You know where the sewer sluice is ..." Briskly, she turned away, listening as the fool jumped to his assigned task. Sile marched boldly over to the dresser and inspected her make-up.

A shudder ran through her as she heard the lapping sounds from beside the bed.

"Stop that, you idiot! I've told you before about lapping out my bedpan. That's disgusting!"

The bedpan clattered to the floor and silence fell in the room, at least for a moment. Then the bedsprings began to squeak.

Turning round, she glared at the drunken jester. He had dropped his trousers, and was now dry-humping her favourite pillow.

"What, by Dagda's sacred chestnuts, are you doing, fool?" Sile demanded, as she raced across the room and lashed out at his naked cheeks with her riding crop. "That pillow is worth more than your sorry hide! Those covers are made from the finest silk, and they cost me more than a good chariot!"

The jester would not release his hold on the pillow, and her repeated beating of his bare buttocks merely urged him on. "I can't help it!" he gasped between thrusts, "Your scent ... it drives ..." he grunted, "... me wild!" His stumpy little body bucked wildly as he gripped the pillow in a death-like grip.

"What is that appalling smell?" Sile gasped, noticing for the first time the heady odour coming off the midget.

"Ah, dat'd be the royal billy-goat, ya Madjeshty," he gasped, still humping away in a mad frenzy.

"You weren't riding the billy-goat, were you?" Sile demanded. She was forced to step away as the stench permeated the room.

"Of course not, your Most-voluptuous! I was only having a wee frolic with the nubile nanny, Mabel, when that coward attacked me. He hit me from behind and knocked me over, just when she was bleating sweetly. The wretched beast wouldn't give me any peace to woo the fair maiden, so we ended up in a tussle. It was a battle worthy of a ballad, I jest you not. We fought like lions. He was armed with those mighty horns of his, and me, I had my trews down around my ankles. Finally, I wrestled him to the ground and smited the monstrosity," Malachi explained between thrusts, clearly proud of his conquest.

"By Arianrhod, you're having a bath ... right now, and I'm sending you the bill for my bedding." Sile marched over and pulled the bell-cord. Charlene arrived quickly with two of the Pink Rose's bouncers in tow. They had been anticipating trouble from the drunken jester.

"Ah, Charlene, you're just in time. Has my bath been drawn?"

"Yes, Mistress, but ..."

Sile cut her off. "You two... don't just stand there. Grab that little runt, pillow and all, and drop him into my bath. I want him scrubbed until he squeaks like a kitten. Do you understand? Wash him thoroughly, clothes and all, and don't leave a single inch of his hide untouched. I want him red raw, from head to foot. Oh, and wash his mouth out with some carbolic soap, while you're at it. He's been drinking potty-water again!"

"No! Not a bath, your Madshjesty!" Malachi begged between humps, desperate to finish his conquest on the ravaged pillow while he still had the chance. Suddenly, he gasped and grunted, his eyes rolled back in his head and he lay still, panting happily.

"I guess it's too late to save my pillow." Sile sighed with resignation. "Charlene, have all of this bedding boiled, will you. Well ... what are you all waiting for?"

They pounced on the jester and despite his protests, dragged him from the room. A loud wail and a splash could be heard from beyond, followed by some weeping and an occasional splutter.

Sile marched into the bathroom, just as the bouncers were finishing rinsing out the jester's ragged locks.

"I'm sorry, Medb. I only wanted to prove myself worthy, so that you'd take me with you," Malachi wailed.

"...With me?" Sile asked. "Where is it that I'm going again?"

"It was all in the message ... the one that you had me to deliver to the General. I'm sorry, your Madjeshhty, but it fell open while I was walking, and I happened to glance at it. I know about your plan to invade the *Fear Ban*. Please take me with you!"

"I don't know, Malachi. It'll be dangerous, and you'll have to be cunning."

"I can be brave, and I can be cunning! Just you wait and see."

"Oh, I suppose so. When was I leaving again? It's slipped my mind," Sile prompted.

"You told the General to make ready your chariot for first light. You wanted to give your horses a good run this morning. The army is to be ready to march on the following morning."

"I did, didn't I? Well done, Malachi. Have some more wine while I get you something more *heroic* to wear. Then, we'll take a ride in my chariot. We'll see just how brave and cunning you can be."

"Really, your Mad-jeshty! You'll take me with you?"

"Of course, Malachi! I could hardly leave you behind, especially after your victory over the billy goat. Maybe we can rustle you up a little sword, too."

Sile hurried from the room. She had much to do and little time to do it.

"Charlene, pack a bag of supplies and hurry. I'm heading for Manquay at first light."

"...But what about your dawn ritual?"

"I haven't got time for that. Listen, I could be gone for some time, so you're in charge until I return. Oh ... and give the fool some food. I don't want him to pass out on me. Now pass me that nose, will you? I'll need to redo this make-up."

Chapter Twenty-Eight: Secrets of the Ice

The morning was cloaked in fog, filling the parade ground with a low-lying carpet of mist that billowed around the stable-hands' ankles and blew from the horses' nostrils like steam from a kettle. Every sound was heightened in the frosty air, and the rattle of harness and the stamp of restless hooves echoed across the open space.

The ostlers straightened when the Queen started across the open space with her diminutive jester in tow. The Queen was bundled up against the cold, but her infamous red hair billowed out behind her as she moved, and they could see her green leather armour occasionally though the gap in her woollen cloak.

The jester had relinquished his usual monochrome motley outfit. Instead, he had chosen to wear black leather shorts and a matching vest. This was topped off with a rakish peaked cap of the same material. He was also armed with a small sword. It was of the type given to young boys for their games of war. A studded dog-collar adorned his neck. Its leash was held firmly by Queen Medb, while in her other hand she carried her chariot-whip. She steered the drunken jester toward the chariot. Occasionally, she would correct his direction with a tug on the leash or a prod of the whip.

Malachi bellowed out loudly "Make way for the Queen! Make way for the Queen! As ever, obscene. A man's wet dream!"

The ostlers tried hard to hide their smirks as they stood quickly to attention. They waited while Medb and her jester mounted the chariot and stowed away their baggage. No one questioned the load, or that the Queen had decided to take her jester along with her for this morning's drive. Those at court were well used to her eccentric behaviour and her fondness for the mad fool.

Lifting the reins expertly, she flicked them to urge her team into motion. The sudden movement caused her companion to stumble, and only the Queen's thigh, quickly pinning him to the wickerwork frame, stopped him from falling out of the chariot.

She drove the chariot with consummate skill. It was the finest chariot in *Tir Pect,* and pulled by the two finest warhorses, bred for generations for their speed and stamina. Even the harness was a work of art in its craftsmanship. It was a wedding gift from Conchubhar. The stable-hands' watched with a mixture of pride and awe at the sight of their Queen. She was an equal to any man in the kingdom of *Tir Pect*, even the High King.

She drove past the training targets, giving the horses their heads as they picked up their pace. With a sure hand, she steered them toward the gateway and out through the portcullis, into the city. By the time she rolled down the cobblestone street, the war-chariot was at a full gallop, and it raced through the city with breakneck speed.

"The gods help anyone who isn't quick enough to get out of her way!" one of the ostlers' remarked.

"We might as well grab a bite to eat," said another. "From the look of it, they'll be gone for a while. There's no point in us standing around like a bunch of garden gnomes in the cold."

No one could argue with his reasoning, but they waited a few moments longer just to be certain. Then, they started back toward their barracks. As they walked across the misty yard, they were surprised to notice a lone figure marching toward them.

The morning air was heavy with low-lying mist, and the sun had not yet raised enough to burn off the morning chill, which filled the parade-ground with a carpet of mist. The fog billowed around the stable-hands' ankles and would have blown from the horses' nostrils in tiny clouds, had they still been standing there. Sounds were still heightened in the dense air, but the rattle of horse bits and the stamp of restless feet no longer echoed across the open space. Faintly, in the far distance, the steady rhythm of horse hooves and the rattling of chariot wheels could still be heard.

The stable-hands stopped when they saw Medb crossing the open space. They did a quick double-take, looking back across the now empty parade-ground. This time, the Queen was alone but she was still bundled up against the cold, and her infamous red hair still billowed out behind her as she strutted toward the dumbfounded ostlers. Looking closely, they could see her dark green leather armour occasionally though the gap in her heavy, woollen cloak. She held her chariot-whip loosely in her right hand. Its long bull-hide lash was well oiled, supple and ready to use.

Queen Medb stopped in front of the stable-hands, irritation clearly written on her face. Her beloved chariot had not been made ready for her, as per her instructions. "Well?" she demanded testily.

The ostlers were struck dumb with a mixture of confusion and terror. Medb was renowned for her temper. "Your Majesty?" the nearest mumbled.

"Where ... is ... my ... chariot?" Queen Medb demanded, each word laden with venom.

"Your Majesty ...!" he repeated, looking across the parade ground where the mist was still settling after the chariot's departure. "Your Majesty ..." he tried again. The others backed slowly away, hoping to avoid the worst of Medb's wrath.

Her whip struck out like a viper, slashing across the spokesman's face and sent him reeling into his companions.

"Somebody had better tell me why my chariot isn't ready... right now, or I'll have you all flayed alive. I'll draw up a roster to make sure there is no respite in the beatings that you'll receive. Now, where ... is ... MY ... CHARIOT!" Her usually pale complexion was mottled with rage.

"You ... I mean ... we ... you just left, your Majesty?" the spokesman blurted out, unable to back any farther away.

With a shriek that would make a *Ban-Sidhe* envious, the Queen fell upon him. Swinging right and left with her whip, she lashed out at the unfortunate man. "How can I have left already? I'm still here, you idiot!" Medb exclaimed, punctuating each word with a blow of her whip. The man had lost consciousness, long before she had finished. Panting lightly from the exertion, she glared at the others, seeking another victim.

"Guards!" she roared, although there was no need to do so. Many of the guards were already arriving, after hearing the commotion. "Seize these cretins, at once. I want them roasting over hot coals until one of them can tell me where my chariot is."

It took a considerable amount of pain, along with the sworn testimony of others within the city, before Medb finally accepted that the stable-hands were telling the truth. Then, her guards sought the whereabouts of the jester, Malachi. She reasoned that, if an impostor had made off with her chariot disguised as her, then another midget must have disguised himself as her trusted jester, too. Another bell passed before it dawned on her that Malachi had been involved in the treachery. A hefty price was quickly placed on his and his unknown assistant's heads. By that time, Sile and Malachi were long gone. Driving the fastest chariot, pulled by the fastest team, there was no one who could catch them, even if they knew which direction to look.

An inevitable delay in the southward march was called, while the King placated his distraught wife and found a suitable replacement. The Queen adamantly refused to lead their invasion on an inferior chariot. She would not be the laughing stock of the known world. Conchubhar knew that the delay was worthwhile, if she and her Bear Clan berserkers were beside him in the moons ahead.

He chafed in silence at the delay and swore his revenge on whoever was responsible. As he repeated regularly to himself over the coming days, "I never did like that damned jester!"

*****

Maerlin had mistakenly believed that she was doing the right thing by bringing the two torturers to High Peaks to stand trial. This, however, as with many other things in life, proved to be a bit more complicated than she had initially anticipated.

Crime on the mountainside was pretty much nonexistent. In the small mountain villages, everyone knew everyone else, and a strong community spirit bound them together. True, there were occasional crimes of passion, but the villagers looked upon these with sympathetic eyes and no big deal was ever made of them. Crimes of greed were unheard of. Everyone knew everyone else's business and generally accepted their lot in life. They did their best to enjoy what fate had given them. Politics were treated with indifference at best, or simply ignored as someone else's problem. That was until now. No one had ever expressed any political interest in the mountainous area, and the villagers themselves had no use for politics. It didn't milk the cows, put food on the table, or cure anyone's ailments.

Formalised religion was treated with similar apathy. The mountain folk were not anti-religious. They merely worshipped in a more casual, unstructured way. They saw the gifts of the gods every day in the sun, the moon, and the weather. They accepted these things as they accepted the mountain upon which they lived. It made no sense whatsoever in their lives to mumble incoherent gibberish each morning or evening, so they just didn't do it.

They woke up each morning at dawn and started to work, and they fell into bed each evening, exhausted from their labours. There was no such thing as a day of rest, to be spent in quiet contemplation. Such a concept was a luxury that they could ill afford. They took time to give thanks at the turning of the seasons, at Imbolc, Lughnasa, Beltane, and the other seasonal celebrations, but that was it. The concepts of worship and politics were foreign to them. They had no need for them. No use for them. "That's da sort of daft stuff dat dem townies get up ta. It can't be good for you," was the general consensus on either topic.

Now, for the first time ever, the villagers had a real crime on their doorsteps, and they were at a loss as to how to handle it. None of the Elders were willing to make a decision on the matter, which left the criminals in the hands of the priestesses.

The philosophies of the Order were generally similar to that of the mountain community. However, the two priestesses on the mountain were exceptions to this rule. Many considered Nessa to be the most worldly of the priestesses of the Order of Deanna. For this reason, it had been her task to seek out new recruits from amongst the population. Ironically, this was the reason that Nessa had been sought out the previous summer. The villagers of High Peaks had requested her aid during Maerlin's 'difficulties'.

Seabhac was also an exception to the general policy of non-involvement within the Order. Her constant clashes with their leadership had been one of the reasons she had finally abandon the Order and sought a life of obscurity. Ironically, by doing this, she had left the world to its own devices, which was exactly what the Order had been arguing for all along.

By that time, however, Seabhac had enough of politics. After the events that led to the creation of the Dragon Clan, she had been happy for the world to leave her alone. That had all changed, however, with the coming of her great-granddaughter. Seabhac's past had caught up with her.

Of all the priestesses of the Order of Deanna, Seabhac and Nessa were the best equipped to deal with this crisis, but that wasn't saying much. Cora, despite her father's fame, was of little help, either. This left the decision in Maerlin's hands.

They didn't have a gaol on the mountain or any other secure place to house the prisoners. None of the doors even had locks, nor were the windows barred. As far as the mountain people were concerned, a door's purpose was twofold. It kept out the worst of the wind and stopped livestock from wandering in, raiding the food, and leaving droppings on the clean floors. They had no need for such things as padlocks, and the nearest thing to one was the humble door-latch. Security was a newfangled 'townie' word, and it sat in the same metaphorical cesspit as politics.

After much consideration, Maerlin finally opted to chain the prisoners up to a post in the hayloft. It was dry there, and at this time of the year, it was nearly empty. She became their gaoler, fearful of an innocent villager getting hurt if they tried to escape.

A council meeting was called, with the priestesses shuttling in the Elders from the other villages so that they could all have their say on what was to be done. The meetings went on for days, partly due to the lack of more urgent tasks to attend to, but also because this was a new concept for the mountain folk, one that they were ill-equipped to deal with.

In fact, had the lambing season not kicked in, thanks to the blessing of Arianrhod the Moon goddess, they could have been there until the spring gathering. As the lambs started arriving, the urgency for a solution became apparent. The villagers could delay no longer.

In a last ditch attempt to gain a common consensus, Maerlin brought the Elders out to what remained of the ghostly village, so that they could see firsthand the crimes that had been committed and the aftermath. The charred remains had long since been buried, but the line of fresh graves could not be ignored. Some were so small that you would have thought that they had been dug for a family pet. The charred crucifixes and burned huts had been left untouched, as had the objects that littered the empty village: old clothes, a stray shoe, a child's doll. These were the items that hardened the hearts of the Elders and strengthened their resolve. A sentence of death was agreed unanimously, but still a problem arose. Who was going to carry out the dreaded deed ... and how?

Maerlin felt the weight of the decision on her shoulders and decided to sleep on it.

*****

"Ah! So you're back. Have you changed your mind, then?" Sygvaldr asked.

Maerlin knew she must be dreaming, again. "Oh bother! Not you again. I haven't got time for this."

"I take it that you're not pleased to see me." His sadness made her look up into those wonderful deep blue eyes. The pain she saw within those pools made her heart ache.

"No, it's nice to see you, really it is. It's just ... I've got a lot on my mind right now."

"Weddings are like that. So much to plan ..."

"What is it with you and weddings?" Maerlin demanded. "You can't go around assuming that every girl you meet is going to be your wife. It's not healthy! Did you propose to the last girl you met, too?"

"Well ... now that you mention it ... actually yes, I did! But ..."

"See! It's not healthy. I bet she ran a mile, didn't she?"

"She confided that her heart was already taken. She told me that she would send the daughter of her blood in her stead. Is your heart taken, also, daughter of her blood?"

"I don't know! I'm too young to be thinking about love. Anyway, as I said, I've a lot on my mind at the moment, so if you could just leave me in peace ..."

"But ... I didn't bring you here. You did that on your own," he said. "I think you came here seeking me out."

"And why would I do that?"

"People occasionally come here looking for answers. I've been around a long time, and I know a thing or two, I'll have you know. Sometimes I can help. I helped your mother, or at least I hope I did. You might have come seeking advice of the heart."

"Listen. No disrespect, but I didn't come here to get love tips from someone who wants to marry complete strangers."

"Something's bothering you. Why don't you tell me what it is?" Seeing her hesitation, he added "What have you got to lose?"

She thought about it for a moment, and then, with a shrug, she explained about the prisoners and the sentence of death.

"And this task has fallen upon your shoulders. Is that it?"

"Yes. It's one thing to kill someone in anger or to defend myself; I've done that before, though it weighed heavily on me afterwards. I knew, however, that I'd done the right thing, but this ... this is murder. It'd make me no better than them. My peers may have sanctioned it, but it still means killing two people in cold blood. What am I supposed to do?"

"It sounds like they deserve to die," Sygvaldr declared.

"They do, but still ..."

"Here, on the Icy Wastes, when someone has done a great wrong and it cannot be recompensed with a suitable fine or deed, they're banished into exile. They are sent out onto the ice. No one can help them in any way, and they are declared outside of the law. No protection is offered them, and they can be killed on sight. Their lives are effectively in the hands of the gods. Whether they live or die is their decision. The gods here are harsh, and they rarely offer forgiveness. Occasionally, the Ice Bears or the Tundra Wolves deliver the death sentence, but mostly ... it's the cold."

Maerlin was silent for a moment. "That seems like a good solution, but I can hardly fly them all the way to the Icy Wastes and dump them on your doorstep."

"Oh, I wouldn't mind. Actually, it'd be no bother at all. Maybe I could get them to look at the plumbing first."

"I'm not sure if they'd be any good at plumbing, but that's not what I had in mind. I was talking about exiling them here ... to live or die at the gods' whims."

"Oh, I see. Well then, you'll just have to find your own Icy Wastes, I guess. Now can we get back to more important matters?"

"Such as...?"

"Well, the wedding, of course! Obviously, this was the real reason you came, admit it?"

"Give me strength. Will you ever give up? I don't know how many times I've got to say this before you'll understand. I'm not marrying a complete stranger."

"...Fair enough ... I see where you're going with this..."

"You do?" Maerlin asked, incredulously.

"Of course! You can't commit fully to our marriage as you don't know me yet. Very well then ... come along," Sygvaldr announced, marching off.

"Wait! Where are we going?"

"You wanted to know me more before we get married. So, first things first, let me show you my kingdom."

"I didn't say that!" Maerlin protested, but her legs moved forward anyway, following him as he scurried along the frozen corridors.

"As you can see, I love ice. Isn't it pretty? It's hard, shiny, and so easy to work with."

"Sygvaldr, why isn't it cold in here? I mean, it's all ice. It should be colder, shouldn't it?"

He gave her a smile that would melt a glacier. "Ah! That'd be the magic. It's just a little something to make life easier. Now, let's go and see my treasury. That's where I sleep!"

Maerlin awoke with a start. The hairs on her arms rose in the pre-dawn chill. Rubbing the sleep from her eyes, she peeled herself away from Cora's arms and reached for her robe. A soft groan of protest came from within the blankets as she slipped out of the bed.

"It's not morning yet," protested Cora. "Come back to bed."

"It's near enough. Besides, I'm awake now."

"Then come over here and kiss me," pleaded Cora, stretching her arms out in invitation.

Maerlin kissed Cora lightly on the lips before slipping away. "I'll get the fire going and stick on the kettle," she said as she headed out. She was just slipping through the door, when she heard Cora's sleepy groan and the pillow hit the doorframe

*****

They sat down to a quiet breakfast after a rather sombre version of the 'Dawn Chorus', led by Nessa who was practising her vocals. The interruptions to their daily chant by a rather over-enthusiastic male magpie had managed to lighten the mood somewhat. His attempts to woo Nessa were failing miserably, but everyone admired his refusal to accept defeat. Cora had even started calling him Sir Gallaghad after a hero of legend, much to Nessa's annoyance.

"Your vocal cords are coming along nicely, Nessa," Cora commented.

"Actually, I haven't got any," Nessa replied. "Don't ask me how I manage to speak as I haven't got the foggiest idea. You'd have to ask the healers on the Holy Isle about that. They might be able to give you an answer. All I know is that magpies don't have any vocal cords."

"But how do they sing?"

"Listening to him this morning, I'd hardly call it singing. I've heard broken-winded horses sounding better."

"Don't listen to her, Sir Gallaghad. I thought it was sweet," cooed Cora.

"I wish you'd stop calling him that! It'll only encourage him, and he needs little enough of that as it is. To answer your question; magpies, and other birds also, sing with their throats."

"Oh, I see. Is that how you do it?

"No. I seem to be the exception to the rule. I just think what I want to say and it comes out."

Maerlin considered this revelation. "So what you do in order to speak, it isn't normal for a magpie. Is that it? Gallaghad couldn't do it, for example?"

"Yes, Maerlin, that's correct."

"Like you're channelling hidden powers in order to speak?"

"I guess ..."

"So, it's like magic then?"

"I wouldn't say that exactly."

"Are you sure, Ness? I once asked you what magic was and you told me... 'That it was like channelling hidden powers toward a desired goal. That it was using the mind, and perhaps certain props and aids, to make the improbable, achievable.' That's what you're doing, isn't it? You're channelling your mind toward a goal: which in this case is speech. Your throat and your beak are your aids."

"Deanna's blessing, Maerlin, I'd never thought of that!"

Maerlin smiled. "So, technically," she continued, "If you can speak, then you should be able to do other magic, too?"

"That's brilliant, Maerlin!" Cora declared with an enthusiastic squeal.

"Let's not get carried away, shall we? It's a good idea in theory, but that's all it is ... theory."

"Well, there's only one way to find out, isn't there. Come on..." Maerlin placed her glass of water in front of Nessa's beak, "Make it move."

Nessa nervously scanned the room. The others were looking at her expectantly. "What ... now?"

"Is there a better time?"

"It's a bit sudden, Maerlin ... that's all."

"Just give it a go," Maerlin pleaded, eager to see if her theory worked.

"Very well then, if you insist." Nessa calmed her mind, using the same exercises that she had taught Maerlin, the previous summer. First, she pictured a plain white screen in her mind and was surprised at how easily it formed and remained solid. Then she changed the colour of the screen, going through the colours of the rainbow, until finally, she had the total blackness of the final screen. Taking a deep breath, she focused on the glass of water, firstly with her eyes and then with her mind's eye. She

329

pictured it upon the blank canvas of her thoughts. She could feel the power tingling in her claws as her magical energies built. Staring deep into the water, she sought out the Elemental within. It was calm and floated gently in the water, but it livened up as she focused her magical energies on it. The tiny Diva stirred and rose up, spinning slowly around its confined space. Nessa encouraged it with a soothing croon, and the water spun faster until a tiny vortex spiralled in the centre of the glass. With an inward smile, Nessa released the Diva, allowing it to slow and become calm again.

"There you go. Are you satisfied now?"

The others were too speechless to reply and didn't get the chance to anyway, as the Elders picked this time to barge into the tavern for their morning meeting.

When they had all settled around the large table, Maerlin spoke "I think I might've found a solution to our dilemma," she announced. "I had a Dream-catching last night, and I was given a seed of wisdom. I was told to cast our prisoners into exile on the Icy Wastes. We place their lives in the hands of the gods. We let the gods decide if they should live or die."

"But the Icy Wastes are hundreds of miles away," Auntie Millie objected.

Maerlin smiled. "Yes, I pointed this out. I was told to make my own Icy Wastes."

"Can you do that shhhort of thing?" Uncle Joe asked, in awe of the wonders he had seen from the priestesses.

"I don't have to, Uncle Joe. The gods have already done it for us."

"They have?"

"It's right outside the door: *Sliamh Na Dia*. The Mountain of the Gods is your very own Icy Wastes."

"You're going to set them free, up there? Isn't that dangerous?" Millie asked.

"How many people do you know who've seen its summit and lived to tell their tale?"

"Me father onceshh told me about a man who'd come down off da mountain. We all thought it was a crock of auld cowpatshhhh," Joe declared.

"We did it ..." Cora pointed out, "... but we used a lot of magic."

"So, the chance of them surviving are next to nothing," Maerlin declared.

"Your Momma survived the mountain," said a hushed voice from the shadows.

"Poppa, is that you?" Maerlin asked. "What did you just say?"

Eoghan Strong-arms walked into the light. "I said that your Momma came over the mountain. I saw it with my own eyes. My heart was lost on the day she walked out of the mists. I thought she must be a goddess, so I did. I've worshipped her ever since."

"Are you telling me that it was Momma who climbed the mountain?" Maerlin asked. "I'd always thought that it was you, or that maybe you'd met at a fair or something. She really scaled the mountain ... on her own?"

"Aye, lass, she did that! She was as calm as the tarn in midsummer, so she was. Not a bother on her. I swear, she came out of the mist and walked up to me like she was just popping in for a cuppa tea. How could I do anything but fall head o'er heels in love with her?"

Maerlin looked questioningly at Seabhac, who shrugged. "She just disappeared one day. No one knew where she'd gone to. She just vanished. They searched, but they couldn't even find her footprints in the snow."

Maerlin turned back to her father. "Poppa ... did Momma ever use magic?"

Her father shuffled his feet nervously like a boy who had been caught stealing apples from the neighbour's orchard.

"Poppa, I need to know. Did she ever use magic?"

"I'm not sure, but I think so. Only on a couple of occasions, when she'd just moved here. I think that she stopped. I think it scared her too much. It's hard to explain ... it's like she didn't want to use it, but sometimes it got the better of her. As she got older, she got better at fighting it. I guess that it was a bit like me with my temper. I was always getting into scuffles when I was younger, but I learned to cop myself on!"

The room was so quiet that you could hear the boards creak under the weight of his body as he shuffled nervously. After a couple of long moments of silence, Maerlin said softy. "Thank you, Poppa. I know how hard that was for you."

Chapter Twenty-Nine: Dawn Raiders

She had driven the horses hard all day, slowing to a trot when the road was quiet and speeding up again whenever there was traffic nearby. The sight of the notorious Queen of *Tir Pect* hurtling along, the scythe-blades of her chariot sparkling in the spring sunshine, was enough to clear any road. Now, her arms and legs felt like jelly, and she was sure the mares were also feeling the gruelling pace she had set. Malachi had long since passed out and was lying forlornly, curled up amongst the packs, after emptying his stomach violently on a number of occasions. Finding a narrow side road, Sile slowed the chariot down to a walk, looking for a suitable campsite. A few furlongs later and far enough away from the main thoroughfare to avoid detection, she found a small brook by a clearing, sheltered by a coppice of hazel, willow, and broom. She barely had the strength to brush down and hobble the horses, but she forced herself to light a fire. It was still cold at night, despite the melted snow, and there was always the possibility of wolves or other night-predators. They would need the fire to deter such creatures and prevent them freezing in the night. Pulling a canvas cover over the frame of the chariot to create a makeshift tent, she woke Malachi and helped him into its shelter.

"You need to eat something," she urged.

"I don't feel well. What did you give me?"

"That's probably all that wine on an empty stomach. I only gave you a mild sedative. I'm sorry Malachi, but I needed your help. In the morning, I'll drop you off by the roadside, and you can walk back to *Ard Pect*. I'll go on alone. You can tell them that you were drugged and kidnapped. It's the truth, after all."

"Are you kidding me? Medb will have me flayed alive. No amount of pleading will appease her. I've betrayed my Queen!" he moaned. Tears rolled down his ruddy cheeks.

"It'll be alright. I'm sure that it'll all sort itself out." Sile now regretted taking the jester along with her. She shouldn't have involved him in her scheme.

"Why! Why did you do this to me?"

"I had no choice, Malachi! I need to stop this war before it gets out of hand!"

"Against the *Fear Ban* ... but they were the invaders? The King and Queen have a right to take back the land. It belongs to them."

"Don't be such an idiot, Malachi. You might wear a jester's garb, but you don't fool me. I can see the sharp mind that hides behind that mask of stupidity. We lost that land two centuries ago. It's time to accept the facts and move on. The Clans of Dragania have merged, Pect and *Fear Ban*, to become something new. We'd not be saving them from invasion, we'd become the invaders. Can't you see that?"

"What you're speaking about is treason," he objected.

"It might be treason, Malachi, but it's the truth. If I don't do something to stop this madness, thousands of people will die. I've not worked hard to see it all go up in flames."

"But the Queen ... she believes that now is the time to strike. The *Fear Ban* are weak. Is this not so?"

"You should make a jester's outfit for her if she believes that. Clearly, her spies are not telling her everything, either that or she's only listening to what she wants to hear. Listen, Malachi, there's a new *Dragan* in the land. He's born and reared and already cutting his teeth. Only this winter, he walked the streets of *Ard Pect*, as bold as brass. The Brocians are calling him the *Ciudachbane*, for he single-handedly slew a *Ciudach*. Not just any old *Ciudach* either, but a full-grown, enraged bull-*Ciudach*, whacked out of its head on Chorthium dust, all of this, from a lad who has yet to grow his first chin-fluff. And there's more ... this young *MacDragan* has befriended a sorceress of Deanna. She is said to be *Uiscallan* reincarnated, and she has already defeated the Dark Mage in battle. You've seen the scarred face of the one who claims to be Dubhgall the Black. You've seen the burn marks and the holes where once he had eyes. That was the work of this young sorceress who is destined to become the next Storm-Bringer. Do you really think that the time is right for the Pects to invade Dragania? Do you think that it will be easy thing to ride down the Northern Highway and reclaim the Plains of the Dragon? They might as well race down the throat of a dragon itself and burn, as it consumes them with fire. This war is utter madness, and it must be stopped!"

"But how are you going to achieve that?" Malachi asked.

"I don't know, I really don't, but I know someone who might, someone who is close to the *MacDragan*. All I can do is try."

"Then I'll come with you. In time, Medb might see the risks that I've taken to save her kingdom, and she may find forgiveness in her heart for me."

For the first time, Sile understood just how deeply the somewhat-deranged jester loved Medb. She had always known of his passionate lust for the Queen. It was for this reason that she had created the disguise she now wore. The fool had paid highly for her to pretend to be Queen Medb so that he could act out his fantasies. Looking into Malachi's eyes, she could now see the fires of love that burned within him for the royal nymphomaniac. She also felt sure that in her own way, Medb held him in her own affections. At least, that was, until this morning. The wound caused this day would be a hard one to heal. Today, the fool had paid far more than usual for the services of the Pink Rose's mistress.

"I'm sorry, Malachi. I really shouldn't have dragged you into this."

"Ach, forget it, Sile. All my life I've dreamed of becoming a hero. Well, my wish has finally come true. I should've listened to my grandmother ..."

"Why? What did she say?"

"I haven't the foggiest idea! No one in their right mind would listen to her. She was madder than a field full of cock pheasants in springtime."

"Maybe it was 'be careful what you wish for.'"

"The last thing I remember her saying was: 'There's nothing more magical than a bumblebee.' I mean ... what's that supposed to mean? Daft old coot!"

They were silent for a long time, and Sile was just drifting off to sleep when Malachi started laughing: real belly-aching laughter.

"What are you laughing at, you fool?"

"...The chariot! I wish I could've seen Medb's face when she learned that we'd stolen her precious chariot. By the gods, it would've been priceless."

"Shut up and get some sleep," Sile commanded with a wry smile.

*****

Conal was up and ready to start his morning run long before Taliesin was due to wake him. In truth, he hadn't slept much with excitement. It was time. All of the waiting, for the passing of the winter moons, was finally over. It was finally time for him to take up the mantle of the Dragon-lord. He was ready to lead *Clann Na Dragan*.

Looking at himself in the mirror, dressed only in his loincloth, he could see the muscles rippling on his lean frame. The rigorous regime of exercise and the strict diet were paying off. He was leaner than his father had been, but he could see the shadow of his father's frame within the reflection, looking back at him. He could see his father's eyes also, but not his father's face. People said that Conal took more after his mother, and facially, that seemed to be true. Not that he could remember his mother. He had been blessed with his father's blonde hair and piercing blue eyes. He also had his father's stubbornness, and the same recklessness in the face of danger. The Dragon flowed strongly through his blood.

Following Declan's advice from earlier in the week, he buckled on his armour. The Grand Marshall advised him that he should treat his training sessions as if he was facing a real battle: fully-armed and armoured. Conal had embraced this philosophy. When he was ready, he lifted up the legendary sword, *An Fiacail Dragan,* and slid it into the sheath that lay across his armoured back.

He was now ready, so he headed towards the door, but stopped when an idea occurred to him. Lifting up the water pitcher, he set off.

*****

The snort of the horses woke Sile, and for a moment she lay still and listened, wondering what had woke her. No further sound came so she closed her eyes and started to drift back to sleep.

Just as she was dropping off, the horses snorted again, and she knew that something was wrong. Cautiously, she rolled out of her cloak and placed a hand over Malachi's mouth. He woke with a start, but she held him firmly and motioned with a raised finger for silence. Releasing the fool, she rose quietly and peeked out of the makeshift tent. Obscure shadowy forms moved in the misty half-light of dawn. They stalked slowly closer to the hobbled ponies so as not to spook them. At first, she thought they might be wolves, but their movements were not the way of the wolf.

The mists cleared for a moment, and she could make out small humanoid forms. Silently, she counted them. There were at least eight that she could see, but there may be more, hiding in the mist. The dawn raiders had hoped to catch them unprepared while they slept.

"Stay here," she hissed at the fool.

Slipping her daggers free, she slipped quietly into the mist. On silent feet, she circled around the camp and approached the intruders from their flank, moving as quickly as she dared. When she was in position, she paused, fixing the position of as many of the shadowy creatures in her mind as possible, and then she leapt into motion.

The first of the creatures turned, sensing her at the last instant, and its eyes widened as her razor-sharp dagger slashed across its throat, severing jugular and windpipe before it could cry out. Sile moved on, rushing at her second target. The creature let out a brief shriek as one of her daggers plunged into its neck and drove upwards. The cry was short, but loud enough to alert the others ... the misty battle had begun.

Within moments they were charging at her from all sides. The first two assailants went down quickly, but eventually Sile was forced to go on the defensive. Only her constant motion and dexterity saved her, as a variety of weapons were thrust in her direction. Spinning and flipping backward and forward, she prevented her opponents from any concerted attack. She even managed to wound a few of them, but she wondered how long she could sustain this frantic pace. She was outnumbered, and they had her surrounded. Hearing a war-cry and sensing movement to her right, she dodged away from the expected blow, still trying to get a clear view of her opponents in the dense fog. She lashed out with a foot, catching one of them in the face and then ducked and spun, hamstringing her stunned opponent.

She heard the clash of weapons again to her right and back-flipped away from the noise, once, twice, before spinning to confront another of the creatures. Her knives rose quickly to block its downward striking club, and her knee rose sharply upwards as she countered. Catching it in its solar plexus, she heard it grunt in pain and smelled its rank breath, before she embedded both of her daggers into its kidneys. She had finally broken free and momentarily paused to catch her breath. She could still hear the strange war-cry amongst the clash of blades. Suddenly, it came more clearly to her ears: "For Medb!"

"Malachi!" she exclaimed, rushing back into the fray. Only the jester's bulk distinguished him from the other creatures as they were of a similar height. She was surprised at the ferocity of the jester's attacks. Armed only with his toy sword, Malachi was forcing a pair of opponents back with powerful blows. Seeing one of the creatures sneaking up behind the jester, Sile leapt forward and dispatched it.

Realising that the odds were rapidly diminishing, the creatures finally broke away and fled into the mist. Within moments, it was as if they had never existed. The dead, however, lay on the ground as mute testament to their dawn raid.

Malachi bent over and groaned in pain.

"Are you wounded, Malachi?"

"I'll be fine, Sile, just give me a moment," he grunted, still doubled over.

"Is there anything I can do, Malachi?"

"It's nothing. The dirty scoundrel kneed me in the plums, that's all ... I don't suppose you could kiss them better?"

Sile grinned, relieved that Malachi was not seriously injured. "I'm sorry, Malachi, but it's way too early in the morning for that sort of nonsense. Besides, since you're no longer the court jester, so you can't afford my services."

"Ouch! Have a little sympathy for a wounded comrade, Sile. D'you have to kick me while I'm down?"

She leaned over and kissed him on the cheek. "There you go, a kiss for my heroic knight, although I'm not so sure about your shiny armour."

"What! I sleep better in the nude! Besides, I didn't have the time to put my clothes on. That get-up you gave me is tighter than a taxman's pity. I'd still be struggling my way into those damn shorts if I'd have tried to get dressed. Anyway ... when you're a fine specimen of masculinity like me, you might as well share it with the world!"

Sile wisely refrained from comment. Instead, she looked down at the creature that was lying at their feet. "What are these things?"

"They're *Na Coblinau-Dorcha* ... Dirty little sneak-thieves, the lot of them."

"Dark Goblins! I thought they were just fairy tales."

"Oh no, they're real alright. There are loads of the smelly critters roaming around on the 'Teeth of the *Draoidin*', but you don't see many of them this far south. There must be a cave complex around here that they're hiding out in. They don't venture out in daylight. It's safer for them to sneak around in the dark. This mist must've been too tempting for them, and they must've smelled the horses."

"How is it that a court jester knows about this?"

"Where I come from, way up in the wild north, there are large bands of *Na Coblinau-Dorcha*, plenty of *Ciudach*, and a few other nasty buggers I could mention. We learn to fight before we learn to walk, if we want to stay alive. My people tend to be a quite reserved bunch due to the harsh environments that they live in. They don't have the same tolerance for fools, dreamers, and poets that you Pects do," Malachi explained. "I wasn't always a jester, you know, although I've always been a bit of a fool. I was cast into exile when it became clear that I wasn't going to be like the rest of them. Somehow, I managed to survive and headed south, looking for a better life. Since then, I've done a lot of stupid jobs over the years, stuff that no one in their right mind would do. Clearly, I was eminently qualified!"

"You mean to say that you're not a Pect? But I thought ..."

"You thought what? That I was some inbred mountain runt, or that my mother had been sampling too many recreational mushrooms and I came out deformed. Is that what you were going to say?"

"Well, no ... but ..."

"Don't worry, Sile. I've heard them all before, and the answer is, no. I'm none of those things. I'm exactly how the Thirteen meant me to be," he declared. "Although I think I was at the back of the queue when it came to brains." Malachi indicated his forehead with a tapping finger.

"So ... you're supposed to be short?"

"Yep, that's probably why they call us Dwarfs."

"Dwarfs! As in ... well, *Dwarfs!*"

"I know ... fairy tales, right?" Malachi grinned and rubbed his arms against the chill.

"But I thought Dwarfs were all supposed to have beards hanging down past their wedding-tackle."

Malachi scratched his chin. "Medb doesn't approve of facial hair, and what the Queen wants ... Anyway, it's hard to be a jester if no one can see your face."

"...I'd never thought of that."

"Well .... I'd better get those shorts on before my plums fall off with the cold. I can feel them creeping up into my throat as we speak."

"I can do better than that, Malachi," Sile announced, stepping over to the baggage. Digging around for a moment, she pulled out a black and white cap, with attached bells. "Here you go!"

"My suit ... you brought my suit!" Malachi blubbered, rushing over and hugging her enthusiastically.

"Please ... put some clothes on first! I know where you've been!" she protested, quickly handing over the rest of his piebald regalia.

Hopping comically from one foot to the other, Malachi slipped into his motley costume, grinning from ear to ear.

"Malachi," Sile asked "Is that really your name?"

"Don't be daft! That's a ... a stage name, if you like. You'd never be able to pronounce my proper name. You'd choke on your tongue while trying to spit it out."

"So why Malachi?"

"When I came upon the first Pectish village on my journey south, I saw something amusing. Three men were standing over an old jack-ass. It was jammed tightly into a water trough. The daft bugger had decided to have a bath to ward off the heat of the day, and he'd got himself stuck. They tried and tried but there was no budging him. He was wedged tighter than a moneylender's charity. They were about to put the dumb critter out of its misery with a lump hammer when I interrupted them. I offered them some silver dust for the ill-fated donkey, and they figured they had nothing to lose. Only a fool would want to buy a dead donkey ... So, thinking that I was the biggest idiot this side of the Icy Wastes, they quickly agreed. We spat and shook on the deal, and they scurried off to celebrate their good fortunes."

"What happened?"

"It was simple, of course! I waited until they'd retired to the local tavern, and then I lifted up the hammer and gave it a mighty swing. It was all over in the blink of an eye. It only took one good blow."

Sile looked shocked. "What did you buy it for, if you were going to kill it?"

"I didn't hit the donkey, Sile! Do I look like a complete idiot?" Malachi asked. "I smashed out the side of the trough, and the ass rolled free, without so much as a scratch. So I climbed onto its back and quickly rode out of the village before they realised their mistake."

Sile stifled a laugh. "What's that got to do with your name?"

"It was the name of the donkey. I rode that old ass all the way to *Ard Pect,* and then I sold him to a dodgy horse-dealer for two silver shillings ... and they call me a fool! He'd been good luck for me so I figured that I might as well use his name. After all, it was as good as any other."

"Come on. We'd best get on our way before those goblins start stinking up the place up."

"They already do ... but I know what you mean."

*****

Taliesin heard the creak of floorboards but paid them no heed. It was still too early, and he was warm and comfortable.

A soft whisper caressed his ear *"Wakey-wakey!"*

He snuggled deeper into the blanket, ignoring the voice, but not for long. Taliesin was brought suddenly awake by the cold, wet shock. Spluttering at the water that was running down his face, he barely had time to catch sight of the assailant. However, there was no mistaking the dark green armour as the culprit raced out of his bedroom, or the sound of his laughter.

"I'll get you for this, Conal *MacDragan*!" he cursed, wiping his face on his sodden bedding. "Just you wait and see. You'll be sorry!"

*****

Maerlin opted to face the mountain alone. This was her burden to carry. Much though the others protested, she was adamant that she would be the one to pass sentence on the two convicts.

As soon as the 'Dawn Chorus' was finished, she bade goodbye and set off, flying northwards on her quarterstaff with the two convicts in tow. She had found that she didn't need to sit on the staff to fly, but somehow it made flying seem less flimsy. Just floating around with the Sylphs carrying her worked fine, but it gave her a bit of the wobblies. Sitting on the quarterstaff seemed more solid. It felt right. She knew that it was irrational, but it was true, nevertheless. This, she assumed, was why other sorceresses had used this option since the first witch had learn to fly. The two men had no such luxury and gazed on in horror as they skimmed over the frozen wastes. Quietly, they flew into the dense fog, and Maerlin's task became more difficult. She created a forward shield to cut through the dense fog, while still focusing on her flying. It seemed deserted up here in the mists, but occasionally, she spotted tracks in the snow beneath her. Not sure what creature had made them, she continued higher, staying far enough off the mountain to ensure safe passage. Whatever lived on the mountain was sure to be dangerous, apart from the rabbits and ptarmigan of course.

Her mind drifted off, and she found herself thinking of Sygvaldr's handsome smile before her better sense shook the thought away. Damn, but that man was annoying! Why was he so fixated on marriage? She was sure that they could be friends, if he could only give up on this ludicrous notion of matrimony. Maerlin had no need to shackle herself to any man, when she had Cora's loving embrace. Cora was her soul mate and understood her completely. She was the sister that Maerlin had never had. Still, Sygvaldr's smile did give her a strange warm feeling inside, despite his missing tooth. She realised that she was still thinking about him and forced herself to focus on the task at hand.

After what seemed like an age of mindless flying, she broke through the mists and entered the world of the gods. It was another beautiful sunny day on the top of the mountain. Enjoying the peace and solitude, she flew around to the far side of the peak and stopped before the two small caves that Cora claimed were the nostrils of the Elder God: *Crom Cruach*. This seemed like as good a place as any to leave the convicts. She released the Elementals and let the torturers drop to the ground.

"Listen up," she commanded. "This is the peak of *Sliamh Na Dia*, the Mountain of the Gods. The Elders have weighed your crimes and their vote was unanimous. Your fate lies here, on this mountain peak. You have been banished from Dragania. Your lives have been placed in the hands of the gods, and it will be up to them to decide your fates." Maerlin fished out a tiny knife and threw it on the ground. "With this, you can cut your bonds."

Maerlin pointed north. "In that direction you'll find the lands of the Pects. They'll probably kill you on sight as you are both *Fear Ban*, and the people of *Tir Pect* have no love for the invaders."

Maerlin pointed east. "In that direction you'll find the Broce Woods. It's the ancestral lands of *Clann Na Broce*. You may know them as the Brocians. They are Pects also, but they have always honoured the Great Truce brokered by the Dragon-lord. However, Lord Boare recently broke that truce. I'm sure that as Boars, you'll get swift justice if you enter their sacred woods."

Maerlin pointed south. "In that direction is High Peaks and your certain death. You have been declared outlaws by the people of the mountain. If you're seen on their mountainside again, the signal fires will be lit and you'll be hunted down like rabid wolves."

Maerlin turned to the west. "Finally, you could choose to go west. Here, you'll find the Sea of Hunger and the Western Isles. However, I doubt that their King will offer you any protection, especially after his daughter tells him of your deeds. If you're lucky enough to survive the journey off the mountain, you might be rescued by a Reaver Dragonship. They know the value of a strong arm, though they'll show you little mercy. As you can see, your options are bleak even if you make it off the mountain, but the choice is yours. Before you begin, you might want to take some time to plead with the gods for forgiveness. One of them might heed your prayers. Your life is in their hands. Should we ever meet again ... I will kill you."

Maerlin flew off without a backward glance. She hardened her heart with memories of the burned-out village.

*****

Conal began his morning run with enthusiasm. He was glad to be away from the hustle and bustle of the busy fortress. As his day progressed, he would always find himself inundated with tedious questions that only he, as the acting head of the Clan, seemed able to answer. It was stupid really, he thought. How was he supposed to know how many barrels of Leithban mead they were going to need over the coming year? His Clan was growing on a daily basis. Stragglers were coming in every day, and he was sure that the spring gathering would bring in a further influx of his scattered clan folk. It was getting harder to remember all of their names and faces. He had learned to appreciate this quiet time alone on the plains each morning.

He kept to a steady, ground-eating pace, feeling the slight burn of his lungs as he made his way through his first circuit of the hill. The building work was coming along nicely, though Conal had many ideas on how to improve the basic structure. Presently, it was built nearly completely of wood. Over time, and with the aid of a healthier treasury, Conal hoped to rebuild it using granite. After all, they were not far from the mountains and an abundance of stone.

Conal was passing the hay barns when a distinctive humming sound caught his attention. Had it been later in the day, he may not have heard the noise above the hustle and bustle of the busy fortress. This early in the morning, however, the silence made the soft hum seem like a shout. Instinctively, he flinched away, and his *Ciudach*-hide armour did the rest. His reflexes had spoiled the shot, and the missile glanced harmlessly off his tough protection, though the power of the blow could still be felt. The arrow bounced off his shoulder padding, causing him to wince. Had he not flinched away at that critical moment, the arrow could have pierced his heart. A second arrow quickly followed the first, and Conal barely had time to dive for cover behind the nearest barn. Two more arrows whizzed past his head, coming from different directions. One of the archers must have fired early, hoping to take credit for the kill. They had been close to succeeding ... too close, thought Conal.

Sliding his sword free, he rolled away as a second volley of arrows flew overhead. Conal kept moving, knowing that he needed to avoid being pinned down. He was too far away from *Dun Dragan* to be heard. Calling for help would be futile, and it would only give away his location to his assailants. He would be peppered full of arrows before the guards were fully awake.

Conal opted instead to take the offensive and bring the fight to his attackers. Moving cautiously, he searched the mist, waiting for the next volley of arrows. Lifting up a broken pitchfork, he threw it to the far side of the barn, where it banged against the wooden sidings. Within moments, four arrows peppered the siding. So there were four of them, at least. Studying the directions of the arrows, Conal knew that his attackers were spread out across the grassland. This gave them a variety of viewpoints to shoot from, but it also lost them the strength of numbers. He marked their locations firmly in his mind and slipped into the mists. Having run each morning around Dragon's Ridge, he had one clear advantage over the archers. He knew this territory much better than they did. This was *his* battlefield. Now, he would become the hunter and they would be the hunted ... they just didn't know it yet.

Slipping quietly through the denser pockets of mist, he crept forward. He would need to dispatch them quickly and quietly, before they realised the flaw in their plan. Still, it would be good to find out who had sent them. Conal was getting close, and he slowed to a crawl as he eased his way through the damp grass. Fortunately, the fort's livestock had eaten the grass near the *Dun* down to stubble, making stealth possible. Conal caught a movement to his right and altered his course slightly, stalking his prey.

The shadow stood, peering ahead with bow at the ready. It was seeking out its target amongst the cluster of buildings that stood out in the mist. The kill was sudden and brutal. Conal leapt the last few feet, sword held two-handed for an overhead strike and cleaved through the archer with a downward blow. He struck with all the force that he could muster. Nevertheless, the attack was not without some muffled noise, which drifted through the mists and alerted the others. Death now stalked amongst them.

"Fallon!" a voice hissed. "Was that you, Fallon?"

Conal moved away, circling around to approach the speaker from a different angle. As he crept forward, his thoughts drifted to a conversation he had had with Cull about honour in combat. "Honour is for the man with an army at his back. He'll soon lose the respect of his army, if his leadership qualities are besmirched. In a dark alley, when you are outnumbered or out-armed, honour is the toll of the death-bell, the sound of Macha's summoning. Honour is the loser's lament. When the time comes for you to lead an army, you won't need the weapons that I can teach you. Until then, they're the passage to your future kingship."

Cull had taught Conal many subtle and underhand ways to win a fight when the odds were stacked against you. Searching for a pebble on the ground, he used one of those lessons now, the art of deception. Throwing the stone low to the ground, he allowed it to skim along, giving the impression of someone moving in that direction. A moment later, he sprang into attack.

The ruse worked, at least partially, as the man was looking in the wrong direction when Conal rushed forward. Still, the assassin was a professional and he recovered quickly. He turned, sensing the danger before Conal was within striking distance, and he loosed an arrow wildly in the Prince's direction.

Conal sidestepped, pivoted on one foot, twisting away from the incoming arrow and then he dived low. Still spinning, he brought his sword around in a wide arc and cleaved away the assassin's legs. Conal sprang to his feet as the man's scream echoed across the grassland. Flicking the assassin's bow out of reach, Conal sighed. "Well, so much for stealth!"

He looked down at the masked figure that was struggling to stem the blood where his legs used to be. Leaving the man to scream in agony, Conal moved off into the mists. The noise would be sure to distract his opponents and put doubt in their hearts. It would also alert the guards on the hill. Again, he circled, changing his point of attack. Soon, the rising sun would burn off the mist, and the assassins were rapidly running out of time.

The sound of horses galloping away surprised Conal, as his attackers still had the numerical advantage. Why had they left so soon? It didn't make any sense.

The answer came to him through the mist. "Gorvagh? Gorvagh! Come back here, you yellow coward! I'll gut ya sorry ass for this!" One or more of his assailants had fled, but how many others were still hiding within the mist. Clearly, there was at least one.

This time, he decided on a different approach. Boldly, he commanded "Throw down your weapons and come out of the fog. Give yourselves up or die a slow and painful death!" Conal moved away again to probe the fog from a different direction.

As he was passing a small hollow, Conal saw two men stepped out of the fog. They were armed with long-swords, their bows now slung across their backs. Conal hugged the grassland and studied them as they walked past. They moved with the casual confidence of professionals. They stalked forward cautiously, staying slightly apart. They were near enough to offer each other support and avoid isolation, but far enough apart to optimise their attacking options. Their heads constantly swivelled, searching for movement in the swirling mists. Conal waited, letting them walk past until their shadowy forms disappeared. Only then, did he hurry after them.

Cull had taught him the importance of details. Always look for weakness or opportunity in your foe. Know thy enemy. Nothing was too small a detail to make a difference. Cull had spent a long time drilling this into Conal, testing him on everything he saw until Conal learned to miss nothing. Conal had learned his lessons well. For example, he knew that both his attackers carried their swords in their right hands, their stronger hand. He had learned that when a right-handed man was attacked from the left side, the swordsman's reaction time would be a fraction of a second slower. It would take him that much time to readjust his position. He would be on his weaker foot during this readjustment and his sword would have a fraction farther to move before it could counter its opponent's strike. He knew that this moment of time could be the difference between success and failure. He needed to reduce the odds and quickly.

Roaring a defiant challenge, he hurled himself at the nearest of the assassins. The assassin spun around on his weaker left foot, as anticipated, propelling himself around with the stronger foot, as his sword whirled around in a wide arc. Had the blow been successful, Conal would have been disembowelled, but the razor-sharp edge of *An Fiacail Dragan* cleaved the assassin's arm away at the shoulder. The assassin's sword-arm flew past Conal's shoulder, missing him by a hair's breadth and falling harmlessly to the ground. Using his forward momentum, Conal crashed his padded shoulder into the injured assassin and sent him sprawling on the ground. There the assailant lay, screaming his lungs out.

Dismissing him from the fight, Conal jumped away to face the remaining assassin. He barely had enough time to block the incoming blow. The attacker was strong, fast, and relentless, and the Prince fell back under the flurry of blows thrown against him. Inch by inch, he conceded ground as his opponent pressed his advantage, giving Conal no respite. Had the attack happened three moons earlier, Conal would already be dead. The daily training sessions with a variety of weapons had honed Conal's reflexes and improved his stamina. However, the assassin was giving him no opportunity to counter. It would only take one mistake on Conal's part for this to end. The attacks were lightning-quick, powerful and varied. The first thrust was to his body, and then came one to his head, followed by a low slash to his ankles. It was a good combination of attacks, high to low and low to high. The assassin created a complex pattern of blows. He was much more skilled than an ordinary soldier, and Conal could do nothing but dodge and parry wildly while he waited for an opening and searched for the key to the attacker's pattern. He needed to understand the pattern before he could find a way to break through it.

The mist was blowing away, and he could hear horns in the distance, rousing the guards. As yet though, no one had come to his rescue. Panting heavily from the exertion, Conal had no breath left to call out, and the injured assassin nearby had finally fallen silent. He had either slipped into unconsciousness or died from blood loss.

Conal's brain tried desperately to come up with a solution. He needed a way past the other man's attacks, or some subterfuge to shake his opponent's confidence and give him some respite. Nothing came to mind. Conal was going to die. It was only a matter of time. Eventually, the assassin would find a way through Conal's weakening defence and it would be all over. All of those years of hard work would be for nothing. All of the time and effort he had expended in seeking revenge for his father's death. All the training wasted. It was a bitter irony that on the very day that he was due to leave for the Gathering of the Clan, he was going to be denied. He would fail to be recognised as a man. He would fail to become leader of his Clan.

After his death, he would be denied a seat in the Hall of Heroes beside his father. As a boy, he could not claim such a merit in the afterlife. This was the day that Macha would claim him. The bittersweet taste of his own defeat amazed him, and he cursed the gods vehemently as he laughed at his own folly. How could he have been arrogant enough to demand his rightful place as the Dragon-lord? Conal: the boy who was babysat by the witches of Deanna. Cull had once described him as an incompetent thief, at best. Where did he get off thinking that he deserved anything from the world? What foolishness.

Laughter bubbled up at his own stupidity. He laughed so hard that he struggled to breathe. It rolled off him in waves and soothed his momentary panic. What did he have to lose? He had already lost everything, and he was about to die. At least he could laugh at his own stupidity. Images flashed through his head: the ferrets in Maerlin's bed, the prank this morning, the drunken stunt in *Ard Pect*. All of the many pranks he had engineered during his time at the tavern in Manquay and on the Holy Isle. Conal thought of all of his petty acts of stupidity and all of his arrogance. Together, they summed up his wasted life. What a useless excuse for a human being he had become.

And yet, for all of his folly and all of his mistakes, Conal was still here, still standing. Defying the odds and defying the damned assassin who was failing to kill him. Damn, but the man was a good swordsman! Conal laughed into the man's face, getting belligerent now.

"Is that it?" Conal goaded. Anger boiled up in Conal, fuelling his dragon blood and renewing his strength. His parries became stronger and more assured. "Is this the best you've got? I'd have thought they'd have sent someone a bit more competent. Surely, I'm worth the expense."

Conal fed his anger into his blows, matching like for like until the assassin was the one giving ground. Conal sensed people around him, shadows in his periphery vision, but he ignored them. All that mattered was his anger and the fight before him. This had become personal. Either he or this assassin would die, and woe betide anyone who got in the way.

"Kill me, you bastard!" he cursed through gritted teeth. "Come on ... kill me! What're you waiting for?"

Chapter Thirty: The Path to Manhood

It was Conal's sword that finally decided the outcome of the duel, as the combatants were too evenly matched. The sword: *An Fiacail Dragan*, which had been carved from the tooth of a dragon and imbued with all the magical lore of the order of Deanna, was far stronger than mere steel. It was stronger than even the assassin's finely-crafted blade. Although neither of the fighters knew it, the fierce combat had taken its toll on the other man's blade. It had become as serrated as a carving knife. Minuscule cuts had been sliced out of it with every blow. Hairline fractures grew and multiplied, despite the many days of folding the steel into a worthy blade. No sword was designed to suffer the barrage of blows that this one had. With a bell-like ring, it finally shattered, sending shards of metal flying in all directions. *An Fiacail Dragan* broke through the assassin's defences and sliced deeply through his shoulder.

At this point, had Conal been able to stop, the assassin might have yielded up some valuable information during interrogation. Conal, however, was far beyond such rational. He had seen his life flash before him and had laughed into the face of death. He'd defied the very gods themselves and dared them to hold him accountable for his arrogance. He was in a state of maddened fury and bloodlust. The dragon blood that flowed through his brain had taken control. It took six more blows before he realised that his opponent had stopped fighting and then another two before he acknowledged the assassin's death. Panting heavily, blood pooling on the tip of his sword and weeping from his armour, he gazed down at the carcass that lay before him. "I guess you weren't that good after all," he mumbled, as the red mist started to clear from his eyes.

Exhaustion washed over him as he lifted his head and looked around, ready to face the next opponent. The meadow was full of people, gazing open-mouthed at the carnage and shocked at the savagery of the combat.

Finally, Taliesin stepped cautiously forward. "It's alright, Conal. They're all dead. You can put up your sword now."

Conal realised that he was still standing in a fighting stance, ready for the next attacker. He slowly let the sword slip from his blood-stained fingers and fall to the ground. He staggered slightly before Taliesin rushed forward and caught him.

"Easy, Conal!" Conal's armour was soaked with blood. "Quick, get me a stretcher!"

Conal shook his head to clear it and grinned up at the bard. "Did I win?"

"Yes, Conal ... you did. Hold still while I get you some help."

Relief washed over Conal. "I won! I WON!!!" A joy so pure ran through the Prince and with the last of his waning strength he roared out a challenge to the world: to the very gods themselves, and to all of his enemies. *"DRAGAN ABÚ! DRAGAN ABÚ!"*

This final exertion was too much for his battered body, and Conal's knees buckled and he slipped to the ground, barely conscious despite the smug grin on his face.

Others rushed forward, and Conal was carried up to the *Dun*. They brought him into the infirmary, where his armour was stripped from his bloody body, and he was washed in warm wine and honey. Conal was surprised at the myriad of tiny cuts that they found. Some were made by the assassin's swordsmanship, while others still held tiny slivers of steel from the shattered blade. Conal couldn't remember being wounded, but they smarted now that the adrenaline rush had waned. Ointments and bandages came next, as each wound was carefully washed out and stitched back together. Conal gritted his teeth and fought off the waves of nausea that threatened to overwhelm him, wincing despite his best efforts to put on a brave face.

Taliesin finally took pity and chased any spectators from the room. When only the wizened surgeon, Declan, and Taliesin remained, Conal asked "Who did this ... did any of them survive?"

Declan shook his head. "All of the combatants were dead before we arrived. It was too late to question them. We have trackers out, hunting the one that rode away, but I don't hold out much hope of success. He had a good head start."

"Which way did he go?"

"His tracks were going east, Sire."

"East ... not south?" Conal had thought the obvious culprit would be Lord Boare.

352

"No, Conal, they weren't Boarites, but that tells us little about who actually hired them. Two of them are Pects, while the other two are blonde-haired and fair of skin. That means that they could be from anywhere in Dragania, or perhaps even Reavers. You can find such sell-swords for hire in any of the major cities, although perhaps not of this quality. The hilt of that shattered sword was definitely from *Tir Pect*, and it was crafted to a high quality. Such a sword would not come cheap, and neither would its wielder."

"So this was the Pects?"

"I didn't say that, Sire. My own sword was crafted by a Pectish blacksmith, as is your armour. Such items can be ordered during a spring fair and collected at the autumn one, if you have the purse to pay for them. You'd never need to set foot inside *Tir Pect* to obtain one of their weapons."

"He went east, you say?"

"There is only one rider, according to our scouts, but he has five horses. That's why I doubt we'll catch him. Whoever got away can relay the horses. He could be halfway to the Bitter Eastern Sea before our scouts had reached the Screaming Plains."

"What of the eastern Clans?"

Declan shrugged. "I doubt we'll ever know. One thing's for sure, however, you were lucky this time."

"Lucky?"

"Yes, Sire ... lucky! You survived. Next time, you might not be so fortunate. Someone who can afford to hire sell-swords can probably afford to hire more of the same. Worse still, one of the assassins' guilds might have a contract out on you. If that's the case, they'll keep sending more men until the job is done. So yes, you were lucky this time. Next time, we'd better be a damned sight more careful, or we'll be looking for a new King."

"I wish Cull was here," said Taliesin. "I'm sure he could shed some light on this."

Conal nodded, knowing that Cull would be the best person to ask. "I want those bodies wrapped carefully, and have the ground outside searched with a fine tooth comb for clues. We'll be taking them with us when we leave. First though, I need some breakfast. I'm famished."

"You're not still thinking of going to the Gathering, are you?" Declan protested. "It's too dangerous. We'd need a small army to protect you."

"It's a good job that I've got one then, isn't it? One way or another, I'm going to the Gathering, and I *will* compete in the games. I need the recognition of the Brehons before I can become the leader of the Dragons. I can't do that if I'm hiding out in the cellars on *Dun Dragan*."

Declan's face fell, but Conal's showed his determination. Eventually the Grand Marshal gave in. "Very well then. I guess you've got a point. Nevertheless, I must ask you to agree with me on a few precautions ..."

"Go on ..." Conal nodded, not agreeing to anything, but willing to listen.

"Firstly ... no more early morning jogs..."

"...You've got to be kidding me..."

Declan held up his hand and continued "...Alone. If you're going anywhere, I want at least a dozen of our best warriors beside you."

"Three ..."

"...Eight."

"I'll agree to six, but only if they keep their distance. I'll need a little space to breathe. I can't hide behind a shield wall for the rest of my life."

"I can work with six. I'll draw up a roster and begin selecting suitable warriors. If we set up four shifts, that'll mean we'll need twenty-four of them, at the very least, plus a few replacements. They can be your elite bodyguards. Think of them as a second set of armour."

Conal ground his teeth in annoyance. "Great ... more minders!"

"No, Conal, he's right," Taliesin placated.

"I know he's right, Tal! That doesn't mean I have to like it. I'd only just got rid of the witches of Deanna, and then I got lumbered with Cull. Now,

354

I've got a whole platoon of bodyguards to deal with. Will I even be able to use the latrine in peace?"

"Certainly, Sire ... after they've checked it first, of course."

"Naturally," Conal agreed dryly.

"Sire, should we give them a name? It needs to be something that will be a symbol of pride to the men and women within the unit. It'll give them a common sense of purpose. What do you think?"

"That's a great idea!" Taliesin enthused. His bard's mind was already working on various options. "What about the Invincible Platoon, or maybe ... Declan's Devastators ... How does that sound? Naturally, they'll need a special uniform and a suitable banner ..."

Although still unhappy with the idea of bodyguards, Conal gave in to the inevitability of the idea.

"They'll be the elite warriors of *Clann Na Dragan*, and as Declan said, they'll be like a second set of armour, so let them be known as the Dragon-scales. We'll have the armourers craft each of them a fine set of scale-mail armour and a helm to match. Let them stand out amongst the other Dragon warriors. Theirs will be an honoured position that others will strive to attain, and they will be feared by my enemies. As for the banner, let them carry Luigheagh's personal banner, the one that I'd normally carry into battle as leader of the Dragon Clan."

"That's brilliant, Conal!" Taliesin was nearly jumping up and down with enthusiasm.

Declan smiled and nodded in agreement. "It shall be done, Sire."

*****

Ceila led the priestesses of the Order in singing the Dawn Chorus. The sun, as if summoned from the earth, rose to burn the mist off the Great Marsh, and the waterfowl and other birds took up the chorus. They had a busy day ahead of them, collecting nesting material and gathering food in preparation for the first hatchlings of the year.

Ceila joined a group of priestesses on the way to the Dining Hall for breakfast.

"Are you sure that this is wise, Ceila?" Madame Muir asked, not for the first time.

"Yes, Muir, I do. Let's not go over this again."

"But we've always kept ourselves isolated."

"Indeed, we have, Madame Muir. Sometimes, this policy has been to our detriment, as thou art quite aware. We need to send a delegation to the fair anyway, with Nessa unavailable, and it's important that we send a strong delegation with the Dragonson claiming his inheritance."

"A strong delegation, yes, but you're stripping the Isle of every able-bodied sorceress we have. All of the Dream-catchers, Healers, and Wild-magicians are going with you. There'll only be me and a handful of old fuddy-duddies to keep the novices from any shenanigans."

"I'm sure that thou wilt be most capable at this task, Melissa. That's why I chose thee for the job. Thou did manage to keep me out of trouble during my wilder years."

"But do you really need them all?"

"I honestly don't know, Melissa, but I'd rather be safe than sorry. I'm sure that a strong presence will help to keep Lord Boare from misbehaving during the proceedings. I'm still trying to make sense of everything that's going on. The one time I managed to get through to Maerlin, she made absolutely no sense whatsoever. It's like she has a wall of fog surrounding her, and the people with her are similarly blanketed. I can't understand it. I've never had so much trouble getting through to another Dream-catcher before."

"Yes, I know. Did she really say that Nessa was a magpie?"

"I don't know how many times I have to tell thee, she definitely said a magpie."

"Bizarre!"

Ceila shrugged and sat down to eat.

"But I still don't understand why we need to interfere?"

"I made a promise to Conal's father that I would protect his son, should the worst happen. I intend to fulfil that promise despite Conal's reluctance to be guided, but it's more than that. It's Maerlin. Her fate and the fate of *Clann Na Dragan* are heavily intertwined, as is Cora's fate. It's as hard to unravel as a piece of knotwork. They are our sisters ... and so too is Nessa."

"...And Uiscallan?"

"That's yet another mystery to unravel. I can only assume that Maerlin was mistaken, but nothing would surprise me."

"It can't be! No one has ever lived that long, even one blessed by Deanna, especially when living away from the Isle. I've checked our archives thoroughly and from what I could make out, Uiscallan must be close to a hundred years old. Yet Maerlin has claimed that she is wandering around the countryside. That's preposterous!"

"Don't forget that until recently, Dubhgall the Black sat at Lord Boare's side He would be of a similar age, if not older. Little is known of his origins."

"Speaking of the Dark Mage, have you heard any more from our sisters in *Ard Pect*?"

"Sadly, no, I haven't. They seem to be afflicted by this cloud of mystery, too. We have always been able to commune with our sisters in *Tir Pect* before, but now, they've disappeared into the mists. We've been forced to rely on doves, and much though they are usually reliable messengers, travelling over the mountains at this time of the year is hazardous. Many die of exposure. However, the mere fact that a mist is blanketing *Ard Pect* causes me some concern. Dubhgall has always been good at hiding in the darkness and the mist."

"You don't think it's true, do you?"

"Heed me when I tell thee this. Until I see Dubhgall burn before my eyes, I wouldn't doubt his ability to rise from a grave. His dark magic may be the most vile and repulsive, but there is no denying his powers. Should he turn up at the spring fair, it will take all of the priestesses of the Order to stop him, but stop him I must, once and for all. We have sat back and been content to watch the Dream-world for far too long. Now, enough of this idle speculation. The boats must cast off if we're to reach the ship by nightfall."

*****

Maerlin had also sung the Dawn Chorus at the start of the day, before preparing for their departure. It had been decided that they would accompany the delegation of mountain folk who were heading to Manquay for the spring fair. Maerlin had a variety of reasons for this decision. Firstly, she wanted to ensure the safety of the villagers on their journey. Secondly, she wanted to meet up with Ceila and the priestesses of the Order there. She also wanted to be there for Conal's Rites of Manhood.

She had decided that it would be nice to just simply walk around for a while. Much to Seabhac's disgust, Maerlin intended to walk the whole way to Manquay. Although flying was fun, it required a lot of concentration. Maerlin was starting to tire of the constant drain of her energy, both mentally and magically. If magic was a muscle that needed exercise, she argued, then so too were her legs and she intended to use them.

Maerlin had realised that over the winter, her use on magic to do menial things had softened the tone of her muscles. She had set about rectifying this. Over the past few days, Maerlin had cajoled Cora into sparring matches. This had brought cries of protest from both Nessa and Seabhac, though for different reasons. Nessa had a motherly concern over the possible risk of broken bones, while Seabhac was of the firm opinion that the use of weapons was beneath a sorceress. As Maerlin couldn't keep everyone happy, she had decided that she would just please herself and let off a bit of steam, so they had sparred daily. Cora had even managed to charm Maerlin's father into making her a trident: the traditional weapon of *Clann Na Rón*. For his efforts, Cora had smothered him in kisses, much to his embarrassment. Maerlin quickly learned that the normally-placid Cora was quite competitive within the sparring ring, with her weapon of choice. Cora had finally admitted that due to having only brothers when growing up, she had spent much of her time, in or around, a sparring ring.

It was now time to leave the village again, and this time, many of the villagers struggled to contain their emotions at her departure. Leaving her father again was the worst, but at least she was departing on good terms. For the first time, Maerlin knew that she would always have a home here in High Peaks. For a girl who had felt so alone, less than a year ago, she now found herself with more homes than she cared to think about. So many places now had a place of her heart. High Peaks and Eagles Reach were high on the list, but there were also Seabhac's cottage and the Holy Isle.

Finally, turning away from High Peaks, she followed the small group of villagers, yearling bull calves, hoggets, geese, and carts full of produce that were making their way down from the mountainside. Last summer, it had taken some time to reach Manquay, as Nessa and Maerlin had wandered aimlessly around the mountainside while Maerlin learned to control her magic. This journey would be shorter than the previous one, but it would still take nearly a week to reach Manquay.

As she walked away from the village, she was pleasantly surprised to notice that one of the boys who were herding the bull calves was Duncan Gammit. They had made peace over the last week, even going as far as having a few 'friendly' sparring matches, which turned out to be not so friendly after all, although this could have had more to do with their competitive natures, rather than any long-held animosity.

"Are you sad to be leaving?" Nessa asked from her perch on Maerlin's shoulder. Maerlin closed her eyes momentarily and brought herself into the white room that she used to mind-speak with Nessa.

"I don't know why you insist on coming in here for a chat. I know you're quite capable of speaking when you want to."

Nessa shrugged. *"It's cosy in here. Anyway, it's the only place I can get any peace."*

Maerlin smiled. *"Is Sir Gallaghad still in hot pursuit?"*

"I wish you'd stop calling him that! It's not his name, you know."

"He's got a name?"

"Of course he's got a name, but I don't think it'd do you any good to know what it was. You can't speak magpie."

Maerlin pulled out her tongue in a very unladylike fashion. *"Nessa?"*

"Yes, dear?"

"Is it me or are you getting younger?"

"I told you that the way you see me would change, Maerlin. Remember?"

Maerlin looked at the young woman sitting in the chair by the fire. The image blurred, and for a moment, it was the magpie that was perched on her shoulder again, and then it changed back to the petite woman with the bold streaks of blonde against the jet-black hair. Maerlin knew that some of what she saw was her mind's perception of Nessa's psyche, but she was sure that there was more to it than that. A lot of what she saw was a younger version of Nessa, despite the blessings of Macha and Deanna. *"You must have been a real heart-breaker when you were younger, Nessa MacTire."*

Nessa flushed with surprise. *"What brought that thought on?"*

"Oh, nothing, I was just thinking, that's all. How exactly did you get to be a crow? I know that Macha claimed you as one of her own, due to the fact that you took on the form of a Dark Angel, but you never told me how you did it in the first place?"

"It's a long story, dear."

"We've got a long journey ahead of us. I've got plenty of time."

Nessa sighed. *"Very well then, if you insist. Where should I start?"*

Maerlin thought back. *"Tell me about the Watchtower. That's where you vanished."*

Nessa began to explain. "As I recall, I was racing along behind Cull. He had just rescued Cora, and the Boarites were breathing down our necks. I knew that I'd never make it to the trees, so I veered away toward the tower, hoping to distract them and buy the rest of you some time to get into the woods. I thought I might be safe there, as they wouldn't be able to follow me"

"Why wouldn't they follow you?"

"Those towers are protected by ancient magic. Only magic wielders can enter them ..."

"Wait! Hang on a moment ..."

"What now?"

"Cora! She'll kill me if she's left out of this. Hang on, I'll just go and get her." Maerlin stopped at the door of the room in her head and looked back at Nessa, sitting in her imaginary chair. *"Ness, do you mind if I invite Seabhac, too? It'd be rude to leave her out."*

"It's your head, Maerlin. Invite the whole village, if you want," Nessa replied, a little tartly.

"Why don't you and Seabhac get along?"

"We get along just fine. We just see things differently, that's all. Seriously, she's welcome. We are, after all, sisters of Deanna."

"Thanks Ness."

*****

It took a number of days to regain control, but Dubhgall knew that his new 'eyes' would eventually give up their resistance and yield fully to his dominance, and he was right. Eventually, hunger and thirst had won out, and the monks had finished their prayers and realised the futility of their actions. Magic had been summoned in an effort to release them, and Dubhgall had been able to swoop in and grasp the reins of control. He had made Gearoid pay for this insubordination, sending waves of pain into the Abbot, again and again until finally hunger overcame his thirst for revenge. He blasted the door apart and marched out, in search of food.

The local craftsmen had been busy in his absence, and a brand new chariot had been crafted for the petulant Queen, to replace her stolen one. Conchubhar had even donated his best team of horses to his wife, to further appease her. They were finally ready to depart. The foot-soldiers and the supply train of the combined armies of *Tir Pect* had already left days beforehand. Conchubhar had hoped to make up some of the lost time by sending them ahead into the mountain pass. Only his cavalry and war-chariots remained, waiting for Medb and the Dark Mage. Now, they were finally ready. They rode through the streets of *Ard Pect*; a majestic parade to appease the masses, before picking up the pace and racing through the hills.

Chapter Thirty-One: An Unexpected Arrival

Taliesin was helping Conal into his freshly-cleaned armour when they heard the sound of running feet, and a page arrived. "I have a message for you, Sire."

"Well don't be shy, spit it out. I'm kind of busy right now."

"Yes, Sire." The boy nodded nervously and went through the message in his head one more time before repeating it aloud, in case he got it wrong. "Your scouts report a chariot heading this way, Sire."

"Is that it?"

"No Sire." The boy looked nervously around, before blurting out the rest of his message "They said that it was Queen Medb, Sire."

"What ... on her own?"

"No, Sire, she has her jester with her."

"No soldiers ... not even an escort?"

"No sire, only one chariot. No outriders."

"How far away are they?"

"They're probably a couple of miles away by now, Sire, and closing fast. The scout was having trouble keeping ahead of them."

"He did well and so did you," Conal assured the boy. "Is my chariot ready?"

"I believe so, Sire."

"Good. Go and make sure, will you. Tell Declan to prepare some troops to ride out and greet her. I'll be right behind you. Taliesin, where's my sword?"

"Right here, Conal," Taliesin answered, handing over the baldric. "What, by the Seven, is Medb doing here?"

"I haven't the foggiest idea but I'm sure we'll find out, soon enough. Another bell and we'd have already left for the fair."

They hurried outside and Conal grasped his reins as he stepped onto the chariot. "Are you coming, Tal?"

Taliesin looked nervously at the war ponies, chomping eagerly on their bits, waiting to run. He remembered some of Conal's training sessions with the pair. "Erm, no thanks, I never did like chariots. I'd be sure to fall off."

Conal shrugged and studied the group of battle-hardened veterans that Declan had selected to be his bodyguards. Each was mounted and armed with a variety of weapons: from the newly-invented crossbows to composite cavalry bows, plus an array of javelins, swords, and axes. They looked a competent bunch of men and women, warriors who would stand toe to toe in the thick of any fight and would not waver. Declan had made good choices. Nodding to the Grand Marshal, who was waiting on a sturdy warhorse, Conal flicked the reins and gave his ponies their heads. "Let's go and meet Queen Medb then, shall we?"

Declan nodded and kicked his heels into the horse's flanks. They were off, racing down the cobblestone road and out, onto the plain. By now, Conal could see the Queen's chariot. Even from a distance, Medb's red hair stood out, flowing behind her like a flame. Watching the way she handled her horses, he acknowledged her skill and dexterity. "Battle lines!" he roared, and the riders flared out with crisp discipline on either side of the chariot.

"Is that wise, Sire?" Declan shouted over the noise of the horses' hooves and the rattle of the chariot. The chariot wheels were quieter, now that they were off the cobblestones and racing across the grassland.

"I won't stand meekly before one of the most famous warriors alive, Declan. If she is racing to my door, then let my strong arm give her pause. Charge!" he bellowed. His ponies leapt forward, eager to bring the battle to the foe. His newly-assembled Dragon-scales kept pace as they raced toward the Queen's chariot.

"Hold your fire!" Conal commanded as they drew closer. He wanted a show of strength in his greeting, not a diplomatic disaster. *"Dragan abú! DRAGAN ABÚ!"*

364

The Dragon-scales took up his shout as they raced headlong across the grassland, praying not to hit a rabbit hole and break their necks, but determined to protect their young leader. Conal drove on, expecting the Queen to pull up at any moment, but she raced toward him without hesitation.

"Damn her! She's going to ram you!" Declan warned.

"Break formation!" Conal demanded, knowing he would need room to manoeuvre if she didn't pull up soon. If the two chariots continued on their current trajectory, it would be a suicide charge. Neither of the drivers would survive a head-on collision. The Dragon-scales followed his command and broke formation, giving him room, should he need it.

Conal yearned to rein in his mounts, but he would look foolish if he did. Damn it, he thought. I'll look even more foolish if I'm dead. Still, if I'm going to die, then at least the bards can sing of my courage. "G'yup!" he cried and flicked his wrists, urging greater speed out of his team.

"Conal, pull them up!" Declan warned.

The Queen, seeing him urging his team on, flicked her whip over her own horses' heads, urging them to one final effort. Great patches of sweat marred their sleek coats, testament to the hard days of travelling they had endured. However, these ponies were bred for war and they picked up their pace, hurtling across the last fifty yards at a terrifying speed. The collision was only moments away...

After the morning's sword-fight, Conal's dragon blood still sang sweetly through his veins, urging him on to even greater recklessness, but thankfully, reason won out. "Damn you to the Nine Hells!" he cursed as he yanked hard on the reins, swerving his team to the left of the Queen's horses. He had barely a moment to spare. The chariot tilted wildly, careening onto one wheel. Conal leaned into the swerve, raising the chariot blades higher. Much to his surprise, the Queen had pulled the same manoeuvre, and the chariots passed within inches of each other, their deadly scythe-blades barely avoiding decapitating the opponent's horses.

Conal pulled his ponies to a sharp halt and jumped off his chariot, fighting back the urge to draw his sword. "Are you off your rocker? What did you think you were doing?" he demanded hotly.

His first response was from the jester. He staggered off the Queen's chariot and vomited onto the ground at Conal's feet. His face had turned a pale green hue as he sank to his knees and continued to heave.

The Queen stepped regally down from her chariot, grasping her daggers lightly as she readied herself for any confrontation. "You're the one that started it, not me! What was I supposed to do?"

Conal conceded that she might have a point there, and his anger receded slightly.

"Drop your weapons, Medb!" Declan warned as his men surrounded her chariot.

"Medb? Oh ... silly me. I'd forgotten all about that! Wait a minute ... this might help." Queen Medb reached up to grasp her flaming, red hair. With a sharp tug, she ripped the wig free and dropped it on the ground. A moment later, her false nose followed. Quickly removing the hair clips, she shook out her raven-coloured locks and grinned at the Prince. "You must be Conal *MacDragan,* I take it?" she asked with a mischievous grin. "I'm looking for Cull. Where is he?"

"Cull?" Conal asked. He was a little surprised to find that Queen Medb wore a wig and even more surprised to find out that she knew Cull. Then again, nothing should surprise him when it came to Cull.

The jester continued to gag.

"Cull told me that he was your guardian," Medb informed Conal as she walked over to the jester. "I warned you not to eat such a big breakfast, Malachi," she reminded him, patting his back.

"Cull told you that?" Conal asked, bewildered.

"Yes, when he came to visit me in *Ard Pect.*"

"He was meeting *you* ... but I thought ...?"

"Didn't he mention me?" The Queen seemed put out.

Conal answered as best as he could. "I'm sorry, your Majesty. He told me that he was going to the Pink Rose. He never said anything about going to the palace."

The jester stopped puking for long enough to emit a weak groan.

"The palace ...? Oh, by the heavens, no!" Medb laughed lightly. It took a moment for her to compose herself. "The wig must have you confused ... and the chariot, I guess ..." she laughed again, "...and the jester, of course. I'm sure he didn't help. My, we seem to have gotten into a right pickle here." She laughed again, before pulling herself together. "Let me make some introductions, your Majesty. This is Malachi, the Royal Jester of *Ard Pect*, or at least he was ..."

Malachi smiled weakly and wiped vomit off his lips with some grass.

"And I'm *Sile Ceathrar-Cioch*, proprietor of the Pink Rose." Sile unbuttoned a few of the buttons on her leather bustier, displaying a subtle amount of her unique assets for the Prince and his bodyguards. "Do tell me that you've heard of me? I'll be mortified if you haven't."

Conal gazed down at her double cleavage and wondered whether the mounds were real. It seemed rude to ask. "Erm!" Conal spluttered, at a loss for words.

At this point, the Grand Marshal saved Conal from any further awkwardness. "The bards and entertainers throughout Dragania sing of the bountiful pleasures to can be had within the Pink Rose, Milady."

Sile turned and gave him a dazzling smile in thanks. "I like him," she declared. "He says all the right things. You should keep him, *MacDragan*. Now, let's get down to business, shall we. Where's Cull?"

"He's in Manquay. He said that he had to go and see someone there."

"What! He's supposed to be here ... with you."

Conal shuffled his feet. "It's my own fault really. I messed up. Taliesin and I got thrown into *Ard Pect's* gaol."

"Mmmm, I can't see that going down well, knowing Cull."

"He was a bit vexed to say the least."

"I can imagine. So, he left you here and piddled off to Manquay?"

"That's about it."

"Damn it! Damn it! Damn it!"

"Anything I can do?" Conal offered.

Sile thought for a moment. "Well, I guess I might as well tell you anyway. It'd take too long to drive to Manquay and back, and you're going to find out one way or another. At least this way, you can prepare yourself, but I'd have liked to have Cull's input in this."

"It must be important."

"Oh yeah, you could say that. Their Royal Majesties are planning on paying you a visit."

"Oh! I seem to be having a lot of unexpected visitors recently."

"This one's going to be a shocker! Conchubhar and Medb aren't coming alone."

"They're bringing an entourage ...?"

"You could call it that ... a big one!"

"I can hold off on slaughtering a fattened bull for the festivities, I take it?"

"Something like that..."

"Let's just make this clear, shall we? We are talking about an invasion here, aren't we?"

Sile nodded. "You've got it in one! Every able-bodied warrior they could lay their hands on."

"So ... why exactly are you here?"

"I want to stop it, of course. Cull has high hopes for you, and a war right now wouldn't be good for business."

Conal nodded. He was a little surprised to hear of Cull's recommendation. He felt a twinge of guilt at letting him down. "...And what about the jester?"

"Ah, it's a little complicated," Sile replied. "I sort of kidnapped him, when I stole Medb's chariot."

"You stole the Queen's chariot?" Declan blurted out. "That mustn't have gone down well."

Sile smiled again at the Grand Marshal. "Probably not, but I didn't stick around for long enough to find out. I'm sure some harsh words will be had, if and when she ever catches up with me and Malachi. He's decided to come along and see if he could help."

"Does he always puke like that?" Conal wrinkled his nose. The smell lingered despite the light breeze.

"When he drinks too much, which is quite often, yes, I'm afraid so! Oh, and I don't think he travels well."

"I can travel just fine ... when the chariot isn't driven by a madwoman with a death-wish!" Malachi grumbled belligerently.

"Sire, perhaps we should continue this discussion within the safety of *Dun Dragan*?" Declan suggested, scanning the northern horizon.

"That sounds like a splendid idea," Malachi agreed. "I don't know about the rest of you, but I'm famished, and I could do with a stiff drink ... for medicinal purposes, you understand. I need to steady my nerves after that stunt!"

"How do you eat so much, Malachi?" Sile asked.

"What! I've got a good constitution, that's all. We Dwarfs are famed for it."

"He isn't really a Dwarf, is he?" Conal murmured.

"So he claims, but he's an outrageous liar, even at the best of times."

"He hasn't even got a beard ..."

"What is this sudden fixation with beards?" Malachi demanded, getting to his feet. "Suddenly, everyone's an expert on Dwarfish facial hair. It's enough to make you want to pull your whiskers out."

*****

"You can't be serious, your Highness," the Grand Marshal protested.

"I most certainly am. We're going to Manquay."

"But the Pects are invading ..."

"Yes, I'm quite aware of that, Declan, but we still need to go to Manquay."

"Whatever for?"

"So the Brehons can declare me a man, of course."

"But can't that wait? The Pects are coming ...!"

"Yes, Declan. I think you've mentioned that already."

"The Dragon-folk already know that you're a man, Sire. They don't need a lawyer to tell them that. They witnessed it this morning on the field of battle. They'll serve you faithfully as they did your father. You are the Dragonson."

Conal smiled with genuine warmth. "You do me a great honour, Declan, you and all of *Clann Na Dragan*. However, it's not for *Clann Na Dragan* that I need to go. It's for the other Clans, the *Seabhac*, the *MacTire*, the *Broce*, the *Stagaí*, the *Béar*, and all the lesser Clans who'll be at the gathering, even the Boarites ... especially for the Boarites. The Pects are coming with every able-bodied warrior they can muster. Without the other Clans, or at least some of them, we haven't got a chance of stopping this invasion. Many of the Clans will be hard enough to win over, even with the blessing of the Brehons. Half of the Clans of Dragania are Pects themselves! They're as likely to fight with the armies of *Tir Pect*, as stand against them. Even the Brocians may balk at taking up arms against their fellow Pects. We must make them understand that they'd be better off in Dragania than as part of *Tir Pect*. To do that, I must go to the Gathering of the Clans. I must do well at my trials and receive the recognition of the Brehons. The Clans won't even listen to me without getting the Brehons blessing as head of *Clann Na Dragan*."

"Conal is right, Declan. I'm not happy about it either, but he's right, nevertheless," Taliesin declared.

Malachi belched and shook a chicken leg in agreement. "Da boy-King is right and full of might! He is correct and stands erect. To the gathering we go, tally-ho!"

"We?" Conal asked.

"Well, ya can't leave us behind, Sire! Her Majesty would feed me to her dogs ... bit by bit! I love the wench dearly but she's not a woman to be crossed, I can promise you that! She's as feisty as a rabid she-bear ... and that's when she's in a good mood."

"What about you, Sile?"

"I need to see Broll anyway, and Malachi's right. I think we need to give Queen Medb some time to cool off ... a decade or two might do the trick."

"You haven't heard then?"

"Heard what?"

A messenger had arrived a few days previous, bringing Conal the news. He'd assumed that Sile would have heard also, but clearly she hadn't. "Broll has passed on to the Otherworld. Cull is now the head of the Beggars Guild."

Sile sat very still as the news hit home. She seemed unable to fully take in what had been said. She reached for her beaker of mead with shaky hands and missed, spilling it.

"I'm sorry ..." Conal mumbled, not knowing what else to say. Conal had never met the Beggar-lord. He hadn't even known there was such a title until he met Cull, but he knew that if he had earned the respect of both Cull and Conal's father, then Broll must have been a worthy man.

Sile fought back the wave of grief. "It's nothing," she said, though her face showed her shock at the news.

Conal nodded and after a moment he added "Very well then, that's settled. Declan, I want you to spread the word. We leave in one bell, and I want everyone ready to go, and I mean *everyone*: no exceptions. I want the old, the sick, the infirm, all of them, packed away on carts and ready to depart by then. I don't want a single shepherd left behind. We'll take all of the stock and anything else of value with us when we leave."

"But what about *Dun Dragan*?"

"What about it?"

"All the work that we've done to rebuild it ..."

"Declan, I know, but at the end of the day it's just a pile of kindling, waiting to be torched. If we leave anyone behind to protect it, we'll be writing their death sentences. We don't have sufficient numbers to protect it, so all we can do is abandon it. We'll leave the gates open so that Conchubhar and Medb won't need to break them down. If we're lucky, they won't waste time destroying it. It might not be much, but it's all we've got. Now go and make the announcement, and Declan, I mean it. One bell, no more. I'll have warriors scour the *Dun* for stowaways if I have to."

The Grand Marshal nodded and marched off. Sile watched him leave.

*****

Gearoid woke to find himself bound securely to a tree. This came as no surprise, and he tested the bonds only briefly before accepting his fate. One of the advantages of being a mindless automaton during the day was that he needed little or no sleep, whereas the *Darkness* that lurked within Balor needed time to revitalise himself. The constant mental struggle to control Balor's mind and keep Gearoid on a tight leash was taking its toll on the Dark Mage, even if he hid it well. Conchubhar and Medb may not realise it, and the cohort of Hedge-wizards were certainly oblivious to it, but Gearoid, who was constantly linked to the *Darkness*, felt it on an intuitive level. It was a weakness, the only one he had found so far, and one he would keep to himself until he had found a way to use it against the Dark Mage.

He wasn't even going to tell Balor, just to be on the safe side. So while Balor and his evil doppelganger slept, Gearoid prayed, and then prayed some more. The moon goddess Arianrhod, in all her silver splendour, rose and still the monk prayed. He prayed to each of the Seven Greater Gods and to a myriad of lesser gods, as well. He beseeched their aid in winning his and Brother Balor's freedom. Finally, he nudged Brother Balor's foot to wake him. He was similarly trussed up across from him.

"Balor, wake up," he hissed softly.

Balor awoke and struggled against his bonds with the strength of desperation.

"Easy, Brother, it's no use. You'll only do yourself an injury."

"Gearoid, where are we?"

"We're somewhere in the mountains. See that road over there?" He indicated with a nod of his head. "That must be the Northern Highway, so I'd guess we're heading south."

"How do you know?"

"Can you see the moss on the trees, Brother? See where the goddess Arianrhod sails in the sky? That way is south. If we were heading north, the mountains would be over there, and the valley in which Crannockmore Lough lies, would be over there. It isn't, so we're travelling south."

"Are you sure?"

"I wasn't always a monk, you know. I was once a young warrior of the Bear Clan. I grew up a little to the east of here, in these very mountains. I dreamed of being a tracker, and I prayed each night to Cernunnos for greater prowess."

"We have to get out of here. We're heading into Dragania," Balor demanded. Panic masked his ravaged face.

"Calm yourself, Brother. You've nothing to fear from the *Fear Ban*. We must, however, use what little time we have together wisely."

"If you say so, Gearoid. What must we do?"

"We must pray, of course ... for a little while, at least."

"Why do you insist on wasting our time in prayer? Surely there's another option?"

"Be at peace, Brother, and trust me. Come; let us pay homage to Macha."

"What's the point? She just ignores my prayers."

"Then you must pray harder. She isn't a servant to be summoned to your beck and call. She's a goddess. You must believe in her and have faith in her. You must make her want to bother with your measly existence and take time out of her busy schedule as the goddess of death, to aid you in your life, Brother. Now, let us pray."

Balor sighed in resignation, not so much out of conviction, but more out of respect for his spiritual leader and friend.

"Blessed Macha, goddess of the darkest shadows and the mother of the last breath, we beseech you as the humblest of your servants ..."

They prayed together until the warriors around them started to stir. Gearoid then signalled that it was time to stop.

"Now what ...?"

"It's time for you to use a little magic, of course, just enough to burn away your bindings."

"... But that will release *him*?"

"Exactly, Brother! It's morning, after all. Too much sleep can't be good for him."

"But we'll be playing into his hands if we use magic?"

"There are many ways to skin a rat, Brother. Remember ... trust me and have faith. These are the paths to your redemption."

Balor struggled against his doubts for a moment before sighing. "If you insist, Abbot. I hope you know what you're doing." He closed his ragged eyelids and dipped into the magical pool of energy within himself. Absently, he noted that the pool was lower than previously, but he didn't get the chance to wonder further about this revelation, as his darker self leapt upon his psyche and crushed it viciously beneath his will.

The calmness in Balor's face vanished and it was replaced by a harsher aspect that Gearoid recognised as the presence of the Dark Mage. "Good morning, Dubhgall. I hope you slept well," he greeted.

The Mage's ropes turned instantly to ash, and with a nasty grin, Dubhgall reached out and grasped Abbot Gearoid's outstretched leg. Gearoid's scream of pain was short lived, before he slipped under the control of the *Darkness*.

Chapter Thirty-Two: Meeting at the Mage Tower

The sun was well up before the last stragglers left the fort, but Conal was determined to leave no one behind him when he evacuated Dragon's Ridge. They made reasonable progress on the cobbled road south, but their pace slowed considerably when they broke trail across the grassland, toward the Mage's tower. It stood like a gigantic finger, rising up into the skyline, and it could be seen for miles, standing against the backdrop of the Broce Woods. It was getting dark by the time Conal and his entourage arrived and set up camp, and it would take another bell before the last of the Dragon-folk made it into camp.

It wasn't long before the Brocians emerged from the trees, carrying seasoned timber for the campfires. The Badger Clan were very sensitive about strangers cutting down their trees, so Vort had arranged a supply of dry timber to be on hand for the meeting. More and more Brocians emerged, and Conal watched in surprise, wondering if they would ever stop. Various tribal banners flew, denoting the different Broce Setts. Leading them was Vort MacAiden, his banner held high. By his side walked his wife, Orla *Ni Tirloch Broce*, and their sons. Following in their wake was the newly-assembled Warrior-mages and the warriors of the Southern Dell Sett.

Conal gripped forearms with Vort in the traditional greeting of warriors. "Well met, my friend."

"I was wondering if you'd forgotten, *Ciudachbane*."

"Something came up at the last moment ... you know how it is."

"Nothing serious, I hope?"

"Well, you might call it that. There's a big storm heading this way. It's on its way through the mountain pass right now, coming down from the north."

"*Ard Pect*?"

"Aye, *Ard Pect*. It seems that Conchubhar and Medb are planning to invade."

"Really, I hadn't heard that. You must have built up a pretty good spy network, Conal. You work fast."

"Not really. I've been too busy shearing sheep, re-building my *Dun* ... oh, and fighting off assassins."

"Assassins ... when did that happen?"

"This morning. I've sent scouts out to chase down the last of them, but it isn't looking promising."

"Who sent them ... have you any idea?"

"Not yet, Vort, but I'll get to the bottom of it."

"So, how did you learn about *Ard Pect*? Cathal's only just back from there and he'd heard nothing. Granted, he was a bit busy selling off the last of the wool. Still, you'd have expected him to hear something."

"I don't know what's got them all fired up. When we visited *Ard Pect* in the winter there was no sign of trouble, but I've heard it from a very reliable source. Come on. I'll introduce you."

Conal led Vort and his family over to where Sile was rubbing down her ponies. Taliesin and Malachi were throwing dice in the back of Medb's chariot.

"Vort, I'd like you to meet *Sile Ceathrar-Cioch*, Madame of the Pink Rose. Sile, this is a good friend of mine, Vort *MacAiden Na Broce* of the Southern Dell Set. He's the Champion of the Broce and their new High-shaman. This fair lady is his wife: Orla *Ni Tirloch Broce*."

"The gods be with you," Sile greeted them warmly in Pectish.

"And with you," Orla replied with the traditional response.

Vort's attention was drawn to the war-chariot. "Is that ..."

"Yes Vort, it is. Sile stole Queen Medb's war-chariot so that she could warn me about the invasion."

Vort whistled softly.

"And this is Malachi: Medb's royal jester."

"I'm sorry, Conal, but now I'm confused. What's her jester doing here if Medb's planning to invade?"

"It's a little complicated, Vort."

"Excuse me," Orla interrupted, trying to bring some clarity to the situation. "Correct me if I'm wrong here, but this winter you've stole Conchubhar's armour and now you've stolen Medb's chariot, *and* her jester. Am I right? That's to say nothing of your wool enterprise ..."

"Well, I wouldn't put it quite like that!"

"Is it any wonder that Conchubhar and Medb want to invade Dragania?" Orla suggested with a sweet smile.

"Is that really Conchubhar's armour?" Sile asked.

"No, actually, it's mine. It was made from a *Ciudach* that I slew during the winter. The armourers, however, mistakenly thought it was being made for Conchubhar."

"I have to say that I'm impressed with the number of enemies you've managed to attain, for one so young," Vort complimented. "I'm sure that with a little effort, you could be really good at it."

"Thanks," Conal said dryly. "Speaking of my armour, where are the Snow Badgers, anyway?

"Ah!" Vort exclaimed with a grin, "They've been a little delayed. They're bringing a present along for the bard."

"...For me?" Taliesin asked, looking up from the game.

"Yes, Taliesin ... for you." A bellowing was heard deeper in the woods. "That sounds like them now."

"Gertie! Is that Gertie?" Taliesin asked, discarding his dice and peering out toward the woods.

"The stable-hands at Broce will be glad to see the back of her. She's a mean temper, that one. Are you sure she isn't at least part *Deamhan*?"

379

The warriors of the Snow Badger Clan emerged from the woods pulling, and in turn being pulled by, a large brown beast. It fought them every step of the way.

"Oh, Gertie!" Taliesin exclaimed, running over.

"What, by the Nine Hells, is that?" Malachi asked in astonishment.

"I think he called it a camel," Conal replied.

Taliesin rushed blindly toward the clearly-deranged beast and wrapped his gangly arms around her neck, ignoring the still-flaying feet, which were trying to disembowel the Brocians. "Gertie, Gertie, by the gods, I've missed you!" he exclaimed, stroking her neck and cooing softly. "It's alright, Gertie. You're safe now!"

To the astonishment of all the onlookers, the creature calmed and stopped fighting.

*****

Daylight came, and the last of the Brocians left the shelter of the woodlands.

Conal looked out across the plain at the myriad campfires and makeshift tents. It was like a Gathering of the Clans already, there were so many people here. "Did you bring your whole Clan, Vort?"

"Most of them ... from the look of it. We normally wouldn't have half as many people here, hardly more than a third, but the word has gone out. Something special is anticipated at this Gathering this year, and no one wanted to miss the occasion."

"Why? What's so special?"

"You, of course, *Ciudachbane*! They've come here to see you claim your throne and become the next *Ri Na Dragan*. Though you might not realise it, this is a big event. Your destiny has been written in the stars, they say. I don't know if that's true or not, but I've seen what you've done already. It's more than many would dream of in a life-time. Take yesterday for example. You started the day by single-handedly fighting off a band of trained assassins. Then, after a light breakfast, you laughed in the face of death and charged recklessly against Queen Medb's chariot. You recruited the most infamous Madame to your side, along with her jester sidekick, and then you came here to meet *Clann Na Broce*. All of this with *Tir Pect's* army hot on your heels. I'd say that wasn't a bad day's work for any hero."

"It wasn't like that! You've been listening to too many of Taliesin's tales," Conal protested.

"Are the four dead assassins in that wagon over there figments of the bard's imagination, *Ciudachbane*? What about the duel you fought in the mists with their leader, the one with the expensive Pectish long-sword? Your clansmen spoke of it in tones of awe around the campfires last night. Was all of that not true?"

"I guess ... but it just happened."

"And this is why the Brocians have come to see you face your Rites of Manhood. Around you things just happen. They want to be there to witness it, so that they can tell their grandchildren about it afterwards. They come so that they can say that they were there, on the day that *Conal MacDragan* claimed his destiny."

Conal shook his head. "You're as bad as Taliesin."

Vort laughed and slapped the prince's back. "Come along, Conal *Ciudachbane*! We need to get these people moving south or we'll miss the start of the fair."

*****

Cull was perched on an old barrel, high up in a disused tannery, close to the city walls. From this vantage point he could look across the broad meadow outside the wall. Preparations were already well underway for the upcoming Gathering. Posts had been driven into the ground, and designated areas were being roped off to create orderly roads and partitioned sections, all across the vast expanse of grass. It was a good time of year for the Beggar's Guild, with many of the poor earning enough during the Gathering to keep them from starvation during the coming winter. The Gathering of the Clans was the lifeblood of the city of Manquay because the city was perfectly situated at the crossroads between the great cobbled roads, which ran east-west and north-south. Added to that was the River Man, and the traffic that sailed on it. River boats sailed down from the shallows at the edge of the mountain range, flat-bottomed boats sailed upriver from the Great Marsh, and even great seafaring ships ventured here from the Western Isles. They all docked at Manquay for the festivities. The revenue raised during this event could fill the coffers of kings, and it could pay a year's wages for their armies.

This, as much as anything else, was the reason why Lord Boare coveted the title of High King. Manquay sat on the edge of the Plains of the Dragon. For Lord Boare to claim any share of the taxes charged here, he needed to have the right to do so by Brehon law. This was *Dragan* country, and the revenue of the Gathering would belong to Conal after his ascension. Once he became the Dragon-lord, he would become rich beyond his wildest dreams, due mainly to the taxes raised at the spring and autumn fairs. Cynical historians would claim that this was the real reason why *Luigheagh An Dragan* sought the Great Truce between the Clans of Pect and the *Fear Ban* in Dragania. The real wealth of *Clann Na Dragan* was not in the sheep, cattle, and horses it bred on the grassy plains, it was in the taxes that the Clan accrued during the bi-annual fairs.

Lord Boare would need to win over the majority of the other Clans, by might or intrigue, to gain the seat of the High King. Only then could he claim the lion's share of the profit of the fair. This was the reason why he had been seduced into challenging Conal's father. The poisoned words of Dubhgall the Black, whispered into his ear to tempt his greed, had torn down the once stable kingdom, and left Dragania on the brink of chaos. It had nearly bankrupted Lord Boare to pay the Reaver mercenaries and sell-swords that he had needed to bulk up his army. Only slavery and the conscription of his own clansmen maintained that army and kept his ambitions alive. He had been very close to winning the High Kingship, but for all this cost, he had still failed to unite sufficient Clans behind his banner. The Pectish Clans within Dragania did not trust him, and they refused his offers of friendship. Even the northern *Fear Ban* Clans rebelled against his leadership. He was commonly referred to as the Usurper-king, especially by the Horse and Dragon Clans.

Since returning to Manquay, Cull had been further undermining Lord Boare's position. Cull's plots to release slaves from his mining camps and the mass breakouts from his gaols had crippled the Boare's economy. Added to this, pirates had been employed to terrorise the River Suile and along the Boarite coastline, until sailing in these waters was only attempted by the bravest or most foolhardy. Many Boarite ships of wool, grain, and beef, would never make it to the fairground. Empty ghost-ships wallowed in the marshland of the Otter Clan, or their wreckage lay shattered against the rocky coastline. The greatest of all of Cull's interventions, however, was the mutinies within the Boare's own army. Without a reliable force to quell his starving people, rioting had broken out in the city of Suilequay. Recent reports suggested that Lord Boare was heading north with his remaining troops, leaving mayhem in his wake.

It had cost most of Cull's resources and a large chunk of his hidden coffers to achieve this, but it was money well spent. It would take Lord Boare a long time to recover from this disastrous winter, and he shouldn't be able to interfere with Conal's claim to his kingship. Conal would have the chance to consolidate his position before Lord Boare could again threaten the High Kingship. Hopefully, by that time, Conal would be strong enough to thwart him.

Cull was close to exhaustion. He had been working day and night to maintain the pressure and assure the collapse of Lord Boare's reign of terror, but his task was nearly over. Soon he would be able to rest. He had taken on Broll's life's work and he had run with it, and his mentor would be proud of all that he had achieved in such a short space of time. All Conal had to do was ride down to the Gathering of the Clans, compete in his Rites of Manhood, stand before the Brehon and be declared fit to rule. Surely it couldn't be that hard, even for Conal. Cull might have his doubts when it came to Taliesin's ability to guide the prince, but he knew that the Grand Marshal would keep him from getting sidetracked. With the soldiers of *Clann Na Dragan* that Cull had released from quarries and gaols and sent north to Dragon's Ridge, and the promise of assistance from *Clann Na Broce Snochta*, Cull was certain that Conal would be safe.

That was until Madame Dunne came wheezing up the last flight of stairs. Cull flicked the remains of his smoke over the city wall and stood. "What is it, Ester?" He knew that she would not be there without good cause.

"We've got trouble," she panted, "The Dream-catchers think that something is up."

Cull was tempted to shrug her fears off, but his time with Maerlin had taught him not to dismiss the powers of the Dream-catchers. It was far from an exact science, but nevertheless, it could be a very powerful tool, and the Order of Deanna had been using it for centuries. Maerlin, although untrained, had produced some startling revelations. "Is Conal in danger?"

"Yes and no! He was attacked this morning, but he survived. He and the Dragon-folk were heading toward the Broce Woods when Ceila sent me the message, but it's not what they see that troubles them, it's what they can't see. *Ard Pect* has vanished beneath the mists."

"I don't understand? What's that got to do with it?"

"The last message we received from the Sisterhood in *Ard Pect* was that a monk-mage had arrived in the city, claiming to be the Dubhgall the Black. That was over a moon ago, and we've not been able to contact them since. Ceila sent a dove to let me know of her concerns. The priestesses will be arriving in the city tomorrow at dawn. They're on the Lurching Otter as we speak."

"Why didn't they take horses? It'd be quicker."

"They aren't enough horses. Every sorceress, healer, and dreamer she could lay her hands on is coming. Cull, she might be a little high and mighty at times, but Ceila's the best Dream-catcher I've ever known. If she's worried, then there's something to be worried about."

Chapter Thirty-Three: Divine Intervention

The whole of Dragania was awash with people, livestock, and wagons filled with goods. They were a flowing river of life, moving steadily toward Manquay from all directions. Many of the groups were small, with little more than a dozen people in them, but others were much larger and more sinister. These were bands of warriors and soldiers, marching to a common purpose. The other travellers on the highways quickly moved aside to let them pass. Some even turned around and headed back home. That many armed men and women could only mean trouble farther along the road. The cost of moving such a force was exorbitant, and any wise traveller knew that such a cost would not be without reason.

Lord Boare's army of conscripts was just one such moving mass of martial power, marching relentlessly north at a steady, uniformed pace. To the fore of the main force rode his mounted units. A long baggage train and the army's camp followers brought up the rear. His arrival for the start of the spring fair had been planned with military precision, and he would not be hampered by such trivia as rioting on the streets of Suilequay.

The invading force from *Tir Pect* was also controlled with some military precision, though without the same degree of planning and detail. Their end goal was not the Gathering of the Clans, or to sell produce at the fair. For the High King and High Queen of *Tir Pect*, their primary objective was to reach Dragon's Ridge and defeat the young prince of *Clann Na Dragan* before he could consolidate his position. Once this mission was successfully achieved, they would create a fortified base camp in Dragania and gradually move south, eliminating the *Fear Ban* Clans, one at a time. Conchubhar and Medb planned to recruit the southern Pectish Clans to their cause as they went, thus strengthening their growing army in preparation for the final conflict. At some point, the Clans of the *Fear Ban* would probably unite to resist the Pects. It was imperative that a critical mass of Pectish warriors had been recruited to face this final resistance. If all went to plan, they would drive the invaders back into the sea, once and for all.

Their plan had two major flaws, as they were soon to find out.

Far ahead of the slow-moving horde of *Tir Pect,* were its scouts. These cunning individuals were sent forward to probe an enemy's defences, gather intelligence, and relay it back to the main force, while avoiding detection. As their opponents normally had scouts of their own, doing the same task with equal skill and cunning, it is often a game of cat and mouse where the scout is unsure which role he or she was playing at any particular time. They hoped that they were the cat, but sometimes, they found themselves being the cheese-nibblers.

They were the eyes and ears of every army command, and runners regularly funnelled their information back to the army, to keep the King and Queen appraised of the dangers ahead. A moving army was like a gigantic wagon, slow to get started, and even harder to manoeuvre when it built up momentum. To make matters worse, they were heading through a narrow mountain pass. It was an ideal place for a small body of skirmishers to ambush the army from the rocky heights on either side of the Northern Highway.

Sile had raced headlong through the narrow pass and crossed the border checkpoint unhindered. Only a madman would stop Queen Medb's chariot to ask her why she had chosen to invade Dragania, single-handedly. That sort of act could get someone killed ... if they were lucky! The border patrol had leaped out of the way of her scythed wheels and thought no more about it. That was, of course, until the *Tir Pect* army arrived. The real Queen had flogged them severely in front of the assembled ranks for their incompetence.

The combined armies of *Tir Pect* took some time to nervously creep through the mountain, and they breathed a heavy sigh of relief when they finally set foot on *Magh Dragan:* the Plains of the Dragon. By then, the scouts had reported that the fortress of *Dun Dragan* lay deserted. This news did not sit well with the army commanders. To make matters worse, the Broce Woods seemed equally bereft of the warriors of the Badger Clan. This was a force that Conchubhar and Medb had been relying on to bolster their own numbers. Their cleverly laid plans for invasion were quickly unravelling before their eyes, the farther south they marched.

They followed the tracks of the Dragon Clan along the Northern Highway toward Manquay. News came from the scouts the following morning, and it only made matters worse. The runner diligently passed on his message, that the army of *Clann Na Dragan* had turned off the road and joined a force of equal number, which had emerged from the woods. It took a few moments before the unfortunate messenger came round. Medb, in a fit of rage, had punched him with a vicious right hook. Conchubhar's worst fears had been confirmed. Standing, looking up at the magician's round tower, he cursed the gods soundly.

He had no option but to continue south. If he returned home, he would be a laughing stock of every tavern in *Tir Pect*. Turning east or west were not an option either, as they would leave his supply train exposed. His only option was to continue onward and hope to intercept *Clann Na Dragan* before he could recruit the other *Fear Ban* Clans to his side. Conchubhar couldn't even take his anger out on the Brocians, as they had slipped away before his army to the safety of their city, Broca: a city that historically had never been defeated. He knew that entering the sacred woodlands of the Broce with his army would be tantamount to suicide. It had cost him more than a dozen scouts to even learn the whereabouts of the missing Brocians, and they had been much better trained for surviving the woods than a horde of warriors blundering around in the semi-darkness. History was quite clear on the effectiveness of *Clann Na Broce* at defending their territory. It was one of the reasons that *Luigheagh An Dragan* had brokered the Great Truce.

*****

Conal's army had little of the military precision of the warriors of *Tir Pect* or the conscripts of Lord Boare. His army consisted of two separate intermingling Clans, with their children and assorted livestock. The Grand Marshal tried hard to maintain order, but even he eventually accepted defeat and gave in to the carnival atmosphere. Taliesin and Malachi led the parade with jovial music and mad capering, keeping the children of both Clans laughing and screaming with delight. Sile was equally entertaining, giving rides to the older children on Queen Medb's chariot, although only after she had agreed to the Grand Marshal's request to remove the scythe-blades. The festive atmosphere and enjoyment of the parade also had its effects on the adults within the march. Cautious gestures of camaraderie broke down the barriers and the deeply ingrained reluctance between the two Clans.

Soon, Pect and *Fear Ban* marched side-by-side in amiable chatter and revelry. For the first time in history, outside of the designated area of the Gathering of the Clans, friendly relations were established. Quite by accident and with the help of his companions, Conal had achieved what even his legendary great-grandfather could not. He had created peace amongst the two tribes.

*****

Captain Bohan's crewmen were on their best behaviour as they sailed the Lurching Otter upriver and into Manquay. The smuggler ship had some very special guests on board, and Bohan would skin any man who let him down. Spinning the helm with the skill of many years, he glided the ship sideways until it nudged gently against the quayside. It had cost him a heavy pouch of silver to make sure that his berthing was reserved, for the quayside was jammed for the upcoming fair. He was confident that his investment would be worthwhile. His cargo was most precious, even more so than the stolen Boarite fleeces that he had stowed away in his cargo-hold. Those should make a fine price at the fair, given the current demand for high quality, lowland wool.

"Make it fast, ya lazy sea-otters!" Bohan shouted, as he marched along the deck. His crew were a nasty-looking bunch of pirates and cutthroats, one and all, but they were all skilled sailors. It didn't take them long to secure the ship and lower a gangplank. Bohan then tapped lightly on the door of his cabin. "We've landed, ladies," he informed in a much more cordial voice.

"Thank thee, Captain. Thou art a saviour," Ceila proclaimed, leading the priestesses out into the fresh air. She smiled sweetly at the old rogue. "If thy men could assist with our baggage, we'll be out of thy way."

"Certainly, Lady Ceila, I'll get right on it. I took the liberty of ordering you a couple of carriages. We can't have your fine priestesses wallowing in the muck with the riff-raff now, can we?"

"I'm sure we would survive the ordeal, but I thank thee for the thought, Captain. As ever, thou art a most loyal servant of Deanna. I hope this token of our gratitude will recompense thee for thy trouble?" The High Priestess dropped a small purse into the Captain's hand. "Come along, ladies, let's be off. It's not far to the *Uisce Beatha* and I'm sure that Madame Dunne will have everything prepared for us."

Bohan watched his men with a stern eye as they unloaded the baggage, making sure that his crew's hands didn't stray to the fine clothing of the priestess and that no baggage went missing. His crew might be well disciplined, but they were, after all, a bunch of sticky-fingered brigands.

As the last carriage headed off into the city, followed by an inevitable trail of hungry children, Captain Bohan finally relaxed. "Bosun, I'll be in the 'Drowned Parrot' if anyone needs me. Have the lads draw straws for this evening's watch, and the rest of them can go ashore. You'd better warn the pox-riddled river rats before they go that I want all hands back on deck and fit for duty come first light. Anyone too drunk to pull his weight will have their wages docked and my boot firmly embedded in their arse. We need to unload those mangy fleeces before the hold is permanently tainted. They're stinkin' up me' bleedin' hold. If I don't get a good price at the fair for 'em, it's the last time I'll be doing a favour for that raggedy-ass Cull fellow. He never said anythin' about it bein' a ship full of mangy auld wool! I hate the smell of sheep. They ain't natural!"

"Aye-aye, Cap'n."

*****

Gearoid woke up soon after being released from his mental imprisonment and quickly tested his bindings. They were as firm as ever. This evening, he was tied to a supply wagon, and escape was not an option even if he wanted it. Looking around, he could see a sea of grassland around him, with a dense forest and a stone tower in the distance. He had no idea where he was, but it was safe to assume that he was somewhere in Dragania and that the distant mountain peaks above the woodland were his homeland.

He wondered how the other monks were getting on back on the island. With the weather improving and the last of the frosts now gone, there would be plenty for them to do if they were to survive another winter. The mead production brought in enough income to cover maintenance costs, but food production was reliant on the monks' labours. Spring cereals would need to be sown, as well as the planting of root vegetables, kale, and soft fruits. Then, there was the replenishment of the medicinal herbs and flowers. It was going to be a challenging time for the remaining monks, with the loss of so many able bodies over the last few moons. He hoped that Brother Seamy would be up to the task, for he had yet to find a way out of his current predicament. Shaking off such thoughts, he focused on his evening prayers. Closing his eyes, he started to recite his benedictions.

He hadn't been praying long when a voice interrupted him "Pardon me, but I wonder whether I could ask a boon?"

Gearoid stopped in surprise. He had not heard any footsteps approaching across the grass. "What's that? Sorry, I was in another world." He looked up at the old man who stood before him. "Can I help you?"

389

"Maybe thou can. It's about all that mumbling. I'm sorry but it's really hard to concentrate with it going on. Canst thou give it a bit of a rest for a while? I'm close to finding the solution to a puzzle I've been working on, but that racket keeps getting in the way."

"I'm sorry to hear that. I was only praying."

The old man smiled warmly. Although his long hair and beard were white with age, he still had the bulky physique and casual grace of an athlete. Had he been a warrior or a blacksmith in his previous years? He still carried himself with that type of calm assurance. "What for exactly ...?"

"Excuse me?"

"... I said what for exactly? What were thou praying for?"

"Oh I see ... er, divine intervention."

"Perhaps I can help thee?" the man offered, slipping a dirk from its sheath and pointing it at the ropes. "Thou seemeth a little ... detained at the moment. Shall I cut thee free?"

"Oh, thank you, but no, that's probably not a good idea. Someone might come along and you'll end up in trouble. The bindings aren't overly tight. I'm fine ... really."

"I see," said the man, a little perplexed. "And the praying ... dost thou plan on doing it for long?"

Gearoid was momentarily lost for words. Finally, he managed "I guess so. I can pray a little quieter if that'd help."

"No, I don't think that'd work. I've got very sensitive ears, and I really must work on this problem."

"Maybe I can help? I'm good with puzzles," Gearoid offered.

The old man looked down at the trussed-up monk. "I thank thee for the offer, but it's far too complicated to explain."

"You'll never know until you try," Gearoid pointed out.

"Maybe it would be better for me to help thee instead. After all, thou art seeking intervention."

"With respect, I doubt that your problem would be any greater than mine. You see, I'm troubled with a dilemma." Gearoid tilted his head to indicate the other monk, tied securely beside him. "My friend here is troubled by an unusual sickness."

"Is it contagious?" the old man asked, stepping back a pace.

"Oh no, I don't believe so. The problem is in his head, you see. One could almost say that he's possessed."

"Ah, that's a tricky business ... possession!"

"Exactly, and I need to find a way to rescue him before it's too late."

"And I presume that he wants to be rescued?"

"Mmm, that's a bit difficult to say, really. You see ... he's wracked with guilt. He doesn't believe that he's worthy of redemption."

"It's a terrible thing ... guilt. It can eat away at a man like a bad dose of gangrene." The old man spat on the ground to emphasise his point. "All men can be saved, if they but believe."

"That's what I've been telling him!"

Sorrow crossed the old man's face. "There may come a time when thou must choose..."

"Choose ... choose what?"

"Choose between the good of thy friend and the good of mankind. Such a choice is hard for anyone to make, but sometimes mercy comes at a price. The best way to save thy friend might be to set him free. His soul will return to the Wheel of Time, and if he's lucky, he can make up for the sins of this life in his next. Perhaps, he'll be reborn as a bumblebee. Wonderful things ... bumblebees."

Abbot Gearoid looked aghast. "I can't do that. There has to be another way! I think I shall continue my prayers and hope that the gods intervene."

The old man sighed heavily. "If thou insist ... did thou want me to do it for thee? He's sleeping quite soundly at the moment, and I'm sure he wouldn't feel a thing. My blade is sharper than Macha's tongue. I could slip it across his throat, and his passing would be quick and painless." The stranger made a swift motion with his hand and the silvery blade shimmered in the light of Arianrhod's moon.

Gearoid shuddered. "No, I don't think so, but I thank you for the offer."

The man shrugged and slid his blade back into its sheath. "Very well then, if thou art sure. Here, take the blade anyway. There may be a time when thou hast a need of a sharp dirk. This one is blessed, and it'll cut through any bond, whether they are the bond of friendship or those of hemp. Take it with my blessing." The man slipped the sheathed dirk up Gearoid's sleeve and into concealment, ignoring the monk's protestations.

"You're too kind," Gearoid finally accepted. "Could I have your name, so that I can include you in my prayers?"

The stranger smiled benevolently. "They call me Dagda..."

"That's an auspicious name. I thank you for your kindness, Dagda. May the gods be with you ... but wait ... what about your own problem?"

Dagda smiled. "It's a trivial matter really, and thou hast enough troubles on thy plate already."

"Please ... share it with me. The distraction might do me good."

"Very well then, but I did warn thee ..." Dagda paused for a moment before explaining his predicament "By all the laws of nature a bumblebee should not be able to fly, and yet it does. One day, while I was trying to understand how these wondrous creatures do this, I saw one of them alight upon a rainbow. How is that possible? *I* can't even do that. It doesn't make any sense!"

Gearoid thought about it for a moment and took a wild guess "Magic?"

Dagda smiled. "No, I thought the same but it's not magic. I'd know if it was magic."

"Mmm, I see your difficulty, but ... does it really matter?"

"Of course it matters! There must be order in the world. Why, without it ... there would be chaos!"

"The teachings of my monastery tell us that there should be harmony in all things, a balance if you will. Surely, a little chaos is acceptable in order to give balance to the order of the world?"

"Thou might have a point, Druid, but still ... I need to understand how it is achieved."

Gearoid thought for a moment longer. "Perhaps ... perhaps it's faith."

"Faith!" Dagda said dismissively. "Faith?" he repeated, this time giving it more consideration. "By Arianrhod's shapely buttocks, I never thought of that! How, in the Nine Hells, did thou come up with that? I've been wrestling over this conundrum for eons. Curse it all! I'll have to go and check this out."

With an audible pop, Dagda disappeared, leaving Gearoid bewildered. He considered waking Brother Balor to discuss what had just happened, but decided against it. The poor man was confused enough already.

*****

Cull was already waiting when Ceila and the other priestesses arrived at the shabby-looking tavern. He had fought off the urge to race up the Northern Highway, knowing that his place was here, in the city. Here, he could achieve more. Already, he had issues orders to the leaders of the Beggar's Guild, and a thousand eyes and ears were alert for any nuance of danger. Nothing was being left to chance; even the *Uisce Beatha* was being watched.

He'd also had meetings with most of the leaders of the underworld: the Guild of the Cutpurse, the Muggers Union, the Silent Intruders, the Order of the Black Dagger, the Toxic-Demisers, the Smugglers Co-operative, and the Oven-Mitts, to name but a few. Although these organisations held no allegiance to Cull or to the Beggars Guild, a mutual respect had been cultivated over the past few years. Many concurred that their futures lay with the young Dragonson. A stable society under strong leadership was good for all concerned.

Cull rose from his bench and bowed formally to the High Priestess. "The goddess be with you."

"And with thee, Cull. It's good to see thee. On behalf of the Order, may I extend my deepest sorrow at thy loss?" Ceila greeted, taking a seat in the booth.

Cull sat opposite her and looked gravely across at the High Priestess. "I gather that you've been having some trouble sleeping?"

"Ah good, Ester relayed my message, then. Yes, it's true. My Dream-catching has been troubled. Conal was attacked a few days ago, but thankfully, he survived. That's all I know for sure."

"How did they get past his guards? What happened ...?" Cull had a hundred questions.

"He was alone at the time. He was out running. Luckily, he was wearing some strange green armour, and he was armed with *An Fiacail Dragan*. Anyway, it's irrelevant! He survived, and they're alerted to the danger. He now has a troop of bodyguards around him at all times. They are like a shadow upon him. They are led by a stern-looking man. There's also a gangly youth who carries a harp across his back."

"That'd be the Grand Marshal, Declan Morganson, and Taliesin the bard. Declan should be able to keep Conal out of trouble if anyone can. I'm not so sure about Tal though. Still, the boy needs a companion, and the bard's a good one."

"They've left *Dun Dragan*, and they should be here tomorrow. Two others joined them before they left. One was a redheaded woman... or was it raven-haired ... I'm not really sure. She drives a magnificent war-chariot and wears expensive armour. Accompanying her is a midget in motley garb."

"A midget, you say? It couldn't be! What the hell would he be doing here?"

"Thou dost know him?"

"I've bumped into him once or twice at the Pink Rose. He's Queen Medb's Fool ... the Royal Jester of *Ard Pect*. He's with a redheaded woman, you say?"

"It's a little hard to say for sure."

"It can't be Queen Medb. That just doesn't make sense."

"Is the Pectish High Queen doubly-blessed?"

Cull looked sharply at Ceila, surprised at her turn of phrase. "She's a fine looking woman, that's for sure. She certainly would be considered full-figured."

"No Cull, that's not what I meant. Does she have a double cleavage?"

Realisation hit Cull like a bucket of water in the face. "By the Seven, it's Sile! Something serious must be going on."

Cull leapt up from his seat and dashed out of the tavern without further explanation. He needed to find a horse, and quickly. It didn't take him long to find a suitable mount. It was trotting down the street toward him.

*****

The young Boarite captain didn't even see his attacker. He hadn't been expecting to have his horse stolen from under him in broad daylight. He had always heard that Manquay was a rough city, but when he awoke sometime later, he realised that the tales were not exaggerated. He was lying face down in the dirt, and he'd been robbed of all his possessions. He prayed fervently for a rapidly reposting to one of the more civilised, southern cities. Not only had he lost his horse, his fine uniform, and his weapons, but they'd even stolen his boots. He was lying there, dressed only in his smallclothes, being prodded awake by an unsympathetic patrolman of the city's Watch.

It took a great deal of time and effort to convince the guard that he really was a captain in Lord Boare's army. Finally, he was escorted to the local barracks, where someone could vouch for his identity. By that time, his horse was already galloping along the Northern Highway, in the hands of a beggar with a broad-brimmed hat. The rest of the captain's belongings found their way to various fences and pawn shops across Manquay.

Chapter Thirty-Four: Freefalling

Maerlin found herself in dense fog and knew that she was dreaming again, but there was something strange about this fog. It came with a strong wind that sucked the air out of her lungs as it hit her in the face. Her plaits whipped away behind her, flapping about like demented puppy-dog tails. Her face stretched with the force of the wind, pulling her lips back from her teeth and rattling her cheeks. She looked down and realised two shocking revelations. Firstly, she was stark naked, and secondly, she wasn't standing on anything. This wasn't wind that she could feel on her face. She was falling, falling through clouds at a terrifying speed. Panic hit her with an adrenaline rush, making her breathing even more difficult. Her nakedness would have to wait for now, she had more pressing matters to deal with.

The fog disappeared in the blink of her watery eyes, and she could see the ground below in the moonlight. Occasional specks of orange depicted fires and only worsened the sensation of vertigo as she hurtled toward the icy ground, far below. She couldn't even get out enough breath to scream as she fell rapidly toward the frozen wastelands. Her eyes were almost shut, but still they streamed water, which froze on her cheeks.

"There's nothing like a freefall, is there? It always gives me such a rush!" an enthusiastic voice commented in her head. "Doesn't it make you glad to be alive?"

It was a voice that she recognised all too well. Maerlin looked around for the strange man who haunted her dreams. What she saw instead frightened her even more than freefalling to her imminent death.

Directly behind her, and also hurtling toward the ground, was an immense scaly head. It was silvery-white in colour and had two horned ridges cresting above it. The teeth ... they tended to stand out ... even when you're falling to the ground and about to die. You couldn't help but focus on those rows of immense, razor-sharp teeth. The gap within the glittering mass stood out even more, its absence protesting to the world of its abnormality. Pulling her attention away from the gaping maw, she looked into the beast's piercing blue eyes. There, she was surprised to find a sharp intelligence within its monstrous, scaly face. She barely registered the enormous slender body behind the head, the huge bat-like wings that were tucked against its frame, or the tail that moved from side to side, aiding its balance and direction as it plummeted toward the ice. Her mind was far too busy doing mental back-flips to take in these details. The mouth opened a little wider. She caught a glimpse of the creature's serpentine tongue and the deep hole, into which she could easily slip into and vanish forever, behind those wicked-looking incisors.

This time, Maerlin did manage to scream. It was one of those deep, take-all-of-your-breath-away-and–leave-you-gasping-for-air types of screams, and it seemed to cause the dragon some discomfort.

When Maerlin could scream no more, the voice spoke in her head spoke again "Sorry to interrupt you, but don't you think it's time we pulled up?"

Maerlin tore her eyes away from the predatory monstrosity and looked again at the rapidly-approaching ground. It was much closer this time, way too close for comfort, and it was getting quickly toward the point of impact, but Maerlin was unable to do anything. Her mind was frozen in terror.

"Oh well!" the voice muttered, with a calmness that clearly didn't reflect Maerlin's current predicament.

The dragon tilted its wings slightly, and a huge silver claw reached out and wrapped itself around Maerlin's waist before she had time to react. She struggled for a moment, but she was held firmly within its reptilian grasp. Then the dragon's wings unfurled with a loud flapping sound like the sails of a ship catching the breeze, and the world slowed its downward spiral toward oblivion.

Maerlin's world tilted as the dragon banked away. It skimmed over the icy ground at a terrifying speed. She could see that they were heading toward a distant waterfall, frozen in time. Was this the creature's lair? Was this where it was bringing her in order to eat her? Would eating on the wing give a dragon indigestion?

Her heart was beating faster than a hummingbird's as the dragon slowed before the falls, hovered, and then lowered itself gracefully to the ground before the frozen edifice. Once it had settled, it placed Maerlin gently on the ground and released its hold.

She found herself standing upon the Icy Wastes, naked and shaking from a mixture of fear and cold. Maerlin waited for the inevitable bite to come, eyes still half-shut with frozen tears.

"You'll catch your death like that," Sygvaldr warned from in Maerlin's head. Maerlin whirled around, attempting to hide her nakedness from his unseen eyes. She scanned the frozen wasteland, looking for the King.

"Sygvaldr!"

"Should I fetch you something to wear, or do you prefer this natural look? I must say though, the goosebumps aren't doing you any favours. It might be all the rage in your warmer, southern climate, but it's not a look I'd recommend up here on the Icy Wastes."

"Where are you?" Maerlin couldn't see the strange man who haunted her dreams, but she could hear him in her head. Could he be hiding behind the dragon, which thankfully had not yet chosen to gobble her up? Turning to face the immense beast, she looked it in the eye, regaining some of her usual defiance. "Look ..." she began. "If you're going to eat me, can we get this over with? It's far too cold out here to be mucking about ... but I have to warn you, I'm going to give you a really bad case of wind!"

"Eat you! Why would I want to eat you? You haven't got enough meat on you to feed a fox, let alone a dragon," Sygvaldr declared. "And besides, it'd be awful rude of me to eat my own bride-to-be before our wedding night ... or afterwards, come to think of it!"

Maerlin looked sharply at the dragon, at its piercing blue eyes and its missing tooth. It suddenly became obvious to her. 'I sleep in the treasury,' he had said. Of course he does! He's a blasted dragon! Maerlin suddenly became acutely aware of her nakedness.

Sensing her discomfort, Sygvaldr summoned a little magic, and Maerlin found herself clothed in a fabulous white dress. It was richly embroidered and sparkled with jewelled decorations. Over the dress, he had chosen a warm ermine cloak. He had even provided some warm, sealskin boots. She immediately felt more comfortable, despite the chilly night air.

"Is that any better?"

Getting over her surprise, Maerlin answered "Yes ... thank you."

"I hope you like it. I just knew it'd look wonderful on you. It was my mother's, you know. It would've made her very happy to see you wearing it."

Maerlin looked down at the beautifully-crafted evening gown. It was a very elegant dress. The embroidery alone must have taken many moons to achieve. The material was literally covered in a fine web of knotwork and pictograms, with jewels cleverly stitched into the fine silk to represent the eyes of different mythical creatures within the gown. *"It's magnificent,"* she acknowledged, *"But it's a bit more formal than I'm used to."*

"Formal ... well of course its formal! Who has ever heard of an informal wedding gown ...?"

"What!" Maerlin gasped. She was half-tempted to remove the gown. *"You've dressed me up in your dead mother's wedding dress! Have you any idea of just how weird that sounds?"*

"But you look positively ravishing!" Sygvaldr protested. *"I know that it's bad luck to see the bride-to-be in the wedding dress before the big day ... but it seemed such a perfect opportunity for you to try it on."*

Maerlin seethed with anger. *"How many times am I going to have to say this?"* she hissed, *"I'm not getting married, to you or to anyone else for that matter. Have I made myself clear?"*

"Well, I must say! There's no need to take that tone with me. I mean ... after all, I did just save you from plunging to your death ... and from frostbite. The least you could do is live up to your end of the bargain."

"What bargain is this? I must have missed that one. Was it the one where the girl gets rescued by a dragon, and he doesn't end up eating her, so they get married and live happily ever after? Did I miss something?"

King Sygvaldr sighed, and a long trail of icy breath blasted the ground to Maerlin's right. *"You don't realise how hard this is for me. After all, it wasn't my idea, you know. It was Uiscallan's. I was already resigned to the fact that I was going to be the last of the Frost Dragons of the Icy Wastes. I was just watching the centuries creep by, waiting for the inevitable and then they came marching into my palace, asking for my help. She was the one who pointed out the prophecy ... not me!"*

"Wait a moment, you're going too fast," Maerlin protested. *"That's the second time you've used that name. Let me get this straight. You're talking about Uiscallan the Storm-Bringer, Priestess of Deanna, correct?"*

"I'm not really sure about all those titles, but she looked a lot like you, if that's any help."

"What exactly did Uiscallan say?"

"I can't remember it all. It was quite a while ago. It was something to do with a prophecy to save the world of Dragonkind and Mankind. There was something about the 'daughter of her blood' being betrothed to a dragon ...?"

"I see ..."

"She's your mother, yes. Am I right?"

"She's my great-grandmother actually, though not for much longer when I get my hands on her."

"Oh dear! I do hope I haven't caused a family feud. They can be so messy, you know ... and such foolishness. It was that type of thing that caused the demise of Dragonkind in the first place. Please don't be too upset. You should sit her down and talk to her before flying off the handle. I'm sure she had her reasons."

"Reasons! I'm just dying to hear what they are. She made some sort of deal, and because of that, I'm supposed to marry a dragon." Maerlin shuddered as the full reality of the proposal hit her. *"I'm not even sure that I'd survive the wedding night!"*

"Oh, you'll be quite safe! I assure you. It was all the rage at one time. Many a beautiful maiden tied herself to the Ice Pillar outside of the palace, in the hopes of wooing a young buck dragon to marry her. It's kept our bloodline going for centuries. It was only when the practice stopped that things started to get difficult. You see, in the end, we became weak from too much inbreeding. The mixing of the blood with that of mankind had kept us strong. Without it, we had fewer children, and many of those were weak and died before they could reproduce. It was a disaster."

"What exactly happened with Uiscallan?"

"Well ... she explained it all to me. It was all to do with the need for the mixing of the bloods of our races. Of course, by then, most of the humans had already left the Icy Wastes. They'd sought a better life over the sea. Virgins no longer petitioned for the chance to marry a dragon. So, Uiscallan offered to help."

"That was very kind of her," Maerlin replied tartly. "Since she was being so generous, why didn't she marry you?"

"Ah! Sadly, she'd already lost her maidenhead to the young man who came with her. We dragons have traditions and a very strong sense of etiquette. It has to be a maiden, you know. One has to maintain a certain set of standards."

"But ... your race was dying out. Couldn't you have made an exception? I mean... I'd have thought you'd be lining them up and breeding like rabbits. After all, it's either that or extinction. Though, now that I come to think about it ... maybe I shouldn't be giving you ideas."

Sygvaldr looked shocked at the crassness of her suggestion, which was no mean feat on such a scaly face. "Whatever must you think of me? We dragons are civilised creatures. We're not monsters, you know!"

Maerlin bit back the obvious comment. "Sorry ... so you were saying ... you needed a virgin ... a willing one, I take it?"

"Naturally!"

"And what did Uiscallan get out of this arrangement, pray tell?"

Sygvaldr thought for a moment, before he answered "Nothing, I suppose. Though, I did help the young man that she came with. It seemed only polite to offer."

"What did you give him?"

"I gave him the gift of my blood, dragon blood, for him and for his offspring."

"How did you do that?"

"Well, it was two gifts really. You see, when a male dragon marries, he bites the bride ..."

"You what! You mean to tell me that you're not content to just marry me, you want to eat me, too?"

"Goodness gracious me, no! Not eat ... hardly that. It's more like a friendly nibble. It's all part of the consecration of the marriage, and it gives the bride the blessing of Dragonkind."

"Oh, that's alright then!" Maerlin replied with a heavy layer of sarcasm. "Why didn't you just say that in the first place?"

"He merely breaks the skin and finds a vein; any vein will do, although naturally, there's a fondness for the one on the neck or the inner thigh. Traditionally, it's done on their wedding night. Usually, the act is performed while in the heat of passion, when the bride is too far gone in the act of lovemaking to notice the bite. It's all part of the ceremony. The guests all applaud, and a wild party is thrown afterwards."

Maerlin could feel the heat flushing into her cheeks. "You mean to say that this isn't done in private!"

"...In private? How would the guests know that the consummation was completed, so that they can celebrate the event?"

"Maybe you could ring a bell or something. I don't know," Maerlin said dryly. She couldn't believe she was having this conversation. "So, anyway, you bit the Prince's neck, is that it?"

"Ewwww, no! No such intimacy existed between us. I merely bit him on his wrist."

"That's it? You bite him and he gets the blessing of Dragonkind?"

"It's a little bit more complicated than that. The male dragon bites himself first, so that his canines are infused with his blood. As the blood of the dragon flows into the blood of mankind, they mingle."

"And how does this benefit the recipient?"

"They become stronger, their reflexes are faster, and they are less prone to ailments. In some cases, they may even take on some other dragon

traits. Some live longer lives than normal, and on very rare occasions, they've been known to have the ability to meld into full dragon form for short periods. My mother was one such human. That's why I can take the human form so easily."

"You mean humans can turn into dragons?"

"It's not unheard of, though as I said, it's very rare. Usually, it's only the ones with latent Form-melding abilities, but they all benefit from the ceremony in one way or another."

"I see," Maerlin said, thinking about all that she had been told. "You said something about a second gift: one for his offspring?"

"Yes, that was the matrimonial gift. I bequeathed him one of my teeth. It was imbued with the blood of a dragon, so that he could pass on the blessing to future generations. All he needed to do was nick his skin with it, cover the tip of the tooth with his own dragon-tainted blood, and then use it to cut a vein on the baby. They'd then have the dragon blood in their veins also, albeit a slightly weaker version, as it passes down the generations. Dragon blood is very strong, and it should still affect his offspring to a lesser degree, even without the blessing of the tooth. It would pass down through his seed, as well as through his blood. The gift of the tooth would only strengthen this blessing."

The Dragontooth sword, of course! Maerlin remembered an odd comment that Seabhac had once made regarding it. It came back to her now, though she couldn't recall whether she had heard it or whether it had been in one of her dreams. She had said: "So they still treat that damn thing like a sword, eh?" Now the comment made sense. The dragon's gift, meant to aid virility and life, was being used to butcher people. She wondered what Sygvaldr would think of such a sacrilege.

Memories of Conal, and of the things that people had said about him and his family, came to mind.

"Sygvaldr ... What other traits do people get from dragon-blood? Could it make them reckless, quick-tempered, or fearless, for example?"

"Those are all possible side effects. Dragon cubs do tend to be fairly exuberant at times, rambunctious even. They like to push themselves to their limits, and they can be a little heedless of their own personal safety now that you come to mention it."

Maerlin smiled. That sounded just like Conal.

"Now that we've got that settled, are you ready to get married?"
Sygvaldr asked hopefully.

"Again ... really? Don't you ever give up?"

"But it's been prophesised! You cannot deny your destiny, so you might
as well embrace it. That's what I always say."

"Mmm!" Maerlin said, doubtfully. "How exactly did Uiscallan agree to
all this ... you know ... me, getting married to you? I'm still not getting
that part?"

"She told me that sadly she couldn't accept my offer. Her heart and her
maidenhood had already been taken, but she foretold that at some time in
the future, a daughter of her blood would come to unite Dragonkind and
Humankind. That daughter would be betrothed to a dragon. As I'm the
only Frost Dragon left ... it's only fair to assume that she was talking
about me ... and as you're her only daughter ..."

"Great-granddaughter ..." Maerlin pointed out absently.

"...But you are 'a daughter of her blood', nevertheless, and the first of
such to come here. So it's fair to assume that she was referring to you."

"Could she have been referring to my own great-granddaughter? Not
that I'm planning on having any children. I witnessed some difficult
births while I was roaming around the mountains. I think that I'll pass on
the whole motherhood thing, if it's all the same to you."

"You mean you're calling off the wedding ... again!"

"Sygvaldr, you're a nice man and all, and I'm sure as dragons go, you're
a nice dragon, too, but I just don't do the whole damsel in distress thing.
You might as well face facts. The wedding is off! In fact, it was never on
in the first place."

"But ..."

"Yes, I know ..."Maerlin interrupted, holding her hand up to stop his
protest, "... Uiscallan's promise and the whole tooth thing, right? Don't
worry about it; I'll get right onto it, just as soon as I wake up. I'll be

having a long chat with Uiscallan about all this, you mark my words. Once I've finished ripping strips off her hide, I'll go and speak firmly to Conal about your tooth. He's going to have to give it back to its rightful owner, whether he likes it or not. Now, if you could be kind enough to send me back ..."

"Pardon?"

"You know ... send me back, so that I can wake up. I've a busy day ahead of me."

Sygvaldr pondered the predicament for a moment and smiled a wicked dragon grin, full of sharp teeth. "Certainly, Maerlin, It'll just take one moment while I change. I can't do this in dragon form. It isn't Dragon-magic that you need. What you need is Human-magic."

One moment, Maerlin was looking into the eyes of a dragon, and the next, she was staring at the handsome face of King Sygvaldr. He stepped closer until their noses were almost touching and placed a hand on her cheek. Lightly, he brushed a stray lock of hair behind her ear. "I'm ready whenever you are."

"Ready ... ready for what?" Maerlin asked nervously. She was getting butterflies fluttering in her belly at his close proximity.

"Why ... for the kiss, of course. It's a crucial part of the magic."

"You've got to be kidding me!"

"Would I do that?"

Maerlin hesitated, but something deep inside her wanted to know what it felt like to kiss him. Eventually, against her better judgement, her curiosity won out. Without even realising fully that she was doing it, Maerlin moved closer, and their lips met half-way. She had meant it to be a quick peck on his lips, but this became extended as she felt herself enveloped in his strong arms. His lips pressed deeper, and Maerlin's body melted into the embrace.

A soft moan escaped her lips as she woke with a shudder. She found herself back in the bedroom, standing over the bed, her mind still half-trapped in the moment of the kiss.

Cora stirred in the bed. "Morning, Maerlin. I see you're dressed already. Nice outfit by the way. I haven't seen that one before."

Maerlin looked down and gasped with surprise. She was still wearing the silk wedding dress and sealskin boots, as well as the ermine cloak. "Sweet Deanna!" the full extent of her Dream-catching hit home. "Uiscallan! I've got to go and see Seabhac."

"But it's still dark outside! She'll be asleep."

"Not for much longer, she won't," Maerlin growled.

"Oh, dear," Cora frowned, sensing trouble in Maerlin's tone. "Hang on; I think I'd better come with you."

*****

It wasn't long before the whole camp was awake. Sleep was not an option as the shouting reached its peak. Seabhac, in her usual abrupt manner, had not been pleased with the rude awakening and had been forthright in her opinion. Maerlin was filled with righteous wrath and refused to be browbeaten. She wanted to get to the bottom of this, there and then. She refused to be put off until later. Seabhac, half-asleep and taken aback by the accusations being flung at her, reacted with predictable stubbornness. Heavy clouds circled overhead as a storm quickly brewed above them. It would have soon broken and flooded the mountainside had Nessa not stepped (or in her case, hopped) into the tent at that point.

"I think that's quite enough from both of you!"

"Stay out of this, Nessa," Maerlin warned.

"Maerlin, sit down ... NOW!" Nessa commanded sharply, and Maerlin stopped instantly. It was so rare for Nessa to raise her voice, but few would ignore her when she did.

"That's right," Seabhac said, smugly.

"I think we've all heard quite enough from you too, you old windbag! Sit down and shut up," Nessa commanded. "From what I've heard, you've got a lot to answer for, so you can get off your high horse and park the attitude in the corner. We're all going to sit down and discuss this matter like civilised people. Is that clear?"

407

Seabhac's face was a mask of astonishment, but she lowered herself onto a stool.

"It's about time someone spoke to her like that!" Fintan murmured from his makeshift perch. *"Never thought I'd live to see the day ..."*

Nessa's sharp glare silenced him.

"Cora, make us all some tea, will you?" Nessa asked. "Everyone else can remain seated and gather some composure. There's a storm brewing overhead, and I hate it when my feathers get wet. It'd absolutely ruin my morning!"

Sir Gallaghad hopped into the tent at this point, carrying a mouthful of worms for Nessa's breakfast. His arrival ruined her commanding presence, but eased the tension somewhat. No one could help smiling at his unrelenting efforts to woe Nessa.

"Oh, for pity's sake! That really isn't necessary, you know," she protested. "I'm perfectly capable of finding my own breakfast."

Gallaghad cocked his head to one side and hopped from side to side expectantly, looking from Nessa to the pre-offered worms.

"Oh, very well then, if you insist!" she sighed and selecting a juicy, fat one. Quickly, and with as much grace as possible under the circumstance, she ate the earthworm. "There ... are you satisfied now?"

Gallaghad waited a moment longer, before realisation dawned on him. This was all the recognition that he was going to receive for his efforts. Quickly, he scoffed the rest of the worms, before they could wriggle away.

Cora returned with the teapot and a tray of cups. She looked hesitantly at Nessa. "Erm, Ness, shall I pour you a cup too?"

Nessa sighed. "Sorry, it's force of habit, I guess! I always found a cup of tea soothing in times of stress. It's one of the only things that I miss about my former self."

"I was thinking about that," Maerlin said. "From what you said the other day, you have the ability to Form-meld, just like Vort does. Or at least you did have when you were human?"

"Yes, I did. It was how the priestesses of the Order first noticed me. That was when I was a child in the Wolf Clan. I first changed when I was about twelve, during a squabble. Since then, I've learned to change into a number of forms. I'd never tried Form-melding into a rat before, but at the time it seemed appropriate. What has this got to do with our present discussion?"

"I thought that would be obvious," Maerlin said. "If you could Form-meld before, then perhaps you still can. We know you can still do magic. It might not be only the blessing of Deanna that you retained. You might still have some of your other magical abilities too."

"She has a point," Seabhac agreed.

Nessa considered it for only a moment. "Maybe you're right, Maerlin, but let's not get sidetracked. Pour some tea, Cora, and we'll focus on our current predicament."

"Which one?" Cora asked. She still did not fully understand what Seabhac and Maerlin were arguing about.

"She's referring to my marriage arrangements, Cora," Maerlin grumbled.

"Thou hast to understand, Maerlin, when I told the dragon about that, I wasn't planning to have children. How was I supposed to know I was going to end up pregnant?"

"From what I hear, you were already playing with fire. Is it any wonder that you got burned?"

"Maerlin, there's no need for that tone, thank you very much. It isn't helping," Nessa chided.

"Maerlin, I'd forgotten about the whole thing until thou turned up wearing that pendant. It was just another part of my past, best forgotten. By the time I found out that I was expecting, Luigheagh had already announced his intention to marry the Princess of the Seal Clan. She was an insipid trollop he hardly even knew. I fled into the mountains and hid from the world. I'd had enough of politics and enough of the *Dragan*. That's when I started using the name Seabhac and built my cottage. I picked a nice isolated spot and vanished off the face of the earth. I prayed that my daughter would never have to pay for that promise. That she would never have to marry a dragon. When she came of age, she married back into the Hawk Clan, and I thought that it was all behind me. Thou hast to believe me. I never intended this to happen."

"What about this prophecy?"

"That! It was just some old manuscript that I found in the library vaults, on the Holy Isle. It seemed to be a way to help *Luigheagh An Dragan* fulfil his destiny. There are hundreds of bizarre documents in that vault. Most of them are complete nonsense, or total gibberish. I'm told that Dubhgall the Black holds great faith in such things, but most people think they're nothing but the collective ravings of drug-induced lunatics."

Maerlin recalled a Dream-catching she had witnessed, a dream which directly related to Uiscallan and a certain nocturnal visitor before the Battle of the High Kings. However, she didn't think this was a good time to discuss it. "So, what are we going to do about it?"

"We do nothing, of course. Dragons are very formal creatures, and he wouldn't force thee into marriage, no matter what the terms. Their folklore is very clear about this. It has to be a virgin, and she has to be a willing bride. Nevertheless, thou might want to consider losing thy virginity sometime soon, just to be on the safe side."

Maerlin face said a thousand words, most of which would only ever be heard inside a dockside tavern.

"It was only an idea, sorry. Anyway, thou hast nothing to worry about."

"That's easy for you to say, but I can't just sit back and ignore this. At the very least, I'll need to give him back his tooth."

"Whatever would thou do that for? He can't put it back in his mouth, can he? What possible benefit could there be from bringing him the tooth back?"

"It just isn't right, that's all. It'd be like stealing, and I wasn't brought up to be a thief. I want no part of it. This might have happened a long time ago, but I'm still tainted by it."

"So what's thy plan? Art thou going to go and ask Conal to relinquish his sword?"

"It wasn't his to begin with," Maerlin insisted. "It was taken under false pretences."

"Knowing his views on thievery, Maerlin, I doubt that he'll agree with you," Cora pointed out.

"Well then ... I'll just have to make him see sense, won't I?"

"That sword has become the symbolic key to the stability of Dragania, Maerlin. You do know that, don't you?" Nessa asked calmly.

"Yes I do, but he'll just have to learn to do without it. Anyway, he still has his dragon blood. That'll have to be enough. One way or another, I'm not going to see Sygvaldr cheated."

"Oh ... so its Sygvaldr now, is it?" Cora teased.

Maerlin flushed. "You know what I mean."

Chapter Thirty-Five: The Gathering of the Clans

Cull rode into Conal's camp at sunset, as the last of the stragglers were arriving from the north. Leaving the stolen horse with one of the young men who were minding the herd, he headed toward the centre of the camp, in search of Conal. Sile found him first.

"You look like a cat that's been dragged through a hedge backward, Cull. Are you getting enough sleep?"

"Not really, but as usual you look gorgeous, Sile. However, you're a long way from home."

Sile shrugged. "You always told me this southern air would suit my complexion." Her tone turned more serious, and she added "Sorry to hear about Broll. I know that you two were close."

"Aye, we were, and you were always his wilful daughter. He could never say no to you. Thanks, Sile. I know he was close to your own heart, too."

Sile shrugged it off, wanting to say more but knowing this was neither the time nor the place. "How fares Manquay? Has your ascension to the throne gone smoothly?"

"I guess. The world conspired to give me the job," Cull grumbled.

"That's because there's no one better suited for it. Broll's legacy was always safe in your hands, Cull."

"I don't know about that, but I've done my best to loosen Lord Boare's grip on the world. But now it seems that Conal has other troubles."

"Ah, so you've heard about Medb and Conchubhar then?"

"I was referring to the attempt on Conal's life, but I'd also heard rumours of a possible invasion."

"The rumours are true, but first ... the assassins. Come on, I'll show you their bodies. I've looked at them myself, but I'll let you draw your own conclusions."

"They weren't just hired thugs then?"

"Oh no, they're the real thing." Sile led him over to a nearby wagon and pulled back the canvas to reveal the bodies beneath. Thankfully, the weather was still cool, and the flies weren't too prolific, but the stench still grappled with the nostrils.

Cull climbed into the wagon and stripped the bodies, thoroughly inspecting every nook and cranny of the bodies of the assassins.

"Well?" she asked as he climbed down.

"They have mixed racial features so it's hard to say. Their calluses indicate that they've been trained in a multitude of weapons. There weren't farmers or common soldiers. That's for sure. They could have come from any one of the Assassins Guilds, or they could be sell-swords from any one of the larger cities really."

"We might be asking the wrong question here. Maybe, we should focus on who hired them, rather than who they belong to?"

"I doubt that it's the Boare's work. For starters, he can't afford it. His coffers must be running dry by now. Secondly, he likes to use his own clansmen for his dirty work. They cost less and they tend to be more loyal, or at least more afraid of failure. The assassins' clothing and weapons indicate Pectish workmanship. As you know, the only city in *Tir Pect* that tolerates *Fear Ban* is *Ard Pect*. That's why I tend to think that they were sent by either Medb or Conchubhar ... it might even have been a joint venture. Medb has always been a rickety trebuchet at the best of times, you never know what madness she might get up to, but I'd have thought better of Conchubhar. He always seemed to be blessed with common sense. His one exception, of course, was marrying Medb and that could have been as much to do with politics as love."

"That's what I thought, but it doesn't make any sense."

"I know. Why pay hired assassins, which don't come cheap, and then stage an invasion? It'd be one or the other ... not both. If they were planning to invade, they'd want the moral victory of beating Conal on the battlefield. They'd need it to have any hope of uniting the Pectish Clans behind them. It'd be as important as the territory they'd gain from the victory. Having Conal die before they invade would only weaken their hand. You're right, it doesn't make sense."

"But who else could it be?"

"I haven't the foggiest idea, Sile. One thing I do know though. It wasn't done by the Order of the Black Dagger. I met with their leader yesterday, and he's pro-*Dragan*. He knows the benefits of a stable economy. That's to say nothing of the good working relationship he has with the Beggars Guild. The loss of that revenue alone would be bad for his business. It made me ill when I looked at Broll's accounts. To be fair to him though, it was money well spent. One thing we can be certain of is that no other guild will attempt to fulfil a contract on the Black Dagger's patch. That could lead to a very deadly situation. The sooner Conal arrives at Manquay, the happier I'll be. I'll personally pay the Black Daggers to protect him, if I have to. That way, we can all sleep soundly."

"Are they really that good?"

"You could say that, Sile. If I had to pay for someone to die, that's where I'd go."

"Would they take on two opposing contracts at the same time?"

"No. That sort of thing is bad for business. If they take on a job, it stays active until completion. There's no going back. If the client changes his mind ... tough! They'll still kill the target, and they make that quite clear before the deal is signed. A 'Death Certification' is literally signed in blood. When the client signs it ... death is a certainty, and we're not talking about the 'we're all going to die in the end' type of thing, either. They take their contracts very seriously. Taking opposing contracts could be a disaster, if word got out. They have a reputation to maintain."

"The guild in *Ard Pect* is like that from what I've heard, though I've never had much dealing with them personally. I could get word to Charlene and have her look into them."

"If you do, tell her to be careful ... very careful. Assassins Guilds tend to like their privacy. Now, let's go and find Conal, shall we?"

"Are you sure you don't want to stop off at my tent first?" Sile purred. "You seem a little tense. I could help you to unwind ..."

"Sile, I've just ridden all the way from Manquay. If I see a bed, I'll want to sleep in it, not use it as a trampoline ... another time, perhaps."

"You're about as much fun as the Grand Marshal!" Sile pouted.

"Declan? Why, what's he done?"

"Absolutely nothing ... that's the problem! He seems to be immune to my charms. You don't think he likes boys, do you? That'd be such a waste."

Cull laughed. "Sile, you're a very bad girl, do you know that! You could do irreparable damage to that poor man. I doubt he'd be used to your inner-city ways."

"I'd be happy to teach him," Sile offered sweetly. "In fact, I'd take a great deal of pleasure in his education."

"What, and have him running for the hills! No, Sile, leave the poor man be. I need him just the way he is. He doesn't need distracting by your charms."

"Ah! So you admit that I have charms!"

"Without a doubt, Sile."

"Then why can't he see that?"

"Have you ever considered that you might intimidate him? You might have too many charms for an uncomplicated man like Declan."

"Are you suggesting that I should be ... coyer? I can do that, you know."

Cull shook his head. "It's not going to happen, Sile. Put him out of your head."

"I could give him back ... when I've finished," Sile offered.

"It's not going to happen, Sile," Cull repeated firmly. "Can we focus on the business at hand?"

They soon found Conal. He was taking juggling lessons from the jester.

*****

The Gathering of the Clans for the spring fair began in earnest the following day, with the arrival of clansmen from all directions. By midday, a tent city had grown outside of the walls of Manquay, and a

416

steady stream of goods and people flowed toward the fair. Some of the deals had already been done before people arrived. Stock and goods of the highest quality changed hands rapidly. People were eager to snatch up a bargain before others could get their hands on it. The fair itself was a cacophony to the senses, with bright colours everywhere, fragrant food, music, dance, entertainers, and varied goods brightly displayed to catch the eye. Merchants fought to out-do each other and attract people to their stalls with promises of bargains and one-day-only sales. Pickpockets, tricksters, and con men, flowed through the crowd, making a killing on the gullible, the naive, and the foolish. Others roamed through the crowd selling a variety of things to pleasure the flesh or the mind.

In the middle of the afternoon, Conal arrived at the fair at the head of a strong force. He was driving his chariot with Cull standing at his side. Driving Queen Medb's chariot was Sile, accompanied by Malachi. At Cull's urging, this smaller more mobile force headed up by Declan's Dragon-scales rode ahead of the main group. That way, Conal could arrive as soon as possible into the relative safety of the spring fair. There, the keeping of the peace was rigorously enforced by the guardians of the ancient laws, the Brehons.

Vort would bring up the remainder of their force with the help of Taliesin. They were not expected to arrive until late that evening. By then, the lead party would have established a suitable campsite. Cull had left Conal in the safe hands of the Grand Marshal, while he headed into the city to speak with the leader of the Black Daggers. If all went well, Conal would have a further wall of protection before nightfall.

Word of the prince's arrival spread like a viral infection, and soon, the whole of the fair was awash with gossip. The guards erected a perimeter around the Dragon camp to keep away strangers as politely as possible, but as firmly as needed. The general message was that Prince Conal was not receiving visitors, and that there would be no exceptions. The Grand Marshal had been very clear about that, not that his men needed reminding after the recent assassination attempt. Nearly the whole of *Clann Na Dragan* had witnessed at least some of the fight with the final assassin, at the foot of Dragon's Ridge. They were all too aware of the dangers that their prince faced.

*****

Maerlin waved farewell to the travelling party from the mountain at the city gates. The villagers would make their way around the city wall to the fairground, while Maerlin, Nessa, Cora, Seabhac, Fintan, and the ever-present Sir Gallaghad, braved the inner city. Their destination was the small tavern owned by the Order of Deanna: The *Uisce Beatha*.

It had been nearly a year since Maerlin had slipped out of the city. Nothing much had changed. The houses still seemed to have sprung up at random, with three-storey dwellings towered over their one-storey neighbours. Thatch mingled with shingle and slate, and many of the houses leaned outward as if straining across the road to reach the other side, leaving the space in-between, dark and foreboding. Dogs prowled in packs, barking mangy creatures with hungry eyes. Children followed, as hungry-eyed as their dogs. They were dirty-faced and dressed in rags.

Nevertheless, Maerlin had changed during her time away. She had grown up considerably. Her opinions of the squalor had not changed, but she was less shocked by it. It saddened her to realise that she had become accustomed to the deprivation. The commotion and crowding in the streets no longer brought palpitations to her heart, and her ears had become numb to the hawkers as they held up choice articles for sale. The depleting daylight, struggling to compete against the torches that hung on rings every few feet, held little anxiety to Maerlin. She was no longer the inexperienced mountain girl of yesterday. She walked with a new confidence. She was now a well-travelled woman of experience, a sorceress of Deanna: a Storm-Bringer.

She ignored the darkened alleyways that cut away from the main thoroughfare, littered with debris. Knowing now the dangers that lurked there, she refused to give them unnecessary attention. Her eyes avoided direct contact with the strangers around her, and her head tilted slightly downwards so as not to provoke confrontation with the denizens of the city. She walked like someone born here, hardened to its degradation. Now, instead of being the novice on this expedition, she was the world-weary guide making sure that Cora did not become ensnared in the city's deadly allure.

"Come along, Cora. Let's not get sidetracked," she advised, pulling her companion along.

"But Maerlin ... didn't you see that?"

"See what, Cora?" Maerlin asked, guiding Cora farther away from the alley.

"That woman ... she was half-naked!"

"Keep your voice down," Maerlin hissed. "There's no need to draw attention to ourselves."

"But ... those men ... they were ... in broad daylight!"

Maerlin smiled, remembering another similar incident on her first day in the city. On that occasion, a man was being mugged. This time, the woman in question was going to earn a few coins for her trouble. At least Maerlin hoped that was the case. Maybe she ought to go back and check, just to be on the safe side.

"Don't even think about it," Nessa warned in her head, guessing at Maerlin's concerns.

"But, she could be in trouble?" Maerlin protested.

Nessa sighed. *"Very well then, I'll go back and check. I'll meet up with you at the tavern. No one's going to notice a magpie lurking about in an alley. You, on the other hand, could get yourself into trouble."*

Nessa flew back down the road, her ever-persistent shadow following in her wake.

"Come along, Cora. We're nearly there. It's just round this next corner if memory serves me right."

"And what if it doesn't?" Cora asked apprehensively.

Maerlin thought for a moment. "Then I guess we'd be lost, wouldn't we."

"Art thou sure that this tavern is a good idea?" Seabhac asked.

"We need a place to sleep, Seabhac, and there's none safer in Manquay."

"Yes, but it's owned by the Order."

"Which is exactly why it's safe, Seabhac. Listen, I know you're nervous about meeting the Sisterhood again after all this time, but it'll be fine."

Seabhac's face confirmed her lack of faith, but she kept her opinions to herself. "Very well, then. Let's get this over with."

Thankfully, Maerlin was not lost, and the ramshackle tavern appeared up ahead. "Ah, there it is!"

"Is that it?" Cora asked, "It looks like a bit of a kip to me!"

"Looks can be deceiving as Nessa always taught me ... 'what we see isn't always there, and what we can't see still exists'."

Seabhac sniffed. "What's that supposed to mean?"

"You'll see when we get there ... come along."

*****

"Maerlin! Cora! My, how it warms my heart to see thee again," Ceila declared, hurrying forward. "The blessings of Deanna upon thee both." Ceila embraced the novices warmly; glad to see them after so long. "By the goddess, thou hast grown up so much while thou hast been away."

Ceila then noticed the older woman, standing hesitantly in the doorway. A large regal-looking raptor was perched on the woman's shoulder. Despite her hesitancy, an unmistakable aura of power came from the woman. This was someone who would not be easily cowed. Ceila disengaged from the novices and smiled warmly as she walked over to great the new guest. "Thou must be Uiscallan, I take it?"

"No. I'm Seabhac, and this is Fintan MacIolar-Mara of the Hawk People of Eagles Reach," Seabhac replied sternly. "The one that thou kneweth as Uiscallan has been gone for a long time."

"But I thought ..." Ceila looked confused and half-turned to Maerlin.

Maerlin sighed and intervened. "You thought correctly, Ceila. Granny likes to be referred to as Seabhac these days."

"I've warned thee about using that term before, Maerlin," Seabhac grumbled, "It's unbecoming!"

Maerlin ignored Seabhac and made the introductions "Seabhac, this is Ceila Dream-catcher, High Priestess of the Order of Deanna and Guardian of the Holy Isle. Ceila, this is Seabhac, once known as Uiscallan Storm-Bringer, my great-grandmother, and this is Prince Fintan of the Hawk Clan ... at least, I think he's a prince. He's the strong silent type, so it's really hard to tell."

"Maerlin!" Seabhac hissed in warning, but was again ignored.

"Now that we've got all of that cleared up, we need to sit down over dinner and sort a few other things out. I don't know about you lot but I'm starving ..."

"Maerlin, where's Nessa?"

"She'll be along shortly," Maerlin answered, heading for the kitchen. "She's spying on a street-walker and her two clients."

The flippant answer caused some consternation, but Maerlin was too tired and too hungry to be overly concerned. She had a to-do list in her head: food, bath, bed, and then retrieve the sword. Everything else was way down the list and would have to wait. Maerlin was feeling cranky at the moment, too cranky to bother with the delicate feelings of others. To top it all, she could feel the unmistakable aching in her lower abdomen. The goddess, Arianrhod, had taken this time to remind her of her womanly blessing of fertility, right on time. Maerlin had been too busy to notice the swelling of the moon, but there was no denying that dull ache.

Just what I need, she thought. Maerlin quickly amended her to-do list: food, some medicinal herbs from Ester's supplies, a bath, a comfortable bed ... and then get the damn sword back off Conal. It might not be a good idea to confront Conal until her general disposition improved, at least a little. They had a tendency to clash heads at the best of times, and he wasn't going to like the idea of giving up his new toy. One way or another though, he was going to give her the sword, whether he liked it or not.

Chapter Thirty-Six: A Hero Rises

Nessa landed on a pile of discarded rubbish, pointedly ignoring Sir Gallaghad, who had perched nearby. She couldn't shake off her new shadow, no matter how hard she tried. By now, she'd even become accustomed to his presence and had started to take it for granted. He was always there, her silent watcher, her admirer.

Turning her attention to the carnal act before her, she watched for a few moments. It was enough time to satisfy her that the young woman was a willing participant in the sordid act. Not that she appeared to be enjoying the task, her eyes attested to her lack of pleasure, but nevertheless, she made suitable noises of encouragement to hurry her clients along.

Nessa had seen enough and was set to take wing when it happened. Her wings, half unfurled, did little to stop the claws that shot forward and ensnared her. She struggled and pecked furiously at her attacker, but this only seemed to encourage it. With a flick of its sharp claws, it knocked Nessa to the ground, stunning her momentarily.

A shadow fell across Nessa's attacker, launching a reckless assault on the alley-cat's head. A flurry of black and white fury squawked its outrage as Sir Gallaghad swooped to the rescue, swooped, and attacked again, never letting up on his onslaught. Talons, wings, and beak struck again and again, distracting the cat to allow Nessa the time she needed to recover.

The cat crouched, anticipating the next dive, its legs tucked in under it, ready to spring into the air. They met with a furious clash, but the tomcat was heavier and more dexterous. Flipping in mid-air, it caught a hold of Sir Gallaghad in its fore paws and bit down with its wickedly-sharp jaws. They landed, locked together with the full weight of the cat pounding onto Gallaghad's chest. His struggle stopped as the cat raked him with its claws and sunk its teeth into his feathery chest.

Nessa felt Gallaghad's pain deep inside her, and she jumped up in a fury. Drawing instinctively upon her magical powers, her body tingled all over as she leapt forward to save the stricken magpie.

The appearance of a wolf in the alley took the cat totally by surprise, and the feline barely escaped with its life. It howled in pain and ran, bleeding heavily from the sudden onslaught of lupine ferocity. Nessa pulled hard on the instincts of the wolf and fought against the natural urge to give chase. Instead, she turned back to check on the fallen bird.

"Gallaghad!" Nessa howled, slipping without conscious thought into human form as she raced to his side. Drawing upon her healing skills, Nessa focused her magic on his battered body and found the life force within. Taking deep breaths to calm her distraught mind, she poured some healing energy into the ravaged magpie. "Live, damn you ... live."

Guilt washed over her as she berated herself for all the times that she had ignored him. He had come to her rescue in her time of need, despite her unforgivable behaviour. Cradling the injured bird to her bosom, Nessa remembered the other man in her life, so long ago. She had rejected him to follow the calling of Deanna. He had become a Dragon-lord, just like his father before him. Now, a second chance of love had come into her life, and she had again rejected it. "No!" she promised herself. She would not let that happen.

Clutching the bird to her bosom, she raced through the streets. Passers-by gawked at the beautiful woman with the strange, monochrome hair, who ran naked past them, but strangeness was an everyday occurrence in a big city and it was quickly forgotten.

Nessa burst into the kitchen, the most likely place to find Madame Dunne. "I need help, fetch me your medicines," she demanded.

Ester turned, surprised to see a naked woman carrying a bleeding bird across her newly-cleaned floor. She was about to object when Maerlin stopped wolfing down stew and exclaimed "Nessa!"

There was no doubt in Maerlin's mind about the identity of the woman in front of her. She had seen her so often during their mental chats. Still, it was a surprise to see her in the flesh. Nessa's distraught expression pushed all other matters aside. She rose from her stool and rushed across the kitchen to Nessa side. "What happened to Sir Gallaghad? Is he alive?"

"Barely!"

Ester was already gathering her medicines, quick to assess the situation. She slid the copper kettle across to heat on the stove as she hurried over to join them. "What can I do?"

"We'll need to bathe these wounds before they get infected and brew a tea to help with any internal injuries," Nessa assessed. "After that, it's in the hands of Deanna."

"What happened?" Maerlin asked.

"I got careless, that's what happened. A mangy alley-cat sneaked up on me while I was distracted. It must have been sleeping amongst the rubbish."

Maerlin inspected the cuts on Nessa's body at a glance. "You need some treatment too, Ness. Those cuts could turn nasty."

"I'm fine," Nessa dismissed.

"No. You're not! You're bleeding all over the place. Sit down and we'll look at you both," Maerlin ordered.

Nessa was about to argue, but seeing Maerlin's fierce expression, she sighed and pulled up a stool. "The foolish idiot, he attacked the cat. He could have got himself killed!"

"He'll be fine," Maerlin assured, hoping that it was true. "He's strong, and you know how stubborn he can be."

Nessa smiled for the first time, a little sadly, as she stroked the magpie's feathers.

Ester placed a bowl beside the stool and poured some boiling water into it. Selecting some of her pots of herbs and tinctures, she dropped ingredients into the water and stirred. "Now, let's have a look at the wee chap, shall we?" she prompted.

Nessa reluctantly released her hold on Sir Gallaghad.

*****

Conal woke early the next morning and prepared himself for the coming ordeal, just like all the other young men who had come of age that spring. Like them, he was here to show his worth to his peers, and stand before the Brehons to be judged during his Rites of Manhood. Despite the myriad number of protectors within the shared Dragon and *Broce* campsite, he would have to walk away from this protection, alone and unarmed, to face his trials. Dressed only in a simple wool tunic and loincloth, he left the tent and headed down the road toward the large marquee for registration. Tradition was very clear on this. He must not have anyone mollycoddling him when he took his first steps into manhood. Others may assist him later with the donning of his armour or the preparation of his chariot, but only where this would be normal for a man to seek aid for such a task. Wherever possible, the youth must complete his tasks independently. He must stand on his own two feet.

Conal walked down the street with other boys, before and after him, to face the day's challenge. He had not even been allowed to carry his father's dagger with him, an item he cherished above all others.

Crowds lined the makeshift streets, shouting encouragement to one and all as the young men walked toward their destinies. Conal had time to study some of his fellow competitors and noticed that they came in all shapes and sizes. Many wore their Clans clearly in their features like banners. The small, lithe boy with the high cheekbones who walked before Conal had the distinctive features of the Hawk Clan. The heavyset boy who lumbered along behind Conal was obviously a member of *Clann Na Béar*. He had the broad shoulders, dark swarthy skin, and the shaggy mane of hair so common amongst the Bear Clan.

Many of the boys had already been decorated with their first tattoos, freshly scabbed-over wounds depicting their Clan's Totem-beast. Their tired eyes showed the strain of the previous night's artwork. They had patiently endured the needle-sharp blades of their male siblings as they had slowly carved the tattoos. They had then rubbed dyes into the bleeding wounds to colour them and create the animalistic effigy of their Clan. It was believed that such tattoos would give the contestant greater courage and endurance during the coming trials. It would imbue them with the traits of the Totem-beast that the Clan held affinity with. In the case of the bleeding bear tattoo of the youth behind Conal, this would be strength and ferocity in combat. Beneath Conal's own tunic, his torso was bare as he had no close kin to wield the tiny blades for him. Taliesin and Declan had both offered to stand in for Conal's deceased relatives, as they would later stand in when needed during the trials. Much though he was humbled by their offer, Conal had declined and remained unblemished.

The Hawk boy stopped at the end of a queue, waiting for his turn to enter the marquee. None of the boys talked or joked. Everyone stood silently, looking straight ahead. This was what they had all waited for, dreamed about for years, and they would meet their challenges boldly. Conal shuffled forward along with the rest, as the mists of dawn drifted away and the day began. The Hawk boy entered the tent, and Conal would be next. A young Brehon appeared and motioned for Conal to follow him to one of the waiting scribes.

"Name?" the bored-looking scribe asked. He was sitting behind a small table and hadn't even bothered to look up from his parchment.

"Conal."

"Conal ..." the man repeated, carefully noting it on the clean piece of parchment, "... and your Clan?"

"The Dragon Clan."

"Conal of *Clann Na Dragan* ..." the scribe mumbled with a bored air, focusing entirely on his lettering.

Conal had been expecting some sort of reaction, but the clerk was too engrossed in the scrolling letters, so he added. "...If you're going to all that trouble to write my name, you might as well get it right. It should read: Conal *MacDragan* of *Clann Na Dragan*"

This finally got the attention of the scribe. He made a mess of his calligraphy as he jerked his head up to look at the Prince. Conal met his stare with piercing blue eyes. "While you're at it, you might as well leave a space at the bottom ... to add Dragon-lord afterwards. I will be *Ri Na Dragan* when this is all over."

The scribe discarded the parchment, throwing it over his shoulder and resigned himself to starting over. "Cocky li'l bugger, aren't you! You do know that many a young man has failed his trials ...?"

"Some may fail today, but I won't be one of them," Conal replied.

The scribe looked up at him, measuring Conal's confident eyes before he nodded. "Aye, I doubt you will. Good luck to you, Dragonson."

Conal was dismissed without further comment, the scribe already re-writing a new parchment. This would be used to tally Conal's scores throughout the various trials.

"That way," directed the young Brehon. He was pointing toward the far end of the large marquee, where the other competitors were disappearing. Conal followed them and found himself in a small holding area. Time passed while they waited, and the area filled. Finally, all the young men had been registered.

"Young men of the Clans of Dragania and *Tir Pect* ..." Conal looked around as the High Priest of Lugh spoke. He stood on a raised platform with his arms outstretched in greeting.

"Yes, I called you young men of the Clans, for that is what you now are. From this day forth, no matter how well you perform in these trials, you ... all of you, will be men in the eyes of the Brehons. How you wear the mantle of manhood is another matter. It's true that some of you will fail in these trials, and some will not be able to live with the shame that they have brought upon themselves and their Clans. I urge you to remember this small piece of advice. Today is but one day in your lives. Do not waste the precious life you have been granted by the Seven, because of any perceived failure you may have this day. It is an important day, that is true, and some can rise to greatness on the success they achieve this day, but others will inevitably blossom later in their lives. Some may only achieve their full potential in ten or maybe twenty years time. Many are weaker of limb or constitution, but they may be mentally superior or be gifted magically. These may take many years to come into their birthright. Today, these young men will only take their first tentative steps on their long journey to find themselves."

He paused, letting his words sink in on the young, impressionable minds before he continued "Today is the first day of the trials, and we will be assessing your basic skills. After this, you will be segregated into varied groups to continue your assessments over the coming quarter-cycle of the moon. Your first task is a gruelling endurance run. On my signal, you will proceed out of that exit, over there. It will lead you to the edge of the city, which you must then circumvent. You may go either left, right, or through the gates and into the city itself. The choice is entirely yours. Each way holds its own perils. Your final destination is beyond the city, where the foothills meet the mountains. In order to get there, you must first cross the River Man. You may achieve this by whatever means you can. You could choose the southerly route and cross at the Man Bridge, but this way adds to the distance you will need to travel. An alternative route is through the rough ground north of the city and the old bridge that still stands there. This is shorter, but harder to navigate and comes with its own dangers. Then, there is the route of the crow, through the city itself.

This also holds dangers for the unwary; as does the fast-flowing river that you must swim afterwards, should you choose this route."

"Whichever route you choose, when you reach the far bank of the Man, you must head west and seek out the setting sun. Once you find it, you will speak to the priests of Lugh there and return to me. You will then be tested mentally. Do not think that the mental tests are less arduous or less dangerous than the physical ones that you must first endure, especially as a fatigued body leads to a fatigued mind. Now, I wish you all the blessings of Lugh. You may be on your way."

It took a few moments for the competitors to realise that the race had started, but after the first few boys turned to leave, suddenly a mass exodus ensued. Some of the weaker ones were knocked flat and trampled, as the stronger youths used their strength to break free of the pack.

The gruelling training regime that Conal had endured, paid off in those first frantic moments, where physical fitness, balance, and boldness paid dividends. Conal barged his way toward the exit, using his elbows, shoulders, and hips, to ward off anyone who might hamper his departure. The Hawk boy was still in front of him, and as they were reaching the bottleneck at the entrance to the marquee, the boy stumbled and started to fall. Acting as much out of self preservation as out of any act of charity, Conal grasped the back of the youth's tunic and hauled him upright, half-carrying him outside. "Watch what you're doing!" he grunted, as he released the youth.

Conal turned to leave, but the boy grabbed his shoulder. "Hey! Thanks for that."

"Forget it," Conal replied. Shaking off the hand, he started to run. By the time he had covered a few feet, the Prince knew which way he would go. This was his city in more than just title. He'd spent a good part of his life here, and he knew it well. He knew alleys that others would not venture down, shortcuts and byways that would make his journey through the city as quick as possible.

*****

Abbot Gearoid had been awake all night and had been unable to utter a single word of prayer. He had spent the time staring at the exquisitely-forged dagger that he had been given. He muttered to himself again and again the mantra "Dagda!"

Surely, it couldn't have been real, and yet, the dagger was there before him as testament to its reality. He had spoken with the All-father, the leader of the Seven Greater Gods, the god who had united the others to defeat *Crom Cruach*.

Gearoid had prayed each night for divine intervention, and he had been given it. It had not come with flashes of lightning and a rumble of thunder, but as a lump of finely-crafted steel with a razor-sharp edge. The irony of the miracle was not lost on Gearoid. The gods had answered his prayers. In fact, the All-father had honoured him with a personal visitation; taking time out from whatever it is that the gods do, to grant him this boon. All Gearoid had to do was complete the job, and his prayers would be fulfilled. A quick jerk of the knife would have his friend's blood spilling onto the ground, and it would mean death to the *Darkness* that controlled Brother Balor. Dagda's knife was more than adequate for the task ... but was Gearoid?

Gearoid had tried. He had freed himself from the cart wheel and had silently approached his fellow monk. He had even got so far as to place the knife against Balor's throat in preparation for the final, fatal act of friendship, but it would have been easier to cut off his own hand. His muscles rebelled against the deed and denied him the strength he needed.

Three times he had tried, only to stagger away in frustration after each attempt. Could the gods be this cruel? There had to be another way. Maybe, he wasn't looking at the full picture. Was he only seeing the obvious solution and not the full meaning of the gift? Dagda's words haunted his brain. "The best way to save thy friend might be to set him free. That way, his soul can return to the Wheel of Time. Maybe, if he's lucky, he can make up for the sins of this life, in his next."

He wondered what Balor would think, and he knew that Balor would agree with the All-father's synopsis of the situation. Balor, after years of worshipping the darker aspects of the goddess of death, was cynical of the blessings of the gods. He would find great amusement in the miracle that Gearoid had prayed so hard for. The miracle would mean that he could embrace the sweet bosom of his goddess, a fate that his darker-self had fought so hard to avoid.

Yet, he couldn't risk speaking to Balor about it. He was too closely linked to his evil shadow, and he might inadvertently warn the *Darkness* within of the possible threat.

That's what it was, after all, wasn't it? It was murder. He was being asked to murder his friend. The act was also likely to cost him his own life, as he was surrounded by the *Tir Pect* army. They would be enraged at the loss of such a valuable weapon in the coming war. It was equivalent of a pawn's sacrifice in taking out the opponent's queen in a game of chess. Such an act would bring down the full wrath of the opposition, and the pawn's days would be surely numbered. Retribution would be swift ... if he was lucky.

Perhaps, the All-father knew this and meant him to take his own life, as well. Surely, the blade would strike true, if he fell upon its tip? That way, his rebellious muscles would not have the chance to deflect the killing blow. But first, he would have to bathe his hands in Balor's blood. He would have to watch him wake up to the feeling of blood spurting from his opened throat. He would have to hear the death-rattle of his friend's last breath.

Gearoid remembered the killing of a kid-goat during the previous summer. It had been fattened and was readied for the feast. He had held its quivering body firmly and was shocked at the trust in the young goat's eyes, when it looked up at him. He had pressed the naked blade firmly to its throat and sliced cleanly, following Seamy's instructions. He had placed his hand over those trusting young eyes, so that the kid could not see the blood that spurted freely onto the ground. The horrible wheezing sound as it struggled to breathe through its torn windpipe was slow torture to Gearoid's heart, as was the final struggle when it realised the betrayal. Gearoid had hand-reared that kid after its mother had failed to produce milk. He had bottle-fed it and laughed gaily as it followed him everywhere, bleating happily. He had become its nanny, long before he became its executioner. He had betrayed this ultimate trust. The foolish decision to complete the task himself, rather than let another do his gruesome work, had nearly his heart. He had never again offered to act as a butcher for the island's livestock. Gearoid couldn't even stomach the smell of goat meat after that day.

And now, the gods themselves had asked him to become an executioner ... a murderer ... a friend-slayer.

*****

Running through city streets was a sure way to get noticed: mugged, killed, or if you were really unlucky ... held for questioning by the City Watch. That is, even if running was a possibility. The major thoroughfares were so densely packed that, at the busier times of the day, even walking could be a challenge, and walking could be far quicker than riding a carriage, which could get cloaked in cobwebs as it drove through the city, such was their speed. Dray horses had been known to fall asleep in their shafts on journeys through Manquay.

There were alternatives routes for those brave enough, but these were not safe for those who were unarmed. Conal knew the alleys, the sewers, and the rooftops well, and he could navigate his way from any point within the city to any other point, quicker than most. However, to attempt some of these routes without the protection of a blade was a daunting task, even for him. Competitors in the Rites of Manhood left without a weapon for the first trial, and every lowlife in the city knew this. You were a sitting duck for the likes of slavers or other miscreants, and there lay some of the hazards that the High Priest had referred to. No matter which route you chose, once you stepped out of the safety of the spring fair and its Brehon protection, you were fair game for the underworld. Many a youth had been carried off, never to be seen again. Sea-raiders sailed up the River Man at this time of year for the opportunity to harvest the weak and the unwary. In recent years, Lord Boare had turned a blind eye to such activity. Rumour had it that he even purchased some of the Reavers' cargo, to work in his mines.

Conal's first task on entering the city was not to hasten to the far side, no; it was to find a weapon. Annoyingly, he had no money to buy one. This was another stipulation of the Rites of Manhood. As he was dressed in only a simple tunic and loincloth, bartering was also out of the question. He didn't even have footwear, and this was another thing he would need to remedy before too long. If he didn't find suitable footwear, he would return blistered and bloody from his long trek into the mountains. This would hamper him in the other events he would face, during the days ahead.

Conal's eyes roamed the gutter, looking for a suitable pointed stick to use as a shank, a broken bottle, or even a leather thong to use as a garrotte. Any of these would be better than nothing. His lessons with Cull had taught him that even the most rudimentary tool could be used as a lethal weapon, if it was in the right hands. He scoured the streets, but in a city where dire poverty was a fact of life, even a broken bottle had worth to someone. Conal had searched for some time without success. His best find was a lump of broken cobblestone. Still, it was better than nothing. Being pocket-less, Conal pushed the rock down the front of his loincloth and carried on.

The most direct route to the river was along the main thoroughfare, with all its congestion. Conal chose instead to use one of the long side-wheels that circled the city and fed off into the poorer regions of Manquay. Wealth congregated, or huddled anxiously, at the inner core of the city. The outer areas, nearer to the defensive walls, were filled with run-down shacks, reeking factories, and dilapidated sweatshops. Finding a suitable deserted alleyway, Conal took a few moments to prepare himself before entering these poorer sections. A few rolls on the ground and some selective smearing of his bare flesh with the ashes of a disused fire pit allowed him to blend more easily into his environment. To the opportunist, looking for a silver piece, Conal would not stand out from the other street denizens. Perhaps, he was a little more fleshed out than the children who prowled the back-streets with hungry eyes, but the muscles he had developed over the last year were now his only armour. They might dissuade confrontation from the more cautious entrepreneurs. He would have to take his chances, if he ran into more dedicated opponents.

Somewhere, either in the city or out in the countryside, there would be people looking for him, hunting him. Of this he was sure, perhaps more than one group. He was sure that Lord Boare would not miss this opportunity to stop Conal from reaching his throne. Then there were the twin leaders of *Ard Pect*, whose army were still marching south as far as Conal was aware. They too may have sent armed men to intercept the Prince during his trials. There were also the recently-killed assassins to consider and whoever had hired them. Cull was confident that whoever the assassins were, they would seek to complete their task. Once such a contract was signed, it stayed signed. Conal had a price on his head, though he was used to that. Lord Boare had placed a price on his head many years ago, and yet Conal still lived. He planned to see the Boare shackled in chains and buried in a deep dungeon for this, and for his other crimes. Lying dead at Conal's feet would be a close second-best option.

The more Conal thought about it, the more he itched for a weapon to defend himself with, and the more he sensed that he was being watched. In fact, now that he thought about it, he felt sure that he was being followed. Casually, he glanced behind him, but could see nothing obvious. He ducked into an alley, and as soon as he was free of the crowd he burst into a run, dodging through the maze of alleys, hoping to lose his hunters. He ran on, ignoring the other alley-dwellers as he put as much distance as possible between himself and those who followed.

Finally, he slowed. Proceeding at a walk, he calmed his breathing and looked around. He needed to get his bearings. This area held some of the poorest dwellings, barely even shacks, and it was hard to gauge his exact location from the lean-tos around him. This part of the city was ever evolving, changing on a daily basis as materials were brought here to be reused as shelters for the poor. Ahead, he could see the remains of an overturned boat, a metal tube sticking out of a hole in its prow to act as a chimney. The walls of the house were made of a variety of items, from wattle to old rags, anything that could keep out the elements and offer some meagre shelter. He had to admit that despite its bizarre appearance, the boat made a good roof for the structure. It was much better than some of its neighbours, and he wondered how they had managed to carry the boat here, through the maze of alleys. There was nothing like necessity to give creativity to the human mind.

He walked on cautiously, and it wasn't long before he again sensed eyes watching him. They were not the haunted eyes of the local people, but other eyes: hunter's eyes. He had not lost his pursuers, whoever they were. He would have to find another way to resolve this. He would have to hunt the hunters. Conal started to run again. This time though, he had a clear destination in mind. He turned sharply left, and then left again at the next junction, heading parallel to his original course, but going in the opposite direction. Soon, he found another left and up ahead he spotted the boathouse. He had come full circle. Crouching and using the shadowy, left-hand side of the alley, he crept forward and hid behind an old water-barrel. He didn't have to wait long to spot his quarry. A shadowy figure dropped down from a nearby building, rolling to lessen the impact of the fall and began to search the ground. Soon, the figure had found Conal's tracks and was heading off.

Conal followed, hugging the shadowy side of the street. It was difficult to make out the details of his hunter. Conal's eyes searched the rooftops and alleys, checking for other pursuers, but the tracker appeared to be alone.

Only one assassin, that didn't make sense, Conal thought. This one must be a tracker, and the rest of his team must be spread out ahead, ready to close the trap. Conal would need to eliminate this threat now and perhaps gain some intelligence of what lay ahead at the same time. Digging into the loincloth, Conal pulled out his only weapon and hoped that it would be enough. He did have the advantage of surprise, however. The hunter had foolishly focused on the trail ahead and not on his own wake.

When the figure slipped around the next turn, following Conal's tracks, Conal broke into a sprint and made up as much ground as possible. He took the corner at speed and was on the startled tracker before he could recover. Bellowing a war-cry, Conal struck the turning head with a crashing blow and was on top of the tracker before he had fully hit the ground. He didn't want to kill him, merely stun and disarm him. He needed intelligence, so he dropped his rock and swung a punch instead.

A second punch followed the first in quick succession, and he was about to strike again when recognition came to him. The face before him looked familiar. He was looking down at a male version of Maerlin, or at least a battered and bloody male version of her. He stopped the next blow from contacting and looked closer. It was the Hawk boy from the trials. Was this his assassin? Surely not!

"What in the Nine Hells are you doing?" Conal demanded, angrily shaking the youth, "I could've killed you!"

The boy spat out a tooth and a mouthful of blood, before answering "Sorry," he finally managed.

Conal jumped off the boy and dragged him to his feet. "Sorry! Is that all you've got to say?"

The Hawk boy gingerly touched his broken nose and winced.

"Hold your head up and pinch the bridge of your nose," Conal advised.

"I know! This isn't the first time I've been punched in the face, you know."

Conal waited, trying to cool his anger. Finally, he could wait no longer. "Well? Why've you been following me?"

Hesitantly, the Hawk-boy tried to explain "They say that you grew up in this city?"

"Who did?"

"People ... storytellers. They say that you lived here, right under the Boarites' noses."

"So? What's that got to do with you following me?"

"You pulled me out of the tent and stopped me getting trampled ..."

"What choice did I have? You were in my way. If you'd have fallen, I would've tripped over you when you tried to get back up. We were both going to end up getting squashed!" Conal replied. "I was just looking out for number one!"

"I saw you heading toward the city. You knew what you were doing. Everyone else was indecisive. No one knew which way to go ... but you: you knew. So I followed."

"You could have got yourself killed wandering around here. Don't you know that?"

"I could've got killed whichever way I went. At least this way I had a guide."

"I'm not your guide, so quit following me," Conal ordered, starting to walk away.

"Wait! You haven't heard me out yet."

Conal stopped. "Be quick about it then, whatever it is."

"This is your territory, your strength. You know this city, so you're safe here, or at least as safe as anyone can be."

"What of it?"

"When you leave the city, you'll be heading into the mountains, correct?"

Conal nodded reluctantly.

"Do you know much about mountains? Do you know how to recognise different animal tracks? Would you know where there are risks of rock-slides, for instance? I know about these sorts of things."

"I can manage ..."

"I'm sure you can, but I can help. I've spent my whole life in the mountains. They are to me like the city is to you. Maybe not these particular mountains, but I know more about mountains than you could learn in a lifetime."

Conal remembered the youth's tracking ability. "How did you manage to follow me?"

"I used the rooftops. I could watch you far easier from up there than I could from the ground, and I had less chance of being spotted. People rarely look up."

Conal scanned the low houses around him, overshadowed by the occasional factory or warehouse. It must have got tougher for the boy to follow him, once he had headed away from the main thoroughfares. "You know about me? You know who I am?"

"Of course! The whole fair is a-buzz with tales of the *MacDragan*."

Conal smirked. "I wouldn't believe everything that you hear."

"But I'd heard about you even before the fair. They spoke about you in my village. Even Eagles Reach has heard about the Dragonson."

"Are you trying to tell me that a storyteller braved the heights of *Sliamh Na Dia* just to tell you colourful tales about me?"

"It wasn't a storyteller. It was my cousin, the young Storm-Bringer. I heard her telling Iolar-Mara about you during the feast. She came to the village with the other witches of Deanna: my great-grandmother and Fintan Blue-wings."

"Are you talking about Maerlin, and about Seabhac and her hen harrier? They were in your village!"

"Yes. They came with the Sea-girl and the magpie-witch. They celebrated Imbolc with my Clan."

"What epic tales did Maerlin tell about me?" Conal asked.

The Hawk boy hesitated, clearly reluctant to answer.

"It can't have been that bad, can it?"

"Maybe she was joking. I only heard a little of their conversation. I was kept busy serving drinks."

"What exactly did you hear?" Conal pressed.

"Something about you being a loud-mouthed thief with bad manners ..."

Conal was stunned for a moment and the Hawk boy shuffled his feet nervously. Then, Conal started to laugh. "That sounds like Maerlin alright. She never was one to mince her words."

"She did say that she thought you'd make a good king, someday .... When you stopped being a complete brat that is."

"Plain-speaking must be a common habit amongst the Hawk people," Conal joked. "Very well then, Hawk-boy, I'll be your guide in the city, and you can be mine when we reach the mountains. Do we have a deal?" Conal offered his hand.

The youth grinned through bloody teeth and spat on his palm before shaking, "We have a deal, *MacDragan*."

"You can call me Conal, Hawk-boy."

"Very well, Conal, and you can call me *Fuath-Dubh*."

"Foot-Dove? What's that supposed to mean? I'm still not very good at the Old Tongue. Tal's been teaching me but I've been kind of busy lately."

"*Fuath-Dubh*, you dumb *Fear Ban!* It means Nightshade, in *Sassenaucht*."

"Nightshade, it is then. Let's get going, Nightshade."

Chapter Thirty-Seven: Riding a Stag

Conal led them toward the centre of the city, away from the poorer sections, but avoiding the wealthy hub. That area would be the most heavily patrolled by the city's Watch. They needed weapons and some other supplies, and these could not be obtained in the poorer sections of Manquay.

"Where are we going?" Nightshade asked.

"You'll find out, soon enough. Just be ready to run if I do."

Conal soon found what he was looking for. It was the type of rundown tavern that served a rougher clientele and only stopped serving when its client ran out of coins, or passed out. "Stay here and keep an eye out for the Watch," Conal instructed.

"What are these 'Watchers' that you want me to watch out for?"

Conal looked sharply at him. It took a moment before he realised that Nightshade wasn't joking. "Mean, fat, ugly-looking whoresons, the lot of 'em. They wear blue tabards over leather armour, and they're usually armed to the teeth. Believe me; you don't want to mess with 'em. Just keep an eye out for trouble."

"Sure thing ... trouble ... got it!"

"This is your first time in a city, I take it?" Conal asked, dreading the answer.

"Yep ... but so far it's been a lot of fun."

Conal shuddered and took a moment to look about. "Alright, I'll keep this simple. Don't look at anyone, and I mean *anyone*. Don't talk to anyone. In fact, don't even think about talking to anyone! Just try to blend into the background and wait here. I'll be right back."

Nightshade nodded. Conal could almost see his brain reciting the instructions. With a shrug, he headed down the alley beside the tavern. With any luck, he'd find an unconscious drunk dumped around the back, and he'd be able to rob the fool while he was sleeping it off. Sadly, the alley was empty, but Conal had not made a small fortune from pick-pocketing and petty-larceny without learning a thing or two.

Taking a deep breath, he walked casually into the crowded tavern, gliding through the establishment with adroit skill as he made his way leisurely toward the front door. The bar was filled to the brim with an assortment of lethal weapons, usually of the discrete variety. Tavern owners and their hired thugs frowned upon customers armed with claymores or war-hammers, but they usually turned a blind eye to knuckle-dusters, cut-throat razors, even throwing knives and small hatchets. The logic behind this was actually quite simple. By the time the client could get the chance to do any real damage with such weapons, the bouncers would have them pinned to the floor and have pummelled them into unconsciousness. If they were lucky, they'd wake up with said implement inserted in their most private parts. That was a slightly improvement on not waking up at all. Tavern owners were more concerned with avoiding the levels of violence that could bring the city's Watch down on their establishments. Having a visitation from the Watch was *very* bad for business.

By the time Conal reached the front door, his loincloth positively bulged with a wide array of weapons, money pouches, and other valuables. He had even managed to slip past the two muscular pillars that controlled the doors before the cry went out "Stop, thief!"

He had learned to loathe those two words. Cursing, Conal didn't waste precious time looking back to see if they were referring to him. Those would be precious moments he could have used more wisely in running, and that's exactly what he did. Whippets would envy Conal at a standing start, especially after his rigorous training regime. Barefoot and with adrenaline pumping through his veins, he was running up the street before he noticed the shocked look on Nightshade's face. "Well, don't just stand there, you idiot... run!" he yelled as he rushed past. He wasn't going to stick around and see if the Hawk boy was following or not. Once the cry went out, the Watch would answer the call. "Stop thief!" rang out again behind him and Conal put on another burst of speed.

Evasive manoeuvres were called for, and Conal raced headlong into the first available alley that presented itself. Clambering over a rickety fence, he continued down the narrow walkway, leaping over the assorted trash that littered the street. A dog snapped at his heels, eager to chase anything that was running away from it. He didn't have time to stop and teach the mangy mutt a lesson, so he was forced to hop away from its frenzied attacks. "Bugger off!" he yelled, taking a passing swipe at the dog's head to emphasise his point.

He could still hear footsteps behind him, so he kept up a gruelling pace as he twisted and turned down a number of alleys.

"I think ... we've ... lost ... them ... Conal!" Nightshade panted out from behind him, and Conal slowed down. The feet that he had heard chasing him had belonged to the Hawk boy.

"Damn but that was close!"

Nightshade stopped, leaned against the wall and dry-hacked from the exertion, while he caught his breath. Finally, he managed to speak. "You certainly lead an exciting life, *MacDragan*! I haven't had so much fun since last spring's egg-poaching."

"So that's what you mountain boys do for fun, is it? You go raiding the neighbour's chicken coop."

"Not chicken eggs, *MacDragan* ... Giant Eagle eggs. They are very protective of their young. If they catch you, they'll drop you off the nearest cliff!" Nightshade replied with a wicked grin. "It's a sure way to get the blood pumping!"

Conal wondered at the sanity of his companion, but he could hardly throw stones. "Come on. We need to find some new clothes. By now, the word will be out, and they'll be looking for us."

"Who will?"

"The Watch, of course! Who else?"

Nightshade thought for a moment and then uttered one word "...Fat!"

"What?"

"You said that they were fat."

"What's that got to do with the price of rotten kippers?"

"Can you climb, *MacDragan*?"

"Of course I can climb. Why?"

Nightshade led Conal over to a nearby drainpipe and gave it a firm tug. Satisfied, he began to scale the wall. "This way," he directed as he climbed. "The fat watchers won't be able to do this!"

"It's not the watchers ... it's the Watch!"

"That's what I said ... Watchers!"

Conal watched the nimble-footed Pect for a moment, before gripping the drainpipe himself. Soon, they were on the roof and skipping along the tiles.

"Which way is the river?"

Conal got his bearings and pointed. "It's that way, but we need to head slightly to the north. We'll need to do some bartering before we leave the city, and I know a good fence near the western wall."

"What do we need a fence for, if there's a city wall? I would've thought that we needed the find a gate.

"Not that type of fence," Conal replied. "A fence is someone who'll exchange goods for other goods or coins."

"In the mountains, we call them traders."

"Well, I guess he is ... sort of, but a fence deals specifically in goods that merchants wouldn't want to deal with, things that may be of questionable ownership, for example, which reminds me ... what's your poison?" Conal removed various weapons from his loincloth.

"So that's why they were chasing you. I'd wondered about that."

"You didn't think all of that yelling 'Stop, thief!' was a hint?"

Nightshade grinned. "I was a bit busy at the time. You'd got a good head start on me by that point."

"Which of them do you want?"

"Really!"

"Look ... we're in this together so I got enough for both of us. Come on, take your pick."

Nightshade's hand fluttered lightly over the collection and settled on a pair of light, throwing knives.

Conal, seeing his questioning look, nodded. "Consider them yours."

Conal selected some knuckle-dusters and a heavy dagger. He slipped these back into his loincloth. "Let's go."

Nightshade looked at the other weapons. "You're leaving the rest?"

Conal shrugged. "I've got what I wanted."

Nightshade paused and lifted up a bone-handled razor. "I'll take this as well then, if that's alright?"

"Sure, knock yourself out."

"I'm ready now. Let's go meet this fencer."

"It's a fence ... he's called a fence ... oh never mind!"

*****

After a short but fruitful barter with a shady character who worked for the Oven Mitts: the local guild of pawnbrokers and fences, the boys found themselves at the river's edge. They looked with some trepidation at the choppy waters of the River Man. Recent spring flooding had agitated the usually calm waters, churning up mud. Occasionally, flotsam floated by, attesting to the river's speed. Neither boy, it seemed, was an overly confident swimmer.

"Should we head downstream to the bridge?" Nightshade ventured. "That river looks angry."

Conal looked down at the treacherous waters. "No. We'll lose too much time if we do that. Besides, it's the obvious place for a trap."

"Trap, what do you mean?"

"Listen, Nightshade ... perhaps you'd be better off making your own way from here. It's not safe for you to be with me."

"What do you mean, trap?" Nightshade persisted.

"There are men hunting me. I've got a price on my head, maybe more than one. So you see, it's not safe for you to be around me. You're only doing your Rites of Manhood. For me, this is much more important. I'm here to claim the right to rule my Clan and with it, take the first step to becoming the next High King, like my father and my grandfather before me. It'd be unfair of me to hold you to our deal. You didn't know what you were getting into, so I release you from it now. Go on... head for the bridge and find a way across the Man. I'll find another way across."

"Do I look like an oath-breaker?" Nightshade accused heatedly. "I'm not a *slíbhín*. We made a pact, you and I, and I'm not going to wriggle out of it."

Conal sighed. "Don't you understand? This is serious! These are trained professionals I'm talking about. I don't want your blood on my hands, so go with my blessing."

"I will stay and fulfil our agreement. That is, if you still want me around," Nightshade said firmly, looking Conal hard in the eye. "If I left and you ended up dead, what sort of man would that make me? Even if I succeeded in my trials, your death would be forever on my soul. Besides, our chances of survival are better if we stick together. There is strength in numbers."

Conal finally nodded. "Very well then, but don't say I didn't warn you. Let's head upstream and search along the bank."

"Why upstream?"

"Look at that river. She's flowing like a horse at full gallop. For every hand's breadth we cross, we'll go two or three down-river, maybe more near the centre where the flow is faster. If we're not careful, we'll end up in the Great Marshes. You really wouldn't like that."

"I've heard that there's a magical island within the marshes, filled with beautiful, young women. That sounds like a good place to get washed up, I think."

Conal laughed, remembering his own time on the Holy Isle. "I've been there, Nightshade. Believe me, it's not all that it's made out to be."

"Then I guess we'll go upstream."

"We need to find a boat to help us cross."

"Wont they have removed all the boats before the race?"

Conal hadn't considered this. "Then we'll need something to help us swim across, a dead tree perhaps."

They walked along the bank for a while and found nothing big enough to float in the river. Eventually, they came to a little pool, filled with flotsam. "Look over there. Is that a log?"

Conal looked where Nightshade was pointing and he saw something floating in the water. "Let's wade in and find out."

As they got closer, their hearts sank. What they had hoped to be a floating log turned out to be the bloated carcass of a dead stag. Its belly was distended, swollen up like a huge balloon, about to burst. Maggots slithered under its skin, making the hide writhe with a life of its own. Flies buzzed all around it, attracted by the odour of rotting flesh. The stag's antlers looked a little like branches, and Conal could see why it had been mistaken for a floating log from a distance.

"Let's keep looking. Maybe there's something better, farther upstream," Nightshade suggested.

"No, this'll have to do. We've wasted enough time already."

"But it stinks!"

"I wasn't suggesting we eat it, Nightshade, just use it as a raft. Have you a better idea?"

Nightshade's silence was his only answer.

"Let's get this over with then, shall we? My toes are getting numb. So much for the new clothes we bought." Conal pointed to the stag's hind quarters. "You grab hold of them, and I'll take the forelegs. We'll push it before us, and if we get tired, we can climb on top and float along."

They pushed out into the current, feeling the sharp pull as the carcass was dragged swiftly down-river. "Kick out with your legs as hard as you can," Conal ordered, "... and whatever you do, don't let go."

445

They paddled on for a few moments before they heard a bubbly, hissing sound coming from under the dead deer, followed by a horrible stench. Nightshade gagged and tried not to retch. "I think it's deflating. It just farted!"

"It's just releasing excess gas. Don't worry about it, it won't sink. Just keep paddling."

"That's easy for you to say! You got the best side, *MacDragan*," Nightshade protested.

Conal laughed. "Quit whining and paddle, Hawk-boy."

They were, by now, halfway across, and they had passed the point at which they had first reached the bank. The current was faster there and choppy, making it hard work to get any forward momentum.

"I need ... to rest ... for a moment ..."

"Not now," Conal ordered. "Keep paddling for a while at least. We need to get out of this central current first!" To make his point, Conal pulled on his reserves of flagging energy and kicked out hard with his feet. The carcass moved, making slow headway. With a groan, Nightshade followed his example and soon they broke free of the faster current. "That's it! We can ease off a bit now, but keep paddling. We don't want to get sucked back into that."

To Conal's left, farther downstream, he could make out the bulky shadow of the Man Bridge getting rapidly closer. He could see vague figures on the bridge, but it was still too far away to see them clearly. Conal climbed onto the dead deer to look over its bulk and gauge the distance to the far bank. It was still some way away. They would pass under the bridge before they reached the far shore, given the speed of the current.

"I can't feel my legs," Nightshade complained. His face was weary with the continued exertion.

"I'm sure they're still down there. There isn't enough meat on them to tempt the pike."

"Pike? What is this pike?"

"They're big fish that live in the river. They have rows of razor-sharp teeth and they're known to attack children and the occasional stray dog. Nasty critters they are from what I hear. I'm surprised that we haven't been attacked yet. Praise the Seven, luck must be on our side!"

Nightshade looked nervously around at the water. "You are jesting with me ... yes? These pike ... they really don't exist."

"No ... I'm deadly serious! Remember what that old windbag of a High Priest told us. 'There are lots of dangers on the journey'. Pike were definitely one of the things he was talking about. Don't you have pike in your mountains?"

"We have trout and salmon in the mountains, and an occasional eel. There are no man-eating fish living in our streams."

"Don't worry, the pike aren't that bad. They'll just bite off the odd bit of flesh. The leeches in the Great Marsh are far worse. They can bleed a man dry quicker than you can piss. If we paddle hard, we'll reach the shore before we get that far downstream."

Nightshade's paddling resumed with increased vigour. He was determined to be out of the fish-infested waters before he lost any extremities to the ravenous creatures.

A cry came from overhead, and Conal saw that they had reached the bridge. Men crowded the wooded rails, looking down at them. "It's him!" one of them shouted and arrows began to rain down around them.

"Quick, get under the carcass!" Conal yelled and took a deep breath. He plunged beneath the murky water, gripping the foreleg firmly and pulled himself under the relative shelter of the dead stag. Arrows hissed through the water, and he could feel the deer shudder as arrows struck it. An arrowhead pierced the stag's ribcage, stopping within a fingernail's distance of Conal's eye. He gazed, hypnotised by the wickedly-sharp barb. He huddled under the deer until his lungs burned with the need for air. Finally he could wait no longer, and he burst to the surface, gasping for air. Nightshade followed a moment later, his face blue with cold and etched with fear.

Conal looked upstream and was glad to see that the bridge was well out of range. His enemies now knew where he was, and they would be quick to follow. "We need to get to the far shore and fast. Can you make it from here?"

Nightshade looked over the arrow-peppered deer and nodded. "Let's go."

They pushed the carcass aside and started swimming for the shore, their adrenaline-soaked bodies giving them the additional strength they needed to reach the far bank. Finally, they crawled amongst the reeds, gasping for breath.

Sometime later, they finally made it into the foothills...

"We need to keep moving," Conal urged, although his own muscles ached. Twice, they had managed to avoid the roaming parties of riders who were hunting them, but the longer they stayed in one place, the more likely it was that they would be found. They were making slow progress, dashing from one hiding place to the next and trying to avoid being caught out in the open. They had made it into the foothills, their eyes constantly roaming the land around them for danger. It was Nightshade who finally realised that something was amiss.

"Conal ... wait a moment!"

Conal stopped, scanning the land below them. He could see no threat. "We're fine! There's no one out there."

"That's exactly my point ... why isn't there?"

Conal gave him a blank look.

"Where are the others? We haven't seen another competitor since we left the fair. Surely someone must have made it this far?"

Conal scanned the horizon. Nightshade was right. Although they had made good time, they couldn't be that much ahead of the others. Something was wrong ... seriously wrong. "Come on," he said, signalling that they should move on.

"But ... where is everyone?" Nightshade protested stubbornly.

"I don't know, but the sooner we get this over with, the sooner we'll find out."

"What if we're walking into a trap?"

Conal whirled around in frustration. "I don't know, alright! All I know is that nothing is going to stop me from completing this task. So, are you with me?"

Nightshade sighed and nodded. "Of course I'm with you. I was just trying to think it through ... that's all."

"That's not a problem, thinking is good. By the Seven, my head's a-whirl with thoughts right now, but sometimes, you just have to grasp hold of the nettle and hang on. So let's go and find this 'sun in the west', and if there's a problem, then we'll deal with it. Let's just take this one step at a time, shall we Nightshade?"

With no other choice, they ran west as fast as their legs could carry them, up into the hills. Finally, they came to a narrow gorge leading toward the setting sun. "I don't like the look of this!" Conal exclaimed, as they paused at the head of the gully.

"Me neither. It's the perfect place for a trap if ever I saw one. Now, it's my turn to be the guide. Wait here and I'll be right back."

Before Conal could protest, Nightshade had scurried off. Conal fought against the urge to follow, but the Hawk boy was right. This was his country, and they must play by his rules. Slipping under a nearby gorse bush, Conal ignored the prickly undergrowth and settled down to wait. It took a while, but eventually the Hawk boy came running over.

"Well?"

"The gorge is a dead-end, and at the far end there's a wall that's carved into a setting sun. There's a Temple of Lugh back there. A few of the priests of Lugh are sitting around, looking impatient."

"So, it's not a trap then?"

"I didn't say that. There are a lot of men hiding in the rocks on either side of the path. They've been there for a while, and some of them have grown antsy. I managed to spot a few, but there may be others that I missed. That place is full of loose boulders to hide behind. It's a disaster waiting to happen."

"Is there any way we could climb down the back wall to the priests, without going through the gorge?"

"If we had some rope, perhaps, but they're bound to see us climbing down. We'd be sitting ducks."

"It looks like we'll have to go in and face the music then, I guess." Conal sighed and straightened his shoulders.

"Are you mad ... we won't stand a chance!"

"Look, Nightshade, I didn't come all this way to give up now. You can stay here if you want, and I'll go on alone. It's me they want, after all."

Before Nightshade could respond, they heard the rumble of hooves coming from down the valley, racing up the hill toward them. "It looks like we don't have a choice. We're stuck between a rock and a hard place."

Conal looked down at the horsemen. There were nearly fifty of them in all, riding in two bands. The leading group was galloping hard up the hill and consisted of about a dozen riders. The second group was harder to make out through the dust, but they too were riding hard and would be up the hill in moments.

"Nightshade, listen up! Stay close to me and cover my back. Whatever happens, keep moving toward the far end of the gully. With any luck, we'll make it as far as the priests and they'll be able to help us ... but if I fall, don't stop. Whatever you do, don't stop for anything. Have you got that?"

Conal drew his weapons and raced into the ravine before his courage could fail him. Surprise was their best weapon, and speed was their best armour. Conal couldn't afford to hesitate, not even for a moment. By the time the first cry went up, he was already moving at full speed and whirling through the narrow gorge. Long hours of boredom had left the attackers slow to respond. The first was hardly on his feet and was still lifting his bow when Conal reached him. He lashed out with the knuckle-dusters and followed up the blow with a thrust of the dagger as he crashed into the surprised assailant. Never stopping his forward momentum, Conal continued, hoping that the man would stay down. Already, he could hear hooves behind him. Time was rapidly running out.

Another man rose from behind a large boulder, blocking the pathway ahead. Conal bellowed his war-cry at the top of his lungs, *"Dragan abú!"* It echoed off the walls of the ravine, bouncing back at him as if other voices had taken up his war-cry.

The warrior was armed with a mace and shield, and he was wearing a mismatched set of chainmail. The man grinned toothlessly, full of arrogant confidence, as he waited for Conal to come into striking range. A dagger and a knuckle-duster were no match for a fully-armoured warrior, and they both knew it. Bracing his feet and raising his shield, the man lifted the mace high, ready to strike as Conal rushed forward.

Conal had no intention of challenging the man to mortal combat, and at the last moment he leapt and raised his feet before him. His feet landed squarely on the shield with all of Conal's weight behind it. Conal bent his knees to absorb the shock and then jumped, sailing over his surprised opponent and continued down the track. Nightshade was still close behind him, and slowed for only long enough to release a throwing knife into the surprised opponent's face. It sailed true and embedded itself deep into an eye socket. By that time Nightshade was also rushed past.

The screams of the dying warrior ruined any further hope of surprise and men began to pour onto the path from all sides, hoping to intercept them. Now they would be forced to stand and fight. Dressed only in tunics, they were poorly equipped for the coming battle. They stood, back to back, catching their breaths and waited. Surrounded and heavily outnumbered, their only hope was to go down with honour.

"Dragan abú!" Conal challenged.

"Seabhac abú!" Nightshade added.

War-cries echoed around the canyon. It was a confusion of noise, screams, and shouts, as the attackers fell upon the two youths. They charged en masse, hampering each other as they fought to be the first to make a killing blow.

One huge giant pushed himself clear of the others and wielding an enormous battle-axe in two hands, he raised it high overhead, ready to cleave Conal from forehead to groin. Conal, armed with only a dagger and with no space to dodge, could only stand helplessly and watch the axe begin to fall. Time slowed, each moment lasting a small lifetime as the axe-man swung. The axe rose to its full height and started to descent.

It was then that an arrow struck the warrior's heart with a sharp thud. It pierced his armour and buried itself up to the feathers. The axe-man died instantly, and his hold on the axe loosened in the moment of his death. Momentum kept it moving forward, as it slipped out of the warrior's grasp and sailed over Conal's head.

Other arrows followed the first, each shot aimed with deadly accuracy and finding targets amongst the tightly-packed group of men around the youths. Still the warriors attacked, and Conal fought desperately to hold his ground. Grabbing a fallen sword, he fought on using a combination of sword and knife to block and counter. *"Dragan abú!"* he yelled again and again until he was hoarse.

A blow struck the side of his head, and Conal stumbled to his knees, dropping his dagger as he battled against unconsciousness. He saw his attacker raise his club again for the final fatal blow, before a throwing dagger pierced the club-wielder's throat. Nightshade, armed now with only a cut-throat razor, crouched protectively over Conal.

Wave after wave of arrows fell around them and more men died. The pile of bodies around the youths was mounting, and it offered them some protection. It hampered the attacking warriors, who were forced to brave the hail of arrows that rained down around them with eerie precision. Finally, the last attacker fell, peppered with arrows. Conal could hear fighting farther down the gully. More men surged into the ravine, their faces flushed with bloodlust and their bodies coated with the gore of battle. They raced forward like berserkers.

Conal tensed for a moment before he recognised the leader of the charge. It was Declan Morganson, and at his side ran Cull. Conal was too weary to stand, but he smiled nonetheless.

Soon, they were surrounded by a protective wall of Dragon-scales.

"Are you alright, lad?" Cull asked.

"I've never felt better," Conal panted, "... what kept you?"

Cull laughed and slapped the Prince on the back. "We got held up at the bridge. Lord Boare had his troops barricading it, and they refused to let anyone across. When I heard that, I smelled a rat and went to get some help. Here, have a sip of this, lad. You look dead on ya feet."

Conal reached for the flask gratefully and took a big swig of the liquid, only to cough and choke as it burned its way down his throat and put set fire to his belly. "What the ...?"

"I said have a drink, not guzzle the whole flask! That's my best poitin you're guzzling."

"I thought it was water!" Conal protested, handing the flask over to Nightshade.

The Hawk boy sipped tentatively at the flask. "That's good stuff."

"Who's this?" Cull asked.

Conal rose shakily to his feet and placed a hand on Nightshade's shoulder. "This is my friend, Fools-Dove. I owe him my life."

"I've told you before, it's *Fuath-Dubh*, you illiterate *Fear Ban!*"

Conal laughed, feeling light-headed on poitin and relief. "Nightshade, I call him Nightshade. He's Maerlin's second cousin, twice-removed or something like that. I think there's a lot of inbreeding on those mountains."

"My cousin was right about you, wasn't she? She hit the nail on the head when she called you a loud-mouthed brat, *MacDragan*," Nightshade retorted with a grin.

Cull nodded his gratitude to the boy from Eagles Reach. "Well met, *Fuath-Dubh*. You have my unending gratitude for your bravery today."

"Are these men all Boarites?" Nightshade asked.

Cull inspected the dead that lay scattered around them. "From the look of them, I'd say they were mostly Sea-raiders. The Boare's men are all out there, at the mouth of the canyon. They were trying to keep us from getting in here.

Conal stooped and inspected one of the dead bodies more closely. Gripping an arrow firmly, he pulled it from the corpse and inspected it.

"Be careful with that, Conal! That tip could still have some poison left on it."

"These aren't Dragon Clan arrows, Cull. We don't use poison."

"They're not. They belong to the Black Daggers."

"Assassins!" Conal hissed, looking around nervously.

"Relax! They're on your side. I took the liberty of hiring some extra protection for you. I hope your coffers can afford it. They are known to take exception to tardy payers, and believe me, they don't come cheap."

Conal searched the rocks, but could see no sign of them. "Are they still here?"

"Probably, but you'll never spot them. At least … I'd be very disappointed, if you did."

"Are you sure that they can be trusted?"

"...Implicitly! Broll has used their services for years. They're the best that money can buy."

Conal accepted Cull's judgement. "That's fair enough. Come on, Nightshade. This is no time to be lolling about." Stretching briefly to shake off his weariness, Conal headed farther into the canyon.

"Where're we going?"

"We're going to find the setting sun, of course. Have you forgotten why we came here?"

Chapter Thirty-Eight: The Return of the Sun

Arm in arm, they wearily made their way to the end of the canyon and looked up at the chiselled effigy of the sun god that was engraved on the rock walls. They climbed the stone steps and stood in front of the cave mouth, where the priests of Lugh were waiting.

"Names?" a scribe asked.

"Conal Dragonson ..." Conal declared, "... of *Clann Na Dragan.*"

"*Fuath-Dubh ... of Clann Na Seabhac.*"

The scribe cleared his throat. "Congratulations. You're the first to reach us." He handed each of them a copper coin with the face of the god, Lugh, stamped upon it. "You're half-way there now. All you have to do is return to the High Priest and present these tokens to him."

Conal looked down at the coin in his hand. Is that it, he wondered? After all the trouble he had gone through, all he had to show for it was a copper farthing: the lowest of all the coins of the realm.

Cull spoke up from behind the youths. "They'll also be the last competitors you see today, Druid."

The priest looked up. "What was that you said?"

"I said ... there won't be any other boys coming here today. You might as well pack up and head back to the city. I think you'll be needed there."

"But that cannot be!"

Cull's face was like stone as he explained "There have been many vile murders committed today, priest. There was wholesale slaughter down at the Man Bridge, and we rode past dozens more bodies on the way up here, scattered across the countryside. We also saw a Reaver Dragonship sailing down the river, packed to the gills with prisoners. This is a dark day in the history of the spring fair ... a very dark day indeed. Come along, lads, you'll be riding back to the city with an armed escort. I'm not taking any more chances today. Woe betides anyone who gets in our way."

Conal considered protesting, but the news had hit him hard. So many young men had been butchered for the chance to kill him. Lord Boare was going to pay for this, as was anyone else who was even remotely involved. "Where's the Boare, Cull?"

Cull looked over and saw the rage that burned in Conal's eyes. "Now isn't the time, Conal."

"Where is he?" Conal persisted stubbornly.

"He's gone, Conal. He scarpered as soon as his treachery was discovered, but we've more important things to worry about."

"More important ..." Conal growled angrily. "What's more important than seeing that rotten bastard impaled on a stake?"

Even Cull was surprised at Conal's venom, but he explained "The combined armies of *Tir Pect* are less than a day's march from the city, Conal. The Boare will have to wait for now. You need to unite the Clans and prepare them for battle."

"Me?"

"Who else is there? Lord Boare has ruined his one chance of getting the other leaders to back his claim for the High Kingship with this botched assassination attempt. They'll be baying for his blood right now. Hell's bells, some of his own clansmen were caught up in this slaughter. The damned Reavers didn't even bother to distinguish between them. They captured any youth they could get their hands on, or shot the ones that looked like they might escape. If someone doesn't bring some order to things, you'll have half of the Clans chasing after the Boare, and Manquay will be left undefended. Conal ..." Cull pleaded urgently, "Now is not the time for vengeance. Now is the time for leadership!"

Conal had long hungered to avenge his father's death, but Cull was right. "Very well, Cull, but I won't forget this. Let's ride."

*****

The horses had been ridden hard and stood, sweat-soaked and weary, when the Dragon-scales reached them. Dead bodies littered the ground around the head of the gorge, testament to the vicious battle that had been fought there. Macha's Dark Angels were already feasting on the dead, cawing raucously when they were disturbed from their meal. The warriors of *Clann Na Dragan* only stopped for long enough to collect their fallen brothers, not even bothering with the traditional looting of the enemy. The crows and the wolves would have the feast all to themselves this evening. Quickly, the Dragon-scales mounted up, collecting the spare Boarite horses and headed back toward the city.

At Conal's insistence, they stopped along the way to gather up the fallen youths that had died trying to attain their manhood. Conal promised himself that they would be given fitting funerals as warriors. He would accept nothing less for them.

Finally, they reached the bridge and the evidence of the earlier battle that had been fought there. Many people were gathered here, and the wailing of mourners filled the air as they rode grimly onward to the fairground. Conal led the procession with a mask of determination on his face as he rode to the marquee of the High Priest of Lugh. Chaos filled the fairground, and the area in front of the marquee was its epicentre. Here, the crowds had assembled to demand justice from the Brehons. They were the keepers of the peace, and they had failed their people today. The heads of the various Clans stood to the fore with anger and shock written across their faces.

When he could ride no farther, Conal slipped to the ground. With a phalanx of the Dragon-scales around him, he pushed his way through to the front. The High Priest stood at the opening of the marquee, hands aloft, trying to call for order. Conal forced his way through until he stood in front of the old priest.

The crowd fell silent, recognising the banner of the *Dragan* that flew behind Conal and the blonde mane of the Dragonson.

When all was quiet, Conal spoke "I've been to the setting sun today, though many of my brothers-in-arms did not make it that far. They were slaughtered as they tried to claim their manhood." Conal threw his copper coin angrily to the ground at the High Priest's feet. "I came to the Gathering of the Clans in peace. I respected the ancient laws of the Brehon in order to claim my right to be recognised as a man. I know that normally the Rites of Manhood take a full quarter-moon to complete, but I haven't got the time to waste on such foolish protocol."

Conal paused a moment, sensing the anger of the crowd behind him. "This evening, I demand to be recognised as a man. What's more, I demand that all those who came here to compete be recognised as men. That way, they may find some peace in the Otherworld and feast in the Hall of Heroes. Could they deserve any less?" He glared defiantly at the High Priest, and the crowd roared their agreement. "I demand justice under the Brehon laws. Will you give me that justice, priest?"

The old man looked sadly at Conal and mirrored his own anger and pain. "You've done well, young *Dragan*, to complete the task that was assigned to you against all odds. By recognising your fallen comrades and speaking out for them, you speak with the voice of a man and not that of a petulant child."

The High Priest raised his voice, so that it carried far across the fairground. "Let it be forever recorded in the Annuls of history that *all* of the contestants in this year's games competed equally. All of them passed their Rites of Manhood and became men. They have become heroes, even. Tonight, we shall hold a wake for the fallen to pay them tribute. In the morning, we'll cremate their bodies at the sunrise and free their souls to fly into the Otherworld. There, they can indeed feast in the Hall of Heroes. May Lugh and the other gods greet them there and bless them."

The announcement went someway towards appeasing the anger of the crowd, but many still sought vengeance on the perpetrators of today's dark deed. Angry cries rose as clansmen bayed for the blood of the Boare.

The High Priest raised his arms again for silence. "I can assure you that the Brehons will investigate these atrocities, and anyone found guilty of these foul deeds will face the full rigours of our justice."

"The Boare is getting away while you prattle on about justice!" someone yelled from within the crowd. Others cried similar accusations.

Conal turned to the crowd and raised his arms high for silence. "Clansmen, Clansmen, listen to me!"

The crowd fell silent, wanting to hear what the young *Dragan* had to say. Knowing the animosity between the Dragons and the Boarites, many hoped that he would lead them in the pursuit of Lord Boare.

"Now is not the time to go Boare-hunting, much though he is well-fattened and ready for the spit!" Conal got a few half-hearted laughs for his wordplay. "We have more pressing matters to deal with. Despite the rage that boils in my blood, the pursuit of the treacherous Boare will have to wait. An army has invaded Dragania from *Tir Pect*. They march south while we stand here, plundering the lands before them as they come."

It was clear from the looks of surprise that many at the fair were unaware of the invasion. "Tomorrow, they will arrive at the gates of this very city, my city, and I for one will stand against them and deny them entry." Conal waited, letting the impact of his news settle over the gathering.

"I know that many of you are from the honoured and ancient Clans of the Pects, and I know that you traditionally hold allegiance with your cousins in *Tir Pect*. Other Clans may feel that it would be wiser to retire to their lands and avoid taking sides in the forthcoming confrontation. I know this and I understand it, but before you make your decisions, let me speak to you all for just a moment."

He paused and looked around at the faces before him. "My great-grandfather, *Luigheagh An Dragan*, believed in this country. He fought hard to gain peace amongst the Clans that live here. He signed a peace treaty between the tribes of the Pects and those of the *Fear Ban*. He believed that it was important ... nay essential, to unite all of the Clans in Dragania. I, like my forefathers before me, believe that too. We have always honoured the Great Truce. If the gods see fit, I will continue to do so. The future of Dragania is in our unity. We are different Clans and come from different tribes, this is true, but we need to respect and embrace those differences and learn to live together ... This is our land ... It doesn't belong to the greedy eyes of Lord Boare ... and it isn't a trophy to be claimed by *Tir Pect!* Tomorrow at dawn, I will fight for Dragania. If you choose to run south to the safety of your homes, I will bear you no ill will. Likewise, if you choose to sneak north in the night and join up with the northern Pects Clans, I will respect the Brehon laws, and you may leave in peace. Tomorrow, however, I will go to war, and I will show no mercy to any who support this invasion. So tonight I bid you all to go in peace and speak with your councillors. On the morrow, I will stand at the gates of Manquay and meet my destiny. Beside me, I would welcome my *Clann* brothers and anyone else who would fight for the unity of Dragania."

*****

Maerlin followed the High Priestess through the crowded street and out of the gates toward the fairground. In her wake there followed a long line of the sisters of the Order, and the crowd parted to let them pass. Maerlin had argued long and hard with Ceila, before finally agreeing to the compromise, but she still wanted to race ahead and confront Conal.

News of the slaughter only heightened Maerlin's urgency, but Ceila had been insistent. Priestesses did not rush. Doing so would only cause panic in the streets. They would walk calmly to the fairground, despite the dire news. Flying was clearly not an alternative that Ceila approved of, no matter how many times Maerlin attempted to browbeat her into acceptance. With gritted teeth, Maerlin followed the High Priestess.

Nessa had pointedly refused to leave Sir Gallaghad's side, and Madame Dunne had also chosen to remain behind. Someone had to protect the tavern against the looters that had started rioting in the streets.

The chaos had spread from the fairground and opportunists were using it to their own ends. That was, at least, until the Watch stepped in and brought some order to the city. A few examples had been made, and the looters' bodies now littered the gutters. The dead looters were left there as a reminders of the Watch's opinions on acts of anarchy.

The sun was setting, and Maerlin was sure that the Watch was going to be in for a restless night, as news of the coming invasion spread throughout the city. Thankfully, news of Dubhgall the Black's part in the invasion had been kept quiet and was on a need-to-know basis.

As the priestesses of the Order of Deana walked, they were joined by the priests and priestesses of the other Gods. It was critical to show a united response as they assisted the priests of Lugh and the Druidic Orders. They all would be needed to bring order to the fairground. With any luck, they may yet avoid a civil war. Maerlin knew that whatever chance she had of persuading Conal to relinquish his sword would become nonexistent if he was too busy swinging it at somebody's head.

*****

It had been a long day for Conal, and he was bone-weary as he sat eating a meal with his trusted advisors. Malachi was telling a hilarious and often raunchy tale about an incident with a she-goat and a minor woodland deity, much to everyone's amusement. Conal was too tired to follow the convoluted anecdote. Even his madcap impersonation of the drunken godling was lost on the Prince, whose heart ached over the day's losses. Although he didn't know any of the young men personally, he knew that they would have survived had they not been born on the same year as the

Dragonson. Their fate was sealed on the day Conal arrived at the spring fair. It didn't matter that the deed was perpetrated by others. The weight of their deaths still sat heavily on Conal's shoulders.

He took a sip of the heady Pectish mead and grimaced. For too long he had dreamed of the day when he could finally be considered as a man. Today that day had come, but at what cost. Pushing the goblet aside, he sat back and closed his eyes, trying to shut out the noise within the tent.

"Sire?" a voice whispered beside him, waking Conal from his slumber. He wasn't sure if he had slept for a moment, or for a bell. Conal looked around, noticing that his guests were still sitting around the brazier, chatting amiably. "What is it, Declan?"

"You have visitors, Sire."

"At this time of night ... you've got to be kidding me."

Conal looked at the concern on Declan's face and relented. "This is important I take it. Who is it, anyway?"

"It's the Orders, sire. They've come to speak to you."

"The Order ... which one?"

"It's all of them, Sire. The heads of the Seven Greater Gods are here, along with those of the Druidic Orders. There are others out there, too."

"Others?"

"Yes Sire. Most of the Clan Chiefs are there, as well as many of their clan folk."

"What do they want?"

"They've come to speak to you, Sire."

Conal looked down at his grime-encrusted tunic, still splattered with blood from the day's fighting. "Give me a moment, will you? Let me at least wash the blood off my hands and change my tunic. Tell them I'll be right out."

The Grand Marshall nodded and stepped toward the entrance. "Oh, and Conal..."

"Yes, Declan. What is it?"

"Maybe the green armour, Sire ... and the sword, too. It's always good to look one's best, when one is meeting important people."

Conal was about to protest but decided to trust Declan's judgement. Peeling off his grimy tunic, Conal poured water into a bowl and scrubbed his face and arms clean.

"Tal, give me a hand here, will you? We're about to have visitors."

His guests looked up from their tale, and a hush fell in the tent. The jester even went as far as to peek through the tent flap. "By the paps of Macha, he's not kidding! It looks like half of the city's out there! I hope they aren't here for a lynching, I'm too young to die!" Malachi grinned like a maniac.

"Don't stand in the doorway, gawking like a buffoon!" Sile chided, smoothing down her gown as she rose elegantly from her chaise lounge. "Come away from there, fool, before someone sees you!" How she had managed to find the couch was anyone's guess, let alone how she persuaded the guards to let her bring it into the Prince's tent. She was, as Cull had said, very resourceful.

"It's too late for that, Sile. I was definitely seen. They've got the place surrounded."

"I suppose we should be grateful that you didn't flash your fat behind at them, while you were at it!"

"I hadn't thought of that, Sile! Do ye think it would help to lighten the mood? I never did understand why you humans find the sight of naked buttocks so amusing."

"Forget it, fool! Sit down and quit your prattling." Sile looked down at her dress, inspecting it for stains or creases. "You really need to invest in a full-length mirror, Conal. I could procure one for you one at a very reasonable cost, if you'd like."

"Not a chance, Sile. I'd have to wait in line to get a look at it!" Conal pulled on a woollen under-garment and motioned for Taliesin to start passing him the *Ciudach* armour. A few moments later, after much

462

fastening of buckles, he added the sheathed *An Fiacail Dragan,* and finally his helm.

"How do I look?"

"You look ready to take on the world. I hope they haven't just come for a game of Toss or you'll certainly be overdressed."

Conal grinned and punched Taliesin playfully on the arm. "I wonder if we can have a bigger version of Malachi's outfit made up for you, Tal, if you're going to keep telling bad jokes. Well ... there's no putting this off. I guess I'd better go and see what they want."

"After you, Sire," Taliesin mocked, imitating the formality of the Grand Marshal.

Conal stretched his shoulders and straightened his back before walking out of the tent. Many torches had been lit around the area, and within their light he could see the faces of those who had gathered. His eyes scanned the crowd, noticing many familiar faces. Ceila stood with a group of women dressed in the ceremonial robes of the Order of Deanna. Behind her, he could see Maerlin and Cora. One lady stood out amongst the witches. She was dressed in a simple homespun woollen dress, and a hen harrier was perched regally on her shoulder: Seabhac. The High Priest of Lugh stood beside Ceila, his acolytes behind him. Conal also noted the leaders of the other Greater Orders. Each greeted him with a warm smile or a nod.

It was the three leaders of the Druidic Orders who stepped forward.

The Brehon Master spoke first, his deep voice carrying easily over the crowd. "Conal, son of the Dragon-lord, today the High Priest of Lugh declared you a man. As Brehon Master, it is my task to acknowledge this before all here this evening."

Conal nodded, unsure as to what to say. He had thought that the deed was already formalised by the High Priest's declaration.

Next, the Chief Druid spoke. "Conal, son of the Dragon-lord, you stand before the people of the Gathering and your words must be true to the honour of your ancestors. Do you understand?"

Conal nodded, but when the Druid continued to wait, he answered, "Yes ... yes, I do. I swear on my ancestors to speak the truth before all assembled here."

The Chief Druid nodded his approval. "Your Clan, the mighty Dragons, have lost their head. A Clan needs a leader to serve his people and keep them strong, a Lord who will protect the weak and punish the wrongdoers. He must defend against invasion and bring fertility to the land. He must be without blemish and a proven warrior. He must be wise, and just, and he must be honourable. He must be the heart of his people, so that through him they too can be strong. To seek such a position, a man needs to be all of these things and more. Do you, a youth who has only just reached manhood, honestly believe that you are such a man? In your heart of hearts ... can you truly say that there is no other, better suited for this task?"

Conal thought long and hard about the question. The Grand Marshal had ruled *Clann Na Dragan* well during his absence, and he was a fitting leader, but Declan had no desire to take up the mantle of kingship. He had made this abundantly clear to Conal. Above all else, one thing was certain to Conal. He believed that he was born to rule. He felt it deep within the core of his being. He knew that he would not find peace in a lesser position. Finally, Conal spoke up with confidence. "I swear to you all that in my heart of hearts, I know that there is no one better suited to take up this task. I am the son of the *Dragan*, the grandson of the *Dragan*, and the great-grandson of the *Dragan*, and dragon blood burns in my veins. I was born to rule the Dragon Clan, and I swear to do so to the best of my ability. I will make my ancestors proud."

"That is good, but nevertheless, we have our doubts. We cannot take the word of one so young at face value." The leader of the Druidic Order turned and addressed the gathered people "Are there any others here who wish to speak on the matter? If anyone wishes to speak, let them do so now?"

The crowd murmured and looked around. Finally, one man stepped forward. "I am Cathal, Head-warrior of *Clann Na Snochta Broce*, firstborn son of Sionna, Elder of *Clann Na Snochta Broce*, and I wish to speak."

The Chief Druid signalled for Cathal to proceed.

"This winter, I travelled to *Ard Pect* with some of my Clansmen. Conal *MacDragan* came along with us. On the way, we were attacked by a ferocious *Ciudach*. Not just any *Ciudach,* but a bull *Ciudach,* maddened beyond reason by Chorthium dust. Some of our warriors died that day, trying to defeat it. Others still recover from their wounds. Many more of my clansmen would have died had the *Dragan* Prince not attacked the *Ciudach* and killed the beast. It was this act of bravery that earned him the title: *Ciudachbane,* amongst my people. So I wish to speak up now and acknowledge his courage."

The Chief Druid spoke then "Thank you, Cathal, but courage alone does not make a king."

Declan stepped forward. "I am Declan Morganson, the Grand Marshal of *Clann Na Dragan*, and I've been the acting head of *Clann Na Dragan* since the passing of the last Dragon-lord. Many have spoken to me about continuing to lead the *Dragans*, but that is not my destiny. I would like to speak up for Conal. I have known him since he was a boy. I trained him in arms and taught him many of the skills of leadership. He is as fierce and brave as his title suggests, but he is more than that. I have seen his hard work and diligence. He made sure that his people were all fed and sheltered during the cold northern winter. He spent the Dragon coffers wisely and rebuilt the fortress of *Dun Dragan* on Dragon's Ridge, when others would have left it to rot. I know that in his heart he is always thinking of the good of his Clan, and because of this his people love and respect him. On behalf of the Dragons, I swear that he is the right man for the position, despite his youthful appearance."

The Chief Druid nodded. "Thank you, Declan, for your words of assurance."

Nightshade stepped forward nervously, clearly unused to speaking before so many people.

"Do you wish to speak?"

Nightshade nodded and looked around nervously before finally mustering his courage. "My name is *Fuath-Dubh,* and I'm a tracker of *Clann Na Seabhac*. I only met the *MacDragan* this morning, but I wish to speak on his behalf. Today, we began our Rites of Manhood along with many other young men. Unfamiliar with the area, I was unsure of the best way to complete the task that we had been set. It was then that I noticed Conal. He showed leadership where others only showed hesitation. So I followed him when he chose the path through the city. I thought I was being clever, but the *MacDragan* found me out and accosted me. We had words and finally agreed on a pact, a pact that as it turned out meant that I survived when so many others did not. I have no doubt that I owe the *MacDragan* my life, but that is not why I wish to speak out. On the way back from the mountain, at Conal's insistence, we stopped and gathered up as many of the fallen youths as we could find. This was done despite the urgent need to return and the danger of exposure. He refused to leave any of the candidates to the wolves and the carrion-birds." He stopped to look apologetically at the rake-thin High Priestess of Macha, "Begging your pardon, Ma'am!"

Her grin was wolf-like as she waved him to continue.

"When we arrived back at the fair, he spoke out for the fallen. He asked ... nay, he demanded that they be acknowledged as warriors, so that they could have peace and glory in the Otherworld. He could have easily claimed the glory for himself for surviving the trials when others had failed, but he did not. By winning honour for the fallen, he diminished his own esteem, and yet, he spoke up. For this I will always call him friend, and I also wish to speak on the *MacDragan's* behalf."

Ceila stepped forward and spoke with calm authority "I am Ceila Dream-catcher, the High Priestess of the Order of Deanna," she announced. "For many years now, I've been charged with protecting the young prince of the Dragons until such time as he reached his manhood and could stand before thee. It has not been an easy task, thou canst be sure. We on the Holy Isle tend to be secular to the world around us so that we may better focus on the service of our goddess. At times, we have been forced to take an active part in the politics of the day, and this was one such time. This task proved to be one of our greatest challenges. We of the Holy Isle are far dissimilar from the feisty Prince of the *Dragan*. I am sure that it was difficult for all concerned, and it took a lot of effort to survive the ordeal..."

Conal grinned at the priestess's diplomatic wording, remembering the raging arguments that they had over his conduct and her choice of guardians.

"Nevertheless, I firmly believe that we made the correct decision when we took on this task, and I do not regret it. I am a Dream-catcher, and I have foreseen many possible futures for Dragania. Some are dire beyond the utterance of mere words, and yet some hold the possibility of hope. I have foreseen Conal Dragonson as a key element in the success and growth of the Kingdom. His is a seed that needs to be nurtured and allowed to blossom to his full potential, not plucked as a weed and discarded to the midden. This was why our Order intervened, and why we will continue to intervene. I firmly believe that it is with Deanna's blessing that we do so. Her hand is ever in this matter. Therefore, I plead with thee, heed my words. Conal Dragonson is the rightful heir to the *Dragan* throne. In fact, he is more than that. He is the rightful heir to all of Dragania, and he should be the next High King."

Loud gasps came from the crowd. The issue this evening was not the election of a High King, but the election of a ruler for *Clann Na Dragan*. However, by speaking so boldly, the High Priestess had planted a seed in the minds of the various Clan leaders.

"I think we've heard enough," the Chief Druid declared and nodded to the Head Bard.

The Head Bard spoke up, his voice reaching far out into the darkness and silencing all of the gathering. "Conal Dragonson, kneel before the people assembled here so that they may witness your humility."

Conal knelt, all weariness gone and his heart in his throat.

"Do you swear upon your ancestors to serve and protect your Clan with courage, conviction, honour, and humility?"

"I do so swear upon the spirits of my ancestors."

"And do you swear to uphold and respect the ancient Brehon laws and abide by them?"

"I do so swear on the blood of my ancestors."

Cora stepped forward, holding a purple velvet cushion before her. On the cushion sat a crown of twisted gold, depicting two dragon heads at its tips. As she stopped before the kneeling Prince, Conal gazed in wonder at the Dragon Torc. He wondered who had been protecting it all this time.

"By the powers vested in us…" declared the Head Bard, and the Chief Druid and Brehon Master echoed his words as he continued "… As the three heads of the Druidic Order, we recognise you as the leader of *Clann*

Na Dragan. From this day forth, let all men know you as Conal Dragon-lord and *Ri Na Dragan.*"

The war-cry of the assembled Dragons rang out across the night, as the golden torc was placed upon Conal's helmeted head.

"Rise up and greet your people, Dragon-lord!"

"Dragan abú! Dragan abú!"

Conal stood and smiled at the gathered people, especially his own clan folk. Removing the crown, Conal took the torc in his hands and pulled at the two dragon heads, spreading them wider before slipping the torc around his neck in the ancient Pectish fashion. The *Fear Ban* had always worn their seals of office as crowns, but he had recently heard Taliesin say that the Pectish rulers wore them around their necks. Conal had thought this a good idea, and on a whim he had decided to emulate the custom. A crown was less likely to fall off in battle when worn that way. To the Pectish clansmen in the crowd, however, the gesture was more symbolic. Unbeknownst to Conal, this simple gesture would help him to further unite the Clans of Dragania.

*****

The war-cry of the Dragons filled the night, echoing off the walls of the city and rolling out across the open plain. Sitting by their campfires, far out on the grassland, the combined armies of *Tir Pect* heard the roar and wondered at its significance.

Chapter Thirty-Nine: Betrayal

The festivities that night were a mixture of a wake for the fallen heroes and a celebration of the newly-crowned Dragon-lord. With the horrors of the previous day and the pending confrontation in the morning, people needed a little merriment, so casks of ale and mead were broken open and drink was consumed in abundance. Conal, despite his tiredness, was the centre of the celebrations. Before long, he was light-headed from the strong beverages and unsteady on his feet. Stumbling and nearly falling off the table on which he had been dancing with Cora, he roared at the moon *"Dragan abú! DRAGAN ABÚ!"*

The roar was taken up by the crowd around him, many of whom were his own kinsmen. It echoed across the plains.

Cora helped him down before he fell. Both of them were in fits of laughter and well the worse for drink. "Come along, your Majesty," she laughed, removing a freshly-filled tankard of ale from his hand. "I think you've had enough of that for the one evening, don't you?"

"Awww, Cora!" Laying his arm around her shoulder, he leaned against her to steady himself, "...Jusshtt one more, Princessh!"

With a sigh she relented. "Very well, but let's get you into bed first, shall we? If you fall over now, you'll drag me down with you and ruin my dress."

"And it's such a pretty dresshh too!"

He allowed Cora to guide him toward his tent, clutching the tankard firmly in the other hand. "Shall we sing a song together, Princesshh?"

"Oh, no, I don't think that'd be a good idea, your Majesty." Cora giggled as she plonked him down on the bed and sat down beside him to catch her breath. "Sad though it is to break this news to you, Conal, but you'll never make it as a bard!"

"Oh! Oh! I'm wounded. That cut me to the quick! Don't you love me, Cora?" he asked, looking at her with forlorn puppy-dog eyes.

Cora felt herself getting lost in the deep blue of his eyes and answered honestly. "Of course I do, silly ... just not your singing!"

*****

"Maerlin! Maerlin!"

Maerlin turned around, trying to find who was calling her amongst the madness of the celebrations.

"Maerlin!" the shout came again, and this time she spotted the caller. Waving, Maerlin forced her way through the crowd. "Hello, Auntie Millie, how's it going?"

"You haven't heard, I see!"

"Heard ... heard what?"

Auntie Millie had worry lines etched into her already-weathered face. "It's my nephew. He's disappeared."

"Who ... Duncan? What do you mean ... disappeared?"

"He went out with the other lads this morning. He was competing in the trials, Maerlin, but he never came back. His poor mamma's worried sick."

Maerlin had seen the awful rows of young men, laid out on tables, wrapped and ready for their cremation in the morning. She wondered if Duncan Gammit was amongst the dead. She had not looked that closely.

"Are you sure he didn't just run off on one of his pranks, Millie? You know what he's like."

"We've checked everywhere, Maerlin. The last he was seen, he was heading toward the bridge. No one has seen him since. This was too important to him to go running off. He was biting at the bit to get his manhood. He's changed over these last six months. He's grown up. Megan, the miller's daughter, and himself, they were going steady. There was talk of him going to work at the mill once he'd completed his trials. He'd got her father's blessing and everything. He wouldn't have messed it all up just for a bit of fun. He's not the same lad that he used to be, believe me."

Maerlin had to admit that Duncan Gammit had changed. Over the last month, he'd shown himself to be a hard worker, and they'd managed to put their past differences behind them. The news of his expected matrimony was a revelation to her, however. Hating herself for mentioning it, she asked "Millie, have you ... has anyone looked in the big marquee?"

The fallen youths had all been laid out in the marquee. It was the only space large enough to hold them all. The priests were busy even now with the pre-cremation rituals.

Millie laid a hand on Maerlin's shoulder. "Aye, Maerlin, I did that myself. You couldn't ask a mother to go into that place. It'd break her poor heart to see all of those young men. Sweet Deanna, I searched every face in that place, and there was no sign of him. Some other boys from High Peaks were amongst the dead, but Duncan wasn't."

"Then, where can he be?" Maerlin asked. Realisation hit her like a knife in the stomach. "Oh no!"

"What is it, Maerlin?"

"The Reavers! I heard someone mention a Dragonship heading downriver. They must have taken him!"

"By the Seven!"

"Don't worry, Millie, I'll get him back, I promise you, even if I have to fly to the Icy Wastes and hunt down his kidnappers. I'll find him and I'll bring him home. Do you hear me?"

Maerlin looked around. She needed help and fast. With each passing bell, the Reavers would be farther away. "I'll be back as soon as I can, Millie. I've got to go and find some help."

Maerlin headed into the heart of the revelry where she had last seen Cora, dancing with the newly-elected King of the *Dragans*. She was sure that she'd be able to find help there. Cull would be there, as well as Vort, and the other companions. Between them, they would know more about the day's events than she did, and they'd be able to advise her.

Ultimately, she would need to catch the pirate ship before it reached the sea, and that meant flying. Ceila, like Nessa, didn't approve of flagrant acts of magic, but on the morrow the priestesses were going to face Dubhgall the Black in battle. A little flying seemed tiny by comparison. Maerlin needed help, however. She needed Cora and Seabhac above all, and she needed them right now.

Maerlin forced her way through the throng of people and spotted Taliesin, sitting by the fire. With him were a raven-haired beauty and an ugly-looking midget in a jester costume.

"Tal! Where's Cora?"

"How'ya, Maerlin!" Taliesin greeted cheerfully, attempting to get to his feet and failing miserably. "Maerlin, come and have a drink with us. Let's celebrate Conal's coronation. But firshht, allow me to introdush ..."

"I haven't got time for this, Tal! Where's Cora?"

"Cora, Cora, how we all adore her!" the jester sung, off-key. Taliesin laughed and took up the tune.

Maerlin fervently wished that her magic could do something useful right now, like turn him into a toad. She briefly considered sending a salamander down his trousers, but she really didn't have the time to torture the information out of the bard. Grasping hold of his tunic, she shook him roughly. "Taliesin, where's Cora? I need her, right now!"

The raven-headed woman beside them tried to speak "That really isn't ..."

Maerlin glared at her. "Do you know where she is?" Biting back her impatience, she added "...please. It's important?"

"She's in there," Sile indicated Conal's tent with a nod of her head, "but you might want to ..."

Maerlin released Taliesin, who fell to the ground, too drunk to hold himself upright. With a nod of gratitude, Maerlin marched towards the tent.

"Wait!" she heard the woman call out, but Maerlin was in too much of a hurry.

"Cora," Maerlin yelled, as she grasped the tent flap. Hearing giggling within, she pulled the canvas aside and called again "Cora ..."

Maerlin stopped dead in her tracks, and the blood drained from her face. The naked back she saw before her and the flowing red hair, she knew intimately. They had stopped at the sound of her intrusion, and the giggling died as Cora looked around and noticed Maerlin for the first time.

Cora gasped in surprise "Maerlin!"

"Maerlin?" a second voice asked. She knew that voice, too. Conal's dishevelled head popped up from behind Cora's naked shoulder.

Maerlin was too shocked to say anything as Cora reached for her discarded robe.

"Maerlin, it's not ..." Cora tried to explain, but Maerlin had already fled. "Maerlin, wait!"

Maerlin had no intention of waiting. She ran through the crowd as fast as she could. She was barely able to see through the tears that clouded her vision.

*****

It was Seabhac who found her, shortly before dawn. She was sitting on a haystack at the rear of the *Uisce Beatha.* "Maerlin?"

"Leave me alone."

Seabhac sighed and climbed up the side of the stack as gracefully as her old legs would allow. Panting from the exertion, she plopped herself down beside Maerlin. "I heard what happened. I'm sorry, Maerlin."

"I don't want to talk about it."

They sat in silence, watching the sky turn pink with the first promise of dawn. "Maerlin, I said that I'd tell thee about my life, about the promise I made to Sygvaldr, and why I didn't take him up on his offer."

"Now ... you want to talk about this now?" Maerlin grumbled, preferring to wallow in self-pity.

"I think it has some relevance to thy current predicament, so yes. Now is a good time."

"Do we have to?"

Seabhac ignored her. "The bard, Taliesin, tells a good tale ..." she began, "but he, like everyone else, knows only a fraction of what really happened on that journey. *Luigheagh MacTorc,* Conal's great-grandfather, was like many of his Clan before him, a stubborn, pig-headed individual. But for all that, he was a born leader."

"Hang on a moment ... did you just say *Luigheagh MacTorc ...?* "

"I thought that might get thy attention. Yes, *Luigheagh MacTorc.*"

"But doesn't that mean ...?"

"Oh yes, Luigheagh was a Boare! It was one of the reasons why he chose a new animal totem for his Clan after the Battle of the High Kings. Luigheagh thought it was important to have separation from his southern cousins, after slaying his own uncle and stealing his throne."

"But that's not what we've been taught?"

Seabhac laughed heartily. "Maerlin, thou still hast a lot to learn about storytellers. They're all mercenary wordsmiths, and they'll sell their tongues to the highest bidder. The High King controlled the royal coffers and, therefore, he controlled the truth. History is always written by the victorious."

"Does Conal know this?" Maerlin remembered Conal's hatred for all things Boarite.

"I doubt it. Knowing Luigheagh, he'd have had the annals of history rewritten before the blood had a chance to soak into the grass. He was far from stupid, even for a Hinterlander. I doubt even Luigheagh's own son knew about it. Perhaps that was one of the reasons why he married that princess from the Western Isles in the first place. She was very naive and very pretty, in a vacant sort of way. I doubt she could write her own name, let alone read a manuscript. She was also besotted with Luigheagh, and bent over backward to his every whim."

"You didn't like her, I take it?"

"Oh, far from it, we were the best of friends. At least that is, until I found Luigheagh in her bed. That sort of dampened our sisterly bonding somewhat."

"Oh, Seabhac, I'm sorry," Maerlin said, keenly aware of the duality of the story.

"It was nothing, really. It was all over anyway, long before then, but that was the final straw, and it gave me the impetus I needed to leave *Dun Dragan*. I'd been putting it off for far too long, foolishly hoping that Luigheagh would come around ... but we're getting off the point here. I want to explain to you about Sygvaldr. As I was saying, the bards know little of what actually happened. It was Luigheagh who suggested that we keep the whole thing a secret."

"Why was that?"

"It started on the journey east, during one of our heated rows. We had quite a few of those. I can't remember what it was about exactly, it was just another silly argument, I guess. Anyway, we were standing, right in each other's face, bawling each other out like a pair of lunatics. We were saying nasty things which neither of us really meant, when all of a sudden we started kissing ... One thing led to another..."

"Sygvaldr said something about that. So you and Luigheagh were lovers."

Seabhac nodded. "Yes, we were. So you see, I couldn't accept the Dragon's offer of marriage, even if I'd wanted to. I'd already lost my maidenhead. I knew how sacred the Dragonkind regard such things. Anyway, I foolishly believed that Luigheagh would marry me."

"Was that why he wanted to keep the journey a secret?"

"Probably ... possibly ... I don't really know. I thought he loved me. By the Seven, I was such a stupid young girl at the time. Anyway, I had to help the Prince win the High Kingship, so I suggested the whole 'marriage to the daughter of my blood' thing to Sygvaldr, and he lapped it up. I was a Priestess of Deanna, Maerlin, and we knew ways to stop unwanted pregnancies, so I thought it was safe to offer him something that was never going to happen, and as I said, Luigheagh needed my help. He needed to bring something back to his Clan."

"But *An Fiacail Dragan* was never supposed to be a sword. Didn't you know that?"

"Of course, we knew. By Deanna, he could have brought back an icicle for all that it mattered. It wasn't the tooth itself that was important, it was the symbolism. A young prince, journeying far on a quest for a magical item in order to win over the throne! By the Dagda's ripened plums! What poet wouldn't sing about such a tale? Luigheagh had won the hearts and minds of the people long before the first war-cry was sounded. By that time, Lord Boare was as mad as a rabid dog, and he was already convinced of his own doom. The man could hardly tie his own boot laces anymore, he was that far gone! All Luigheagh had to do was get close enough to run the old dribbler through. Although, as it turned out, the Boare did manage to put up a bit of a fight in the end."

"So what happened between you and Luigheagh?"

"I've asked myself that same question many times, and I've yet to come up with a good answer. He told me on the way home that we should keep our affair a secret until his throne was secured. Once he'd won over the other Clans, he could choose whoever he liked as his Queen without creating a public scandal.

"Why, I don't understand? You helped defeat Lord Boare."

"Maerlin, don't be so naïve! We're talking about politics here, and remember, this was a long time ago when the Pects and the *Fear Ban* were constantly at each other's throat. This was before the Great Truce with *Clann Na Broce*, and the first tentative steps toward peace between the two tribes."

"Seabhac, I still don't understand?"

"I was a Hawk, Maerlin; a *Pect* from *Clann Na Seabhac*. The High King couldn't choose a Pect to be his Queen. There would've been rioting in the streets."

"But was he still planning to marry you?"

"So he had me believe while we were travelling, but when he got back to the *Dun,* something happened. He started acting strange, distant even. At first, I thought it was all part of the plan, a ruse to keep people from guessing about us, so I played along. We only slept together one more

476

time after that. It was on the eve of the Battle of the High Kings. That was when he gave me the pendant, the one that you now wear."

Maerlin touched the silver merlin absently and remembered the dream that she had had of Uiscallan and Luigheagh's heated lovemaking. Except ... it wasn't Luigheagh that Maerlin had seen leaving the tent. It was Dubhgall the Black. "Damn it! Seabhac ..."

"Hang on, Maerlin. I've nearly done. This is only the second time I've ever told anyone about this, so be quiet and let me finish ..." Seabhac insisted. "After a moon or more, I started to get sick. I knew what it was, of course, but I was silly enough to still hold out some hope. I kept the pregnancy a secret, even from Luigheagh, though by then we hardly spoke to each other. The right time to tell him never arose. By the time I'd realised my predicament, it was already too late. Luigheagh had announced his intention to marry the Princess. By then, I was too far gone to stop the pregnancy. I could already feel the child moving inside me. I was an emotional wreck, Maerlin, so I did the only thing I could think of. I ran away and hid in the mountains. If it wasn't for Fintan, I'd probably have lost her during childbirth. That would have been the end of the dragon legacy, but he chanced along and saved us both. Maerlin ... thou art probably better off without the Dragon-lord or the Princess for that matter. They may have always been destined for each other. History has a wicked way of repeating itself."

"Seabhac, listen to me! I'm sorry, but I should've mentioned this sooner ... I forgot all about it!"

"Forgot what, Maerlin?"

"Luigheagh wasn't the father of your child ... Dubhgall was."

"What on earth art thou talking about? Don't be absurd!"

Maerlin told her all about the Dream-catching. After all that Uiscallan had been through, she deserved to know the truth.

Chapter Forty: The Reavers

They walked in a silent procession from the fairground to a small hillock nearby. Here, a huge windrow of dry timber stood waiting. The sky was blossoming pink with the coming dawn and the promise of fair weather as the priests of Lugh led the way. They were followed by the leaders of the six other Orders. Behind them came the people of the Gathering.

"Have you seen Maerlin?" Cora hissed.

Ester looked sternly at the novice, before relenting. "No, I'm sorry."

"What about Nessa?"

"She refused to leave that magpie's side. Anyone would think it was human, the way she's going on!"

"Is Sir Gallaghad alright?"

"He'll be fine. From the look of it, he'll be as right as rain. He lost a lot of blood, but he'll pull through. He's already showing signs of improvement."

Cora was relieved. She had always liked the little magpie. "What about Seabhac? Why isn't she here?"

"No one's seen her, either. They've both vanished. Without them, we could end up with some real trouble on our hands, even with the support of the other Orders. We need a figurehead to fight behind, and Uiscallan would have been ideal. If Uiscallan isn't here, then Maerlin would be the next best thing. She might be young, but no one can deny her power. I wouldn't like to be in her bad books ..." Ester declared, then seeing Cora's crestfallen face, she added "... I mean ... oh, never mind!"

The bodies were reverently placed onto the long pyre, and the priests chanted to their god as they watched the sun crest the horizon. Soon, the funeral pyre was ablaze, and smoke billowed up into the dawn skyline. The gathered crowd stood for a few moments in silence, waiting for the fires to collapse in a shower of sparks and the bodies of the fallen heroes to be consumed by the flames. The priests and priestesses of the Seven Orders pooled a small amount of their magical energies to encourage more heat into the pyre. Finally it was done, and the gathering broke up. They headed back to their camps to pack up their possessions, and prepare for the coming day. Some prepared for battle, while others prepared to flee.

*****

"You can't seriously want to meet them out on the open plain, Sire," Declan protested.

"That's exactly what I'm suggesting we do, Grand Marshal."

"But wouldn't it be safer to fight them from behind the city walls? They were built for just such a purpose, after all. The Pects haven't the troops or the equipment to attack the city. They'll know this."

"Your reasoning is sound, Declan, but you're forgetting two things. Firstly, my first act as Dragon-lord cannot be to hide behind walls as if I'm afraid. Secondly, we can't afford to be locked in a protracted siege. We need a show of strength if we're going to get the backing of the other Clans."

"But what about their chariots, Sire? The Pects love to go to war on them, and you're suggesting a battlefield that's ideal for them. They'll decimate your troops if they're allowed to use those chariots. Behind the walls, their chariots are useless."

"Then we'll have to find another way to defeat their chariots, Declan, but we can't fight this battle from behind the city walls. Is that clear?" Conal ordered. He was too tired and irritable to continue the discussion.

The Grand Marshal bit back his response and nodded his head. "It will be as you wish, Sire."

Hoping to appease Declan, Conal added "We can dig pits and line them with stakes. Build an embankment outside the city and make the Pects come to us on foot. We can still win this, Declan, without it becoming a siege."

*****

The combined armies of *Tir Pect* were camped a few miles north of Manquay. Few of the *Pectish* warriors had slept well. They had listened to the war-cries echoing across the land, long into the night, and then, as they had prepared their breakfasts, a bright flame lit up the horizon. As the sun god brightened the sky, they could clearly see the smoke ahead.

"What, in the Nine Hells, are they playing at?" Queen Medb demanded, looking at the pillar of smoke.

"I haven't the foggiest idea, Medb, but I'm sure we'll find out, soon enough," Conchubhar grumbled. He could see the tension in his wife's eyes and sensed her hunger for battle. He looked out across his army and wondered if he would have enough warriors to win the day. His ancestors were looking down upon him and failure would bring a heavy toll. Stretching his broad shoulders, he raised his fist high into the air and signalled to the army. Horses snorted and harnesses creaked as the war-chariots rumbled forward. The wind was blowing lightly from the west, barely ruffling the grassland. It was a peaceful morning, a mockery of the day's future. Birds were happily singing, and the occasional startled grouse burst up before the army, squawking its protest at the disturbance.

"Spread out!" he commanded "Battle formation! Let's not have any surprises." The chariots fanned out on his command, forming a single long wall of bladed death. Scouts rode ahead and flanked the marching army on sturdy mountain ponies, while to the rear, jogged the warriors on foot. No two warriors looked alike. They carried a diverse range of weaponry and armour, a myriad variety of shields and multi-coloured banners depicting the various Clans of *Tir Pect*. In truth, they were not an army, they were a rabble of half-drunk warriors, but they were no less dangerous for their lack of crisp, military discipline. Like the Pectish clansmen who dwelt within Dragania, they were feared for their ferocity.

In the forefront of these warriors was the large group that marched directly behind Medb's chariot. These were her Bears: the warriors of *Clann Na Béar*. These warriors were big-boned and heavyset for Pects, with some of them equal in height to the *Fear Ban*. Renowned for their berserk rage, these men and women were Queen Medb's pride and joy and the backbone of the Pectish army. They were the steel gauntlet which would tenderise the opposition. Next to them ran Conchubhar's Wolves of *Clann Na MacTire*. Smaller and leaner than their burly cousins, they were no less deadly. With quick reflexes and wiry strength, they were famed for their stamina and cunning. Where the Bears fought as brave individuals, the Wolves fought as a pack. They did not engage in one-on-one combat in the traditional Pectish style. They fought as a combined fighting mind, working in unison. They regularly hunted *Ciudach* in their mountain homeland, working cohesively to whittle away at the beast until it was overcome. *Ciudach* hunting was a long and exhausting challenge, but one in which the warriors of *Clann Na MacTire* excelled. Other less important Clans took the periphery of the marching army. These were followed by the supply wagons and a solitary coach, which held Dubhgall's group of hedge-wizards.

*****

Conal led the disciplined soldiers of *Clann Na Dragan* to the northern wall of the city and stopped by the roadside. There, they looked out at the dark shadow on the distant horizon. "They're coming."

Conal looked back at his own small force. Beside him stood Declan's Dragon-scales and the rest of *Clann Na Dragan*. They had been joined by the sleek horses of the *Clann Na Copall*: the Horse Clan. Always a loyal neighbour to the Dragon Clan, they were the best light cavalry in Dragania. Their horses were taller than the native Pectish ponies, but still had enough of the ponies' breeding in them to make them tough and durable. They carried composite bows, as well as lances, short swords, and bucklers. On open grassland, running at full gallop, they could be devastating.

Vort and many of his Brocians had also stayed. They were helping to dig a long trench in front of the city walls, piling the earth on the southern side to create an embankment. The priestesses of Deanna were nestled under the shadow of the city wall behind Ceila, while the other Orders had taken up positions along the ramparts above.

They were a good force, but they were too few and Conal knew it. His scouts had reported the size of the *Tir Pect* army, and even at a glance, he knew that he was outnumbered. He would have to tip the scales in his favour by whatever means possible. It was time to pull out some of Cull's devious tricks. The pre-dawn discussions would now come into fruition.

He looked out across his chosen battlefield. On his western side, the ground was rough scrubland, covered in bushes. The city had been built on the very toes of the mountain range. Queen Medb's legendary chariots would not be charging from that direction, at least. Their wheels would shatter on the stony ground, even if they could make it through the shrubbery with any momentum. It wasn't even suitable for cavalry, let alone chariots. Vort had assured him that some of his Brocians were hiding in the thickets, ready to ambush any infantry foolish enough to

482

assault from that front. Perhaps that was why so few of the Brocians were visible. He knew the preferred warfare of *Clann Na Broce* and standing on an open plain in broad daylight was certainly not their chosen form of combat, despite their undoubted bravery. Conal recognised that they, like the other Pectish Clans of Dragania, would have some difficulties with today's confrontation. Their allegiances were, at best, divided. Many, he knew, would choose to abstain from the field of battle.

"Conal, have your men move away from the ditch. They'll be all day like that."

The Dragon-lord looked around at the group of priestesses who had come forward. Leading them was a striking woman with piebald hair. She had a bedraggled magpie perched on her shoulder. For some reason, despite its evident injuries, the creature looked positively smug, if such a thing was possible.

"Are you deaf, Conal, or are you still addled with drink?" Suddenly, he recognised the voice. Cora had mentioned something about this yesterday, but he'd been too drunk to take much notice.

"Nessa, is that you?"

"Of course it's me, but we haven't got all day for idle chatter. After last night's fiasco, that might be just as well! Now, get your soldiers out of that ditch."

Conal flushed and hurried to obey. Clearly, his coronation meant nothing to the likes of Nessa *MacTire*, but that was no surprise. He wondered if anyone in the city had not heard about his fling last night. Shaking his head, he spoke to the Grand Marshal. "You heard the lady, Declan; get those men out of the ditch."

It wasn't long before the earth was pouring forth at an astounding rate as the Earth-sisters of Deanna worked their magic. As the men hurried to set sharpened stakes into the newly-made trench, other priestesses summoned fire to scorch and harden the tips of the stakes. Conal watched in amazement, as his fortification sprang into existence. Smoke drifted lightly across the battlefield when the priestesses burned the stakes, and Conal recalled the funeral pyre and all of the fallen youths. Would this be his day to die, too? Would he receive a decent burial? Shaking the doubts from his mind, he marched over to Vort.

"It's a fine morning for a battle," Vort greeted enthusiastically. Conal had to admit that it was a wonderful spring day, but his pleasure was tarnished by the expectation of the day's events.

"Aye, I guess. Vort, I wonder whether you can help me. I've just had an idea."

"Sure thing, what is it?"

"You said that you had some warriors hiding in that scrubland. I was wondering if they could clear some of it for me."

"Clear it? This isn't the best time for landscaping, Conal. Why would they want them to do that?"

"One of the things that Cull taught me was to know my battlefield. I grew up in this city, so I know how rocky the ground is under those shrubs. I'm betting my life on it that Medb's charioteers don't. With a bit of luck, some of them will be stupid enough to try charging across it."

"That's a possibility, I guess."

"It is, especially if you use a lure to sweeten the trap."

"I like your thinking, Conal. Leave it with me. I'll go and track down Cathal's *Broce Snochta*. What were you thinking of using as bait?

"I hadn't got that far yet ... why?"

"I'd use archers. Charioteers *hate* archers. It's sure to get their attention. Oh, and perhaps it'd be better to leave that area without a pit. Make it look as if you didn't have time to finish it. I'd leave a pile of dirt and a couple of shovels sticking out of the end. That'd be sure to catch their attention."

Conal grinned. "I'll get right on it ... oh, and Vort ... have them pile the brush up in a long windrow on the western edge. That should discourage them from sneaking around our flank."

"Consider it done."

"... Oh, and Vort!"

Vort looked back.

"... Thanks again ... for everything."

The Brocian grinned and trotted off into the shrubbery. In no time at all, the gentle slope was being swept clean, leaving only the rough grass behind. Conal was surprised at the number of Brocians working there. There were far more than he had expected, but even with them, he was still outnumbered. Turning away, he hurried over to the Earth-sisters before they could complete the trench. The shadow in the distance had grown, and he could now make out the figures of men and horse within the dense mass.

*****

The gates creaked open, and from within its dark shadows emerged two finely-crafted war-chariots. *Sile Ceathrar-Cioch* drove the one that she had recently stolen from Queen Medb. She was dressed in her green leather armour. As always, she looked magnificent. By her side stood the jester, Malachi, dressed in the traditional motley costume of his trade. With none of Sile's grace, he clung nervously to the wickerwork frame. The other chariot was Conal's, and it was being driven by Cull. They stopped a few yards from the gate, and Conal walked over to join them.

"Good morning," Cull greeted.

"Morning, Cull. What are these for?"

"They'll be needed during the negotiations, of course," Cull explained.

"What negotiations?"

"Conal! There's always a parley before battle. It's a tradition. You need to issue your terms of surrender and reject theirs. I thought you knew that?"

"But what's the point? They didn't come all the way here just to head back home again without a fight, and I'm certainly not considering surrender."

Cull sighed. "There's always a small chance that we can avoid all-out war. Even the slightest chance is better than none. Anyway, if it doesn't work, you'll still have the chance to put Medb's nose out of joint. She'll be furious when she sees her beloved chariot in your hands."

"My hands, but that's Sile's chariot?"

"Not today it isn't, lad. Today, you'll ride in the Queen's chariot. Sile and Malachi will use yours."

Conal looked confused. "And why's that ... this isn't their war?"

"They've both come a long way and risked an awful lot for the chance of avoiding bloodshed today. The least we can do is let them be impartial witnesses during this parley."

"Oh, I see!" Conal replied, though clearly he didn't.

"Just in case the parley doesn't work, I've also brought you some reinforcements," Cull informed. On his signal, people started to pour out of the city, poor people dressed in rags and armed with kitchen knives and makeshift clubs. Some were street urchins and others were dockside harlots.

"Cull, who are these people?"

"These are your clansmen, Conal," Cull advised with deep sincerity. "They are the poor of Manquay, the hungry, and the destitute. They are the sick and the orphaned. They are the underworld and the dregs of your city, but they are, all of them, Dragons. Manquay is your city, despite your ancestors' habit of ignoring it, preferring the cleaner air of *Dun Dragan*. They might be unwashed and starving, but they have chosen to come here and fight ... for you. Much though your ancestors have failed in their responsibilities, these people will still help you in your time of need. They are still loyal to *Clann Na Dragan*. They haven't forgotten who they are!"

Conal was humbled by their gesture. "But they have no armour ... no training in warfare, nothing. By the Dagda, many of them haven't even got weapons. They'll be slaughtered if the *Tir Pect*s get their hands on them. Cull, you can't ask me to use these people. It'd be a massacre."

Cull's face hardened and he grabbed Conal's cuirass. "Listen to me, boy. The only thing standing between these people's homes and that army out there is you! Do you think that they'll survive, if you lose today? They're *Fear Ban* and those that aren't are half-bred bastard sons and daughters of *Fear Ban*. They have as much right to defend their homeland as you do, so use them, for crying out loud! Did I teach you nothing, lad? Look around you, Conal. You're outnumbered. They might not look like much to you, but they're your best hope of winning today. Don't let their dishevelled appearance fool you. I taught you better than that. They've known pain and suffering every day of their lives. When the going gets tough and your pretty little boy-soldiers think about running, these people will be standing and fighting to the bitter end. They've nothing to gain by running and nowhere to go, so they'll fight like cornered rats. *Use them* ... and by the Seven, you'd better remember their sacrifice when this is all over!"

Conal had never seen Cull so passionate before. Seeing the Dragon-scales' threatening stance around him, Conal signalled to them to stand down, as he gently removed Cull's fist from his cuirass. "You're right, of course. I meant no disrespect. I'll take all the help I can get at the moment, and it's much appreciated, Cull, but how am I going to use them?"

Cull looked around as he considered his answer. "Form up your infantry units now, before the Pectish scouts get any closer. Form them four ranks deep, and then use the rest of your men to create the sides of your phalanxes. Fill the centre of each phalanx with some of my people. That way, they can benefit from the armoured warriors around them, and they'll give the illusion of you having a bigger force than you actually have. If you have any spare helmets, shields, or spears, now is the time to break them out. They'll be no use to you tomorrow."

"I guess it's worth a try. I'll get right on it. Can you organise them for me? Have the strongest stay here and join the phalanxes, and put the weaker ones on the parapets with the magicians. If nothing else, they can make a lot of noise. I pray that it won't come to using children to fight my wars for me."

Horns were blown to signal the troops to form up, and bellowed commands had the well-drilled troops form into three strong phalanxes of infantry. They stretched from one end of the city wall to the other. Conal placed the Horse Clan on his right flank and a strong contingent of archers on his left. Another rank of bowmen stood behind his infantry. More of Cull's raggle-taggle army were interspersed between and behind the priestesses of Deanna. Conal was ready, or at least, as ready as he was ever going to be. Climbing onto Queen Medb's chariot, he looked at the imposing-looking army at his back, standing in the shadows of the city walls. They made an impressive sight.

Gazing out across the grassy plain, he compared his force with that of *Tir Pect*. He could see the long row of war-chariots clearly now, their scythe-blades shimmering in the sunlight. With the morning sun behind him, Conal had an advantage. His archers would not have to fire their arrows into the glare of the sun and, therefore, their bows would be far more accurate. The Pects would have to shade their eyes or squint to see through the glare. With the solid walls behind him, he would only have to worry about his two flanks. The spiked pit before his army limited his manoeuvrability, but it was well worth the cost. It cancelled out the effectiveness of the devastating Pectish war-chariots, and it would be hard for the Pectish warriors to cross with any momentum.

There was nothing left to do but wait...

*****

Fintan led the way, his hawk eyes missing nothing as they flew downriver. Maerlin and Seabhac followed, scouring the river banks. They were hunting for Dragonships, hoping to find Duncan Gammit amongst the captured youths that had survived the slaughter and now faced an unknown future in slavery. Occasionally, they slowed and swooped down to inspect a riverboat or seafarer, but so far, they had been unsuccessful.

Fintan screeched overhead, and they followed his gaze. The craft below looked promising. It had the distinctive square sail and narrow hull. This was no flat-bottomed river boat. It was one of the infamous Dragonships of the Northmen: a Reaver ship, feared throughout the land. Its sleek design was built for speed, and its strong structure was crafted to withstand the worst of the stormy Bitter Eastern Sea. Its striped sail was fully unfurled to catch as much of the light breeze as possible and speed it through the sluggish waters. They were close to the Great Marsh, and the choppy waters farther upstream had slowed significantly as the River Man widened and filtered into the fenlands.

They flew overhead, and Maerlin could see people manacled to the decking, but they were too close together to make out individual faces. Whoever the unfortunate captives were, they were certainly prisoners and Maerlin was in no mood to be polite.

"First things first ... let's get their attention, shall we?" Maerlin muttered to herself as she channelled some of the raw emotions that coursed through her body. "Burn, my sweet salamanders!" she commanded and released some Fire Elementals to do her bidding. The small flame flew from her palm, and it grew and grew as it raced toward the Dragonship. A fireball hurtled into the single sail and consumed it within moments. The salamanders hungrily ate through the last of the striped canvas and began eating the hemp roping of the rigging with ravenous greed. Soon, they would eat their way into the mast.

Remembering Captain Bohan's colourful phraseology, Maerlin hovered near the ship and bellowed out "Heave to, ya scurvy dogs!"

A half-hearted volley of arrows came in response, but Seabhac quickly deflected the shots into the murky river.

"You really shouldn't have done that," Maerlin growled through gritted teeth.

She'd had enough to deal with this week with stomach cramps, nausea, and headaches. That was to say nothing of finding her best friends in bed together. She was in no mood for people firing arrows at her. Summoning Air Elementals, she created a force wall and sent out the Sylphs. They blasted across the deck and pushed a few of the armoured warriors into the sluggish water. The giant leeches were quick to take advantage of the swimmers in the sluggish waters and attacked the fallen. The water broiled into motion around the victims.

Maerlin waited until the last blood-curdling screams had been swallowed up before she shouted again "Heave to, I said! This is your last warning! Heave to or you'll all be taking a bath with the leeches."

The huge Reaver who controlled the rudder pulled hard on the wooden handle, forcing the ship away from the main river current and into shallower waters. Maerlin aided him with a little magical assistance, and the ship hit the riverbank with a ground-shaking shudder.

"Release your prisoners..." Maerlin ordered, as the crew climbed back to their feet, "Do it now!"

"Mayhaps ve should kill dem all instead, eh, vitch?" The Reaver captain grabbed the nearest captive by his hair and pulled him up, sword poised to strike.

Thunder rumbled loudly overhead and the air filled with the scent of ozone.

"I haven't got time for this nonsense," Maerlin growled. She moved her staff closer so she could leap onto the deck.

Her hair stood on end and hissed with electrical charge as she marched up to the Reaver captain. He was nearly twice her size and heavily muscled, but her fearless stare gave him pause, and his sword hovered in mid-air. Standing inches away from him, her nostrils flared at the heavy musk of sea, sweat, and sheep fat that permeated the air.

"Either put that sword away ... or use the bloody thing. I haven't got all day."

"I varn you … one more step and I'll run him through!"

"I'm right here in front of you. Why don't you kill me instead?"

The Reaver tossed the frightened boy aside, his sword point turning towards Maerlin.

"Well, what're you waiting for?"

The moments ticked by, and the sword stayed where it was.

"Come on, big guy ... do it! Let's see if your sword-arm is quicker than my magic, shall we?"

The Reaver and the Storm-Bringer glared at each other.

"You really are a bat-shit crazy, vitch-voman, aren't you? Do you know dat?" With a grin he motioned for his men to release the prisoners. "You must have da heart of en drakon, ya!"

"In more ways than one," Maerlin murmured, absently thinking of Sygvaldr.

"So now vhat?" the Northlander asked. "You've robbed us of our catch. Vhat are ve supposed to do now?" His accent was thick, and at times it was hard to understand what he was saying.

"Once your prisoners are released, you can be on your way. Heed my warning, though. If you fish in these waters again, you'll suffer my wrath."

The Reaver looked at the remains of his sails and his scorched decking. "You breathe fire like da drakon too, ya! Alright, vild voman, but der are plump pickings here. If ve don't fish here, den others vilt come, and dey vilt steal yur little fishies, ya?"

"Then, I'll just have to sink a few of their ships until they get the point, won't I?" Maerlin replied with a defiant glint in her eyes.

"I bet ye vould, 'n' all!" The Reaver smiled. "A man vould be happy vith such a voman to come home to. A man might even consider giving up da sea and be happy vit only da one mistress."

"Is that supposed to be a proposal?"

The Reaver leered. "Vell ... at least I vouldn't be going home empty-handed. Vinters can be long and harsh on da Icy Vastes vithout a little company to warm da bed."

"What is it with you lot? Are you all obsessed with marriage? By Deanna! You're nearly as mad as Sygvaldr!"

The ship fell into deathly silence, and the Reavers looked at Maerlin with a mixture of awe and terror. Finally, the huge Reaver spoke again, though even he looked shaken "You know Sygvaldr? *Konungr Sygvaldr*! Sygvaldr da drakon?"

"Of course I know him ... big guy ... frosty breath? You could say I know him very well, if it's the same Sygvaldr we're talking about. His Royal Highness King Sygvaldr of the Icy Wastes ... is that the one you mean...?"

His face became as pale as an iceberg.

"...He keeps asking me to marry him, too."

The Northlander turned quickly and barked out urgent orders to his crew in his native tongue. Maerlin had trouble recognising half of the words he shouted, but the urgency was clear. The slaves were quickly released and nearly thrown overboard; such was the sudden haste to clear them off the ship.

"Forgive me my poor manners, *Frú!*" the Reaver pleaded. "I beg you to forgive my stupidity. Let me assure ye, ve vilt find fresh vaters to fish in future ... far, far avay from your shores! Ve vilt not trouble you again."

"So does that mean the marriage proposal is off?" Maerlin teased, sensing his discomfort.

The Reaver was visibly shaken and laughed half-heartedly. "Please ... dat vas just a jest, ya... a joke if you vill! I'm sure ve von't need to trouble *Konungr Sygvaldr* about dis little ... misunderstanding, vill ve? Ya! Vith ya permission, ve vill be leaving now ... ya?"

Maerlin hopped onto her staff and hovered for a moment, looking at the nervous Reavers. Seeing that all the prisoners had been released and were now standing on the riverbank, she summoned a little magic and pushed the Dragonship back out into the current, where she watched it slip away, downstream. Oars were quickly dipped into the water, and a steady drum rhythm sounded to hasten the vessel along.

Chapter Forty-One: The Battle of Manquay

The *Tir Pect* army stopped only a few spear-throws away from the embankment, and for a few moments everyone just stood in silent anticipation. Only the soft rustle of the wind in the grass, the chomping of horses' bits, and the rustling of Clan banners could be heard. Everyone was waiting, some with calm indifference, others with nervous apprehension.

Finally, Cull broke the eerie silence "I guess we'd better go and get this over with."

Conal signalled for Malachi to raise the parley banner.

After a moment a similar banner was raised on the Pectish side.

"Oh well, here goes nothing," Malachi mumbled as Sile drove Conal's chariot into the middle of the battlefield. She stopped and turned the chariot side-on, signalling to the army generals where she designated no-man's-land to be. It was time for the parley to proceed.

"And ... they're off," Taliesin joked nervously. He was standing beside Conal in the Queen's chariot, having pleaded to be allowed to witness the parley so that he could record it accurately for future generations. As the station of a bard was considered neutral, he would not affect the delicate etiquette of the occasion. Conal was sure that Conchubhar and Medb would also employ a bard for the occasion. The Monarchs of *Tir Pect* were proceeding across the grassland at a stately pace. Riding in the King's chariot was a man dressed in the seven-coloured cloak of a Bard.

"It's just the two of them," Taliesin added, signalling that Conal could only select one of his trusted advisors to go with him.

Conal looked at Cull and Declan before deciding. "Mount up, Declan. Let's see what they have to say for themselves."

From the look on Cull's face, Conal knew that he had made the right decision. To leave Declan behind would have been a heavy insult to the man and to the rest of the Dragon-scales. Much though Cull itched to be at the meeting, he acceptance of the decision and joined Ceila and the priestesses. From here, he would have a good overview of the battle, should it come to that.

Conal drove sedately forward, fighting the eagerness of the war-ponies and holding them firmly to a walk, despite their protests. They snorted their dissatisfaction, but he refused to give them their heads.

"That's it, Conal ... nice and slow. Act like you've got all the time in the world," Taliesin coached softly. "Head up and shoulders back. This is just a casual stroll, nothing more. Pretend that you're at a Ball and this is a slow motion dance ... on wheels!"

"Tell that to the horses," Conal murmured out of the side of his mouth.

Taliesin laughed loudly and slapped Conal on the shoulder.

"Smile and laugh along. You've just told me a hilarious joke," Taliesin informed him and continued to laugh."

Conal smiled nervously. "I did?"

"I said smile, not grimace. By the gods, you're hopeless at this!"

"Hey, cut me some slack. This is my first time."

"Exactly, Conal, but you can't let them know that, can you? Now smile, you idiot!"

Conal laughed. Though butterflies danced like dervishes in his stomach, he laughed loudly.

"Not too much," Taliesin advised. "We don't want them to think you're touched."

"What do you mean ... touched?"

"You know... touched in the head... away with the faeries."

Conal scowled at the bard. "This is a pile of pig's dung! Can't I just tell them to bugger off back to their mountains, or better still, hit someone with my sword?"

"Conal. There are times when you need to show diplomacy, and this is one of those times. You can't just go around hitting everyone who annoys you. People will think you're a psychopath."

Reluctantly, Conal had to concede that Taliesin had a point, but his nerves were frayed, and his temper was getting the better of him. He was tired, hung over, and in no mood to pass pleasantries with an invading army.

"That's better. Draw the chariot around in a nice slow arc and pull it up beside Sile, so that the right side of your chariot is facing their army."

"Why do I need to do it that way?"

"That's your sword hand, silly. It wouldn't be the first time someone's broken a parley and attacked their opponent. It's better to be safe than sorry."

Conal guided the horses around, watching King Conchubhar do likewise, with Queen Medb's chariot following suit and stopping between Conchubhar and their combined army.

"It looks like Conchubhar will be their elected spokesperson. That's probably a good idea considering the look on the Queen's face right now."

Conal glanced over and saw the mask of seething fury that marred Medb's complexion. The Queen was so preoccupied that her horses stepped over the invisible line of protocol and had to be firmly pulled back into position.

"It's a nice day for a drive ..." Conchubhar greeted warmly.

Conal inspected the High King of *Tir Pect*. Conchubhar stood a fraction taller than Conal. Years of combat and training had made him heavily muscled. His long, dark mane was held back from his face by two long plaits, flowing from his temples. Both his hair and his drooping moustache were peppered with the first frostings of grey, but they added to his handsome features. He was dressed in a long cuirass of scale-mail armour, and his forearms were protected by wonderfully-crafted leather greaves, and across his back hung a pair of finely-honed swords. Conchubhar had chosen a light set of armour that gave adequate protection, but still left him with a good degree of flexibility and speed.

The Queen's armour was a perfect match of Sile's, even down to the buckle details, though whereas Sile was armed with an array of deadly knives, Queen Medb was armed with a formidable twin-bladed battle-axe. The rumours appeared to be true about her ability to fight in a berserk rage. A battle-axe was a formidable weapon in the hands of a berserker.

Taliesin nudged the Prince with an elbow, bringing Conal out of his daydream.

"Aye, it's a fine day, indeed. It's a shame that you missed the festivities," Conal recovered quickly. "The mountain passes must have slowed you down. It's always hard to travel with such an excessive entourage. Still, with all of those *Ciudach* roaming around in the mountains, you can never be too sure, can you? These are dangerous times."

Conchubhar looked pointedly at Conal's *Ciudach*-skin armour. He recognised the rare hide immediately and noted the fine Pectish craftsmanship. "We heard some cheering last night, and we wondered at its cause. Are we too late for the spring fair?"

"I'm afraid that the fair has been cancelled for this year. A tragedy occurred, so we thought it better to call off the rest of the Gathering. You also missed my coronation, but I thank you for your gift. It was most thoughtful of you both."

"...Gift?" Conchubhar struggled to hide his confusion.

"Yes, your gift. It's not a bad chariot as they go, and the ponies aren't too shabby, either. It was most considerate of you to send emissaries on ahead, when you realised that you were going to be detained in the mountains." Conal smiled warmly at Sile and Malachi. He could hear Queen Medb choking on her anger, but resisted the urge to look over at her. He was sure that Taliesin would fill him in later, if they ever got out of here alive, that is.

"Ah, yes, the gift ... right, of course ... ermm ... so glad you liked it!"

"We missed your arrival at *Dun Dragan*. Sadly, I had some pressing affairs of state to attend to, and I just couldn't wait any longer. I do hope you found the note I left?"

"Note ... we saw no note."

"Oh really, what a shame. It was right beside the big sign that I'd planted at the foot of Dragon's Ridge. The one that read: *Trespassers beware. Keep your filthy hands off my grass!*"

Conchubhar flushed slightly. The Queen's throat made a noise like a death-rattle.

Finally, Conal acknowledged her presence. "Your dear wife seems to be choking on something, Conchubhar, perhaps she swallowed a horsefly. This grassland is swarming with the little blighters at this time of year. It's hell trying to sleep around here in the summertime. Anyway ... it's been fun, but I really have to go now. I've important things to do. Traitors to hunt down ... you know ... kingly stuff! I presume, you'll be able to find your own way back home ... or do you need me to provide you with an armed escort? We wouldn't want anything untoward to happen to you during your state visit."

Conchubhar's face flushed again, and his eyes bored into Conal's, but Conal's smile never flinched for a moment. He stared straight back with casual confidence. The moments ticked by with painful slowness before Conchubhar's eyes turned away. With a flick of his wrist, his horses moved off, leaving his Queen open-mouthed in astonishment.

"Hang on!" Medb objected. "Where are you going? He stole my chariot, and you're just going to leave ...?"

"Forget it, Medb ..." Conchubhar murmured, "... just leave it be."

"Leave it be? Leave it be! Are you mad? This is what I think of leaving it be!" Grabbing her axe, Medb raised it into the air and hurled it across at Conal with all of her might.

"Look out!" Taliesin yelled, diving across the chariot and knocking Conal out of the way.

The ponies had been constantly fighting against Conal's control, chomping on their bits. They sensed the tension of battle in the air, and these ponies were bred for war. All the slow prancing and standing around was irritating them. As Taliesin crashed into Conal, the chariot lurched forward and the reins slackened. Highly-strung by nature, the war-ponies took their chance and bolted. Luckily, they were facing across the battlefield, rather than toward the enemy lines, but they careened headlong across the grassland toward the stony ground that had so recently been cleared to ensnare chariots. Conal grappled with Tal, trying to get free of the tangle of limbs, but the bouncing of the chariot wasn't helping and neither was the bard. "Get off me, Tal!" he cursed, pushing Taliesin aside.

Sile had been quick to respond, and her chariot raced after Conal's ponies, cutting them off and bringing them round to face back toward Manquay. She called out to calm them, and they responded, recognising her voice after many days of travelling under her command. They slowed to a trot, still tossing their heads, but her calming voice soothed them and allowed Conal to regain his footing. Grabbing the reins, he steered the chariot toward the gap in the ditch and into the relative safety of the fortified embankment.

Sile pulled up alongside him. "That was close!"

Conal was furious. Queen Medb had broken the parley and damned near sliced his head off in the process. He looked down at Taliesin. The bard was lying in the bottom of the chariot, looking even paler than usual. Conal was surprised to see blood flowing along the floor of the chariot. "Tal! Are you alright?"

Taliesin tried to rise but his legs were like jelly and he slipped back down again. "I feel a bit light-headed, that's all..." he mumbled, "... just give me a moment!"

"Tal, you're bleeding!" Conal crouched down beside the bard and pressed his hand to the wound to stem the flow. "Sile, go and get the healers."

"I'm fine ..." Taliesin protested. "I'm just a little dizzy, that's all! I'm sure it's just a nick, Conal."

Conal raised his bloody hand to Tal's face. "Shut up, Tal. This is not just a nick!"

Taliesin gazed down at the blood that was dripping from Conal's fingers before his world started to slip away. His eyes rolled backward in his head, and he slumped into unconsciousness.

"Tal? Tal! Damn it!" Conal cursed.

"He's fainted, ya Majesty. I'll look after him for you. Ye haven't the time for this right now."

Conal looked up at the jester, Malachi, and nodded.

"Go, Conal. Your army's waiting for you," Malachi advised. The Dwarf's voice was filled with disappointment. All of their efforts to stop this war had failed. All Sile had done was help Conal be prepared for it.

Taking one last look at Taliesin, Conal rose to his feet and looked around.

His army watched him silently, hardly breathing ... waiting.

Medb had scored first blood. Conal swore that she would pay for that. Rage boiled up in him as he slowly drew *An Fiacail Dragan* from its sheath. It shimmered in the morning sunlight. Fuelling his anger into his shout, he hurled his war-cry toward his enemies *"Dragan abú!"* Marching to the head of his troops, he yelled it again across the battlefield *"DRAGAN ABÚ!"*

"DRAGAN ABÚ!" responded his loyal Dragon-scales. The phalanxes immediately took up the war-cry.

"DRAGAN ABÚ! DRAGAN ABÚ!" The roar echoed off the battlements. Cull's makeshift army waved their assorted weaponry and roared their defiance.

"Are you alright, Sire?"

Conal looked up at Declan. "I'm fine, but Taliesin has a bad gash across his back. What happened to you?"

"When your horses bolted, Medb tried to pursue you. I had to give Sile a chance to catch you, so I intercepted the Queen. It's a good job that the demented Bear-sow had thrown her battle-axe away or I'd still be out there. When she ran out of javelins, she was forced to head back to her army for another weapon. It was either that or throw ponies at me. Mind you, nothing would surprise me when it comes to Medb."

Further conversation was useless as the forces of *Tir Pect* charged across the battlefield with a blood-curdling yell of pure hatred.

"Archers!" Declan bellowed over the din. Horns blared in response, carrying his command farther than the human voice ever could.

The waiting archers responded instantly, stepping forward and raising their bows.

"Fire!" Declan yelled, and the humming of angry hornets filled the air as wave after wave of arrows arced high overhead. Some of the chariots crashed into the dirt as the air filled with the squeals of dying horses. Still the wheeled wall of death rumbled onward, ever closer, building up momentum as they raced across the grass.

The Pectish warriors ran along behind. They knew that the longer it took to cross the battlefield, the more arrows would rain down upon their heads, so they ran as if pursued by the hounds of the Nine Hells.

Declan dismounted, slapped his horse on the flanks and grasped Conal's shoulder. "Quickly Sire! We need to join the phalanxes."

Conal hesitated, standing defiantly in front of his army, but then the chariots cast their first volley of javelins. They were hurled into the sky and fell, some landing around the newly-crowned Dragon-lord. Luckily, they'd been released too early to be accurate. Finally realising his danger, Conal followed Declan to the safety of the nearest phalanx.

"Shields!" Declan ordered and the *Dragans* raised their shields before them, ready for the next wave of missiles.

The archers fired a final volley at the racing chariots before diving for cover behind the heavily-armoured phalanxes.

Conal and Declan barely made it into the unit before the first hail of javelins thudded into the phalanx. The *Dragan* shields had been designed to protect the upper body and were oval in shape with an iron banding around the rim. Javelins pierced the thick, oak planking or ricochet off the ironwork. Inevitably, some found gaps in the shield wall and pierced the flesh beneath. Men died, unable to fall because of the tightly-packed mass of warriors around them.

"Forward, half-pace," Declan yelled. "Lower spears!" The units responded with crisp precision and moved to the brink of the embankment. There, they readied themselves to defend their position against the onrushing warriors.

The chariots, their javelins now dispensed, split left and right to avoid the ditch. One enterprising fellow spotted the gap in the ditch where the road headed toward the gate, and charged headlong into the phalanx protecting it. The horses crashed onto the braced spears, but with so much momentum behind it, the bladed chariot bit deeply into the tightly-packed phalanx. Many Dragons died. The charioteer was thrown from his vehicle and landed heavily behind the phalanx, where the archers and Cull's ragtag mob were waiting. They fell upon him like a pack of rabid dogs, and he died screaming.

Smoke drifted down from the hillside and closed over the battlefield like a fog bank.

"Hold the line!" Declan encouraged the troops, before speaking directly to Conal "Follow me, Sire We can't see what's happening from here."

Declan led Conal toward the city wall, and the waiting Dragon-scales. Here, the ground was higher, and they had a better view of the overall battle. Conal watched the riders of the Horse Clan nip at the heels of the retreating chariots. They had skirted the defensive ditch and were now hounding the chariots as they retreated toward the Pectish side of the battlefield. The cavalry peppered the undefended backs of the charioteers as they tried to break clear. Many of the drivers died, and some of their unguided teams careened wildly through the heart of the Pectish foot-warriors. Scythe-blades cut through the massed ranks.

As the last of the chariots disappeared into the smoke, the cavalry wheeled away and returned to the defence of Conal's right flank. During their brief combat, they had inflicted heavy losses on the prized chariots of *Tir Pect*.

Conal turned to the other flank, where smoke now billowed heavily and drifted across the battlefield. The chariots on that flank had turned into the smoke, and the screams of horses testified to the rough terrain hidden within.

"Where did that smoke come from?" Declan asked.

"The Brocians must have set fire to the scrub," Conal replied with a grin. The *Snochta Broce* disliked sunlight on their sensitive eyes, and Cathal must have seen the opportunity to counter this. Conal was sure that within the smoke, the Brocians would wreak havoc on the stranded chariots. It was a stroke of genius, even if it did negate the effectiveness of his archers.

Now, the battle would begin in earnest. It would be told by the brave men and women who stood, toe to toe, at the edge of the embankment. The phalanxes were outnumbered, but had the advantage of height and a spiked pit. They would need to hold and repel the combined forces of *Tir Pect*. It wasn't long before the first of the Pectish berserkers reached the defensive line. Jumping the stake-filled ditch, they battered against the shield wall of the phalanx with swords, axes, and hammers. Many were skewered on Dragon spears as they leapt across the ditch. Others stumbled, hesitating at the last moment, and fell or were pushed, into the pit. The ditch quickly filled with the dead and the dying, pressed down by the mass of warriors treading ever forward. The Dragon phalanxes creaked under the strain. In places, the Wolves and the Bears even gained a foothold on the embankment, before being repelled back across the body-strewn ditch.

The first ball of fire hurtled over the heads of the Wolf Clan and engulfed the left phalanx, incinerating combatants within the blink of an eye. Fireballs rained down around the embankment before the priestesses of Deanna and the other Orders could counter with their own magic.

Declan was constantly sending runners to his various commanders, strengthening a point of weakness, or countering a probe. Ceila was likewise coordinating the magical defences, while Conal could only stand by helplessly, feeling impotent. The battle had descended into a chaotic cauldron of madness, a maelstrom of death and destruction, and he was forced to watch it unfold before his eyes.

Dubhgall the Black was winning the magical combat, despite the poor resources at his disposable. Many of his hedge-wizards had already collapsed. They had been unable to take the mental strain of the cohesive attack and counterattack which Dubhgall had demanded of them. Despite their inadequacies, Dubhgall had one clear advantage over the Seven Orders. He had lived for generations and dedicated a vast amount of his time to the study of combative magic. The Orders, on the other hand, had abandoned this particular facet of the magical arts for other more productive forms of magic. Many of the magicians of the Seven Orders had learned little or no combative magic during their times as novices. They had studied it even less after their graduations. This made Dubhgall quicker to react, more efficient in his use of his powers, and far more effective. The army of the Dragon-lord were suffering heavily from this disparity.

The phalanx on Conal's right wavered and threatened to collapse under the combination of magical attacks and the ferocity of the attacks from *Clann Na Béar*. Their line bowed inwards, as more and more of the Bear Clan gained a foothold on the embankment.

Conal could see that his reserves were already stretched thin. Without a moment's hesitation, he leapt into the fray, hoping that the Dragon-scales would follow. Pushing his way to the front of the phalanx, he saw the cause of the disruption.

It was Queen Medb. She was red-faced and frothing at the mouth. Her battle-axe was cleaving left and right in great arcs, clearing ground for her kinsmen. Conal watched her cleave through a soldier and take another step forward, already moving her axe into a backhand sweep for the next assault. She would have to be stopped, and quickly. However, Conal had no idea how to do this. He looked down at the fallen men and dismissed the idea of grabbing a shield. The wreckage of several lay scattered on the battlefield, mute testament to the devastation of her axe. It cleaved through the oaken shields as if they were made of tin. Entering that ever-moving arc of steel would mean certain death, and in the tightly-packed combat, dodging was out of the question.

At a complete loss for solutions, he did the first thing that came to mind. He roared the war-cry of his forefathers and charged. For too long had he sat back and watched this battle unfold with growing frustration. Now was his time for action.

"*Dragan abú!* Long live the Dragons!" he yelled as he moved within the arc of the double-edged axe. As it swung toward his head, he raised his sword in a two-handed grip and struck out at the flying axe. The shock rode up his arms and shuddered through his shoulders, but the axe slid upwards along *An Fiacail Dragan* and away. He stepped a little closer and watched the axe's counter-arc. This time, the blow held more power, but again, he deflected the axe and moved, inch by inch, closer. Recognition flickered across Medb's deranged face, and she re-doubled her efforts, forcing Conal backward into the press of men behind.

He bided his time and waited for the burst of adrenaline to fade, before pressing forward again into the swinging axe strokes. Retreat was not an option. He needed to get within her strokes to have any chance of victory. He needed to slow the momentum of the ever-moving battle-axe. Gritting his teeth, he ignored the jarring ache in his shoulders and pushed forward. Once twice, three times, he deflected the horizontal axe strikes away from his head, forcing the whistling axe upwards away from the killing blow. With each deflection, he edged closer.

His only warning was a subtle movement of her hips, but he'd been trained thoroughly by the Weapons-masters of *Clann Na Dragan*. In fact, he had been anticipating just such a move. As the axe slid for the fourth time off his blade, the Queen changed her line of attack, and the blade arced around and over her head. Had he tried to deflect the next blow, his wrists would have shattered, and the axe would have been buried in his body. He watched the axe swing up in its killing arc. As it reached its pinnacle and began to descend, Conal leapt forward.

Realising that he didn't have the space to manoeuvre his sword around for a killing blow, he improvised with one of Cull's unorthodox lessons in combat. Springing under the arc of the descending axe, he crashed his helmeted forehead into Medb's face with all of the force he could muster. Her nose shattered on impact, and momentarily stunned, the axe slipped from her grasp. Quickly, Conal grabbed her flaming red mane and yanked her head back to expose her throat. His magical blade pressed against her jugular, hungry for her blood

"Yield!" Seeing the stunned look on her face, he repeated his command. "Yield, Medb! Yield or die."

The fighting around them stopped as both sides waited in anticipation. In the distance, the battle still raged and the dying continued, but here, time stood still as Conal waited. His blade was pressed lightly into Medb's neck and blood trickled from its razor-sharp point.

Queen Medb glared up at her captor with baleful eyes as the realisation of her predicament finally sunk home...

504

Chapter Forty-Two: The Final Cut

"But I thought the plan was to get the Dragontooth back from Conal. I thought that was the whole point of going to the spring fair in the first place." Seabhac asked.

Maerlin replied with her usual frankness. "It was, Seabhac, but I don't trust myself at the moment. I'm so angry, I might do something stupid. It'd be wiser for me to walk back to Manquay and use the time to gather my thoughts. Maybe in a moon or two ..."

"What about the battle? It'll have started by now."

Maerlin sighed, feeling the weight of expectation pressing down on her. Destiny, like everyone else, was just going to have to get along without her for a while. She'd had enough of being a puppet to Fate. "If Conal can't win a little skirmish without me holding his hand, then he needs to rethink his career choices. This time, he's going to have to fight his own battle, besides ... he's got Cora and the other priestesses to help him. He doesn't need me."

Seabhac embraced her great-granddaughter. "I have to go, Maerlin ... thou knoweth that, don't thee?"

Maerlin nodded. "Of course I do..." then she added, "... be careful, Seabhac."

"Uiscallan."

"Pardon?"

"Thou had better start calling me Uiscallan. I think it's time for me to stop hiding behind a mask and faced my destiny."

Maerlin stood with the freed prisoners and watched as Uiscallan flew away. When she had disappeared from view, Maerlin looked around at the young men. It was only then that she realised that Duncan wasn't amongst them. Her heart sank, realising her failure. If he wasn't on the Dragonship, then where could he be?

*****

The battlefield was easy to find. It was hard to miss the heavy pall of smoke and the sounds of war. It had been a long time since Uiscallan had witnessed such ferocity, and it made her feel old to see it again. There was always too much futile loss of life, all for the sake of petty politics and greed. It was time to put an end to this, once and for all. She waved a silent farewell to Fintan and landed at the rear of the *Tir Pect* army, where Dubhgall was coordinating the magical battle.

Lifting her staff, she hiked up the small hillock to confront her nemesis. As she drew closer, she caught sight of his ravaged face. Life had not been kind to the Dark Mage of late, and he looked diminished from his former self. Her gaze flickered to the slack-faced man who stood alongside Dubhgall. He had evidently once been portly, but had recently lost a lot of weight, and his skin hung loosely from his body. His face was a blank façade. Only his eyes moved, sharp and focused as they studied every nuance of the battlefield. Dubhgall's right arm was clasped firmly onto the shabbily-dressed monk's shoulder.

"Dubhgall!" Uiscallan shouted.

The Dark Mage gave no indication of hearing her, but the eyes of the monk swivelled around and bored into her own. The Mage spoke "I'm busy ... come back later."

His casual dismissal lit a fuse within her temper. The sky darkened and thunder rumbled loudly in response to her anger. Gritting her teeth, she sent out a blast of force that rocked both men backward. "This won't wait, Dubhgall. I want to speak to thee ... now!"

With a look of surprise, Dubhgall turned. "Uiscallan, is that really you?"

"Thou tricked me, Dubhgall. Thou stole my life from me, and then thou tricked and seduced me," she accused. "I've come to make thee pay for that."

"Uiscallan, Can't you see that I'm busy right now. Come back later, and we can talk about it then. I haven't got time for this!"

"Make time!" Uiscallan growled, sending a bolt of lightning arcing from the heavens directly at the Mage.

This time he was ready, and he deflected the strike.

"Uiscallan, I don't want this. I never wanted this. You have to understand!"

Uiscallan was tired of his mind games. She was tired of his lies and trickery. She summoned Elementals and cast bolt after bolt of lightning from the sky.

They had both had a busy day, and had been using their powers since daybreak, so their reserves of energy were depleted. Uiscallan fed off her anger to fuel her need, while Dubhgall drained the last of his cohort in an effort to block her assaults.

Realising that discussion was futile; Dubhgall quickly went on the offensive. Energy bolts shot toward Uiscallan. Soon, the whole battlefield stopped fighting to watch the epic struggle between the two legendary magicians.

The ground shook and the heavens roared. The winds swirled in madness around them and rain fell in torrents, as fire and lightning arced back and forth. In reality, the battle was over in moments as they were both quickly drained of power, and yet, it seemed to go on for an eternity.

Uiscallan felt a burning sensation deep within her chest and pain shot up her arm, causing her to stumble. She summoned the last of her magic to deflect Dubhgall's barrage of assaults. She would rid the world of his evil, once and for all. She could hear her heart beating like a demented bodhrán in her head. Her eyes were misting over, as the pain enveloped her body like a cloak. Finally, her weakened heart stuttered to a halt, and she fell to the ground, clutching at her bosom. She lay there gasping for breath, her face a rictus of pain as the shadow of the Mage fell across her.

"Uiscallan, together we could've ruled the world!"

Uiscallan the Storm-Bringer looked into his ravaged face and laughed at the bitter irony of his statement. All she had ever wanted, he had taken from her, and his only thoughts were for world domination. Letting out a long sigh, she closed her eyes.

No one heard the shriek of rage that came from the stormy skies. They never saw the grey shadow of death that fell like an arrow to strike the Dark Mage's face with razor-sharp claws and beak. Fintan had reluctantly watched from on high, but when he felt Uiscallan's spirit leave this world and the connection between them break, his mind broke too. He attacked without thought or care for his own safety. Uiscallan had been his life, and now she was gone.

Dubhgall staggered back under the assault, raising his hands to protect his ravaged face from Fintan's attack, while he summoned the last shreds of his magical powers. He never even felt the razor-sharp knife that plunged into his ribs and pierced his heart. He wasn't aware that in his moment of panic, he had released his grip on Gearoid Brightstar. Dagda's blade sank deep into Dubhgall's chest and stole away his life in the blink of an eye. He could not deny the power of the All-father's blade.

Dubhgall fell to the floor beside Uiscallan, his dead face a mask of surprise.

The Hen Harrier landed nearby, shrieking out to the world at the pain of his loss.

Gearoid sank to the floor and began to weep. "I'm sorry, Balor. I'm sorry!"

Time stood still. The swaying grass had stopped its dance, and an old man popped into existence. Humming softly to himself, he meandered through the statue-like warriors, toward the grassy knoll.

He paused for a moment, sensing Fintan's grief. Dagda had the power to take away Fintan's pain, but he was wise enough to know that the pain was part of the grieving process, so he stayed his hand. "I'm sorry for thy loss, Fintan MacIolar-Mara, but Uiscallan has gone to the Otherworld now, and thou cannot stay here. Fly, Blue-wings, fly and be with thy people. Thy task here is done, but thy family will need thee in the days ahead."

Fintan hesitated. He was reluctant to leave, but the will of the god was too strong to resist. With a final screech of loss, he took to the skies.

The All-father watched patiently until the majestic bird was a mere speck on the western horizon, before turning away. Gently, he stooped and prised the blooded dagger from Gearoid's hand. Such a weapon must not remain in the hands of a mortal, even one with so pure a heart as the Abbot. "Come along, Brightstar. Let me take thee home."

Gearoid was too grief-stricken to protest, and Dagda led him away from the frozen battlefield. Once they were clear of the chaos of war, the All-father absently clicked his fingers, and the battle came back to life.

Epilogue

Sliamh Na Dia trembled and shook as the caged god, *Crom Cruach*, vented his rage. He had worked hard for many years for this chance to escape, but the All-father had thwarted his machinations and removed the Elder God's bishop from the board of play.

Long before Dubhgall the Black had approached Macha, he had sworn allegiance to *Crom Cruach*. When Dubhgall was only a frightened slave, he had sold his soul to the Elder God. Having found an ancient manuscript, the young slave had preformed the dark ritual, hoping to win his freedom. Little did he realise that it would enslave his soul for generations.

The snake-god had nurtured and developed him, before sending him into the world to create chaos. It was *Crom Cruach* who had sent a vision to Dubhgall. It was he who had urged him to seek out the Temple of Macha. Dubhgall had always been a double agent against the Seven. He had always been loyal to his original dark master, the god who lurked deep within the darkness of his soul. Dubhgall had managed to fool Macha, but the All-father had somehow become aware of this duplicity, and he had taken steps to eliminate the threat.

Deep within the bowels of the mountain, the snake-god stirred. It was time for a new piece to enter the game, more than one in fact. Huddled, shivering in the shelter of *Crom Cruach's* nostrils, starving and near to death, lay the two torturers. Into their delirium-filled dreams, the Elder God slipped. He offered them their wildest dreams and all for such a small price. It would only cost them their souls.

Soon, *Crom Cruach* would unleash not one, but two Black Knights onto the board.

... And so ends Book Two of the Storm-Bringer Saga.

Other books by Nav Logan:

The Storm-Bringer Saga: -Book One

The Storm-Bringer Saga: -Book Two

The Storm-Bringer Saga: - Book Three

(Due for release in late 2014)

Learn more on: -

https://www.facebook.com/

And on my website: www.navlogan.com

Learn more on: -

https://www.facebook.com/StormbringerSaga

And on my website: www.navlogan.com

*****

Glossary

For a full glossary of the Storm-Bringer Saga go to: -
http://navlogan.wordpress.com/2013/10/16/glossary-of-the-storm-bringer-saga/

*****

A Final Note from the Author

Thank you very much for taking the time to read this book. I hope that you enjoyed it and that the story has lived up to your expectations.

With my profound thanks

Nav

About the Author

Many years ago, when I was just a small boy, gazing in wonder at his first pubic hair, I decided that I was going to become a tramp. I was going to drop out and go to Strathclyde. Why Strathclyde, many asked? The gods only know, but every man must have a goal in life. Being an engineer or a pilot didn't cut it for me. My soul was filled with wanderlust and the need for adventure.

So, after leaving home, I dropped out. I even went to Strathclyde, passing through it in a sleepy haze while being rocked gently to slumber in the passenger seat of an unknown truck.

Since then, I have done many things and seen many places, always following my instincts and trusting in my destiny. I am self taught in many things, a jack of all trades and a master at none, but I've always got by. A strong self-belief, confidence, and my stubborn Ulster will, has brought me through many adversities. I try to be the best I can be and often fail, but I continue nevertheless.

I have been writing since I was that small boy, my mind always wandering. Mainly, it has been poems and the occasional short story. Maerlin's Storm was first written over a decade ago. It wasn't something I planned to do. I didn't wake up and say, I am going to be an author; far from it. Like many things in my life, it all started with a dream. The next morning, I wrote a poem about it. Later, the poem became a story. It grew from a small seed and suddenly became a beanstalk. People read it and enjoyed it, but then life became busy again, and for many years the story sat, collecting dust.

I tried writing a follow up, but it initially petered out due to other commitments. It would have stayed on the shelf, forgotten, but for my wife. She bought me a Kindle. (She may live to regret that moment of madness, but I love her dearly for it).

29159645R00312

Made in the USA
Charleston, SC
04 May 2014